Anonymous

Garfield memorial volume

Tribute from the citizens of Jersey City to the memory of James A. Garfield

Anonymous

Garfield memorial volume
Tribute from the citizens of Jersey City to the memory of James A. Garfield

ISBN/EAN: 9783337131593

Printed in Europe, USA, Canada, Australia, Japan

Cover: Foto ©Raphael Reischuk / pixelio.de

More available books at **www.hansebooks.com**

GARFIELD MEMORIAL VOLUME.

A TRIBUTE

FROM THE CITIZENS OF JERSEY CITY

TO THE MEMORY OF

JAMES A. GARFIELD,

LATE

President of the United States.

PUBLISHED BY A COMMITTEE APPOINTED FOR THAT PURPOSE.

JERSEY CITY:
DAVISON & CO., PRINTERS, 27 MONTGOMERY ST.
1881.

PREFACE.

UPON the death of President GARFIELD, the Mayor and Board of Aldermen of Jersey City designated several places in the city, at which public services would be held and suitable expression given of our great sorrow, and of the Nation's loss of its Chief Executive Magistrate.

One of these meetings was held at the Reformed Church on Bergen Avenue.

At the conclusion of the meeting, the following resolution was unanimously adopted:

"*Resolved*, That the Chair appoint a Committee of Three to consider the propriety of publishing a pamphlet containing the proceedings of this memorial meeting, or to join with any other committee or committees to prepare a more extended publication if such should be deemed advisable, and if such publication is made, to put the same on sale for the purpose of defraying the cost, or to solicit subscriptions for the same."

The Chairman of the meeting appointed the undersigned as such committee.

When the committee entered upon the discharge of the duties assigned to it, there was an expression given through the press to the effect that the volume should embrace the whole city, and that a sufficient number of sermons and addresses should be selected and published which would make a fair representation of the feelings and sorrow expressed on that occasion.

In accordance with that wish, the committee have made as broad a selection as possible consistent with a proper sized volume.

The work of arranging the various sermons and addresses in the volume devolved upon Mr. Weart, who took charge of editing the same.

All the addresses made at the meeting at the Reformed Church, where the resolution was passed, which has called forth this memorial volume, have been inserted first, and the other matter has followed as the editor could best arrange the same.

Nothing has been inserted in this volume except the matter solicited by the committee, and the committee extended as wide a call as the space in the volume would permit, and the work is submitted to the public with a hope that it will keep alive in our memories the virtues of this great statesman, and stimulate the rising generation to greater exertions, and a broader christian philanthrophy.

JERSEY CITY, OCTOBER 21, 1881.

JACOB WEART,
JOHN J. TOFFEY,
JOHN M. JONES,
Committee.

PROCEEDINGS

OF THE

Garfield Memorial Meeting

FOR THE

FIFTH DISTRICT, JERSEY CITY, NEW JERSEY,

HELD IN THE

Bergen Reformed Church,

MONDAY EVENING, SEPTEMBER 26th, 1881.

Notice having been given through the columns of the Jersey City papers, and the several congregations of the city having been invited through their pastors, an immense concourse of people filled seats and aisles of the Bergen Reformed Church, and hundreds were turned away from the doors, unable to gain admittance. Seats were reserved in front of the pulpit for Van Houten Post, G. A. R.

Promptly at 8 o'clock, a solemn dirge was rendered upon the organ, by Mr. HARRY BRIGHAM, Organist of the Church, during which the Hon. G. D. VAN REIPEN, President of the Board of Aldermen took the Chair.

The Choir of the Church, led by Mr. A. D. JOSLIN, then sang a beautiful requiem by Sphor, beginning with the words "Rest in the Lord."

A fervent prayer was offered by the Rev. F. C. PUTNAM, Rector of St. Paul's Protestant Episcopal Church, on Duncan Avenue.

The Rev. H. H. WAITE, of the Second Congregational Church on Summit Avenue, read an appropriate Scripture Lesson.

The Rev. J. V. N. TALLMAGE, D. D., Missionary of the Reformed Church in America, at Amoy, China, read the following hymn, prefacing the reading by reminding the congregation that it was written by the poet Montgomery, on hearing of the sudden death of a Missionary, at his post of duty :

> Servant of God, well done !
>   Rest from thy loved employ :
> The battle fought, the victory won,
>   Enter thy Master's joy !
>
> The voice at midnight came :
>   He started up to hear :
> A mortal arrow pierced his frame ;
>   He fell, but felt no fear.
>
> At midnight came the cry,
>   "To meet thy death prepare,"
> He woke and caught his Captain's eye ;
>   Then strong in faith and prayer,
>
> His spirit with a bound
>   Left its encumbered clay :
> His tent at sunrise on the ground
>   A darkened ruin lay.

The hymn was sung by the congregation, led by the Choir and organ.

Addresses were then delivered by Hon. JACOB WEART and ISAAC S. TAYLOR, Esq.

After which the Choir rendered with touching tenderness the recitative "Come Unto Me," by Bradbury.

Addresses followed by Rev. P. G. BLIGHT, Pastor of the Emory M. E. Church, and Hon. WILLIAM BRINKERHOFF.

Mrs. DE CARLO then sang Holden's Arrangement of "Nearer my God to Thee."

Rev. A. S. GUMBART, of the Summit Avenue Baptist Church then addressed the meeting.

He was followed by a duet sung by Mrs. DE CARLO and Miss CHRISTIE, "Sleep thy last sleep," by Barnby."

Hon. JONATHAN DIXON, Justice of the Supreme Court of New Jersey, and Major Z. K. PANGBORN, Editor of the Jersey City Evening Journal, made the closing addresses.

An eloquent and impressive prayer was offered by Rev. E. W. FRENCH, D. D., of the First Presbyterian Church, Jersey City Heights.

The resolution relating to the publication of the proceedings, as quoted in the preface to this volume, was carried unanimously; and after singing the familiar hymn—

"My Country, 'tis of thee,"

the congregation was dismissed with the benediction by Rev. CORNELIUS BRETT, of the Bergen Reformed Church.

Besides the Pastors of Churches who took part in the exercises, Rev. E. L. STODDARD, of St. John Free Church, and Rev. I. W. HATHAWAY, of the Westminster Presbyterian Church, were present during a portion of the evening, and a large number of prominent citizens were noted in the audience.

OPENING ADDRESS BY THE CHAIRMAN,

HON. G. D. VAN REIPEN.

———

FELLOW CITIZENS—

Called upon to preside, as I have been this evening, and as there are a number of eminent gentlemen to address you, I will only state that this meeting has been called for the purpose of giving expression to the dominant feeling evinced by all, in the great loss sustained by the country in the death of the President, JAMES A. GARFIELD, and whose lifeless remains have this day been laid in the silent tomb by gentle hands, and the tears of fifty millions of honest mourners are baptising the republic anew.

He had everything to live for; a loving family and a lofty place, but when the awful summons came to leave it, all he simply said, "I am ready," and died, surrendering to God the life he gave.

The Nation is to-day stricken in grief, and has assembled around the bier of our late President, to drop into his open grave, tears more tender, and expressive of greater sorrow, than any tears shed around the grave of any martyred patriot, except it may be that of our lamented Lincoln; for in Lincoln and GARFIELD, our two martyred Presidents, are embodied the deepest woe, and the most sublime sympathy, the Nation can lay upon any altar.

A land in grief. Our Star Spangled Banner draped in black, and at half-mast on every flagstaff. The Capitol of the Nation shrouded in mourning, and upon the great piles of marble such as only Nations can raise heavenward, down to the most humble cabin in the land, the weeds of mourning are exhibited, and as the train speeds its way from the Capitol, bearing the ashes of the dead to their final resting place on the beautiful shores of Lake Erie, made memorable by the valor of a Perry, who won national renown for bravery on the placid waters of that lake : the railroad track is strewn with flowers, and at every city, town, and hamlet, large masses of human beings assemble, with uncovered heads, or humbly kneeling, and with tears flowing, salute the passing train, and pay their reverence and respect to God's dead President.

Looking at the dark cloud, which so suddenly lowered over the Nation on the second day of July last: when we saw the flash of the assassin's pistol, and beheld our President prostrate and bleeding, just as he was entering upon the threshold of a journey, which was expected to be one of great pleasure and joy : our Fourth of July was turned into a day of sorrow : the Nation was bowed at the throne of mercy, pleading for the life of our President: but still the great black cloud hung over us, and for eighty days we watched and prayed, and finally the life which was so

9

dear to us, faded away, and our cherished GARFIELD was no
more.

Was there no silver lining to this cloud, "No balm in
Gilead"? Yea, my friends, God always displays at the
proper time the silver lining to the darkest cloud ; and un-
folds to us in due season, the hidden secrets which at the
time, seem the most mysterious workings of His Providence.

Behold the Apostle Paul a prisoner at Rome, bound down
in chains, and sending out from his prison walls those epis-
tles which have enlightened the Christian world for nearly
twenty centuries, and will continue to do so until the end
of time. Paul, a prisoner at Rome, might have been a very
mysterious stroke of Providence to the feeble Christian
Church of his time, but to us to-day, his imprisonment is
but the blaze of the noon-day sun ; Paul, a prisoner, that
he might have the time and opportunity to put on parch-
ment by the divine inspiration those precious truths which
were to evangelize the world.

Martin Luther, in his dungeon, beside his flickering ta-
per, at the time of the Reformation, might have been looked
upon very mysteriously by the handful of followers who
gathered around him, when light was breaking upon the
gloom of the dark ages ; but to us to-day, the mystery is
all unfolded, and the silver lining of that dark cloud is
lighting the path of the Christian, and leading the nations
on their journey of Christian enlightenment and civilization.

Bunyan, for twelve long years in Bedford Jail, because
he had espoused the cause of Christ and preached a free
religion, and dissented from the Established Church, might
have appeared as a very mysterious stroke of Providence
to his devoted wife, who was pleading in vain for his release, and to the small band of Baptist followers in Bedford, who gathered around him when he preached the Gospel ; but to us who have come after to see God's plan and
government of the world unfolded, it appears differently ;
for we see that Bunyan in prison is writing his Pilgrim's
Progress to be a guide along the pathway of the Christian ;

a book that has gone through fifty editions, and in the early life of Abraham Lincoln fell into his hands, and was in his log-cabin his chief educator. Bunyan in prison penning those lines which were to fill the heart of Lincoln with that love of Christian liberty, which was to make him the great liberator of the world, and gave him the heart and manhood to strike the shackles from the slaves of his countrymen, when the hour arrived for him to strike.

My stricken fellow-citizens, may we not look for the silver lining in this dark cloud? may we not look and see the Providence embraced in this stroke of God's hand? Individuals are but God's instruments to carry out His great work of creation: individual lives may come and go, as the waves upon the sea shore, ever rising and falling, but the great mass of humanity remains: just as the great body of the ocean remains calm and peaceful, while upon the shore the waves are dashing against each other in fury.

In this instance, a little more than a year ago, JAMES A. GARFIELD was singled out to become the most conspicuous figure in American politics.

He was put in nomination for the highest office in the gift of the people: and then it was that the American people began the study of his life and character; and as they took up the study, his life was unfolded to them with a constantly increasing richness, and a growing beauty. His past speeches were brought out, republished, and circulated; and all of his utterances were found to contain a richness, a fullness, and a depth of meaning in them, which was convincing to all; and we learned to know that he spoke upon political and national topics as no other man had spoken in his time.

His character as it was studied and examined, grew brighter and brighter until it stood out, as embodying all that is best and noble in the American citizen. Born in poverty, reared in adversity, educated by the money earned by the hardest of manual labor, his study was of the severest mental toil, he became the first scholar of his time, and carried to the Presidential chair more learning than any man who had preceded him; and as a son, husband, father,

and friend, he had no peer in all this broad land : and when
he took the oath of office as President of these United States,
he kissed the Bible of the God who created him, and then
turned and kissed the lips of the aged mother who gave
him birth. The first kiss is registered in the high courts
of heaven, the second kiss is registered in the hearts of
his countrymen, and in the Manhood of the World ; and
will be recorded in history as the highest filial affection of
a son, and the deepest love that can be displayed by man.

If we are wise to-day, we will look into our own hearts,
and try and learn the lesson taught us by this great bereavement. All nations have been led and governed by
rulers. The most savage nation on the earth has its chief,
and the most enlightened Republic its President. So it ever
has been, from the earliest formation of society. Governments are ordained of God, and the government set up
here, was created by men of prayer, devout men, who revered God, and looked to him for guidance and support:
and God has protected this government and people. The
government established here has withstood all assaults,
foreign and domestic ; and we have been steadily working
out the great evils that existed in our body politic.

Our greatest social evil was slavery, but God in his providence put it away, but at the cost of the most precious
blood of the nation, and by the expenditure of vast amounts
of treasure, and as the crowning act of sacrifice, God took
from us our beloved LINCOLN ; but the nation was spared.
True, it was left in a discordant and disjointed state. A
solid North, and a solid South were elements to be dis-
carded from the body politic, but how to do it, and unite the
people, was the problem. For sixteen long years the deep
wounds made by civil war have been healing, and who can
gainsay the fact that in the fullness of time, the hour had
arrived when we should have a restored Union ; in fact, as
well as in name ; when in our devotion to our Constitution
and laws, we should know no North, no South, no East, no
West, but a united Nation, striving for the welfare of all.

If the life and death of JAMES A. GARFIELD shall be the
means of fully accomplishing this great end, it will not be

in vain that he lived and died, and a thoroughly united nation may be the silver lining to the dark and mysterious cloud of this day : and may give to him that high place in history about which he seemed so anxious, when he contemplated that his life was to be so early cut off. Certain it is, that no man in modern times burst so suddenly upon the American people, and so attracted and centralized upon him the public gaze both North and South, as did President GARFIELD.

No event in modern times has sent such a thrill through the heart of this nation, as was done by the bullet of the assassin, when President GARFIELD fell. No event has brought this Nation so devoutly to the Throne of Grace, as this event did. No event has so thoroughly united the whole nation in one common petition to God ; that petition being a prayer that the life of the President might be spared.

All this united action must bear its own fruit : all this fervent prayer will not return to us empty and void. The life of our President was not spared in answer to our prayers, for the autopsy disclosed the fact, that the wound was mortal ; but while we lose our President, if we gain a thoroughly united and restored Union, with the bitterness of the late civil war all wiped out, with a more deep and devout reverence for Almighty God awakened, and a firmer reliance placed upon him by our people ; results such as these will be a full atonement for our loss, and an answer to our petitions.

As the nation watched by the bedside of the dying President from day to day, a bond of a more united brotherhood was created and began to grow ; and every bulletin issued from the attending surgeons' hands, was a fresh root striking down deep into our hearts, and extending to the remotest bounds of our country ; daily and hourly binding and welding us together as a nation, so that by the time he reached the portals of death, and could see the gates of the celestial city opening to receive him, this people were bound up in a union of hearts, a union of sentiment for our Constitution and laws, a union of States, and all cemented together by the blood of JAMES A. GARFIELD. This Union will stand : I do not believe now that there is any power on earth sufficiently strong to tear us asunder.

In relation to this subject matter :—death of our rulers, we as a people have much to be thankful for. Our first State Constitution was adopted July 2d, 1776, two days before the signing of the Declaration of Independence. Our Second Constitution was adopted in 1844 : under these two Constitutions we have existed as a State for one hundred and five years, and I have no recollection that any one of our Governors has died in office. A most remarkable favor of divine providence to us as a State.

As to the United States, President Washington was inaugurated April 30th, 1789, and the first President to die in office was President Harrison, which occurred April 4th, 1841 ; so that for a period of fifty-two years the government was administered by the person chosen by the people to perform that duty : and for a period of nearly one hundred years we have only lost four Presidents by death, and on each of these occasions the government was transmitted from the dead President to the living Vice President, chosen by the people to succeed to the office, and on each occasion there has been a peaceful transfer, without any commotion in the country, and without a ripple upon the body politic; which is one of the events in our history as a nation, which has been the amazement and wonder of the other nations of the world. For these great blessings, we should be devoutly thankful to Almighty God.

Chester A. Arthur is now the lawful and constitutional President of the United States, as such he is entitled to, and we should extend to him our hearty and cordial support. Placed in his present position by the people, he has a right to look to us to aid him in the administration of the government, and we have a right to look to him for a wise and able administration, and I have no doubt he will give us such an administration. When King Solomon commenced his reign, he prayed to God for wisdom that he might rule wisely, and be able to judge between good and evil, and because Solomon asked this thing, God heard his prayer, and because he did not ask for himself long life, great riches, or the life of his enemies, God made him the wisest man in all the earth, and added unto the gift both riches and honor, so that there was no King like Solomon in all his days.

Let us pray to God that He will give unto our President wisdom, so that he will be able to rule wisely and well; and let us all remember, that God reigns; that the Republic lives; and the Nation is constantly ascending on a higher plane of civilization.

There are times when—

> " Words, like Nature, but *half* reveal
> And half *conceal* the soul within,"

and never are words to be more distrusted than when invoked to the expression of *grief*. The heart, that knows its own bitterness, and would fain give vent thereto through the medium of speech, finds but little relief in language ; and yet the commingling of sentiment from sympathetic minds *is* the greatest balm for stricken hearts.

To-night, while the great National heart, of which ours are integral parts, full of, and *knowing* its own bitterness, is seeking consolation, let us endeavor to gather from each others words reminders of the past and assurances for the future that can gild the dark cloud which has so long hovered over us, and, bursting, has scattered sorrow over our land.

We come fresh from the grave of a murdered President —in which we have buried not merely a respected and honored Chief Magistrate, but *one of us*, who was enthroned not only in the place of power, but in the *affections* of this great People—and *so* enthroned therein that naught except the hallowed word "LOVED" can express the earnestness with which those affections clustered about him.

Had you, Mr. Chairman, been commissioned to examine and test the truth of this assertion, and could you have been enabled to penetrate each Commonwealth, City, and hamlet of our vast domain, and explore each valley, and traverse each mountain-side within our land, wherever man has made his habitation, and could you have probed each heart, your report would be : Yes—they all LOVED him. I saw it attested by the outburst of horror and sympathy

2   17

when the assassin's shot was fired—I have seen it attested
throughout the eighty days of anguish as the bulletins were
watched from hour to hour and hope and fear were alter-
nately depicted in the faces of the myriad watchers. I saw
it attested at the Fireside and in public as petitions inces-
santly ascended to God for His sparing mercy, and I saw
the whole fifty millions of the land bow together in sackcloth and ashes, pleading with the King of Kings for the
preservation of that *one* life.

I saw it attested by mournful countenances, yes, by gush-
ing tears, as the message "he is dead" was flashed from
the shore of the sea that sang his requiem.

I saw it attested by the hush and silence of busy mart.—

I see it now attested by emblems of mourning from structure grand and hovel mean,—from stately ship and tiny
craft,—from Iron Horse, and humble Ragman's cart inscribed "He loved the Poor—and I revere his memory".

I hear its attestation in tolling bell, and cannon's roar—
and Art, and Science, Pulpit, Press and Rostrum all bring
tribute and attestation.

Verily his nation *loved* him—and kindred nations across
the seas had learned to love him too,—and *their* tributes
come in deeply sympathetic forms, assuring that America
is not alone in her sorrow.

Such, I say, would be the truthful Report.

Then, ere yet the sod that was opened for him has been
replaced, we would water it with affection's tears, and plant
in each surviving breast, at least one flower from the garden of his life.

But where, amid the profusion of flowers that bloomed
in that fair garden, shall we begin? They are *all* flowers
of virtue,—and all of most brilliant hue—and, unlike those
which Nature permits to thrive only in more sunny climes,
and will not bear transplanting, these are all indigenous
to a common humanity, and each little cutting may live and
bloom in another life than his.

Affection — Patience — Perseverance — Patriotism—Bravery—Heroism under suffering—Humility—Fidelity—Uprightness and Christian Character, all charm us as we seek
a choice.

Take one—take all—ye people, and nurture each, that each one of you may have a life-garden in which others may find delight.

But especially adorning, it seems to me, are these three which attained well nigh unto perfection, if not perfection. in GARFIELD's life—*Humility, Fidelity* and *Uprightness.*

How the first was developed, and how it adorned the rest!

Never was deed performed or word spoken by him which could be construed to indicate that he deemed himself worthy of honor.

To himself he was but a man—and every man his peer.

Never did he seek an office—and when office sought and found him there was no elation which bore him beyond the reach of all.

He ever tried to *learn*, not deeming himself possessed of all needed lore.

He sought Divine assistance—and thankfully accepted suggestions from the experience of men.

In his view, his was but an humble life in the service of his country—and ever acknowledging superiority in others he became oblivious of self.

Gifted with Rhetorical powers which he could wield with master tongue, he was never obtrusive in their use, but his words of sense and wisdom in Legislative Halls were always addressed to the considerate thought of others and were never used as the lash of a Party Leader.

And how shall I speak of his *Fidelity?*

Was ever more faithful servant than he? Trace him. from Schoolmaster to the Senate of his State—thence to the din and roar of battle and Chickamauga's bloody field —thence to the National Congress, and onward and upward to the Presidential Chair, and nowhere can you find a single swerve from duty's path, or hesitation to perform his *entire* duty.

No trust committed to him was ever allowed to suffer— It was a constituent part of his nature to be faithful.—

By day, by night, at all times and in all places he recognized his duty and sought to perform it. Even when his poor, tortured frame had writhed in agony for well nigh the eighty days that God permitted to elapse between the assassin's shot and the relief of Death, his mind, so wonderfully clear and composed, turned toward those whose servant he was, and his wasted lips gave utterance to his welling thoughts as he exclaimed—" *The People, the People —my trust.*"

Eloquence indeed was this—All the Eulogies that gifted Oratory can pronounce could not so well assure us that he was devoted to us and our interests, as these few words from the dying Hero—and we know that the response "The President, the President—our hope" welled up from every heart, and ascended to the Throne on High, in unison with supplications in his behalf—Truly, he was faithful unto death.

As mountain towers above mountain, uniting to form one grand Panorama of Majestic beauty, and the highest peak crowns all with sublimity, so, towering over all the other virtues of him of whom we speak, and crowning all with their sublimity we see—not shrouded in mist, but glistening in pure light—his *Uprightness* and *Christian Character.* He acknowledged God in all his ways, and placed his reliance upon the strong arm of the Most High, while his heart rejoiced in the efficacy of Christ's atonement for sin.

Simple, unaffected Christianity pervaded his life, and purity of purpose and love of God and fellow-man actuated his every deed.

On such a Christian foundation, laid in youth, he reared the grand structure of his life—and thus was enabled, when he knew his days were fast numbering—aye, in the very presence of Death, to submit himself to the will of his Heavenly Father, with those touching words of confidence —" It's all right."

God be praised for such a life.

Gather from it the lessons it teaches, and profit by them —and treasure the inheritance it leaves—that GOOD *name* which the American People now have to perpetuate beside those of their own Washington and Lincoln—and may we in truth be enabled to say—

"On God and Godlike men we build our trust."

And now as in sorrow we turn again to the cares and duties which await us, we hear the dead yet speaking to us as he says—"*God reigns, and the Government at Washington still lives*"—Esto Perpetua—Let all the people say Amen— and give to their Country and its Rulers their prayers and their devotion—and as to our Hero whom we bury, let us with the Poet Laureate, say—

"Hush—the Dead March wails in the peoples ears:
The dark crowd moves, and there are sobs and tears:
The black Earth yawns: the mortal disappears;
Ashes to ashes—dust to dust:
He is gone who seemed so great.
Gone; but nothing can bereave him
Of the force he made his own
Being here, and we believe him
Something far advanced in State,
And that he wears a truer crown
Than any wreath that man can weave him.
But speak no more of his renown,
Lay your earthly fancies down,
And in the mausoleum leave him—
God accept him, Christ receive him."

The life and character of President GARFIELD have been fully and beautifully spoken of by the gentlemen who have preceded me, and while there remains but little for me to say, still it is a privilege to have an opportunity to add a few words expressive of one's thoughts upon the subject matter of this meeting. I however ask your indulgence and leniency because of thoughts and words chosen at this time rather than to a prepared address suitable to the occasion.

As I walked along the streets of the City of New York, and our city, this morning, I was reminded of the universal and sincere observance of the day : public buildings, places of business and private residences clothed in mourning for the dead : an absence of the usual stir and excitement of a week day : citizens of all classes absorbed in deep thought, their countenances indicative of grief. All feel the nation's loss. Grief is not confined to any section or State—to our own country. We all mourn—"the nations of the earth mourn." From the day the assassin's bullet pierced the body of our late President, regret and sorrow became universal. Recitals of sympathy came not only from within our own borders, but from the whole civilized world. This morning's newspapers inform us that three European Courts —Great Britain, Belgium and Spain—have gone into mourning for the death of President GARFIELD. This is the first time we have heard of such evidences of respect and royal etiquette by foreign nations.

President GARFIELD, from humble birth and poverty— fighting against adversity—raised himself to position in society and state. As a defender of the nation's honor on the field of battle, he bore a conspicuous part ; as a member of the Council of the Nation, he became the leader of his political party. As the Chief Executive Officer of these

23

United States, he stood boldly for the maintenance of good government, in the full confidence of the people, and before we reaped the full results of his labor, the assassin's bullet did its part, and to-day we meet to mourn the loss of him whose name will go into history as one of our ablest and wisest statesmen. When he became President of these United States, he became President of a nation of which you and I form a part; when he died, he died not as the President of any particular political party, but as President of these United States. All good citizens regret his death, honor his memory, and would drop a tear upon his new made grave. Who did not admire his executive ability, his manly qualities? Firm and inflexible as a statesman, tender and loving as a husband, father and son. Brave in the field of battle, brave in the hour of death.

But he has gone, and another occupies his position at the head of the government. The affairs of the nation move on as though the blow had not been felt. Each department performed and performs its respective labor as thorgh nothing had happened. What other nation could, with so brief a political existence, have withstood the shocks received by this nation—civil wars, conflicts with other nations, financial crisis, assassination of its Presidents—disturb us as individuals, but the government remains the same. The stability of our government is assured to us; its institutions are permanent, and its form and system are adapted to the people. May we find consolation in the fact that our conduct as a people, the uninterrupted business of the departments of government during these trying times, have elevated us as a nation : that this bereavement has hushed party strife and feeling; has called forth expressions of good feeling from home and abroad; has drawn together all classes in closer relation; has justified us in believing that we are respected and honored by all.

In considering the great loss sustained by us, let us not forget that wife who during those days of anxiety stood beside the bed of him whom she loved, and there showed that patience, care, tenderness, fortitude and allegiance which none but a true and loving wife and mother can give; that wife whose life has been rendered most miserable: forget not the sons and daughter; forget not the aged mother, to whom we are indebted for a GARFIELD; that mother who lived to see her son the Chosen Representative of a Great People; that son when he took his oath of office, and delivered his inaugural address, forgot not his mother, but first prepared a place for her that she might give him, in that trying and eventful hour, a mother's support.

Our loss is great: but can it compare with the loss sustained by that wife, those children, and the aged mother?

May the life and character of GARFIELD be not forgotten by those who live after him.

"Know ye not that there is a Prince and a great man fallen this day in Israel."

These words spoken many centuries ago, find an echo in our mournful souls to-day. We stand in the presence of a great crime. That terrible tragedy which opened in Washington on the eve of the Nation's greatest festival, closed on Monday night on the Jersey shore.—President GARFIELD is dead.

Change is written on everything with which we are familiar.

History repeats itself.

This is not the first time that this great nation has bowed its head and wept over the lifeless body of its Chief Magistrate—(sad to relate)—struck down by the dastardly and forever infamous assassin.

This sad event which has filled every home and heart throughout this broad land with the shadow of death, is not without its parallel; and many a mind has dwelt upon the two events in mournful comparison.

Sixteen years to the rear for a few moments.

On Saturday the 16th day of April, 1865, a dark cloud —a storm cloud—broke upon the heart of this great Republic.

The country was startled from sea to sea with the sad tidings of the attempted assassination of that "Prize Man of the Woods"—ABRAM LINCOLN—the night before.

---

* The Committee solicited from the Rev. Mr. Blight his Sermon preached on the occasion to his Church and Congregation, instead of his address delivered at the Bergen Reformed Church ; portions of which were embraced in the same. The Sermon, therefore. takes its place here as the tribute of the Emory Methodist Episcopal Church of Jersey City Heights, which will not have assigned to it an independent chapter in this volume. —EDITOR.

Another flash of the wires told the excited people that the President was dead.

That was a dark day in the history of the Republic.

The smoke of battle like a dismal fog-cloud hung over the field yet crimsoned with the blood of heroes who cheerfully laid down their lives that the "Stars and Stripes" might live.

On that memorable Saturday, when the Spirit of our Martyred LINCOLN went up to God who gave it, and New York City seemed ready for the scenes of the French Revolution, a loyal host gathered in front of the doors of the Custom House in Wall street.

The speakers on that occasion were heroes, patriots and statesmen.

Among that noble company stood one, with a small flag in his hand, and beckoned to the crowd, and raising his right arm sky-ward, spoke out an electric appeal. Alas! the hero of that day, is the martyr of this.

The speech of General GARFIELD before that great assemblage was brief.

There was not much time for speech-making. Manhood —integrity—and patience in well-doing were the demands of the hour. "The rights of liberty and equal laws" must be upheld.

And remembering as we do to-day, that those lips which spoke so well then, are now forever closed in death, we cannot refrain from using his own words in reference to the death of President LINCOLN. "In taking away that life," he said, "They have left the iron hand of the people to fall upon them. Peace, forgiveness and mercy are the attributes of this government; but justice and judgment, with inexorable tread, will follow behind them. This nation is too great to look for mere revenge, but for the security of the future I would do everything."

How strange! yet how true. President GARFIELD has followed the immortal LINCOLN, after sixteen years full of noble service for his country, has gained his Crown of Martyrdom—the murderous Guiteau has accomplished his infernal work—a disappointed office-seeker has slain another of the World's Best.

The villain full-grown that slew JAMES A, GARFIELD, 'has exposed himself to the iron hand of the law : and though " peace, forgiveness and mercy are the attributes of this government—he being dead yet speaketh—"Justice and Judgment, with *inexorable tread*, MUST follow behind them, for the security of the future we must do everything."

JAMES A. GARFIELD expired at thirty-five minutes past ten last Monday night.

"God reigns, and the government at Washington still lives."

For many weary weeks the President of the United States—the victim of a crime second in villainy to only one other in our history—lingered between life and death. The illustrious sufferer for eighty days bore his sufferings with a patience, a courage, and a calm, which seemed to fill the heart of the nation with hope, that ere long he would hold in his mighty grasp again the reigns of government.

But that brave fight for life, which the whole civilized world watched with tearful eye, throbbing heart, and anxious soul—failed at last.

A great ship has suddenly gone down into the black waters of death—capacious, well built, carrying precious and valuable freight.

It is well that the nations put on weeds of mourning. Ay! the world has lost a friend.

Be it remembered, a great and good man, like the sun in the heavens, is the property of no sect, race or clime. He belongs to the whole world. Humanity feels the influence of his life, and mourns his loss this day.

JAMES A. GARFIELD makes his transit from this life to the next, while the nation reverently and tearfully stands at his bier.

And not only the fifty millions of this Continent presenting everywhere emblems of sorrow—Yes, the sable badge of woe drapes window and column and mast—the North and the South alike : the whole land is in mourning.

But Europe also bows her head, and the people of every land pause in the presence of this great calamity.

A bright light has gone out in the death of President
GARFIELD, and the gloom falls upon the shores of all the
continents of the globe.

Bravely did he fight in the great struggle for life. A su-
perb specimen of heroic manhood. At last, that great temple—the body — (battered and broken by the assassin's
bullet), suddenly fell at Elberon, "and all is over."

Thus passed from this life, one of "Nature's noble men."

Beholding that life as we do to-day, with the mists of
prejudice and party feeling swept away by the hand of
death, what can we do but stand up before the whole world
and say—" He was a Man."

He is gone, and has left "foot-prints on the sands of
time."

—The romantic life of JAMES A. GARFIELD began in Ohio
November 19th, 1831, and was therefore not yet fifty years
of age.

GARFIELD the Boy — the Soldier — and the Christian
Statesman, are the pictures we hold to your view to-day.

His birth-gifts were of the best. He entered the race of
life grandly furnished to make a splendid run, and this he
did. A sound mind in a healthy body, a wholesome constitution. Heaven has nothing greater to give a man when
he is born.

A grand old mother stood behind him with her prayers,
and whenever he looked backward, he beheld virtue, industry and frugality. That mother behind his boyhood, who
had learned the art of trusting God, pushed him upward
and onward, till at length he stood alone—

> " The pillar of a people's hope."

—Diligence robed his young life, and never did he cast
the garment aside. Beginning life in the shop of hard
work he never went out of it. Grit and perseverence made
him master of that, which to all appearance for a time
seemed to be his only portion—humble toil.

It was a struggle against fearful odds for years ; his path
was rugged and up hill. He fought against poverty and
conquered, obscurity, and came up to shine among the

stars destined to burn for ever—Washington, Jefferson, and Lincoln.

The boy born to poverty, and left fatherless when a child in his mother's arms, rises from the "tow-path" and the carpenter's bench to eminence in professional life, and before some men begin to live, he sits a cultured Christian gentleman, at the head of a great institution of learning.

Hiram College received a benediction in the year 1857, when Mr. GARFIELD became its President ; and the students were inspired to nobler deeds.

One of them writing on this point recently, said :— "There are men and women scattered over the United States, holding positions of honor and wealth, who began the life which led them upward, by the voice and with the assistance of Mr. and Mrs. GARFIELD." Certainly it is no overstated tribute when we say, that the active, generous, and pure life they led for two years at "Hiram," will bless generations yet unborn.

In him we to-day lament, lofty patriotism found a home. Hence the soldier—"General GARFIELD"—when war was declared, and the integrity of the United States trembled in the balance.

It was perfectly natural and logical that GARFIELD should be one of the first to offer his services in the National Cause. He loved his country, and entered the conflict at the head of the gallant Forty-second, and bounding across the Ohio into Eastern Kentucy, he confronted General Marshall at Middle Creek. Born to win, he won at Middle Creek.

When shall his glory die ? Wrapping himself in the mantle of glory, at the great battle of Chickamauga, and was promoted Major-General for "gallant and meritorious" services in that engagement.

On that September afternoon, memorable 19th day of September, 1863, witnessed the deeds of a hero. Alas! that on the anniversary day of that great victory, September 19th, 1881, should witness the death-struggle of JAMES A. GARFIELD, President of the United States.

A true patriot he toiled in his country cause—" nobly

bled, and his deeds as they deserve, receive proud recompense. His name we give in charge to the historic muse, who, fond of its treasures, marches with them down to later times; and sculpture in her turn gives form in stone, or more enduring brass, to guard him and immortalize her trust."

He was a man of good education and attainments, marked independence of character and thought, and possessed the concomitant virtue of courage.

Though not indifferent to popular opinion, as no sound mind is, he had much of the spirit of that old hero who said—" Where there as many devils in Worms as roof-tiles, I would on."

In the character of President Garfield there was almost everything to admire, and almost nothing to condemn. His intellect was clear, powerful and logical; his speeches were marked by clearness of expression, and force of utterance, and always commanded attention.

His professional, military, political, and home life, gives ample proof that he was every inch a man.

One step higher—

"The Christian is the highest style of man."

It was the crowning glory of our President that he was a Christian. His feet were firmly planted on that Eternal Rock where stood in other days the martyrs who endured poverty, scorn, and death, rather than disobey conscience. The foundation of his Christian life was laid on Christ; and as the outside life went up, there was a corresponding elevation of soul.

He cultivated a devotional spirit which was not marred by mysticism, or chilled by doubt. Like Caleb, the son of Jephunneh, who was of "another spirit" from the timid spies ; like Joshua, who resolved " As for me and my house we will serve the Lord;" the glorious principles of the " Gospel of the Blessed God" filled his soul. Hence his courage in danger, magnanimity in distress, submission in suffering, and a hope full of immortality in the prospect of death.

A hot political canvass oftentimes burns the virtues of a man, and too often throws their ashes into the péoples eyes. Lies are rapid travellers, and men sometimes call them facts. They shall perish. Truth is immortal. History will write the name of our dead President among the best of the world's Christian Statesmen. " His mausoleum is the American heart, his renown is safe in the bosom of a great nation that cannot forget him, and out of love of him must find new paths to glory."

He has gone from us forever ; he has finished his course. With rapid steps he moved to the front, and reached the end with the sun shining in a noon-day sky. The Crown of martyrdom was given him at the shrine of duty. He has fought his last battle, suffered the last disappointment, and beyond the reach of murderous hands—no more delirium, nor rigor. He is at home, and at rest in our Father's house, robed, crowned, and immortalized. He has gone from us forever—Whither has he gone ?

The world's Commander-in-Chief has said to our Chief Magistrate, " Come up higher," and the Presidential Chair was vacated last Monday night by President GARFIELD, for a seat at God's right hand—

"To him that endureth to the end, will I grant to sit with me on my throne."

" And I heard a voice from heaven saying—Write, from henceforth blessed are the dead which die in the Lord. Even so saith the Spirit, for they rest from their labors."

Death is another life, and when we whispered "he is dead"—" The angels were singing, a man is born."

Brothers—Let us learn to cultivate friendship, and communion with God.

He can be better to us than all earthly friends. Let us anticipate the eternal enjoyment of God, and of our friends in heaven.

Our friends are not lost, they are only removed from a tabernacle to a mansion.

They shall come again.

" Beyond the smiling and the weeping
      I shall be soon,
Beyond the waking and the sleeping,
Beyond the sowing and the reaping,
      I shall be soon.
Love, rest and home—
Sweet home,
Lord, tarry not, but come."

Brothers—a great and good man has been taken from the head of the government.

His gain is our loss—his freedom makes us prisoners of grief, but not Hopeless Prisoners.

THE CLOUD IS SILVER-LINED.

In the mid-night of our sorrow, with tearful eye, we look toward our strong tower, and cry—" Watchman, what of the night?" Is there no answer? Nothing seen but ebony clouds rolling across the sky? No sound heard save the voice of vexed thunder amid the mountain of sorrow?

" Watchman, what of the night?" " The morning cometh." The eastern horizon flames with light. " Sorrow may endure for a night—Joy cometh in the morning." It must be so: immortal lips have declared it.

God governs the world for man's benefit, and though he does permit crime, he can make the wrath of man to praise him, and in his own good time he will do it.

God is never in a hurry—therefore be of good cheer.

The villainy of one man cannot wreck this great Ship of State, and although the Captain in a thunder storm perish with his hand on the wheel, she will outride the storm and brave the tempest.

Changing the figure :

This Republic is not an arch, held together by a keystone, and if removed, the confronting halves fall in ruinous heaps, shattered into ten thousand fragments.

No one man is indispensible to the life of this government. President GARFIELD living was a column of strength, but his death has enlarged and cemented a universal brotherhood.

"The deeds that men do live after them." Guiteau—
"Doubly dying, shall go down to the vile dust from whence
he sprung—unhonored, unwept, unsung." Our beloved
President GARFIELD has left a memory which smells sweet,
and shall blossom in the ashes of the tomb.

Nations, like forest trees, may grow stronger by the rude
blast sweeping through them, whose roots strike deeper
into the tenacious soil.

If we are wise, this big cloud which some fear so much,
"May break in blessings on our head."

Brothers—methinks I hear a voice to-day, calling us to
duty, reminding us of something almost forgotten (by the
people of this country, who instinctively make haste to
be rich.)   •

PERSONAL RESPONSIBILITY in the affairs of the Nation :

Everything is left in the hands of Professional Politicians, who have planted and fostered a Upas tree whose
deadly shade is upon this day. Root out from the field
of American Politics the "Spoils System." That the
"Spoils belong to the Victors," is heathenish, and should
not be permitted to raise its unsightly head in the light
of this last quarter of the nineteenth century.

Selfishness has been a devil in man in every age, whose
crimes have blackened the page of history.

There is a cure for all this. I read in the signs of the
times that we as a Christian people—perhaps—must not
have more politics in our religion, but MORE RELIGION in
our politics.

Who says that religion and politics must never be mar-
ried. No decent body. There are two enemies of the
race—father and child, who object to the union—Rum and
his Satanic Majesty.

"Keep politics out of religion." Why? Why, for the
same reason that the thief would like to see all the officers
of the law appointed to watch the North Pole. Everybody knows the wherefore of this. Guilt is a coward.

RELIGION, NOT SECTARIANISM, we must have in our "Town
Meetings," and all the way up to the "White House."

Christianity is not that effeminate thing, that some little

pious souls think she is, which must always be wrapped up in the napkin of some "ism."

She was born in a storm, and the thunder of the waves has ever been sounding in her ears. She has always received rough treatment, and she is built for it. She has iron shoes, and she can stand in them at the poles. She is fitted for legislative halls, the palaces of kings, and the courts of queens. Ay! She has stood like the ocean's rock, which throws off the insulting wave in harmless spray.

Joseph in Egypt, Daniel in Babylon, Paul before Felix, John Knox in the presence of Mary, Wilberforce on the floor of the House of Commons, and JAMES A. GARFIELD in Washington. •

Religion and politics are not oil and water. They can, ought, and must live together.

We must not make God the author of sin, nor say of this great crime, "A divine Providence." There is no Providence in it. God, as the moral Governor of the Universe, does not deprive his creature the freedom of his will. Right and wrong are before every man. He can go two ways, up and down. Guiteau took a long and fatal step downward, and laid low our President.

My hearers, I can trust God for the government of this world. The Republic is safe—"God reigns." He speaks to-day and lifts the veil.

He whom we lament, once said—

"There are times in the history of men and nations, when they stand so near the veil that separates mortals from immortals, time from eternity, and men from God, that they can almost hear the beatings and feel the pulsations of the heart of the Infinite."

> "The lives of good men all remind us,
> We may make our lives sublime;
> And departing leave behind us
> Footprints on the sands of time.
>
> Let us then be up and doing,
> With a heart for any fate:
> Still achieving, still pursuing,
> Learn to labor and to wait."

It is impossible to give expression to the feelings of an hour like this. We have passed through nearly three months of alternate hope and dread, which could scarcely have been exceeded to each one of us, if the shadow of death had hung over our own households. That suspense culminated in an event which filled with sorrow the hearts of fifty millions of people, and touched in sympathy the whole civilized world. And what was this event? One man had died—But such a man, and such a death!

Fifty years ago, in a log cabin in the northern part of Ohio, where the trees of the primeval forest were still sighing to the breezes from Lake Erie, was born a child of poverty and toil. No unusual sign distinguished his birth from the advent of the thousands of infants who, that day, first saw the light in the dwellings of the poor.

Ten years pass by, and this child has become a school-boy, trudging with brown bare feet to his daily task. Still he is but one among his comrades, and not the fore-most one, unmarked by any prophetic trait of future greatness. For him, as for ten thousand others, a widowed mother struggles in her round of anxious labor to give him bread, and such training as may fit him for the humbler walks of life. Trust in God, whose blessing she invokes upon her offspring, and the love of those she nurtures, are alike her strength and hope.

And now another half score years have departed, and this youth of twenty stands upon the threshold of Hiram College. Through manual toil at the counting desk, at the carpenter's bench, at the wood-pile, at the canal, he has emerged; a gleam of light had flashed upon that watery highway, which seemed to him the finger of the Almighty, shining through the gates ajar, and beckoning

37

him to higher spheres, And now, obedient to the vision, he approaches the Pierian Spring, whose waters never quench the thirst that brings the spirit to their fountain, and with a soul fired by worthy ambition, he seeks for knowledge and the power which that supplies. Now, first, he stands forth, apart from the common throng, stirred by a 'noble rage' which 'chill penury' cannot repress. Poverty is indeed still his companion, but cheerful industry brings a smile even to her sullen face, as she walks hand in hand with this determined youth, at once a student and the janitor of his *Alma Mater*.

Another decade rolls away, and Sumter's gun has echoed from sea to sea through this broad land. Rebellion, with horrid front, stands menacing the nation. Patriot cheeks are blanched with fear; but they glow again with healthy blood when the clarion voice of the undaunted Lincoln is heard summoning to arms the valor and loyalty of his countrymen. The summons penetrates the seclusion of the class-room at Hiram, where the *quondam* janitor presides, training the studious in the lessons of peace. Ten years of college life, scarce broken by a sally into the forum of debate when Freedom sought a champion, had fostered his mental growth with the learning of the centuries; his tastes and aspirations had all pursued the paths of civil life, and the blare of the martial trumpet grated on his ear. A young wife had set up for him a domestic altar garlanded with the flowers of grace and love, and the mother, who had taught his infant feet to walk and guarded all his boyish years, was now leaning upon his strong and willing arm. But the cry of his country reaches him, and notwithstanding all his culture of the arts of peace, not withstanding, nay, applauding him, his wife and mother, he quits the quietude of study, the sanctity of home, and the safety of the Senate, for the din and danger of the field of war.

Now ten years more of history have been fulfilled. The child of the log cabin, the barefoot school-boy, the toilsome student, and the patriot soldier has become the representative of his neighborhood in the capital of the nation. Once more Peace has resumed her sway, and this cultured man has come to take his place among the leaders of the people. Already has his right to prominence there been recognized. His learning, his wisdom, his eloquence, his integrity, and his patriotism, have fitted him to bear a worthy part in rebuilding the shattered fabric of the Union. Nobly has he helped to break the fetters on the bondsman's limbs, to restore the honest industry of freemen to its wonted channels, to give security to wealth, to quench the fires of sectional animosity, and to make government a blessing and not a burden, through all the borders of the land. And to this purpose his life seems now devoted; for if you watch him through the coming years, you shall see him in these legislative halls, never idle when there's work to do, never silent when a word is needed, never faltering when danger threatens, never weakening under heavy burdens, if his hand or tongue or heart or brain may advance the cause of righteousness and truth.

And now the snows of half a century have fallen, since this man first breathed the breath of life; and behold, he stands among his countrymen crowned with unequalled honors! While yet he holds the legislative trust which his neighborhood confided to him, his great State calls him to a higher plane, and bids him perform her part in the Supreme Council of the Union. While still this office remains an honor only, and has not yet become a duty, the Nation summons him to be her Chief Magistrate. And so, with the triple wreath upon his brow, as Representative, Senator and President at once, he attains the summit of human greatness.

But he knew that the path of glory was not a path of ease, and girding himself for that of which he never hitherto had come short, his duty, he entered with simple dignity upon his lofty functions. One-twelfth of his administrative course was not yet run, and all the people's hope had ripened into assurance, that, beneath his sway, the Republic would suffer no detriment, when the peaceful morning air is startled by a pistol shot, and

" He that is in his glory falleth, and that by a contemptible enemy."

All the problems of his life are solved, and he is face to face with death's tremendous issue.

Now gather round his stricken form the sympathies of every heart. He had been willing to give his life for his country: What is his country not ready to give for his life! Can any human skill preserve him? May wealth not buy some years of living for him? Can prayers reverse the sad decree? He wished not death, for his own high purposes seemed unfulfilled: but he feared him not, knowing that the immortal part within was far beyond his shaft. Through eighty days the unequal struggle lasts. In vain. Death conquered; and the will of God was done. Civilization bowed in awe and grief. From the lowliest hut of the slave-born freedman, and the royal chamber of the God-blest queen alike, the reverent wail of sorrow rose.

To-day we bury him. But let us be not dismayed. Such lives do not end in the grave. They constitute the Nation's history, and pass from generation to generation among the most valued jewels in our political inheritance. And even such a death is not without its uses. It hallows all the memories of the life before it: and it enforces a lesson we had already learned, that no single man is essential to the country's progress. As the fathers fall, you shall see the sons whom the example of their virtues has begotten, nurtured and trained, step forward in their stead to take their places in the government of this great people, as it leads all the nations of the world to liberty and light.

SERMON BY REV. A. S. GUMBART.*

" He being dead yet speaketh."—HEB. xi. 4.

On the night of April 14, 1865, the crack of the assassin's pistol was heard, and swifter than the wind the cable flashed the terrible news—LINCOLN is murdered. The great chief of a great people had fallen : a canopy of darkness veiled our land in sorrow : a thrill of horror troubled every loyal breast.

On the morning of July 2, 1881, when the people of our land were preparing to celebrate the 105 Anniversary of American Independence, another shot was fired from an assassin's pistol—a shot that was echoed throughout the world. Again the nation was horrified. JAMES A. GAR-FIELD, the President of the United States, the man who sixteen years before had by his courage and eloquence stilled the wild tumult of an indignant people when the death of LINCOLN drove them almost to madness, was himself plucked from the head of this people by the hand of a murderer. It is mysterious, deeply, terribly mysterious. Over his grave we repeat the words of Gen. Butler on the occasion of LINCOLN's death—" He died in the fullness of his fame." But in the midst of our sorrow how forcibly are we reminded of Mr. GARFIELD's own words of encourage-ment, when fifty thousand people crowded about the Wall Street Exchange sixteen years ago, when the news came that the President had been murdered. I quote in part the words of a distinguished public man who was an eye-witness of the scene—" The people were wild with excite-

---

*The Committee solicited from the Rev. Mr. A. S. Gumbart his Sermon preached on the occasion to his Church and congregation ; portions of which were embraced in his address at the Bergen Reformed Church. The Sermon, therefore, takes its place here, and is also the tribute of the Summit Avenue Baptist Church, to this volume.—EDITOR.

ment. Two men who a moment before had said, ' LINCOLN
ought to have been shot long ago,' were not permitted to
say it again. The next moment one lay dead and the other
dying. A cry had been made to burn the office of the
World. It was a fearful crisis. With a small flag in his
hand, GARFIELD stepped to the front, and with one hand
lifted up to Heaven, spoke out loud and distinct—'Fellow-
citizens, clouds and darkness are round about Him, His
pavilion is dark waters and thick clouds of skies—Justice
and judgment are the establishment of His throne—Mercy
and truth shall go before His face. Fellow-citizens, God
reigns, and the government at Washington still lives.' The
effect was tremendous. As the boiling waves subside and
settle to the sea when the strong wind beats it down, so the
tumult of the people sank and became still." These words
of our dead hero are our consolation and encouragement
in this hour of our Nation's affliction—" God reigns, and
the Government at Washington still lives." Truly, he being
dead yet speaketh.

But my intention this evening is not so much to eulo-
gize our dead President as to draw a few plain and practical lessons from his life and death, which may serve to
make us better men, better citizens, and better Christians.
" He being dead yet speaketh."

The life of our dead President speaks to us, 1st. Because
it reminds us that man's possibilities in life do not de-
pend upon the social nature of his birth. Every man is
in a measure the architect of his own usefulness. Especially is this true in this land where individual energy and
earnest labor may lead a man from the lowest and humblest
to the highest and most honored social or political position. It is one of the blessings of our American Institutions that every man in a certain sense begins life upon the
same plane. Whatever may be his social position he has
placed before him the same possibilities of success. In no
land as in our own land is personal merit so apt to receive
its full and just reward. For a moment let us look back
over the history of the Nation's Martyr. Where did this
noble life begin? What were his surroundings, and what

his apparent possibilities? The scene opens in Northeastern Ohio. On a clearing in the midst of a forest stood a log cabin. At the time when our sketch begins, Death had stricken down the strong man, the husband and father of those that dwelt within. It was a sudden blow. The mother with her children was left alone in the world. The youngest a boy of eighteen months was to be the future President of the United States. Such was the beginning of the life of JAMES A. GARFIELD, the murdered hero, over whose body the heart of the nation bleeds and mourns. It was a beginning of sorrow and hardship. It was a beginning so humble as probably few if any who are here to-night have had; and yet there are young men here to-night—and old men too—who murmur and whine because nature has not given them a "fair start" in the world. Here was a man who was four years old before he wore his first pair of shoes. Here was a man whose early life was a continual struggle against poverty and position. From a tow-boy on a canal he became a student. From a student he became a teacher. From a teacher he became a College President. From a College President he became a State Senator. In time of the country's need he became a Soldier. From a Soldier he rose to the rank of a Major-General. Then a United States Senator, until at last he sat down at Washington as the Chief Magistrate of the people, whom he had so faithfully served as a Citizen, Soldier and Statesman. Surely he being dead yet speaketh. We need but have the willing ear to hear.

Does not the life of Mr. GARFIELD put to shame the complaints of those who charge their failure in life to the want of social position?

Nor has the life of Mr. GARFIELD been an exceptional one in this respect. In the political life we have the names of Lincoln, Grant and others, who were all of humble birth and meagre advantages; and in secular life, who shall number the names of those who while in humble station reached out for the grand possibilities that God places before every man, and by dint of persevering, earnest labor, reached the goal in triumph. True, we cannot all be Presidents, but each man in his own sphere may become the hero of circumstances. But GARFIELD did not *dream* himself into prominence. His advancement and success were the outcome of honest toil and persistent struggles. There are but few men who do not *desire* success, but there are many who seemingly have not learned to *work* for it. We are told that when Mr. GARFIELD was but a mere lad, that the backwoods schoolmaster said to him by way of encouragement, "Now, James, my boy, if you will learn, you may grow up to be a General. He knew little what it was to be a general, but he replied earnestly, O, yes, sir, I'll learn and be a general. Two weeks after the schoolmaster remarked, James is a perpetual motion—but he learns—not a scholar in the school learns as fast as he." And so throughout his whole life, until that life was ended by the bullet of the assassin, GARFIELD seemed indeed to have been a perpetual motion. His life was a life of industry and toil, and his example worthy of emulation. So we mourn not only because our *President* has been stricken down, but because a *Man* as was a man, and one whom the nation could ill afford to spare has been taken from us. " But God reigns and the government at Washington still lives."

But in speaking of the early life of Mr. GARFIELD, I cannot but pay a tribute of respect to that heroic woman, the mother of our deceased President. It is said that great men are the sons of great mothers. In the life of our President this saying has indeed been verified. The historian tells us that just after the death of Mr. GARFIELD's father the corn was running low in the bin, and it was yet a great while before harvest. So the mother measured out the meagre supply, and in order to give her children three meals a day, she went to bed for many weeks without her supper. " But their little mouths were larger than she had measured," and by and by she omitted her dinner also; and thus this noble woman labored and toiled, oft-times sewing for the neighbors and living on one meal a day— " One meal a day and she a weak, fragile woman"—O wonders of a mother's love. Thank God this woman lived to see the little boy whom she had pressed to her bosom in the hour of her sorrow, promoted to the highest position in the gift of the greatest nation on the face of the earth. Forty-five years after, this woman stood upon the platform at Washington and congratulated her son before the people with a hearty kiss; and now as she weeps over the grave of her dead boy, may God bless her and comfort her, and while she mourns because her son is no more, may she remember the words of the buried hero—"God Reigns." Yes, God still reigns, and *her boy still lives*, not only in the hearts and memories of his countrymen, but what is better still, lives and reigns where there shall be no more death, no more tears, no more struggles.

Again: the life of our President speaks to us in his death, inasmuch as it places before us an example of unselfish industry. One of the chief characteristics of our dead President was the benevolence with which he considered the good of others. Unlike many who have pressed forward merely to enrich themselves, or to increase their own fame, it seemed to have been the life purpose of Mr. GARFIELD to labor for the good of his fellow men. President Hinsdale, Mr. GARFIELD's successor at Hiram, bears this testimony. In speaking of our dead President, he says—"He drew near to me and entered into all my troubles and difficulties.   *   *   *   In a greater or less degree this was true of his relations to his pupils in general. There are hundreds of these men and women scattered over the world to-day who cannot find language strong enough to express their feeling in contemplating GARFIELD as their old instructor, adviser, and friend;" and so throughout his life, whether as a teacher, soldier or statesman, his chief object seemed to be to advance himself in order that he might serve others. No man serves his own interests so well as that man who with a true generosity has a mind for the interests of others. No man has so many friends as he who makes himself a friend of others. It is by blessing others that we ourselves receive a blessing.— What a different world this would be; how much less of pain and poverty if men would learn to consider the welfare of others. It is one of the written laws of the Gos-

pel that men should not live for themselves alone, but
for others as well, and the man who has not this spirit
within him has not the spirit of Him who for the sake
of others gave his own life as a sacrifice for sin.

O how many there are who feel that the world owes
them a living, but seem entirely unconscious of the fact that
they owe the WORLD something. The man who is so shut up
to himself that he has no care for others, is not WORTHY to
live, nor is he FIT to die. It is one of the great principles
of life which every man should recognize, namely, that
every man must take care of himself. But man is not to
take care of himself to the exclusion of all others. Self-
care and care for others are sister graces : it is the second
great commandment—Thou shalt love thy neighbor as thyself. There is but one commandment greater than this—
Thou shalt love the Lord thy God with all thy heart and
with all thy soul and with all thy mind.

Again : the life of our President speaks to us in his
death, inasmuch as it reminds us that Godliness and politics need not necessarily be separated from each other ;
and in speaking of this I do not propose to speak of a
"State religion," I merely wish to impress you with the
fact that a politician in the true sense of that term *can* be
a Christian. Mr. GARFIELD was a Christian. Not only
was Mr. GARFIELD a professor of religion, but he had
been buried with Christ in baptism. He believed in the
old fashioned Gospel baptism. But more than this,
Mr. GARFIELD was a preacher of the Gospel; he had
stood before dying men pointing them to a crucified
Savior. In view of these things his death seems all the
more mysterious. But I remember that the great King
of kings himself was betrayed by a traitor and nailed to
the cross by a mob of murderers, and the "servant is
not greater than his Lord."

The life of our President is an evidence of the fact
that religion and politics need not necessarily be divorced
from each other. We sometimes hear men say that the
dividing line between religion and politics is not clearly
enough drawn, but it is just here that the Church of Christ

too often makes a fatal mistake. *There should be no dividing line.* Let us wipe out the line altogether. If religion
has the leavening, the purifying, the elevating power that
we believe it has, let it permeate and saturate our politics
through and through. As long as we attempt to keep
religion *out* of politics just so long must we expect our
politics to be currupt. Of course there are politicians
who tell us that Christians have no business to meddle
with politics. But why do they tell us this? Ah! they
recognize the fact better than we do ourselves that if
Christian men should come to the front and do their duty
as Christian citizens, corruption would be crowded out o
office. If it is right that Christian men should have a
government—if it is right that we should be loyal to that
government, is it not right, I ask, that Christians should
help to make that government? In one of his speeches
Mr. GARFIELD said, in speaking of those who fought for
American independence: "The men who pointed out the
pathway to freedom by the light of religion were the fore-
most promoters of American Independence." So to-day
and in ages to come, the lamp of religion should guide us
in political paths as well as in all other paths of life.
But you say, "politics are corrupt." Well, it is the
business of the Church in the sight of God to purify that
which is corrupt. The more Christ we can bring into
politics the stronger the government and the greater our
assurance of God's protection and blessing. How deeply
our dead President recognized the power of God in the
history of nations is seen in an article from his own pen,
entitled, "The Providence of History," in which he says :
"No man can understand the history of any nation who
does not recognize in it the power of God." A nation
without a God cannot prosper. But what is true of the
nation is true of the individual; without God there is no
hope; without God in our hearts we cannot hope for the
protection and blessing of the Almighty Father. God's
law must be above every other law in the government of
our individual lives, and the light of the gospel of Christ
must guide us in every path of duty. The nation cannot be

better than its subjects. Mr. GARFIELD once said: "The American people are very much like one giant human being." This suggests to us the thought, that inasmuch as every part goes to make up the whole, so every citizen is a part of this giant being. The honest, the pure, the righteous, the benevolent, are the good healthy blood of this giant; the dishonest, the corrupt, the sinful, the selfish, are the boils and tumors that weaken his power and corrupt his purity. So, then, if we are to be a God-fearing, Christian nation, we ourselves must be God-fearing, Christian men and women. The government is the *head* of the nation, but the people constitute its *heart*, and regeneration must begin at the heart. God grant then, that the lost image of God may be restored in our souls through faith in Him whose precious blood cleanseth us from all sin, so that when the time comes for us to die it may be said of us as of our dead President, "he died in the faith." O that Christ would so reign in every individual heart here to-night, that we might not only be made better citizens of the land we love, but that in the life to come we would be recognized as fellow citizens with the saints and of the household of God.

Again: the life of Mr. GARFIELD still speaks to us, inasmuch as it warns us of the uncertainty of life. During his life the President, we are told, seems to have cherished the idea that his end would come in some sudden and violent manner. It was a strange fatalism from which it seemed impossible to rid himself. He confessed that he thought it foolish to harbor any such thought, but it clung to him in spite of himself. More than this, it was his firm belief that he should not live to be older than his father, who died at the age of forty-five, and when the President overlived that age he was in constant dread lest he should fall between the cars, or be killed in some other violent way while traveling. And yet for all this, how suddenly, how unexpectedly the blow came. At a time when great opportunities seemed to await equally as great qualities; at a time when a great work seemed laid before able and willing hands, in an unexpected hour a

murderer's dastardly deed finished a life of usefulness and
dignity. Little did the President dream, as he left the
executive mansion on that fatal morning, that before
evening he would be carried back mortally wounded, but
such is the mystery of life and death, such is the
uncertainty of our being; in the morning we arise in the
full vigor of manhood and womanhood, and at evening-time
we are numbered among the dead. There are times in
life when we seem to be very near death's door, but by
God's grace, human skill is permitted to fan the flickering
flame into a brighter light, and God spares us for a time.
But O there comes a time when the skill of earthly physicians can do no more, and the struggling spirit takes
its eternal flight. Here was a man at whose bedside gathered some of the most skillful physicians of the land.
They had at their finger's ends all that medicine or science
could do for the sufferer. The purse of the nation was
open to their bidding. But at last the heart refused to
do its office work, and with a gasp the hero expired. He
was dead.... O how soon the time may come in your
.life or in mine, when anxious friends will turn away from
our bedside sobbing—he is dead. How true are the
words of the poet—

> "Down the vista of the ages,
> Saints and sinners, fools and sages,
> Marching onward, slow and solemn,
> Go in never-ending column ;
> Here the honest, here the knave ;
> With a rythmic step sublime
> To the grave. "

So there may be times in our lives when God in answer
to prayer may spare us for a season before we go hence.
But there comes a time when God shall say, No—The appointed time has come. The last of the numbered days
is fading into night. Here, for example, was a man for
whom a nation prayed, aye prayed *as no other nation ever
prayed before*, and it seemed as if God *must* spare, but God
said, No—and we bow submissive to His will—for if we

4

have prayed aright, we have prayed that God should do what seemeth him good. If we have prayed aright, we have said, Nevertheless, Thy will, not our's be done. It has been God's will to take him away; we cannot understand it, but this we know, He doeth all things well.

JAMES A. GARFIELD is dead. DEAD, did I say? Nay, over this sad truth I write in golden letters of God's eternal truth—JAMES A. GARFIELD still lives. And from out of the tomb I seem to hear the voice of sixteen years ago—"God reigns and the government at Washington still lives." May God lead us forth in majesty, enrich us with his blessings, and protect us by his might. Amen.

At midnight "there was a great cry in Egypt, for there was not a house where there was not one dead." Thus runs the record of the visit of the destroying angel, in that awful midnight thousands of years ago, to the dwellings of the doomed in that land of fame and eld. One week ago, at midnight, a great cry arose in this land, a like exceeding great and bitter cry of mourning, "such as there was none like it nor shall be like it any more"; for although in that sad night the death angel crossed the threshold of only that one cottage down by the sounding sea, and the fatal arrow from his dread quiver smote but a single life, yet that one stroke pierced through a nation's heart; and as in the land of the Pharaohs there went forth from every house the wail for their first born stricken, so here and through this vast republic it was as if in every home there had been one of its own household dead. It was as if the nerve center of the nation were smitten, and the heart of a great people crushed. The tolling bell which broke the stillness of that midnight hour, needing no interpreter to say, "GARFIELD is dead," marked the first impulse of a mighty wave of sorrow which has swept the continent from sea to sea, and its bitter waters are surging still to-night upon the hearts of millions.

I recall another story of another scene, also of the olden time : "There was a dead man carried out, the only son of his mother, and she was a widow ; and much people of the city was with her." To-day from out a great city by the far-off western lake another dead man was carried out, and he too was the beloved son of his mother, and she a widow ; but he was more than that ; he was the chosen leader of a great nation, the representative of its power and pride and glory,

"The pillar of a people's hope,
The center of a world's desire."

51

And what shall we say of the "much people" who went to-day, in presence or in heart, with that mournful cortege which bore to its final earthly resting place all that was mortal of the murdered President of the Republic. Never before in the history of the race have so many mourners gathered around one coffin; never have tears from so many eyes bedewed a mortal's grave. From all hearts to-day goes up the lamentation, "How is the strong staff broken and the beautiful rod"? Fifty millions of people are bowed beneath the weight of a common sorrow, in all the land, North, South, East and West alike; the bells toll solemnly; the minute guns boom sadly; the funeral drapery waves; men, women and children weep. Nay, not only this, but in lands beyond the sea, millions more are mourning with us, and the great globe is girdled with the thrill of sympathetic sorrow. The sun in his circuit to-day found no country so vast, no people so remote or obscure, but some are there who share our grief. The whole civilized brotherhood of man is moved. Kings, queens and courtiers, scholars, statesmen and soldiers, artisans, laborers, men of all professions and callings, loving womanhood and tender childhood, all mingle their tears at GARFIELD's grave. Toward the draped and bowed figure of Columbia weeping to-night over the tomb of her chieftain fallen, are outstretched the hands of sympathy from all lands and climes; from the shores of our mother, England, from Russia's snows and the hills and vales of Germany, from the vine-clad fields of Italy and France, and from farther India and the islands of the sea, come the greetings of heartfelt condolence, the tribute of tender tears. Why this extraordinary manifestation, this unprecedented, world-wide sorrow? Is it because a single human life-lamp has gone out; because a single human ruler has dropped forever the scepter of command and power? No, for that has often occurred before. But it is because of the exceptional character of the man and the ruler; because of the peculiar circumstances, expectations and hopes which surrounded him; because of the unexampled baseness and cruelty of the deed which wrought his sufferings and death.

We know, and the civilized world knows, that a great man, and a prince among men, has fallen this day in Israel; that a great mind has suddenly ceased its grand work in mid-career; that a noble heart, whose every pulsation beat with high and pure aspirations for the good of humanity, is stilled forever.

JAMES A. GARFIELD, twentieth President of the United States, was born November 19th, 1831, and was reared amid the very humblest and scantiest surroundings, on the frontier of Western life. He lived, to rise, by his own efforts, from poverty and obscurity, to the most exalted station which may be attained by mortal man; he lived to illustrate in his own person and career, the noblest possibilities of integrity, perseverance, courage, fidelity and genius, fostered and aided by the free institutions of a government of the people, by the people, and for the people; and having done this, he was foully and wantonly assassinated on the 2d of July; and having endured, for eighty days, the keenest pangs of mortal suffering, with a heroic fortitude and Christian resignation, which evoked universal and tearful pity and admiration, he died September 19th, in the hushed presence of a grief-stricken nation, and with the sorrowful sympathy of all civilized mankind. This is the brief, sad, touching, yet proud story. Henceforth it is a part of history. What shall we learn from it?

First, that though dead he yet speaketh: that his life and its work are not dead, and need not, will not, die.

"Can that man be dead,
    Whose spiritual influence rests upon his kind?
    He lives in glory; and his speaking dust
    Hath more of life than half its breathing moulds."

It is safe to say that the name and fame of GARFIELD will live and his influence be felt in all the coming time; and the best of this consolatory thought, is the assurance that that influence will be for unadulterated good. GARFIELD left no example which men ought to shun. His whole career was one which any man may worthily strive to imitate, however far he may fall below the high ideal after which he strove, or the actual which he attained. Yet there is this peculiar feature about the life and the success of GARFIELD; he was not great nor will he be chiefly remembered for any single or brilliant achievement; he did not, like Washington, lead his countrymen through war to independence and nationality, and set them on the pathway to future greatness; he did not, like Lincoln, safely guide them through the wilderness and wild tempest of treason and rebellion, nor make his name immortal by striking off the shackles of the slave: it cannot be said that GARFIELD was the originator of any single, conspicuously great public measure; it was not in this way that GARFIELD has won his place in his country's affections, and his high niche in the temple of Fame, among the bravest and the best. It was rather by the rounded fullness and symmetric excellence of his whole character, by the consistent and unvarying manliness and high purpose of his life, by his proving himself equal to all emergencies and *facile princeps*, easily the chief, among his fellows, that it comes to pass that to-day all men say of him; in every public position this sincere Christian, this patriotic soldier, this broadminded statesman, this faithful chief magistrate:

> " Hath borne his faculties so meek, hath been
> So clear in his great office, that his virtues
> Will plead like angels, trumpet-tongued against
> The deep damnation of his taking off."

One of the strong points in his character and chief sources of his deserved popularity was his marked nationality—his intense, distinctive Americanism. JAMES A. GARFIELD was an American of the Americans, one of the completest types and examples of our best American civilization, culture and patriotism. None of the patriots or statesmen of the earlier days, not Israel Putnam, Ethan Allen, or Benjamin Franklin; not Henry Clay, or Daniel Webster, or even Abraham Lincoln, was more redolent of the free soil of America than JAMES A. GARFIELD, and he was, under favoring circumstances, a better example than either of what manner of man may be the product of our free institutions,

and the opportunities this republic affords to the poor and
struggling aspirant for worthy fame and exalted place.
Every fibre of JAMES A. GARFIELD'S nature thrilled with
love of his country, and with patriotic purpose.

It took him, with cheerful zeal, from home and wife and
children, when his country called, and set him in the forefront of the battle for the Union and for liberty and law.
The same instinct of devotion and patriotic sacrifice marked
his whole public life, and it moved his half unconscious
soul, when in his dying hours, amid his torturing pains, he
murmured, "*Strangulatus pro respublica*"—"Tortured for the
republic." He was indeed tortured for the republic, and
he died at last for the republic, as truly as he would, had
he fallen in the storm and shock of battle on the hard
fought, well-nigh lost, but finally well-won field of Chickamauga, which his wisdom and daring valor did so much to
save. A vile assassin slew him; the soaring eagle slain by
a mousing hawk. Let it so stand, nor inquire further.
'Tis said of one of old that he climbed a mountain height,
where God's finger touched him, and he slept. GARFIELD
had toilfully climbed life's mountain to its summit; the
murderer's hand—not God's—touched him, and he sleeps.
A truer patriot never lived; a nobler American has never
died.

In all his public life, JAMES A. GARFIELD followed the
rule of right, and had the courage of his own convictions.
From these he never swerved. He won distinction, but
never by the low, mean ways by which men so often mount
to place and power. He would forfeit any present or pros-
pective advantage rather than demean himself or lose his
self-respect. He showed conspicuously these traits on
many occasions. When the conflict took place in Indiana
between the civil and the military authorities in relation to
the trial of the accused "Knights of the Golden Circle,"
a traitorous organization, GARFIELD took strong ground
against the military interference, and was one of the de-
fenders and counsel of the accused. Judge Jeremiah S.
Black at that time said to him: "Young man, it is a peril-
ous thing for a young Republican in Congress to advocate

such doctrines, and I don't want you to injure yourself."
To this Gen. GARFIELD replied: "That consideration does
not weigh with me; I believe in English liberty and in
English law."

When the fiat money, Greenback craze invaded Ohio,
and had taken a strong hold in GARFIELD's district, he was
a candidate for renomination for Congress. Some of his
cautious friends advised that he should not commit himself
to the honest money cause, "as an indiscreet word might
cost him the nomination." True to his honest convictions,
he stood by his colors. He answered, "Much as I value
your opinion, I here denounce this theory that has worked
its way into the State as dishonest, immoral, and unpa-
triotic, and if I were offered a nomination and election for
my natural life on this platform, I should spurn it. If you
should raise the question of renominating me, let it be understood that you can have my services only on the ground
of honest payment of the national debt in coin, according
to the letter and spirit of the contract."

In a long and most agreeable interview, which it was my
privilege to enjoy with the late President, during the week
prior to his assassination, I had most ample proof, in his
frank and decisive declarations relative to the then existing
political situation, that JAMES A. GARFIELD, as President,
was as honest and courageous, as true to his own convictions
of duty and impulses of patriotism, as he has always been
in every public station. Had he lived he would have given
us the most brilliant National Administration in our history.

There is neither time nor space now to recount the virtues of the dead President, nor review his life. Leave that
to the more careful and possibly more just historian of the
future. From no history of this age will the GARFIELD
chapter be omitted—and as the years roll on his record
will brighten. He trod, while here, the pathway of the
just, which shineth more and more unto the perfect day;
in the full splendor of that day he now rejoices—and there
is no night there. Turning sadly from the grave of the
beloved and honored, second martyr President, let us re-

member that we need shed no tears for him. As he said himself, scarcely more than a year ago, of his own dear, dead, soldier comrades :

" We hold reunions, not for the dead, for there is nothing in all the earth that you and I can do for the dead. They are past our help and past our praise. We can add to them no glory—we can give to them no immortality. They do not need us, but forever and forevermore we need them."

We may weep, because we must, for ourselves, for the widow, the fatherless, the mother bereaved, for a country smitten and afflicted, but not for him.

> " Not for him, who in dying left millions in tears,
> Not for him, who has died full of honors and years,
> Not for him who ascended Fame's ladder so high
> From the round at the top he has stepped to the sky."

> " He has outsoared the shadow of our night ;
>   Envy and calumny and hate and pain,
> And that unrest, which men miscall delight,
>   Can touch him not nor torture him again ;
> From the contagion of the world's slow stain
> He is secure, and now can never mourn
> A heart grown cold, a head grown gray in vain ;
>   Nor when the spirit's self has ceased to burn,
> With sparkless ashes load an unlamented urn."

One thought more and I have done. Death, the reaper, gathers the bravest and the best, but it takes not all. Death could stop the beating of that grand Christian heart, but it cannot rob the nation and the world of the example of his noble life. And that country for which he lived and died, remains to us and our children, with all its freedom and its possible high and glorious destiny. Let us comfort ourselves in this hour with the wise, calm, hopeful words which fell so lately from his lips, now sealed in death :

" Individuals may wear for a time the glory of our institutions, but they carry it not to the grave with them. Like rain drops from heaven, they may pass through the circle of the shining bow and add to its lustre, but when they have sunk into the earth again, the proud arch still spans the sky and shines gloriously on."

Sermon by the Pastor,

REV. P. D. VAN CLEEF, D. D.

Text—II Samuel 1 : 19.

"The beauty of Israel is slain upon thy high places; how are the mighty fallen!"

Saul, the king of Israel, is dead. Raised up in the providence of God to rule the chosen nation, his first duty was to lead her armies against an invading force of hostile neighbors. He answered the call in the hour of his country's peril and distress, routed and destroyed her enemies, and was hailed on his return from the battle as the idol of a grateful people.

But the reign of forty years, begun so auspiciously, was to be terminated in disaster. His sun, so glorious in its rising, went down in the darkness of ruin and despair on the fatal field of Mount Gilboa. The defeated and sorely wounded monarch put an end to his own fast ebbing life by falling upon his sword. David, having been anointed by Samuel at the command of God, was now the king of Israel. The first intelligence of Saul's death was brought to him by an Amalekite, who pretended to have escaped from the camp of Israel, and boasted of having slain the king; in proof of which he presented the monarch's crown and bracelet. The sight of these royal insignia, in connection with the strange words of the man who produced them, filled the heart of David with grief and indignation. He exclaimed: "How wast thou not afraid to stretch forth thine hands to destroy the Lord's anointed? Thy blood be upon thy head; for thy mouth hath testified

against thee, saying, I have slain the Lord's anointed."
Without waiting to inquire into the sanity of this self-
confessed murderer, or the truth of his story, David took
him at his word, and ordered his execution on the spot.
Justice having been vindicated, the grief-stricken king
gives vent to his feelings in that pathetic lamentation over
Saul and Jonathan which is acknowledged to be one of the
most touching and beautiful elegies in existence. Over-
looking the faults, and even the crimes of Saul, he beholds
in his person the "anointed of the Lord," and bewails
his tragic death as the monarch and head of the nation.
"The beauty of Israel is slain upon thy high places; how
are the mighty fallen!"

These words suggest a fitting theme for our reflections
in view of the cruel death of our beloved President. He
is fallen—slain upon the high places of the nation. The
bullets flew thick and harmless around him on the field
of Chickamauga. He was not permitted to die the death
of a soldier. It was reserved for him to devote his splendid talents for eighteen years to the civil service of his
country, to win and wear her highest honors, and then to
fall by the hand of an assassin. To-morrow, amid the
tears of the nation, the remains of JAMES A. GARFIELD, the
twentieth President of the United States, will be committed to the tomb.

Our service to-day does not require an extended biogra-
phy of the late Chief Magistrate. Several memoirs of him
have already been published. The newspapers which are
read by all classes of the people have been filled with
accounts of his life and labors, his sickness, sufferings and
death. Let these papers with heavy black lines be preserved in every household. The future will enhance their
value as relics of a period in our history of which the generations to come will read with wonder and fond admiration.

But the pulpit has an important duty to perform; it is
to interpret the events of God's providence in the light of
his word, and to comfort his people in their sorrows. We
know that God reigns. We have been brought face to face

with this truth in a remarkable manner during the century of our nation's existence. Never have we seemed to be brought closer to the Eternal throne than during the past three months of anxiety and prayer for the life of the President. God comes near and speaks to us :—" To-day, if ye will hear his voice, harden not your hearts."

Among the touching sentences woven into the mourning drapery that speaks a nation's sorrow, none would be more expressive than the words of David—" The beauty of Israel." Saul as the anointed King, and Jonathan as a prince, a soldier, and a statesman, were the beauty of Israel. If the ornaments of our nation are her patriotic citizens, her brave soldiers, her wise legislators, her just and fearless magistrates, then we may lament our late President as the beauty of our Republic, slain upon her high places.

We do not say that there are no others like him. We are proud to believe that our country can produce many a man who, if called to pass through the same trials, would prove as true, and pure, and noble as he. In the providence of God a special honor was reserved for him among other citizens, like that which fell to the lot of the martyrs among other Christians. He was assigned to a special duty in working out the destinies of the country. It was given him to win by his own merits a bright record in history, and by his sufferings to secure a lasting place in the hearts of his fellow-citizens. It is a great satisfaction to speak of the dead, as we can to-day, untrammeled by the fear of exaggerating their virtues, or the necessity of concealing their vices.

No one can study the life of our lamented President without discovering in his character the elements of true greatness. Born and reared amid hardships, compelled to labor and struggle for the positions he gained as he rose from poverty and obscurity, cheerful in his humble lot, but inspired with a laudable ambition to rise above it, with an innate love of knowledge, and a native energy that triumphed over every obstacle in his way, he grew into greatness as naturally as he grew in stature and increased in years. His career from boyhood furnishes a bright example to the youth of our country. It teaches young men that there are honorable and useful positions in life for those who will qualify themselves to fill them, and that these places of honor are prizes, not for the lucky holders of tickets in the lottery of fortune, but for the honest, industrious and brave men who earn them.

"Christian is the highest style of man." In early life JAMES A. GARFIELD became a disciple of Christ. He was not ashamed to be known as a professor of religion, or to speak for his Master. He made no effort either to conceal or to display his religious convictions. He acted out what he thought and felt in an honest, consistent Christian life. When in college, says a classmate, he never retired until he had kneeled in prayer, no matter who might be present.

When the holy day of rest came, though it brought no repose to him on his bed of suffering, he said, "This is the Sabbath; how I reverence that holy day". During his illness his heart was with the little church of which he was a member, and in whose humble sanctuary he always worshiped. A nation can have no richer blessing than God-fearing rulers, and no greater curse than irreligious magistrates. The history of the kingdom of Israel is full of instruction on this subject for all nations, monarchies or republics. Happily our country has been favored with a line of Presidents who have respected the Christian religion. Most of them have been regular attendants at some Christian Church, and several have been communicants, if not while in office, at least soon after their retirement from the cares of State. Even Jefferson, who was denounced as an infidel, framed a moral code for his rule of life from the Sermon on the Mount.

The Christian sentiment of the nation, irrespective of party, gladly responded to the election of Mr. GARFIELD, on account of his religious character. There was a restful feeling throughout the country because the Chief Magistrate was a man who feared God, and believed in the Lord Jesus Christ. We can afford to leave religious dogmas out of the Constitution, if we have Christian faith and practice in the living representatives of the government.

We feel more secure when men of God are at the helm, and so in view of the loss of our President we must take up the lamentation of the prophet:—"The breath of our nostrils, the anointed of the Lord, was taken in their pits, of whom we said, under his shadow we shall live among the heathen."

Our lamentation to-day is over the loss of our President. The death of one who, after an exciting political campaign which is always a severe strain upon the delicate machinery of government, has been elected to the office of President, is a bitter disappointment. When a Presidential election is over the country always breathes more freely. No matter which party succeeds we are quite certain to have an able and patriotic President, and the people settle down to their ordinary pursuits, and the nation adjusts itself to the new order of things. Such was our condition on the 4th of March last. When this peace was disturbed, and the hopes reposed in the new President were crushed, it was, to say the least, a sad loss. The experience of the past rendered the prospect of another Vice-Presidential administration far from agreeable or reassuring. The death of the Chief Magistrate of the nation, with the prospects of a brilliant and successful administration before him, was therefore a deplorable event.

When in addition to this we remember that the President was a man whom the people were learning to admire, to love, and to trust, his death becomes in every sense a sad bereavement. The nation has lost not only a Chief Magistrate, but also a citizen who, irrespective of his position, was one of the ornaments and pillars of the Republic. Had he not reached the Presidency his usefulness would have been very great in the Senate of the United States, to which august body he had been promoted by a constituency that knew his talents and his character, and who having tried him as a representative and found him faithful, said to him: "go up higher."

But that which adds bitterness to our lamentations is the fearful manner of his death. Had he sickened and

died, or perished in some general calamity by which the
good and the bad together are taken out of the world,
the stroke would not have seemed so hard, but that this
noble man, whose life was so precious, should be shot
down like a dog in the street, by a worthless wretch whose
last excuse for his crime is that the President had in-
sulted him; this is more than we can patiently endure.
O why was such a foul crime permitted? Why must that
valuable life be thus sacrificed? This is one of the mysteries of Providence before which humanity stands dumb.
"Could not he who opened the eyes of the blind have
caused that even this man should not have died"? Yes,
Jesus could have prevented the death of his friend Lazarus,
but that which happened afterward proved the wisdom of
the Saviour's plan. "God is his own interpreter." What
thou knowest not now thou shalt know hereafter. But
while we recognize the mystery and the hidden wisdom of
Divine Providence, and are satisfied that the Judge of all
the earth will do right. we cannot but look with abhorrence
upon what man has done. The assassination of a ruler,
even in despotic Russia, is a terrible crime ; how much
more heinous the deed when committed against the chosen
President of a free Republic, a man who occupied his
position by no accident of royal birth, but was one of the
people, who could sympathize with the poor and with the
toiling masses because he had been one with them, who
employed the gift of eloquent speech in advocating the
truth and the right on behalf of the oppressed, who always
endeavored to elevate the lowly, and was the friend of those
who needed a helper. The bullet that struck that man
struck the heart of the nation.

Our lamentation is tenderly saddened yet more by the
thought of the sufferings which our beloved President endured. We were sure that he must have suffered as his
flesh wasted away, and the poison in his blood sapped the
foundations of life, but none knew how much he had patiently endured until those months of weariness and pain
were ended, and the condition of his body gave evidence
of the terrible struggle through which he had passed, and
the havoc it had wrought.

But there is a comfort in the thought that during these months of pain the sympathies of the nation and of the civilized world have been drawn to the sufferer. History may furnish parallels to the murder of the President, but the feeling it has evoked throughout the world has no parallel. We recall the tragic death of Lincoln. We think of the murder of the good Prince of Orange, William the Silent. He, like GARFIELD, had been watched and followed by the assassin who had long meditated the foul deed. Balthasar at one time struck his dagger with all his might into a door, and exclaimed—" Would that the blow had been in the heart of Orange." At last he found his opportunity, and shot the Prince as he was passing from the dining-room to his private apartments. William was entombed amid the tears of a whole nation. "Never," says Motley, "was a more extensive, unaffected, and legitimate sorrow felt at the death of any human being." These words applied to the lamented Lincoln. They apply with fresh and added force to our President whose remains will be entombed to-morrow amid the tears of more than the nation that gave him birth, and now mourns his death. "There is sorrow on the sea." There is sorrow in lands beyond the sea. Three European Courts in mourning—bells tolled, and minute guns fired, and tokens of sorrow displayed on private and public buildings in the principal cities of Europe, Japan, and even in the heart of Egypt—these things have never happened before to mark the death of an American citizen. The tender words of the Queen of England to Mrs. Garfield will never cease to vibrate through the heart of this nation—"May God comfort you as no other can." There is nothing remarkable in the simple fact that one good Christian woman, who has never emerged from the shadow of her long widowhood, should sympathize with another over whose heart and home the same dark shadows have fallen, but there is something sublime as well as touching in the correspondence between these two sisters in sorrow. It is a link added to the chain that binds the two Christian nations they represent more closely to each other. May that chain never be broken. The floral tribute of affection

5

which the hand of the Queen, by her minister, has laid
upon the bier of the President, will wither, but the sentiment it expresses can never be forgotten. May the sad
day be far distant when America will lay her grateful tribute upon the tomb of Victoria.

But there are lessons which this day of lamentation
brings to our hearts as a stricken and humbled nation.
We have not time now to review them at length. But let
us first of all remember our national sins. God has chastened us—let us draw near to His throne of grace in godly
sorrow that worketh repentance. Let not this universal
mourning prove to be but an empty show. Let there be a
complete reconciliation between the North and the South.
Let there be a kindlier feeling between rival political parties. Let faction cease. Let there be no revengeful Esaus
to say in their hearts "The days of mourning for my father
are at hand; then will I slay my brother Jacob." Let
there be a higher standard of political action, and of civil
service reform. Let all animosities and jealousies be buried in the grave of GARFIELD. The public mind is now
absorbed with the idea of public loss and bereavement.
We stand bewildered with amazement as we gaze upon the
solemn pageantry of woe. How grand and overpowering
in its effect upon the imagination is this great national
mourning. Let not this outward manifestation of grief
dull the sense of inward sorrow, or prevent its sanctifying
influence upon the hearts of the people. There is a great
blessing which now seems almost within our grasp—it is *a
revival of religious life throughout the nation.* O how much
we need the presence of the Holy Spirit to sanctify to us
the lessons of Divine Providence. Let the prayers of the
nation now ascend to heaven for the living President and
his constitutional advisers. His first official act is the
appointment of a day of humiliation and prayer. May
that God whom he has thus publicly acknowledged as the
sovereign of the nation endow him with all the wisdom and
grace which he needs in the duties and responsibilities
devolved upon him under circumstances so trying and
difficult. In the task before him he will need the sym-

pathies, the prayers, and the loyal support of all good citizens. That the people will support the government we have no doubt, but, brethren, be as loyal to God as you are to your country and all will be well. When you stand before the Great Tribunal, the judgment seat of Christ, where nations as such are not known, but where we must all appear as individuals, where all human hearts will be unveiled, and all human actions weighed in the balances of truth, O let it not then appear that you have only rendered unto Cæsar the things that are Cæsar's, and not rendered unto God the things that are God's.

May the death of the President produce a chastening effect upon the minds of all the people. May it be sanctified to the nation's welfare, and be made the means in the hands of God of advancing true patriotism and pure religion, that the righteousness which exalteth a nation may be the crowning glory of our Republic.

GARFIELD.

BY HENRY D. HOLT, M. D.

STRUCK DOWN! what means this cry of fear,
   This tale of blood and dastard crime,
   The stain and horror of the time,
That startles all the world to hear!

A ghastly terror moves the land,
   And millions ask with bated breath,
   If 'tis indeed the stroke of death :
Has fate instructed murder's hand?

Hope's trembling pulses feebly move ;
   Must patriot worth untimely bleed !
   Are we a land bereaved indeed,
And doomed to mourn the chief we love?

The prayer that importunes the sky
   As from one yearning soul ascends,
   And fear to faith persuasion lends,
To urge the agonizing cry,

Till whispered from that couch of pain,
   Where tireless love holds tearful watch,
   Faint words of feeble cheer we catch,
And patriot hope revives again.

NOT DEAD ! thank Him whose watchful eye
   Marked the assassin's black intent,
   And his protecting angel sent
To turn the cruel missive by.

NOT DEAD ! not yet insensate hate
   Has wrought its consummated spite
   And reached the life it aimed to smite,
And wound the peace of all the State.

69

In guardian kindness o'er him bend,
 And by his bed of peril stand,
 A ministering angel band,
To succor, comfort and defend.

HE LIVES : and swelling to the sky
 The voice of thankful praise ascends ;
 And in harmonious chorus blends
The psalm that bears our joy on high.

A people's thanks be His, whose hand
 Controls the dial-mark of fate,
 Who rescued our imperilled State
And bade rejoicing fill the land.

—But may we yet o'er peril past
 Exult with joy that knows no fear,
 Nor dread the cloud yet hovering near
That may in blackness spread at last?

The tearful watchers hold the glass
 With fainting heart and trembling hand,
 And fear to see the final sand,
The last of earth, in silence pass.

The struggling hope and yearning love
 Wherewith we strive and agonize
 Would even swerve the Only-Wise,
And Heaven's own perfect counsels move.

But vainly we prolong the strife
 Of tearful prayer with death and doom ;
 We may not shut the waiting tomb
And win the martyr back to life.

The shadow gathers dark and deep ;
 The hour has came for rest and peace ;
 The prisoned spirit seeks release—
"GOD GIVETH HIS BELOVED SLEEP."

And thus the blow has fallen again
 That robs us of the chief we love,
 And GARFIELD walks the courts above,
Fit brother for our LINCOLN slain.

Now, precious in the sight divine
   Be his, our new-made ruler's life,
   From all assaults of hate and strife,
And every dark and mean design.

And many be the peaceful years
   Ere patriot pride shall blush again
   At vision of the crimson stain
That woke our wrath and moved our tears.

Thy will be done, Thou Only Wise,
   Whom good and ill alike shall praise,
   Whom e'en the guilt of man obeys,
Just Ruler of the earth and skies.

—To him who wrought hell's vile behest,
   Who foully smote, nor smote in vain,
   His be the kindred mark of Cain ;
Let sleepless conscience work the rest.—

Now be the fount of sorrow dried ;
   Our bootless grief is more than vain,
   His deeds, his virtues, live again—
The soul of Garfield has not died !

And purer praise and worthier fame
   The coming years shall never know
   Or wisdom's verdict e'er bestow,
Than truth shall weave round Garfield's name.

FIRST BAPTIST CHURCH OF JERSEY CITY.*

Sermon by the Pastor,

REV. WHEELOCK H. PARMLY, D. D.

THE THRONE OF GOD ENVELOPED IN MYSTERY.

TEXT—"Clouds and darkness, are round about him : righteousness and judgment, are the habitation of his throne."—*Psalm* 97: 2.

It has been frequently stated, that after the brutal assassination of President Lincoln in 1865, when all classes of the nation were horrified and indignant at the atrocious act, and thousands of the populace, exasperated by the foul wrong done to an honored Chief Magistrate, stood ready to wreak their vengeance on any supposed sympathizers with the hostile and Confederate States, amid the throes of that chaotic period the Hon. JAMES A. GARFIELD presented himself before a multitude, quelled their tumultuous ravings, and quieted their fury by declaring : "God reigns, and the Republic lives."

In like manner to-day, more than fifty millions of American people mourn together over our crushed hopes, and the lifeless form of our assassinated President GARFIELD,

---

*1. In this house was held a meeting, called by the Pastor, in accordance with the Governor's Proclamation, on September 8th, 1881, from 11 to 12 A. M. to offer *Special* Prayer for the recovery of President GARFIELD. The audience was large, and the *Solemn* Services were participated in by Ministers and many of the best citizens of different religious denominations, and political creeds.

2. Another meeting was held in the same house, on the evening of September 26th, 1881, called by Mayor Taussig and the Aldermen, in which addresses were delivered by Rev. Messrs. Van Cleef, Thompson, Pastor Parmly, and others, *commemorative* of the life and death of President GARFIELD.

yet it behooves us to thank God that his purposes will stand, and that our government survives.

Millions of prayers have been offered, and thousands of sermons have been preached since the day of that fatal shooting, all teeming with the one hope, that our beloved Chief Magistrate might recover. Far too much time, in my judgment, has already been devoted in many sermons, to the despised outcast who perpetrated the horrible deed, and the facts connected with the murder, as well as the execrable wretch guilty of it, are too familiar to need much comment to-day.

We stand in the presence of a great calamity. Our heavenly Father seeth not as man seeth, and so while we were upon our knees in prayer for his life, He has taken our ruler to himself. His body awaits burial, and we are a nation of mourners. Yet we mourn not alone ; this grief is not all ours, for the electric wires have flashed the news of the tragic event to distant nations, and the civilized world, which has been waiting for months past in almost breathless anxiety, bow and weep with us under our terrible bereavement.

A great man—a mighty leader hath fallen, and such an event ought not to be allowed to pass without improvement. Less public events indeed, teach the same momentous truths. Such events we have experienced in our homes when loved ones were taken from our sight by death, and all before us seemed midnight darkness. We have experienced them also, by removals from the church, when the strong pillars were stricken down, and those who remained exclaimed :

"Our fathers! Where are they?"

And many were trembling for the Ark of God, and cried out, " By whom shall Jacob arise, for he is small ?" From behind the dark surroundings, our God replied : Psalm 46:10, "Be still, and know that I am God, I will be exalted in the earth." At this hour, in the midst of our great national sorrow, let us pause and devoutly consider :

I. Some of the dark dispensations which envelope Jehovah's government.

"Clouds and darkness are round about him," is highly figurative language, and like very much besides, which is employed in the Old Testament, and doubtless is borrowed from events which are recorded in its sacred, historical books. For instance, if you examine the appearances of Jehovah to the saints and patriarchs of ancient times, you will discover the origin of this text, for all these appearances were accompanied with clouds and darkness. The cloudy pillar which went before the Children of Israel in all their journeyings, was dark on one side and light on the other—a pillar of fire by night, and of cloud by day. Ex. 14 : 19, 20.

Again, when the Temple of Solomon was dedicated, we are assured that the glory of the Lord so filled the house, that the priests could not enter in. 1 Kings, 8 : 10, 11.

Again, when the Law was given on Mount Sinai, the Lord descended in thunders and lightnings, and there was a thick cloud upon the mountain. Ex. 20: 18, 20, 21. You find also that clouds are emblems of obscurity ; and darkness is an emblem of distress. In both of these we are groping as a nation to-day: The ways of Jehovah are also beautifully illustrated in Psalm 18 : 9, 11, where it is said : "He bowed the heavens also, and came down : and darkness was under his feet,"—" He made darkness his secret place : his pavilion, round about him, were dark waters, and thick clouds of the skies." Then, in Duet. 4: 11, the same word indicates a great commotion, and upheaval, at the appearence of Jehovah. Surely, no language can be more expressive of our condition as a people.

2. Without dwelling further upon ancient times, or events, as illustrative of the mysteries connected with Jehovah's government, let me inquire : Why was permitted, that long, dark night of African Slavery, to settle upon this fair continent for more than two hundred and forty years ;—i. e. from A. D. 1620 to 1863 ? Why was the

"dark continent" ransacked and pillaged, to gratify the White Man's greed of gain? Why were families, and even whole villages broken up, and innocent victims stolen from home, and sold into hopeless bondage, so that the route for more than a thousand miles from the interior to the coast —as Dr. Livingstone asserts—was lined with the skeletons of the miserable beings, who had perished under the hands of cruel slave traders, and resounding with the groans and cries proceeding from broken hearts? And more terrible still, was the fact, that these sufferings were only the precursors of still more bitter sufferings in the lands of bondage into which they were sold. Was all this what might have been expected from a God of infinite love and mercy? Nay, nay, who can fathom the dark abyss of these horrors, perpetrated and continued for centuries? I cannot fathom it.

3. After we as a nation had risen in righteous indignation against this giant wrong which another has called "the sum of all villainies," had sacrificed hundreds of thousands of precious lives, and had waded through seas of blood to rid ourselves from this fearful scourge, why was it that a *mad* assassin was permitted to cut off President Lincoln, the "*Great Emancipator*," and so prolong the internecine strife?

We could not read then, and we cannot read now, the divine counsels, and so we bowed, and *now* bow, exclaiming: "Even so, Father, for so it seemed good in thy sight."

4. Standing at this time as a nation, at peace with each other and with all the nations of the earth, under the clear sky of hope, and with returned and increasing prosperity, why, we imploringly ask, was our beloved Chief Magistrate cut down in the midst of his days by the hand of a miserable miscreant, and a nation thrown into mourning? Echo answers, Why? We know from experience as well as from revelation, that our Father is a God of love, and delights to confer happiness on his creatures, yet we find ourselves oppressed with calamities, and surrounded by miseries.

As a special cause of grief for President GARFIELD, we mourn to-day the death of a *Christian* statesman. Jeroboam, and many of his successors on the throne of Israel are handed down to succeeding ages, as those who caused Israel to sin, and other nations of the earth have had abundant reasons to *rejoice* rather than *mourn*, when vile rulers, who were only leading the people into deeper iniquity were taken from their thrones. But in this instance, not only a statesman, distinguished in every department of the national government, but an eminent servant of God, has fallen from the heights of Zion. It has been truthfully said that he was the type of our American manhood. Certainly ; and we were proud of him. Born in adversity, cradled in poverty, surrounded by opposing circumstances, he reaches the highest place in the nation and in the world, by the sheer force of his own pluck and the power of his own talents. "The place is cheerfully accorded to him, and we proudly point to him and say to the world :

> "The elements
> So mixed in him, that nature might stand up
> And say to all the world : this was a man."

But he was more ; he was a *renewed* man. General GARFIELD was an humble Christian, putting his trust firmly and unreservedly in a Crucified Redeemer. Such an example of piety was needed in Washington. His profession and godly life were a perpetual and potent rebuke to the intemperance of senators and representatives, the blatant blasphemy of prominent politicians, and the low standard of personal integrity produced and encouraged by modern party machinery. Both his words and example taught the wholesome lesson that Divine laws could not be safely impugned, either in private or public life. Surely under the loss of such a ruler, and amid the clouds and overwhelming calamities which environ and threaten us, does it not behoove us as a nation, and as individuals, to pray : "Help Lord, for the godly man ceaseth ; for the faithful fail from among the children of men." Ps. 12 : 1.

II. The only ground of confidence and security, "righteousness and judgment are the habitation of his throne."

We have been walking in the dark ever since the fatal bullet entered the body of our President, for we have been assured by those who made the autopsy after his decease, that we have been praying for a miracle, and that by no *human* process could that wound have been healed. Granted that it may be so. Let us turn then to the strong contrast, to the *only* sure confidence of a Christian people—to *God*. He has said: "At the brightness that was before him his thick clouds passed." Ps. 18 : 12. It is reported that after that most devoted wife of our President, had held the hand of her dying husband, till the last ray of life had expired, she looked heavenward imploringly, and inquired: "Why is this heavy blow sent upon *me?*" She could not answer that question; neither can you or I answer it under similar circumstances, when death has cast its dark pall over all our hopes and prospects. But it can be answered, and through the riven clouds, that answer descends from the Throne of the Eternal God: "What I do thou knowest not now, but thou shalt know hereafter." John, 13 : 7.

Blessed Assurance! Can you, stricken mourner, believe and rest upon this promise? What are some of the reasons which should induce us to trust this promise and feel *secure?* In reply, I remark :

1. This assurance proceeds from Jehovah himself, and is written for the comfort of his afflicted people. And what stronger argument can we employ, either before Satan or a gainsaying world, than : "It is *written*," or "*He* hath *said* it." It is reported that on one occasion, when the life of Napoleon Bonaparte was endangered by an unruly horse, a private soldier stepped from the ranks, and at the risk of his own life, protected that of the Emperor. Napoleon gratefully appreciating the act, said to the soldier: "Henceforth you shall be one of my *body-guards*." When the soldier, immediately after that, presented himself to the master of the guards, and claimed his place, that officer demurred, and

called the man insane. But when the man pointed to the emperor, who was fast receding from their sight, and declared : " *He* said it ; *he* said it," all opposition ceased, and the soldier took his place among the body-guards. Shall the word of a *human* commander be so respected, and that of the Almighty be ignored ?

2. "Righteousness and judgment," are not only the nature but they are the very essence of Jehovah's character. He is unchangeable, consequently, all the divine conduct is equitable, and every event which transpires, however painful and inexplicable to us, must be regulated by a rectitude and judgment which cannot err : And besides this, God is not bound by justice, either to prevent these evils, or to correct them, when perpetrated. All moral government has its foundation in laws and motives, suitable for creatures who possess judgment, understanding, and volition. All, then, that can be justly asked is, that the law shall be equitable for the government of a reasonable creature, and that the creature has the power to obey. These points are readily granted as to the laws of God ; hence the responsibility, for either obedience or disobedience, falls upon man as a moral agent.

3. Notwithstanding Jehovah is not bound by justice to correct and spare, and save men ; yet we do find that, in his love, and pity, he has proposed and matured a plan of salvation, sufficient to save to the uttermost, all who repent and come unto *Him*, by Jesus Christ ; and it does not militate against that plan, that so many evil-doers are found in our world, or that fearful and giant iniquities abound here, our heavenly Father can afford to wait for the time of the execution of his violated laws. It is indeed a most melancholy thought, that a life so precious, and so seemingly necessary for our national prosperity, can be put out by a creature so absolutely worthless and despicable. The poet J. G. Holland has most *aptly* expressed this idea in the following words :

"A wasp flew out upon our fairest son,
And stung him to the quick with poisoned shaft,
The while he chatted carelessly, and laughed,
And knew not of the fateful mischief done,
And so this life, amid our love begun,
Envenomed by the insect's hellish craft,
Was drunk by Death in one long feverish draught,
And he was lost—our precious, priceless one!
Oh, mystery of blind, remorseless fate!
Oh. cruel end of a most causeless hate!
That life so mean should murder life so great!
What is there left to us who think and feel,
Who have no remedy, and no appeal,
But damn the wasp and crush him under heel"?

But our God has brought, and can still bring, order out of confusion, and from this, almost overwhelming sorrow, is able to extract his own glory: "Surely, the wrath of man shall praise thee, the remainder of wrath shalt thou restrain." Ps. 76: 10.

III.   Let us turn briefly, to some *lessons* derived from this great calamity.

1.   Our heavenly Father by these means seems to be *training* us for higher and holier purposes. In our joy, at the exaltation of our Ruler, we seem to have forgotten the brittle thread on which hangs mortal life ; and so to-day our joy is suddenly turned to grief. To the soul of our murdered President, death was a glad release :—from the tongue of the slanderer :—from the shafts of envious office-seekers ;—and from the wicked devices of political aspirants. We may, each of us, properly lament, and exclaim : "Weep, nation weep" ! But our beloved and lost Leader, has entered that land where weeping and sorrow are all unknown, and whence, he might, were he permitted, appropriately, turn to us and say : "Weep not for me, but weep for yourselves and for your children."

2. We are taught by this event, that life is measured, not so much by years, as by usefulness. He fell in his prime ; yet what an amount of labor he has performed during his brief life ;—as a man, as a teacher of young men ;—as a military officer ;—as a representative of the people ;—and finally, as a Statesman and Ruler, with broad and comprehensive plans for the highest welfare of his nation. Not permitted, himself to execute them ;— future generations, must teach their wisdom, by carrying them out. We learn,

3. That trust in Jehovah will *pay*. It is said of lord Dartmouth, one of the State officers of George III, that on one occasion, when early in the morning, the king and a number of noblemen who composed a hunting party, waited a few moments for him to join them ;—as he approached from his castle, one of the noblemen chided him for keeping the party waiting ; his ready reply was :—" I have learned to serve the *King* of kings, before I pay my devotions to my earthly sovereign." The king overhearing the answer, remarked to one near him, "that man can be trusted." Such a record might be truthfully made concerning our lamented President GARFIELD ; for, from his early life, both in public and private, he seems to have placed the service of God as *Supreme*. And the influence of such a life will live in the annals of history. Impelled by a sense of obligation, both to God and men, he inaugurated a greatly needed reform in the civil service of his government. Being dead, his example will speak in that direction, to the generations yet to come.

4. He taught also a lesson of *filial* reverence—in a time of growing irreverence to parents,—which ought never to be lost, specially upon the youth and children of this nation.

When GARFIELD was inaugurated as President, a memorable incident occurred which revealed the true character of the man. In the presence of the representatives of States and other high dignitaries, and a promiscuous as-

6

semblage, he took the prescribed oath of office, swore
fealty to the Constitution, and attested his sincerity and
faith by kissing the Holy Bible. Having first properly
recognized his Creator, he turned and kissed her who bore
him, and who had impressed on his young mind the sanctity
of the oath he had just taken. In this hard and selfish and
prosaic world there was something touching in this hearty
recognition of the relationship of mother. To see the
Chief Magistrate of the greatest Republic that ever
existed, unabashed, in such a presence, paying this tribute
of filial affection to the aged mother, who had followed him
with intensest solicitude from the hour of his birth to his
entrance upon the honors and responsibilities of such an
exalted position, was a spectacle worthy to be commemor-
ated by painter and historian.

5. Another lesson impressed by this awful event upon
the entire people of this land is a greater care in the
selection of the *future* Vice-Presidents of the nation. Four
times have our Presidents been removed from office by the
ruthless hand of death ; four times have our Vice-Presidents—the second officers in the government—been *exalted*
to fill the vacancies. With what results, *three* of them have
presided are matters of history, too well known to need
comment to-day.

It has doubtless, been a peculiar mercy, that our late
President was spared to the nation so long after the fatal
bullet was fired. By this prolongation of life, we have
been brought to our knees, and at this moment lie humbled
in the dust, as never before. And still it becomes us, in
deep humility to pray : "Not our will, but thine be done."
But if our Vice-President Arthur, who *now* takes his seat
as *Chief* Magistrate, has not received lessons from the
course of events during the last three months, as well as
from reading his obituary, while he is still in life and
health, then I despair of his aptness as a scholar to learn
anything. It behooves us as individuals, and as a nation,
earnestly to pray for, and sustain him in the *proper* performance of the duties of his high office.

6. A final lesson which I will name, is the necessity of some adequate protection for the life of our Chief Magistrate while in office. In that exalted position he is not a *tyrant*, but the servant of the people, to execute their will. The choice of fifty millions or more of free-men is not to be treated so lightly, that the meanest wretch living, can thwart all their plans, and cast them into the depths of mourning. It is but a poor consolation, that we can take the life of so miserable a wretch after he has committed the horrid deed, but there should be a law so framed, that the *attempt* of any sane person upon the sacred life of our Chief Magistrate, would surely doom the would-be assassin, to the hangman's noose, or to the headsman's sword. Then, and only then, can we hope for freedom from so fearful a crime.

When—after so many weary weeks of watching and praying, and anxious waiting between hope and fear—the tolling bells aroused us from our slumbers, I cannot express the sadness and disappointment which filled my soul. The following lines from some unknown hand, breathe so nearly the feelings of my heart in that hour, that I venture to quote them here:

Toll! toll! ye solemn midnight bells,
From spire to spire the thrilling echo swells;
And to our hearts the mournful story tells—
        Gone! Gone! Gone!

Millions of watchers list with bated breath
To iron tongues that speak our martyr's death.
"Is this the end?" each to another saith—
        Gone! Gone! Gone!

Is this the outcome of our prayers and tears?
The harvest of his honest toil of years?
Buoyed by strong faith, and ne'er a prey to fears—
        Gone! Gone! Gone!

And has it ended with the assassin's blow?
Why has it been permitted so?
We feel that only God can know.
        Gone! Gone! Gone!

A finished life! More perfect in its plan
Than would have been devised by man,
Perfected as only God can.
              Gone! Gone! Gone!

Had he remained upon the chair of State,
He scarcely could escape the fate—
Envy and misjudgment—which attends the great,
              Now gone! Gone! Gone!

But his sublime patience on a bed of pain
Has bound all hearts as with an iron chain—
He has not suffered thus in vain,
              Though gone! Gone!

What richer gift could bless him from above
Than the whole nation's undivided love?
Without one voice that will dissenting prove,
              Now he is gone!

His upright life has stood each crucial test;
His *living* every mortal blest,
His saintly death completes the rest.
              Gone! Gone! Gone!

No more his voice a guiding star can be,
But his great soul lives in eternity,
And his pure life is a reality,
              Though gone!

Like the ripe sheaf that is cut and bound,
Homeward along its path is found,
Broadcast, rich grain upon the ground.

So all along the path he moved
He found in hearts of those he loved
Rare memories which his goodness proved.

God heard our prayers, not as we would:
His great love better understood,
And answered as a Father should.
              Gone! Gone! Gone!

Weep, strong men ! ye have lost a friend !
With heads uncovered to your Maker bend !
He fashioned that great soul,
He destined this great end.

In conclusion :

1. It only remains for us, tearfully, tenderly and affectionately, to follow the loved form to its last resting-place, and there leave it to await the morning of the resurrection.

2. From the grave of our buried hopes let us turn to, and spread our wants before *Him* who cannot die, and humbly pray, both for our *new* President, and for the perpetuity of our noble Republic. Amen.

PARK REFORMED CHURCH.

Sermon by the Pastor,

REV. J. HOWARD SUYDAM.

Our friend　*　*　*　sleepeth.—JOHN xi : 11.

He is dead! From millions of lips these significant monosyllables have dropped in hushed and solemn tones. From the rude fisherman on the extremest coast of Maine, the mongrel Creole of Louisiana, the fierce Apache of New Mexico, the Northman of Alaska, the words have passed from mouth to ear: "He is dead"! In every dwelling, in every public office, on every mart of trade, in every institution of learning, on the threshhold of every church, though all knew it, yet in place of the usual salutation were the words: "He is dead"! By the lightning's flash the news was borne across the seas, and in the hovel of the peasant, the palace of the noble, in the parliament and the court, there was no need of explanation, as the words were uttered: "He is dead"! Beginning with Great Britian, with which nation, by reason of language and religion our relations are the closest; and Republican France, our friend and ally in the Revolution and our disciple in her form of government; and through all the imperial chambers of Europe as the message is brought "He is dead"! Emperor, King, Kaiser, Tsar and Sultan order the official business to suspend, and the representatives of the people bow their heads in respectful sorrow : and as the intelligence reaches the remotest regions of China, Japan and India, throughout Asia, throughout Africa, Australia, New Zealand and the islands of the sea, as soon as they are spoken, the words are understood: "He is dead"!

Never before have the people of the world assumed such propriety of a man, except the immortal Lincoln, as of him of whom we now say : "He is dead"!

There was that in his career, in his character, in his endowments of mind and heart, in his conduct in public and private life, in his Christian faith, profession and practice, in his statesmanship, in his courtesy and philanthrophy which removes him from all class association and renders him equally admirable to crown and subject, to wealth and poverty, to the cultured and untutored, to the free-born and those aspiring to be free ; at home with all, all claim him as their own kindred.

He is dead! Yet we prayed that his life might be spared. We wanted that grand man to live through the period of administration for which he had been chosen.

We wished it for his sake. The people were of one mind that he was receiving his just deserts, not by the usual mode of caucus and pledge, not as the result of bargain and sale, through no corruption by bribery, by no smoothly spoken promises, but, notwithstanding well-laid plans and arrangements, deemed complete, by which to secure for some other aspirant the coveted prize—accidentally, as some said, providentially, as the world now declares, he was borne on the arms of the people to the chief place of honor in our nation. And all the people rejoiced. They recalled the youth struggling for subsistence, the student bearing off the highest honors of his college, the teacher of youth and principal of an educational institution, the senator of his state, the colonel and major-general in the army, the hero of Chickamauga, fifteen consecutive years in Congress, and there the acknowledged leader of his party, United States Senator—they recalled the man who had risen through all these gradations, who had "held his own" amid his peers in every station, who, though not free from fault or error, made the drift of his life and public service to tend in the direction of all that was pure and elevating, and of all that seemed for the best

good of the people of the whole country, and they said:
"This is the man whom we delight to honor." If by
reason of long and faithful service, character and qualifications it can be said of any, of none could it be more
truthfully spoken than of him, that he merited his position.

Not only for his own sake, but the country's good, the
people lifted to God their voice in prayer that his life might
be spared.

Untrammelled by pledges, his sentiments upon all matters of political reform well understood, the country agitated by fears that it might pass under control of a faction
which should rule chiefly to secure unrighteous spoils, the
mass of the people were greatly relieved, and felt in his
election that they had a man at the helm of government
whom money could not corrupt, nor flattery weaken, whose
life was based upon high-toned principles ; strong, clear-
headed, courageous, who having announced his policy dared
to attempt to carry it into effect. This was in the minds of
the multitude of those who thought as they prayed of the
relations which he bore to the whole people of our country.

Nor was it without sympathy with his family that they
lifted up the heart with the voice during those eighty days
of agony and suspense, beseeching God that the President
might be permitted to live. On the contrary, the picture
of that little white-haired mother—who this week attained
her four-score years—was constantly before their minds.
That loyal and faithful wife, uncomplaining and cheery—
true type of millions of wives in our land not so conspicuous
—was also in their hearts as in their thoughts. And those
growing children stood as we could imagine our own without a father. And so as those bound by a common tie of
humanity, all the best and sweetest traits of human nature in
the ascendency, feeling for others in their watchings, griefs
and anxieties as others have felt, and as we wish others to
feel for us in like extremity, we prayed to God for them,
that the dutiful and loyal son, the large-hearted devoted

husband and the father, whose example and precepts might be expected to rear a noble family, should have his precious life spared to them.

And not the least among the motives influencing our prayers, and those of the whole world beside, was that he was a Christian, a real, pronounced Christian. We greatly desired it to be manifested—we wished it forever after to be conspicuous—that a man could rise through all the gradations of the public offices, take possession and retain them with proper dignity, and invoke the respect of the world and the confidence of this great nation, and maintain not only a Christian character, but remain an humble member of the Christian Church, and deem it a privilege to renew his consecration to Christ by sitting every Sabbath at the sacramental board, and in obedience to the Master's command, "Eat the bread and drink the wine in remembrance of Me." Without ostentation, with no utterance of cant religious phrases, with no desire to obtrude either his views or his practices into places where no good could be accomplished, he was always the type of a hearty, manly disciple of our Blessed Lord and Saviour Jesus Christ. And we hoped and prayed that our brother might grace his position of exalted eminence by four years of Christian example and devotion.

But "He is dead!" All this volume of prayer has ascended. From true and earnest hearts have these petitions proceeded. From the closet, the family altar, and from churches of every name here and in foreign lands—Protestant, Roman, Greek, Mussulman and Jew, the prayer has gone up to the throne for eighty days, "God save the President." "He is dead!"

Are then all those prayers in vain? Has God forgotten us? Or, is there no God? Such questions arise, but they are immediately hushed into silence as savoring of blasphemy. For who are we that we should sit in judgment of God's dealings? What do we know of His ultimate designs? That His ways are "past finding out" we are well assured:

and that He is a God of justice, which blossoms into love, we also know. It is not ours to dictate, but rather to submit to the decrees of Him whose pathway is in the deeps and whose mercy is over all. We are children, and God is our Father. We therefore never call upon Him in vain. You, as wise parents, give to your children what is best for them and not everything that they ask for. In the best sense you often grant their requests when you deny their special plea. And so like reasonable, loving children we bow in reverence, kissing the hand that smites as the hand that bestows, and say "It is well." "Should it be according to *thy* mind" is the question God often puts to us. Or should it be according to His own devisings, purposes, plans, which in their long reach and ramifying influences, shall bring about the most desirable results?

This is of the essence of true prayer. And Jesus presents us an example in himself. In the garden He cried once, twice, thrice, "If it be possible let this cup pass from me," but He added, "Nevertheless not my will but Thine be done." So we have entered our Gethsemane. We have taken the case of our beloved President before God and cried once, twice, thrice, "If it be possible spare him to us;" and all the people responded with a loud "Amen." But at the same time, with the filial spirit of Jesus, conceding all wisdom to God, and never doubting His infinite love we added, "Nevertheless not our will but Thine be done."

We know not what of good is concealed beneath this stroke of His hand, but we think we are able to see, though dimly, something which has already, and which shall in the future, be recognized as a blessing.

Thus we may say that we prayed for the man, for his life—and what is God's answer, if we limit our query to this? We have a glorious parallel in the Scriptures to show that God gives more than we would presume to ask for. Solomon asked for light whereby he might be enabled to discharge his duty, and God replied " Because thou hast asked this thing and not for thyself long life, behold I have done this and more beside." And in another place He says, "Thou hast asked for life, behold I have given thee long life." If we desire the man to have the best that could be for him, behold he has it in glorious revelation at this very time that the whole world weeps and "the mourners go about the streets." God has given more than we asked for.

The Chief Justice of the Supreme Court of the State of New York in an address to his political associates, exclaimed over and over again, with arms uplifted and with tears flowing down his cheeks, "God is greater than our prayers!" We amend by saying "God is better than our prayers."

Think of it! Should God grant our specific petitions in our way, everything would be in confusion. The winds of the ocean would blow from all points of the compass at the same time. There would be drought and famine, floods and disasters, and very few would ever die. Such prayer as dictates to God is founded in ignorance and conceit, and is wanting in filial love and humility. No! It is best; it is certainly best for him whom we loved. We may ask with the Jews at the grave of Lazarus: "Could not this man which opened the eyes of the blind have caused that even this man should not have died"? But to all the Lord speaks as to Martha: "Said I not to thee that if thou wouldst believe, thou shouldst see the glory of God." In that special instance it was for "the glory of God" that the dead should be brought to life. Let us put the emphasis in the proper place; "*for the glory of God;*" not for the immediate gratification of those lonely and weeping sisters, nor for satisfying the curiosity of the multitude, nor for silencing the cavilings of the few surrounding skeptics, but "*for the glory of God.*" The whole transaction had a reach through the centuries, and served as a foundation stone in the structure of Christ's kingdom, which is to have no end.

And so this great grief of ours may have relations to a greater good to this whole people than we have ventured to include in our prayers, circumscribed, as they have been, by the little horizon which our vision may compass. And yet for him who is dead there is now more than we asked for.

What contrasts the contemplation of the solemn event presents!

Six months since he was installed into his high office. We witnessed with pride the grand pageantry, the triumphal arches spanning the broad avenues, each bearing the symbols of the States comprising the Union; soldiers and sailors in brilliant uniform, and led by their commanders, whose names are already crystalized in history; a hundred thousand citizens filling the air with huzzas of delight, music from a hundred bands, cannon booming from the military posts and ships of the navy; the Senate chamber crowded with the representatives of all the nations of the globe in the resplendant regalia of their several courts, the commanders of our army and navy, judges of the Supreme Court in their official robes, senators and members of the House of Representatives, and people of every grade and from every section of our land; the man standing on the eastern portico of the Capitol, before acres of humanity, addressing the multitude with his strong voice, swaying to and fro his grand form, while with famous eloquence he gave expression to the sentiments of his heart and the judgment of his mighty intellect, telling truths wholesome, politic, indicating a policy which should best subserve the good order, the elevation and future prosperity of our great Republic, taking the oath of office, kissing the leaves of the open Bible, and then turning, and in the sight of all the people, acting from the impulses of his nature, never lost from infancy, kissing his aged mother, and then with the true chivalry of his manhood saluting the wife who had traveled by his side all the way up the ascent to this glorious summit.

What a contrast! Only six months gone, and "he is dead"! Dead by the hand of an assassin! This good man slain! This great man shot down while in the discharge of the duties of his grand mission! Now he is no more with us, and the whole land mourns. The dastardly crime causes the flag to fall from the staff. Liberty bows her head as if for shame, and tears fall from the blinded eyes of Justice.

In that same city where he was crowned with the only diadem a free people can confer, by whom a citizen for a time is set apart as the chief among equals, we behold him led to his chamber, and for weeks his life hangs suspended as by a thread. The best medical skill of the land is put forth for his healing. Nothing that science could invent but is brought into service. Nothing that professional hands and hands of affection could do to minister to his comfort, but it is tendered gracefully, tenderly and at whatever sacrifice. In the first moments of seeming convalescence he is removed to the pure airs of the ocean. A brief invigoration—hopes raised—the people elated—but suddenly a change, and that great light is extinguished! *"President Garfield is dead"!*

Again the throngs gather and bow in humiliation and prayer. The public offices, the stores, the workshops, the palatial residences on the avenues, the crowded tenements of the alleys are draped in mourning. The bells again send forth their sound, but it is the funeral knell. The cannon becomes the minute gun. The soldiers and sailors march with arms reversed. The *gloria* changes to the *miserere*. All shouts are hushed. With uncovered heads the masses stand at the stations and witness the draped procession of funeral cars as it speeds along on its iron pathway. And to-day Ohio receives again all that remains of her most distinguished son, while the little mother prays for death, and the stricken widow and orphaned children cling to each other in speechless sympathy, and wonder what is the meaning of " *Glory.*" What a contrast!

Lay him away. Erect above him the monumental shaft. In view of the place where the aspiration first seized him to become a man, near the spot where he put forth his earliest efforts, not far from the home his own hands builded for his mother, and that little farm house at Mentor where his heart always remained, there raise the column which shall forever tell the story of a well-spent life, of a proper, manly ambition, of the rewards of industry, honesty and piety, of the great man who was also the good. Henceforth his memory belongs to the world. The sisterhood of States join hands around the tomb and say, "He was ours;" the larger sisterhood of Nations approach and cast violets upon the sod, and say, "He was ours;" people of all classes look proudly through their tears and say, "He belonged to us," and the Christian Church rises and extends her hands over all in benediction, and says, "He was also of us."

Let him sleep! Let him have his rest who said "I am so tired." His work is done. His sun has set while it is yet noon. "He is not" for God took him. Let him sleep until the day when God shall reanimate the dust, and in the full glory of a perfect being he shall go to be forever with Him who said "I am the resurrection and the life."

I have dwelt, as a refrain, upon the words "He is dead." But let us not rest in this reflection. The Christian life is a paradox. So that, we may say in truth, a good man never dies. In a sense, high and true, and by the Christian unquestioned, President GARFIELD is not dead. There is a sense too in which the unbeliever can assent to this, in common with those of the Christian faith. We say, upon the authority of Divine revelation, that this man lives in his personality, in his identity, and that to-day he is in possession of the same faculties as before his heart ceased to throb in the cottage by the sea on last Monday evening. We believe, upon the same authority, that he inhabits a land—a far more glorious and happy land, than the most favored of the many beautiful oases in this world. We believe that he dwells in a home among the "many mansions" which Christ has prepared for his loved and loving disciples far happier than the happiest homes on earth. We believe that he is where none need ever say "I am sick;" and "where the wicked cease from troubling." We believe him to be at rest in glory. And we believe that there will be a continuity of all that is good, and true, and elevated in that sanctified being, and that it will develop, and that he will be engaged in glorious activities forever. These are some of the articles of the Christian's creed.

But in another sense he is not dead. The unbeliever will admit this kind of immortality. The Scriptures give it expression: "His works do follow him." What he was and what he did *that* follows him, and President GARFIELD will be remembered more for what he was than what he did. Yet what he did by way of achievement will be the inspiration of many a youth. What he accomplished in the midst of the most unfavorable circumstances will be to many a perpetual spur and encouragement, and that with all and through all he maintained a clean character, cherished and shaped his course of life according to the purest principles, and was imbued with the spirit of implicit faith, and sustained by daily prayer, will be rehearsed from generation to generation, and will be to young men at once a rebuke to impiety and moral cowardice, a guide to the highest goal in life, and a quickening impulse to all noble yearnings and energy. *After all, he lives !*

There is one passage in the Bible which is singularly solemn and impressive. It is found in the Book of Job, and is this: "My purposes are broken off." How we devise and plan as if we were to live forever! Sometimes in our selfishness all is intended to produce some future temporal advantage for ourselves; or, at farthest, for our families; and sometimes in the spirit of the Master it is for others, for those who are contemporary, and also for those who shall come after us. But in either case how few are permitted to witness the consummation of their hopes, aims, and expectations? So that we are compelled to say with Job, "My purposes are broken off."

Through the press, and in the eulogiums which will be pronounced by statesmen, it will be shown what grand purposes lay in the mind of our departed President, and which he intended, so far as might lie in his power, to carry to their completion. His inaugural address indicated some of them, such as—to maintain the supremacy of the nation, to secure the freedom of the ballot, to protect our environs from foreign encroachment, to reform the civil service, to break up the foul nest of Mormonism, to secure national aid to agriculture, to stop the course of corruption through the Postal and In lian rings, and to encourage immigration and home industries. His views were large, patriotic and philanthropic. But "his purposes are broken off." They may be carried forward by his successor and the enlightened public mind making itself felt through the people's representatives. It is to be hoped, and this is our prayer, that the grand course toward the general good of our beloved country may not suffer even a temporary check.

Yet for him, "his purposes are broken off."

It is a solemn lesson. Alas, for human greatness! We are a democracy at birth and in death. We lie down alike in the dust. O sad ending, if this were all! Aye! *if this were all!* But, friends, God's purposes stand. And hence we may say, in the words of the deceased President, when on that other occasion our beloved chieftain fell by an assassin's hand: "God reigns and the government at Washington still lives." The wheels are not for a moment checked. One is removed, but another takes his place. One dies, and another assumes the responsibility. There is no revolution. There is no disturbance. We bury our dead in silent sorrow, and the world moves on.

Not for you, aged mother, the continued pride in the earthly elevation of your son ; nor for you, brave and loving widow, the brilliant career of the National capitol ; not for you, orphaned children, the counsel and the example of such a father ; but for you all the sympathies and the prayers of millions, and better than all, the sweet faith in a blissful immortality and inseparable reunion. We come to this at last. And it is the best. We die, but we live again. We live forever; for Christ brought life and immortality to light. And he that believeth on Him shall never die.

> "Death is the crown of life ;
> Were death denied poor man would live in vain.
> Death wounds to cure : we fall, we rise, we reign,
> Spring from our fetters, fasten to the skies,
> Where blooming Eden withers from our sight,
> This king of terrors is the PRINCE OF PEACE."

7

ADDRESS BY WILLIAM L. DICKINSON, ESQ.,

Superintendent of Schools of Jersey City, delivered at Hedding M. E. Church.

I am at a loss to determine which side of the character of that great and many-sided man, our dead President, I shall present to you.

I will not speak of him as a soldier, although his record as a leader of armies, brave, ready and full of resources, is one of which the greatest of generals might be proud. The world has rarely seen in the history of its wars any thing more wonderful than when the obscure school-master of Hiram stepped from the marshalling of boys and girls at the blackboard, to be a successful leader of our armies, and stand at once in the front line of great captains.

I dwell not on his fame as an orator, although with argument, learning and rhetoric all on fire with intensity of feeling, he swayed "listening senates at his will."

I need not refer to his wisdom as a statesman. All men, not excepting his opponents, recognized his pre-eminent capacity in affairs, and looked for great results from his administration.

Why should I talk of his patriotism, in which he shone forth a light of the purest brilliancy, like thousands of his fellow citizens; nor need I dilate upon the "deep damnation of his taking off," and his cruel sufferings, although in this respect he is worthy to be ranked among the greatest and best of those who have died in the service of their country.

Passing over all these, I see in the character of our beloved President, something which is the crown and glory of them all, which doubled their lustre, and more than doubled their usefulness.

The roll of honor of our nation has not upon it many blank spaces. It is crowded with the names of those who have been illustrious in every department of human activity. Warriors, statesmen, orators, poets, historians, men wonderful for their attainments in art and science, justly claim our admiration, and many have earned the undying gratitude of all patriots, for services done to the country. We honor them; we are proud of them for the virtues they possessed, and the good they did.

But how many of these are there of whom a father can say to his son: "My son, behold the man whose private life is worthy of imitation; pure, spotless, untainted in all public relations; so also is he in all social and private associations. Give him your approbation; follow in his footsteps, and you will never go astray."

How often must the teacher, in discoursing before his pupils of our great men and their illustrious deeds, be careful lest he unveil too fully the vices and defects of their lives, and so hold up to the youthful mind examples of folly.

Do we not all acknowledge that the example and influence of some of our great men has been ruinous to many? How often must we, like the sons of Noah, walk reverently backward and cast the mantle of our charity upon their sins?

But for GARFIELD we may claim the crowning glory, that while standing in the front rank of those who have honored their country and made themselves illustrious, while his laurels gained on the field of battle and in the councils of the nation will never fade, yet in no one act in any of his relations as son, or pupil, or teacher, or father, or husband, or private citizen, has he soiled his record, or diminished by one jot the brightness of his character. We may safely hold him up before the youth of our land for their model, to be their type of a true American.

Great were his deeds, but how much greater they look, how much greater they are, accompanied by such a constellation of virtues.

To all young men who find the battle of life a hard fight,

I say, remember the self-denial and privations of GARFIELD in his younger days, imitate his courage, his industry, patience, honesty and truthfulness ; seek to be right and to do right, and all other needful things shall be added unto you.

Have we lost GARFIELD ? Yes ; just as we have lost Franklin and Washington and Lincoln. Their examples and teachings will remain for ever a never ceasing source of inspiration and comfort to all aspiring souls.

GRACE CHURCH (EPISCOPAL), OF JERSEY CITY.*

Sermon by the Pastor,

REV. SPENCER M. RICE, D. D.

TEXT—And afterward, when David heard it, he said, I and my kingdom are guiltless before the Lord forever, from the blood of Abner, the son of Ner.—2 SAM. iii : 28,

There was, my brethren, a very broad and striking contrast, between the civil polity and constitution of the people of Israel and the civil polity and constitution of the modern governments of the nations.

The modern nations, for the most part, far exceed in numbers, the highest point ever reached by the Israelitish nation.

The necessities and civil interests of the modern nations are, also, far more complicated and their legislative enactments are far more numerous.

The civil code of Israel was extremely simple, and was suited to the simplicity of the times and to the necessities of a simple, pastoral and agricultural people.

But that code had this important feature. It was not the work of human legislators. It was a *divine code.* It

---

*The Committee sent an invitation to Grace Church, requesting the Church to furnish their Pastor's sermon delivered on the occasion of the death of President GARFIELD, for the GARFIELD MEMORIAL VOLUME. Upon this request, the Vestry of the Church took action and selected the sermon delivered by their Pastor on the Sunday after the wounding of the President. And the Vestry of the Church having requested the Committee to accept the same instead of the sermon asked for, the Committee have acceded to the request, and the sermon selected by the Vestry is the one printed. No apology need be offered by the Committee for this substitution, as the same is the only sermon in the Volume expressive of our feelings at that time.

originated in the wisdom of God. God was the first legislator for man, and His code was undoubtedly designed not
only to constitute a body of civil law for that immediate
people, but to serve also as a model to the legislators of
the nations to come. It is important, therefore, in this
view, to observe that the laws embodied in that Divine
code are all of them distinguished for their brevity, their
simplicity and their positive character. "A wayfaring
man, though a fool could not err therein." And that
code, had, in particular, two cardinal and distinguishing
features, the one of which was the prevention of bloodshed, the shedding of innocent blood, the killing of men,
made in the image of God. And the other was the repres-
sion of wrongs, and of every kind of injustice. Modern
legislators have recognized the excellence and the binding
force of this ancient and divine code by incorporating its
provisions into their codes, but they have so diluted and
weakened them by amplifications and by amendments and
by correlative laws, that law is no longer the simple thing
that it was when it came from the hand of the Divine Law
Maker and the first Law Giver. That divine law would
not permit Ahab, though king of the realm and the monarch of Israel, to possess himself of that little plot of
ground which belonged to Naboth, without the free consent of the owner, much as the king desired it for his con-
venience and pleasure, and for his purposes in building.
But law in our day, so far from protecting the modern
Naboths in the possession of their property, are expressly
framed to dispossess them of their real property whenever
it happens to lie in the path of the interests of the kings
of our time! And in regard to the shedding of innocent
blood, the divine law was so positive and rigorous, that
when a man was slain, the whole nation became instantly
interested in purging itself of the guilt of bloodshed, well
knowing that, if it did not so purge itself, then, what was,
in the first instance, the crime of an individual, became a
crime which attached to the executive and to the whole
nation, and the whole people had reason to apprehend
dire chastisement and punishment.

It was such an incident which gave rise to the words of David in the text. Joab, one of the officers of the king, had assassinated and treacherously slain Abner, another official of the nation. The consternation of the king, when he heard of the crime, was very great, because he knew that, in view of the exacting and rigorous character of the divine law, how liable he and his people were, before God, and he felt the necessity of protesting instantly as he does, in the text, his own and his people's innocence of this great crime, exclaiming in great alarm : "I and my kingdom are guilt-less before the Lord forever, from the blood of Abner, the son of Ner." And he issued a proclamation, calling on the people to "Rend their clothes and to gird themselves with sackcloth, and to mourn" for the murdered Abner. And the king himself followed Abner to his burial and wept over his grave and lamented over him, saying, "Died Abner as a fool dieth"? "Thy hands were not bound, nor thy feet put in fetters." "As a man falleth before wicked men so fellest thou." Such was the conduct of David and of his people, on the occasion of the base and cruel mur-der of Abner. They wished to purge themselves of the blood which had been so treacherously shed in the land and which they had just cause to fear would, otherwise, be required at their hands. The king and the people very well knew, that it was not necessary, in order to their being involved in the guilt of this murder and to their being held responsible for the blood which had been shed in the land, that they should have known of it and have been privy to the crime. They knew that, though they had had no hand in it, and that though they had been absolutely ignorant of the designs of the man who had committed the deed, they might still be held responsible for it, if it had been provoked by bad government, by a government which makes men mad by oppressions and frenzied by wrongs! And happily, for the king and the people, it was, in this case true, as David, in the text, protested, "I and my kingdom are guiltless, before the Lord forever, from the blood of Abner, the son of Ner." But it is not every government which can so boldly assert

its innocence before the Lord when such crimes are
committed within their jurisdiction. They may show, perfectly, that they have not been privy to the crime, that
they had been absolutely ignorant of it until the moment
when it has made itself known, by the blood which it has
shed, and so, though they may justify themselves before
men they cannot justify themselves before God. It is one
thing, and it may be, a very convenient thing to be able
before men to say, "I and my kingdom are guiltless before
men," but it is quite another thing to be able to say, as
David did, "I and my people are guiltless before the *Lord*,
forever." The eye of the great and final Judge penetrates
beneath the surface and beyond the surroundings, to the
causes, if there are any, which have *led up* to the crime.
And if there *are causes*, which the people have created, or
have allowed to exist, then God holds them guilty just to
that degree in which they have made themselves responsible, and they must atone in punishment and suffering for
the blood which has been shed.

In our country, at least, no charges of direct oppression
can be alleged against its government. And if such a
charge were made, it would immedia'ely fall to the ground,
because there are no prisons, no bastiles to substantiate it.
We have no Siberias, or penal colonies or settlements ; no
scaffolds, with their weekly concourse of victims; no
torture chambers, with their whips and racks and screws.
Every citizen has a direct voice in the *creation* of the government, and therefore, in this country, in particular, more
than in others, are the people directly responsible to God
for any and every evil which exists in the government.
And in this view it is a thing of very grave concern to the
people that there *are* evils in our government; evils which, if
not numerous, are of enormous magnitude, and which have
just led to a crime which has, or which will, as they come
to hear of it, startle and astound the people of the whole
civilized world. We had a chief magistrate freshly elected,
who had just come to us from the people; a typical American; a man born and reared in poverty, but who, with
energy, industry and economy, had qualified himself for

any position or responsibility to which his country might call him. His is one of the examples full of beneficent instruction for "our struggling young men" and such as thoughtful parents employ for the improvement and encouragement of their sons. But that man, just inducted into the one great matchless office of the world has been stricken down, in open day, by the bold hand of an assassin! And if he still lives, it is not because the depraved criminal did not take a steady and fatal aim. The President is so near to death, that, if he should survive his wounds all Christian men will feel that God, while he has allowed the nation to be awakened by the crime to a sense of the evils they have permitted in the government, has protected the victim from what must, ordinarily, have proved a relentlessly fatal wound.

In the crisis of this awful event, it becomes men and citizens, not to allow a natural and justifiable indignation to blind them to the procuring causes of this crime, and which may procure others, as disastrous, unless remedies are applied and the evils removed. And the one great evil to which this crime invites especial attention, and to which this crime will undoubtedly be traced, lies in the principles upon which the offices and patronage of the government are dispensed. We do not need, I am sure, to enter here into an explanation of those principles. No intelligent man is, or can be ignorant of them. Every such man, in his heart and conscience knows and appreciates the evil tendencies of these principles. They introduce an unnecessary and unhealthy vehemence into the politics of the country. They occasion bitter and exasperating assaults, through the public journals, upon the public, and even the private life of public men. They constitute a direct temptation to the commission of frauds upon the ballot boxes, and to the practice of bribery and to corruptions of every kind. They cause the officials of the government to be pursued and haunted by impecunious and, often, by the most worthless men, who seek from the government the means of living without labor, or at least without that kind of labor which God has ordained. They

divert our public officials from their legitimate duties, and
embarrass them seriously and injuriously in the discharge
of their trusts. They occasion offices of importance to be
filled with incompetent and often by bad men. They hu-
miliate men, and degrade them. And, as in the nature of
things, all cannot be gratified who apply for government
positions, these principles upon which the patronage of the
government are distributed, occasion a resulting poverty
and disappointment, and exasperations and deadly hatreds.

And, finally, they lead, not merely to the crimes of corruption and bribery, to disappointments and poverty, but
to violence, to assassination, to crimes such as this which
now spreads its gloom and horror over our whole broad
country. If our President dies, he will have fallen a
martyr to this mischievous and degrading and indefensible
feature of our political system. The crime now in question
was committed upon a high theatre, and there is, I believe,
no man so obtuse in intelligence, as not to be able, and
even to be compelled to see the connection between it and
the evil which we arraign and denounce.

We have arrived at a point in our political history
when members of Congress, senators and representatives,
claim to own and to control the patronage of their respective states and districts, and that positions must be filled
by the Executive only by men whom they have selected.
This is to usurp the power of the President, and to take
from him a responsibility which the constitution has
explicitly lodged in the Executive.

President GARFIELD determined upon coming into office,
that the Executive should not be so shorn of its constitutional powers and duties. He determined to exercise the
power of appointment and of nominating officials himself,
according to the terms of the constitution, but when he
did this, when he attempted to recover that of which the
Executive had virtually been deprived, then followed the
scenes and the political controversies which during these
last weeks have so disturbed and agitated the country.

Assassination and murder startle and convulse the
nation, as well they should. The crime which has just

been perpretrated will reverberate round the world on
account of its atrocity, but judged from the standpoint
of its actual effect upon the well-being of the nation, it
is by no means the deadliest style of crime. It will not,
even if the President should die, have that character. It
deranges business and wounds our feelings, but thanks to
the wisdom of our fathers and to our noble constitution, the
government will live. The crime will not be fatal to the
nation. Atrocious therefore, as the crime is, it is far less
injurious in respect to actual evil, than a single act of
flagrant corruption or bribery, or of the depravation of
legislation. These inflict injuries which reach the very
integrity and vitality of the nation. The constitution has
no remedies for the wounds which these inflict, as it has
for such as that which now threatens the nation, and if
the assassin of a *man* should be punished with swift and
exemplary severity, how much swifter and sorer punishment should pursue relentlessly and even to death, the
man who attempts the life and integrity of the nation,
and the welfare of the whole people, whose happiness is
bound up in the integrity of the government?

This is a time, a crisis, in which the people ought to
awake, and in which the pulpit ought, as it seems to me,
to do what it can to aid in awakening the people to a
sense of the perils which are threatening them from the
directions we have indicated, and which are constantly
increasing with the increase of the wealth and greatness
of the country, and the consequent increase of the patronage which the government has to dispense. Let no man
now shut his eyes to the facts, made more apparent within these few weeks than ever, if that were possible, that
to this question of offices, and especially to the manner of
their distribution, must be traced all the unhealthy political
excitement, the resignations and the election of senators,
and the multiplying dishonors which are humiliating us
in our sight, and degrading us in the sight of the world,
and which in the present instance have culminated in
a bold attempt on the part of a most depraved and
wicked scoundrel to divert into other hands, the govern-

ment and its patronage by the murder of the President.
And if the scenes of these last weeks and days, now baptized in blood, do not have the effect to awaken the people
to their duty in dealing with this evil, they cannot plead
that they are guiltless before the Lord of the crimes which
have been committed, and they must share in the responsibility for the blood which has been shed, and in the crimes
which are sure to be committed in the future, by the
continuation of the temptation to commit them. We, in
our reflections, are apt to merge our personalty in the
mass, and so to hide, or seek to hide from ourselves our
personal responsibility for crimes which so fall out, as this
has done. But God distinguishes. He distinguishes one
hair from another, and every one sparrow, in the field, from
its fellow, and so his knowledge extends down to each individual unit which goes to make up the nation. And, so
no man escapes, in His sight, his own just share of responsibility, and every good citizen will care much more how
he is to stand before God than how he stands in the sight
of a political party, or of men whose interests are the
attainment of offices with their honors and profits. In
politics, as in all the acts and callings of life, we should
act, as in the sight of a just God, and then, when crimes
fall out, we may lay our hand upon our heart and say, with
David, in the text, "I and my kingdom are guiltless before
the Lord forever," of the crime that has been committed,
and of the blood that has been shed.

Sermon by the Pastor,

REV. THOMAS C. MAYHAM.

OUR NATIONAL SORROW.

TEXT—"And all Judah and Jerusalem mourned"—2 *Chron.* 35 : 24.

The whole sentence from which I have taken my text reads : "And all Judah and Jerusalem mourned for Josiah." Our whole nation mourns for JAMES A. GARFIELD. While there are many dissimilarities found in the two men and in the causes for National mourning, there is also much in common. Josiah was king of Judah. GARFIELD was President of our Republic. Josiah sought God in early life and left the brightest name for piety of any of the successors of David. GARFIELD early gave his heart to God and has left the purest record for religious devotion of any of the successors of Washington. Josiah broke down the altars of Baalam and the images, and cut down the groves where idol worship was carried on, and GARFIELD used the axe of his power to destroy " Bossism," and also struck heavy blows to cut down systems which have shielded knaves while stealing from the government. Josiah was pierced by an arrow and GARFIELD by a bullet. Each died from the effect of his wound and both greatly lamented. It would not be difficult to trace out other analogies but these are enough for our purpose.

Our whole Nation mourns for GARFIELD and other Nations are touched by the shadow which rests upon us. A wail of sorrow goes up from the whole civilized world. Ever since the firing of the fatal bullet the electric current has been utilized to express the profoundest sorrow of Nations and of men, and to bring assurances of sympathy for the sufferer while he lived, for his family, and for our whole Nation.

To-day we are a Nation of mourners. An aged mother wondered why any one should want to "kill her baby," and fifty millions of people are amazed and ask why should any one wish to harm an honored son of this Republic? Many and even some ministers of the Gospel have argued that God sent this distress upon us to humble us and to chastise us for our sins. That kind of argument implicates God and makes Him responsible for the crime of Guiteau. I deny it; it was not the work of God but of the devil. God operated upon Guiteau to induce him not to commit the crime, dissuading him from shooting through the window of the church where the President worshiped, and again touched his sympathies for Mrs. Garfield when she leaned upon her husband's arm in the same dépôt where the shot was fired two weeks later. But Guiteau was a free agent, and continuing to harbor his evil designs he let the devil get full possession of him, and thus by his own consent he became the wicked instrument of the evil one. God brings good influences to bear upon us to induce us to give up our bad designs, but he does not break down that free agency with which he has possessed us. So God used good influences upon Guiteau, but I repeat God did not break down his free agency. That wretch was not in the employ of God at all. Our kind Heavenly Father does not employ wicked men to assassinate a good man, a wise statesman, an esteemed and beloved President. We have our National sins it is true and many of them, but for these God never has and never will employ assassins to shoot our Presidents.

Our Nation is in mourning because a great crime has been committed and our chosen Chief Magistrate is dead. An aged mother mourns the loss of her illustrious son; a devoted wife is in bitterest grief over the death of her affectionate husband; and loving children weep because their fond father "sleeps the sleep that knows no earthly waking." But in the death of JAMES A. GARFIELD there is

more than a family bereavement. Our whole Nation is
stricken. Every family over this broad land has sustained
an irreparable loss. Among all our public men no one was
so endeared, and occupying as he did the highest office in
the Nation and filling it so ably the death of no other man
could have produced such universal sorrow. His powerful
and well-trained intellect, his bravery as a soldier, his
wise statesmanship, and his faithful discharge of his duties as President made him the peer of the best kings and
emperors of the earth. Nor had he come to his exalted
station as kings come to theirs, but by earnest hard toil
he honorably and successfully struggled from obscurity
and poverty up the hill of learning and of fame till he
reached the highest summit of glory as the world views it.

As a son he was obedient and reverent to his widowed
mother, as a day or month laborer he was faithful to his
employers, as a pupil he was studious, thoroughly mastering whatever he undertook, as a teacher he was wise and
successful, as a soldier he was judicious and brave, as a
legislator he early took rank among the ablest, and was
soon recognized as a leader, as President he in a few short
months won the admiration of all his countrymen, save an
ignoble few, as a sufferer he bore his pains with Christian fortitude, and dying we trust he has joined the blessed company of the blood-washed in heaven.

It was my privilege to be a visitor at the Chicago Convention, which nominated him for the Presidency. He
was not himself a candidate, but in a speech which made
a deep impression upon me at the time, and which I was
sure I had never heard equaled, he presented the name of
another to the convention. His speech differed from all the
others which I heard on that occasion, in that he acknowledged the real worth, and paid a glowing tribute to the
abilities of every other candidate before the convention.
And indeed, this was characteristic of the man during his
whole life. JAMES A. GARFIELD never sought favors for
his friends by speaking lightly of their rivals, nor did he
ever seek honors for himself, and when they were thrust
upon him he always wore them with credit, and faithfully

8

and conscientiously did his duty. After his election to
the Senate a friend of his wrote congratulating him, and
expressing the hope that he might be further promoted, to
which he replied: "As to the hope you express, that I
shall be called higher, I can only say that my idea of the
highest ambition of a public man ought to be to discharge
fully the duties of the position to which he is already
called. A man is not in position to discharge his
duties fully and without bias if he is aspiring to higher
places, and laboring to secure them. The post of greatest
usefulness ought to be the place of the highest honor."

GARFIELD was in no sense a politician as that word is
now commonly understood. His election to the Legislature of his own State was not asked for by himself. His
first nomination for Congress was made without his
knowledge, and while he was bravely fighting for the flag
of his country, and when the time came for him to take
his seat in the House of Representatives at Washington
he greatly preferred to remain in the army, but the urgent
requests of Lincoln and others, who knew how much his
services would be needed in procuring legislation to successfully carry on the war, together with the circumstances
under which the people of his district had elected him, in-
duced him to resign his major-general's commission and
enter Congress. Some of his subsequent nominations were
made when it was known by his constituents that he
differed from them in measures of great importance, and
after he had assured them that though he had great respect
for their opinions, he could not change his honest convictions nor act in opposition to his own judgment and
conscience to retain his seat in Congress.

His election to the Senate was the golden seal of ap-
proval by his state, of his course in the lower house, and
a fitting expression of confidence in his wisdom and his
integrity, and his nomination to the Presidency against his
most earnest protest, followed by his triumphant election,
placed him in a position for which he was eminently
qualified, and in which he shone with a brilliancy surpassed by none of his predecessors. Every American

citizen may with national pride and personal satisfaction contemplate that pure and that successful career, and each of us may learn profitable lessons, and take great encouragement from it.

But he is gone; cut down by an assassin in the midst of his greatest usefulness. The people, who hold the sovereign power in this country, at a national election chose him to hold the helm and guide the ship of state for four years, but a ruthless hand drew a weapon of death upon him, and defeated the popular will. The Stars and Stripes float at half-mast and habiliments of mourning are upon and within our churches, our homes—everywhere. Our countenances are fallen, and our hearts are sad. The good and true man, the conscientious and wise statesman, our beloved President, JAMES A. GARFIELD, is dead.

My friends it is eminently fitting that we devote this morning hour on this holy Sabbath day to paying our respects to our Nation's honored dead. The tears will fall nor should we try to prevent them. It is the way we feel and our cause for weeping is our justification for doing it. Our loss is great, our grief is indescribable and our sympathies mutual. That the fiend who shot our noble Chief Magistrate is caged is not enough to assuage our sorrow for that does not restore the life of him we loved. That the Constitution provides for a succession to the Presidency and the office is already filled may in some degree calm our fears about the public welfare, still we are not without grave and serious apprehensions. We believe our system of government is the best ever devised by man; we know, however, that it is not without its dangers and we therefore feel safest when men of known ability and of unimpeachable integrity are in official positions. President Arthur may prove himself wise and efficient and discharge the duties incumbent upon him with entire satisfaction, and let us fondly hope and earnestly pray that such will be the case; but President GARFIELD had already definitely proved both his ability and his determination to so administer the affairs of government that all sections should receive their just rights, and the best interests of our common country be conserved, and his loss can therefore only be viewed as a great national calamity. Bringing as he did to his high office ripe scholarship, stern integrity and long experience in public positions, extraordinary expectations were entertained in regard to his administration, but his Inaugural Address convinced the most sanguine that their brightest hopes were to be more than realized, and during the brief time of his active service he won the admiration of all true lovers of good government. The North paid him homage, and the South hastened to bring their tribute of praise. Sectional differences and animosities were rapidly disappearing and the era of good feeling inspired a public confidence which was helpful to all branches of business and betokened general prosperity. The feverish condition of the illustrious patient after he was shot produced the same condition in business, and the pulse of the Nation became irregular, but his heroic endurance of suffering and his calm Christian fortitude during eighty days furnished a noble example of quiet repose, and did much toward allaying the popular fears and preventing disaster in business circles.

What a blessing that he lingered so long after he was wounded, giving time for the excitement to subside, for business men to gradually become cool and confident, and for the people of this country to survey the public interests and prepare their minds for accepting his constitutional successor. Who will say that this was not the way God answered the prayers of those who called upon Him? Certain it is that this nation is better prepared for the change now than it was on the sad second day of July.

What might have been the result had our beloved President died the day he was shot God only knows, and looking toward Heaven this morning we should smile through our tears, and from the depths of our hearts praise our Heavenly Father that GARFIELD lived so long. We deplore his loss, but we have season to rejoice that from his first entrance into public life till the day the assassin's bullet struck him, he served his country faithfully and well. The results of his labors will never be lost. The influence of his pure life will not be forgotten. Our legislators will study his character, and be influenced for good by it; they will investigate the measures which he advocated while in Congress, and learn much which will be helpful for wise legislation in the future. His speeches will be read with interest, his votes carefully noted, and his whole career examined, and though he may have made many mistakes, much will be found which will be ardently treasured and woven into the legislation of the future, and thus the good that he did will in a two-fold sense bear precious fruit in the oncoming years. Nor will his conscientious discharge of the duties and trusts of his public life fail of fruitage, for many will be charmed as they contemplate it, and not a few will consider it worthy of imitation. Then too, his Christian life will not fail of making a deep impression. His reverence for God, for the Sabbath, and for all that distinguishes Christianity from skepticism and infidelity, will challenge investigation and result in great good. The religion of the Bible had in JAMES A. GARFIELD a faithful exponent, and he was not ashamed to carry it into his public life. He believed in the Fatherhood of God, and the brotherhood of man, and in Christ as the only mediator between God and man, and believing, he accepted Jesus Christ as his Saviour, and recommended him to others. True to God, he detested intrigue and sham under the pretension of religion, hence his outspoken words in his inaugural address against Mormonism which not only defies the laws of our country, but is an insult to God and a reproach upon Christianity. Had he lived he would have wiped that foul blot from the face of our land. But his purposes will not be lost, and what was in his heart to do will yet inspire the hearts and nerve the hands of others to accomplish, and when Mormonism shall be exterminated it will be said that he gave it its first mortal wound.

Indeed I take no great risk in affirming that all the plans of his wise head and good heart for God's glory and our country's good will yet be carried out, for while his noble deeds will never die, so also some one will if not immediately, certainly in the near future, consider it both a privilege and an honor to execute his great plans, for his plans as well as his memory are enshrined in the hearts of the American people. His earthly life is ended but the benefits of that life will long endure.

It is but natural that we should ask ourselves why he could not have lived, but this is not the time for arraigning any one for having contributed toward disturbing the public tranquility. Such a dissension in this presence and upon this day would not be in accord with the spirit of the Gospel nor in keeping with the universal sorrow. When the obsequies shall be ended and the body of him whose departure we mourn shall be laid in its last resting place, then it will be in order to fix the blame where it belongs and by voice and vote express our candid judgment and leave it with history for the benefit of future generations. We must do this if our present sorrow is sincere.

GARFIELD'S own native Ohio will sacredly keep his mortal remains, but our whole Nation will canonize his memory and while the green grass continues to grow and the sweet songsters to wing their flight over his grave, we shall continue to reap benefits from his pure life and patriotic deeds.

Future historians will vie with each other to emblazon his fame, and poesy will sparkle with gems of beauty to his praise. The chisel, the pencil and the brush used by skillful hands will perpetuate his memory, and the oncoming millions of this Republic will rise up and call him blessed. Let historians write of his greatness and poets rhyme his glory; let artists paint and sculptors chisel; let monuments be raised so high that they meet the orb of day in his coming, but all this can never fully express the love of the American people for JAMES ABRAM GARFIELD.

St. Matthew's Episcopal Church of Jersey City.

Sermon by the Pastor,

REV. RICHARD M. ABERCROMBIE, D. D.

Text—It is expedient that one man should die for the people.—*St. John* xi, 50.

This expresses both a principle and a prophecy. There is nothing more marvellous in the providence of God and the history of our race, than the fact that the suffering and death of one, even the innocent, are the sources of life to the many. The doctrine of this vicarious atonement enters into the religious creed and sacrificial system of every nation on the earth. It is the burden of song and story in olden time. It glorifies the martyr and the hero. It reconciles us to our burdens and sorrows, and it magnifies the over-ruling providence of God; and yet its very universality and accepted expediency suggest that there must be some grand truth, some central fact on which pivots all this conviction and action, and at once we turn our gaze to the suffering Christ; at once we are reminded of the words which Caiaphas, with all his power and position, would not have dared to utter, if it had not been an acknowledged principle. It is expedient one should die for the nation. But it had a double force from his lips. Joseph Caiaphas, as his real name was, was high priest that year, and therefore having most weight with the council, and occupying an office of inspiration, God used him as the organ of prophecy to tell the world it had a Saviour, and that he should die to gather into one the children of God. The fact and the prophecy do not exonerate Caiaphas from blame. The vindictive jealousy and injustice with which he did evil that good might come; the falseness of his opinion that because Christ could be a

119

king and rebel against Cæsar, therefore he would be the
base ignoring of Christ's innocence and worth, and the vile
appeal to the prejudices and selfishness of the mob, have
made him justly an object of scorn and aversion. But we
have not to do with his temper and motives, but with the
great truth he unconsciously stated, and its wonderful influence on the destiny and progress of our race.

What is the witness of Scripture? Ought not Christ
to have suffered these things? Was it not fit and expedient in the eye of that all-wise Being, who has constructed
the plan of human salvation, and who controls all the
events of time and eternity?

Christ hath once suffered the just for the unjust to
bring us to God.

It became Him for whom are all things, in bringing
many sons unto glory, to make the captain of their salvation perfect through sufferings.

We learn to hate sin by looking unto Jesus, who knew
no sin, yet who was made a sin offering for us. The evil
are taught thereby to consider and tremble. If God spared
not his Son, who had to take our flesh and suffer in order
to save us, what will be the end of those who despise the
sacrifice and trample on His gospel? We cannot search
the Almighty to perfection in his government, but even in
this life we see distress and death shared by the innocent,
as well as many reaping the blessings of other's virtues.

The trials and martyrdom of the purest and best in the
ages past for the defence and salvation of others, reveals
that trouble and Death love shining marks, for a shining
mark draws attention and illuminates a lesson that would
else fail to be learned.

The death of the immaculate Lamb of God was the
most malicious and diabolical act on record. With what
a terrible punishment its perpetrators met; but Christ, as
is truly said, "lives to-day surrounded with the halo of a
pure and ever resplendent glory reflected from the very
fires in which he suffered." His cross is now the symbol
and teacher of a grand doctrine, and the setting sun of
righteousness spans the clouds of human sorrow and

calamity with the bright bow of hope and promise. The over-ruling providence of God has become an article of public belief. Then learn to bow, even in the darkest hour of national or private tribulation, to the connection, that terrible and seemingly cruel as the sacrifice and suffering may be, harsh and fierce as the storm may be, there is a cleansing and purifying redemption in it, a sweet blessing God intends to bestow. It would be fearful to look back upon the past history of the world and not realize this lesson. Take from me the revelation from God, and all is terrible and dark. Come and bring it, and interpret that revelation by the cross of Christ, and my faith is clear and comforting and stimulating.

Christ's death was the life of the world. It was a light and example that never could be lost to the world. It arrested the wrath of God, and brought his spirit and blessing. It gave unity to the race, the only possible unity to be achieved. We are all brothers by the death of Christ. It gave faith in God, in the principles of liberty and truth, hope in the future of man, and it gave what the world had never learned before, love, which should rise superior to all the diversities of interest and opinions, and learn the possibility of universal sympathy and one spirit in the bond of peace.

But this great principle and experience applies to Christ's body, the Church, and to every member thereof, and the whole scheme of society betokens the same. The solid conviction that God allows his judgment in the earth that his people may learn right, ensures that he allows the foundations to be cast down to test the faithful, and makes the very wrath of man to praise him, is producing under the benificent teachings of Christianity, marvels in self-control and unity of purpose, better government, better laws, and grander feelings and results.

And can we, shall we, in this day of our bitter national sorrow, refuse the consolations and hopes which come from this teaching. All the world sat at the pulse of our dying President; all the world mourns to-day his death. Is there one in our land who is not touched to the very

heart when he thinks upon the strange and fearful sacrifice? Who does not feel all the force and tenderness of
an affecting relationship when he reads the touching
description of that death scene, when the ocean intoned
its dirge, and the nation wept by the cold form of
their chief ruler? Men dared not trust themselves to
express the curse and indignation in their hearts against
the vile wretch who had perpetrated the awful murder.
Men who thought they never could weep, let fall their hot
tears as a willing tribute to the great sufferer and victim.
Was there ever such a spectacle of national woe? Who
can look upon the vast display of grief, and see the eagerness of every hand and heart to hang up if only some
little symbol of the sorrow that makes all one; who can
think of the aged parent of the President, just exulting
in the prospects of a proud motherhood, stunned by the
blow and wishing to go down into the grave with her son,
mourning; the stricken wife and children in their parox-
ysm of grief, robbed of their hopes and the light of their
homes; God have mercy on the desolate ones! Who can
remember the mighty and untiring efforts to save his life
and ameliorate his sufferings, the prayers of every class,
the prayers of nations, the tributes and hopes of other
lands, as if the world's destiny hung upon his life, and
not feel that not to sorrow would be a crime?

He dies, but he leaves the world as a grand sunset, with
grateful long lingering light, flashing its glory even on the
clouds, and enkindling the human mind with the potent
contact of his spirit; the principles he exemplified have
not died out. The influence of his life and example will be
felt, and while America shall be a Union, and the world
progress in civilization and liberty, his counsels will be
studied, his character admired, the impress of his genius
be seen, and the influence of his labors and examples be
known and felt in every home. Heroic in life, heroic in
death, how is he among the martyrs.

Great in war, great in peace, great in the hearts of his
countrymen and the world.

But is there no blessing in this curse? We would not

draw the curtain of mysterious dealing; but does not a nation's tenderness often prove a nation's loyalty. In the interests of political principles we may become excited by bitter contests, and resolve not to yield an inch of the platform on which we stand; but when the hour of suffering or calamitous visitation comes, the passions subside in the higher, calmer and controlling reverence for and trust in the stability of our government, and the mutual interests of her people.

Who, but God, could count the throbbings of the heart of our national family, when the news flew over the iron nerves that telegraphed that our Chief Magistrate was murdered, murdered when unconconscious of danger—defenceless—in the path of duty; struck down by assassination, the foulest crime on record. But that death has been overruled to the consolidation of our republic, and hearts that were alien have been united in an universal sorrow.

But a few months ago the suffrage of this country placed the supreme authority in the hands of one who had shown what American industry and integrity could accomplish. With no borrowed plumes of hereditary greatness, but the self-made grandeur of nature he stood at his post the embodiment of energy, fidelity, honest purpose and perseverance. He was the true type of progressive American life. While majestic in public counsel, he was true and tender in private life, faithful to duty, calmly submissive and heroic in death. We will not believe that the prayers for his recovery which rose in every part of the world were unanswered, but that those prayers have, like David's, returned into our own bosoms freighted with the pledges of forgiveness and mercy, unity and blessing, on this land of God's adoption.

Never would God allow such sacrifice without designing to honor it, and (as we learn righteousness thereby) to pour out his benefits upon us. Scarce had that brilliant light of our Christian civilization begun to set in death beneath an earthly horizon, when ten thousand stars shone brightly on the banner of hope.

There has been a greater recognition of Providence from the humblest laborer to the decree from the Capitol at Washington. We have been knit together as patriots, closer than ever. The homage of the world encircles the Presidential office, and on the very sackcloth of our woe is written : "In God we trust."

But shall this sad teaching result only in these effects, or in the evaporation of the sentiment that life is short and uncertain? Is there not in the marvelous event, and the outpourings of a people's grief, a witness to the greatness which never can be lost upon the world? What a spur to holy ambition in these benedictions of the free, these lamentations of a people. Well may we echo the words : "It is something to live for ; something to die for."

Oh may we learn to humble ourselves before God for the sin that brought death into this world, and all our woe.

May God accept, through his dear Son, our Redeemer, the sacrifice of our tears and sorrow! May this nation learn righteousness by the things it suffers. May the blood of its martyrs be the seed of a better growth in every fibre of our national system, and notwithstanding our political differences, and social and personal distractions and interests, bind us closer in our sorrows and joys in the one great brotherhood of man, through Him who as God over all, made of one blood all nations, and gave his life to redeem and unite them.

GARFIELD.

BY FREDERIC W. PANGBORN.

Burn low, O lamp, and let your glamour fall
With gentle lustre, on the pallid brow
Upon the pillow, peacefully at rest
Reclining, once so pained, so placid now.

As one, who, wearied with a long borne care,
Hard toiling in the fullness of the Sun,
The day's work finished, finds the evening shade,
Burn low, O lamp, upon this sleeping one.

Time was, when, in the busy ranks of life,
You sleeper used the fullness of the light ;
Erect he strode, with heart and hand at work,
A noble, mighty hero in the fight.

Not cold ambition, nor conceit of self,
Nor greed of gain e'er marked him, as he trod ;
As husband, father, brother, Ruler, son,
He lived for man, for duty, and his God.

There is no man so good, no soul so grand,
But walks the land in peril from his birth.
The carping envy of a fool's blind hate
May strike the noblest mortal to the earth.

And so he fell, the victim of a mind
Disordered by a petty party strife ;
Alas, that blind unreason should demand
The needless quenching of a useful life.

Could we but know the working of our deeds,
But tear the veil apart and see the end,
The horrid climax of some petted scheme
Might turn us from a foeman to a friend.

"Large was his bounty and his soul sincere,"
The Nation called : he served it to the end ;
He gave to man ('twas all he had) his life,
"He gained from Heaven ('twas all he wished) a friend."

Hark ! 'tis the tolling of a midnight bell ;
From pole to pole the sorrowing bells reply ;
They ring the knell of the untimely end
Of one, so fit to live, so fit to die.

A million hearts take up the mournful knell,
A million souls are filled with sad despair,
A million tongues forget the voice of prayer,
And sobs of anguish load the solemn air.

Perchance, to some, who, wavering in their faith,
Their prayers made mockery by yon midnight toll,
A still, small voice, like that at Horeb's Rock,
May come, to calm the anguish of the soul :

"Lament not thus, oh ye of little faith,
Nor let your sun go down in sorrow dim ;
If ye would strengthen still your trust in God,
Gaze here, and learn the lesson well from him."

"Lament not thus, your woes, indeed, are vain ;
Death is the common lot of all. The knell
That peals to-night, peals for a happy soul ;
'God reigns, the nation lives,' and all is well."

Toll forth, O bells, your brazen midnight knell,
Your solemn message to the nations toll,
Toll forth to Earth a hero's mournful end,
Toll forth to Heaven the triumph of a soul.

The lamp burns low ; the flickering flame is dim,
A star above the Ocean rises bright ;
Deep gloom within, a holy gleam without ;
A soul is passing through the silent night.

BERGEN REFORMED CHURCH, JERSEY CITY HEIGHTS.

Sermon by the Pastor,

REV. CORNELIUS BRETT.

TEXT.—And the archers shot at King Josiah ; and the king said to his servants, Have me away ; for I am sore wounded.

His servants therefore took him out of that chariot, and put him in the second chariot that he had ; and they brought him to Jerusalem, and he died, and was buried in one of the sepulchres of his fathers. And all Judah and Jerusalem mourned for Josiah.—2 *Chronicles* xxxv : 14-15.

We have here in the quaint terse language of our English Bible, the sad story of the violent death, and the national funeral of one of the noblest, grandest, most heroic kings who ever sat on David's sacred throne.

Josiah was but eight years old, when the conspiracy of Jewish nobles against his unworthy father put the sceptre in his baby hands. He was at first, as we may well suppose, king only in name : but with singular precocity he applied himself to an earnest preparation for his work, and was hardly of age, when the astonished regency was set aside, and the young sovereign asserted his manhood by inaugurating radical reforms.

The Temple was cleansed and purified; the Book of the Law recovered from its dusty hiding place, and read to the people ; the worship of Jehovah was re-established in its purity; the Passover observed with ancient divinely appointed rites ; idolatry was punished; symbols of false worship destroyed ; and the depravity, which had grown like a foul fungus on the unclean stock, supplanted by a purer and healthier national life.

The better class of the people responded heartily to the efforts of their chief, and showed their appreciation by an earnest co-operation.

127

He was hailed by the thousands who had never bowed the knee to Baal, or sacrificed in high places, as a man divinely appointed for the work of the hour, as a reformer, who united in himself the prophetic and royal prerogative; and as the revival of interest in the land roused the servants of the Lord to the importance of their obligations, his administration prospered, and his popularity increased.

For nineteen years had this good work been going forward, but such a crusade as that in which Josiah enlisted is never finished; there are always pests to be exterminated and stains to be cleansed; no matter how much has been done, still more remains to be accomplished. Like

> " Freedom's battle once begun,
> Bequeathed from bleeding sire to son,
> 'Tis never lost, but always won."

But the king was still young and vigorous. He had not reached his fortieth year, and if he might attain the age of some of his pious ancestry, ample time there would be to rear a whole generation of disciples, who might take up the work when in the course of nature he was called to lay it down, and permanently establish the pure and undefiled worship of Jehovah in the land of Judah.

But at the very height of Josiah's prosperity, and in the midst of an era of good feeling such as had not been known since the disruption of Solomon's Empire, came the fatal blow which crushed so many brightest hopes.

The king was a brave man, as well as a faithful servant of the Lord. The invasion of a neighboring province by Pharaoh Necho threatened the autonomy of his own state, and he placed himself, at once, at the head of an army to resist invasion. His practiced statesmanship penetrated the Machiavelian diplomacy, with which Necho sought to allay his fears. He knew the treachery of the conqueror, and realized that there was but *one way* to meet it. Force must be opposed by force, even if sacrifices be required, and risks demanded. Living or dying the anointed servants of Jehovah belong to Judah and Jerusalem.

The story of the battle at Megiddo is briefly told in our text. The archers of Egypt shot at the royal leader of Judah, and he fell mortally wounded. They brought him *dead* to Jerusalem. Such a funeral had not been known for generations; never had so many hearts so sincerely sorrowed for a king. They lauded him as a hero, and canonized him as a martyr. All the nation mourned for him, city and country vied with each other in lamentation, and highest of all the honors which chroniclers record, the prophet Jeremiah led the minstrelsy of the land in an ode of sorrow.

You have ere this noted the resemblance between this sad calamity, which opened the fountains of tears in Judah, and that other untoward event which has clothed our whole land in widow's weeds.

As then, so now, the head of a great people is laid low by a murderous shot. As then, so now, he prays for removal, and cries in the bitterness of spirit: " Have me away ! Have me away !" As then, so now, he is carried from the scene of assassination to die, and the "second chariot that he had," harnessed with fire and steam, (and no king had ever swifter coursers, or grander chariot), bears him to the sea. As then, so now, he expires away from his capital, and is carried thither at last in the unyielding embrace of death. As then, so now, he is buried with his kindred in the sepulchre which he had marked for himself while yet alive. As then, so now, the hero died in the stern discharge of duty, as much a martyr to the sacred trusts imposed upon him as the brave Baker, who fell with a bullet in his massive brain, on the fatal field of Ball's Bluff. " Strangulatus pro Republica." As then, so now, a God-fearing, large-hearted, liberal minded, largely endowed and brilliant statesman is taken from a people who had learned to honor and to love him. As then, so now, in the very height of his popularity, he ceaseth among men. As then, so now, a man in the prime of life, who gave promise of

9

increasing usefulness, as a skillful administrator of affairs, is suddenly snatched from his post. As then, so now, the land is full of mourning, and the people bow, chastened before Jehovah, crying, "Oh Lord, how long, how long?" Lamentation is heard on every hand; great poets like Jeremiah weave their wreaths of verse; humble men singers and women singers, set them in tearful requiems; eyes unused to weeping are strangely red, and great sobs break away from hearts too full for utterance; orators pronounce eulogies; associations formulate their grief in resolutions of sympathy; the people suspend their work, to hang out from shop and dwelling the emblems of woe; children troop with sad faces from their schools, and the little ones hush their laughter while they clothe their dolls in crape. Men who voted for him, and men who did not, clasp hands in a community of sorrow, shame, and fear for the Republic; women who know what it is to hang over their own sick, and have been watching with tenderest solicitude at Washington and Elberon, find the old scars of home grief reopened in a new bereavement.

Sympathy that is cheering, and speaks volumes for the brotherhood of man, comes from abroad. Royalty lays a floral emblem on his bier. The English court goes in mourning, as though the head of some ancient house had been taken; and the parish bells of England, which know so well the blithe and merrie chimes of the people, *toll* now with solemn tones, while the widow of Balmoral prays for the widow at Cleveland.

Said the patient sufferer, a day or two before he gave up the noble spirit, "Do you think I will have a place in the history of the world?" "There can be no doubt of that," was the response; "your place will be a grand and noble one."

Over his catafalque, as he lies in state near the home city, where he is to sleep the last long sleep, we say "Amen, and Amen."

"His name is an ordinance in our land forever."

We are, in this land of ours, prone to hero worship, and too frequently set up on high places, heroes unworthy of our homage. It often happens that before he dies, the great man has his opportunity, is found wanting, and is as eagerly cast down, as he was aforetime set up. But JAMES A. GARFIELD has fairly, and honestly earned every honor with which he has been crowned. Every promotion has been awarded, because of work well done in the "few things" already entrusted to him. In the heat of a campaign, to praise broadly was partizanship; but since he has been the nation's watch and care, languishing from a cruel wound, we have been reviewing carefully, and in all its remarkable details, a life full of hard work, cheerfully performed; and are amazed at the vast resources of his scholarship, and the extent of his public service. The more we know of him, the more he grows upon us, and that is an apt description of his career and character which he once quoted from the favorite poem of his favorite author, as a tribute to his predecessor in martyrdom, Abraham Lincoln:

" As some divinely gifted man
    Whose life in low estate began,
And on a simple village green ;

Who breaks his birth's invidious bar,
    And grasps the skirts of happy chance
    And breasts the blows of circumstance
And grapples with his evil star ;

Who makes by force his merits known,
    And lives to clutch the golden keys,
    To mould a mighty State's decrees,
And shape the whispers of the throne.

And moving up from high to higher
    Becomes on fortune's crowning slope
    The pillar of a people's hope,
The centre of a world's desire."

With emphasis we may say that the whole of GARFIELD'S active life belongs to his country. He has no record, apart from the early preparatory struggle, save that which is written in the civil and military history of the Republic.

That struggle to fit himself for work was a hard one; on farm and canal boat, as well as in the severer discipline of the school-room, through which as teacher and scholar he must needs pass, it carried him beyond the average age of graduation : but it made a *man* of the stripling scholar; and when in 1856 he went forth with the diploma of Williams College in his hand, he was abundantly prepared for the work which was waiting for him at the very portals of Alma Mater.

Only three and a half years he remained in private life, a teacher in Hiram Academy, when his fellow-citizens summoned him to represent them in the Senate of Ohio. Even this interval was spent in setting forth, with his divine gift of oratory the stirring theme of the hour. He was not a politician in the ordinary acceptation of that term. He suffered four years of his majority to pass without depositing a vote, because neither of the old parties were committed in opposition to the enormity of African slavery; but when the Pathfinder of the Rocky Mountains was placed at the head of a party whose watchword was "Liberty," he was one of the kindred spirits of the time, who were swept away on the rising tide of an enthusiasm born of principle. He made his first political speech during the Fremont campaign, and after the defeat of his champion, continued from time to time, to plead for the freedom of the virgin territories of the Great West; and thus in a humble way served his country before he had held an office. Once while working his way up towards the education, which then seemed so far distant, he applied to a rustic trustee for permission to teach a district school. He was rudely repulsed, and then and there resolved never again to ask for an office. He kept his vow; and yet from the first of January, 1860, until the curfew rung for the ending of his life work on the 19th of September, 1881, he was never out of the public service. Aye! we all remember during the early days of this very year of grace, how he was at the same hour, acting Member of Congress, Senator-elect from Ohio, and President-elect of the United States.

When in 1861, the national unity was assailed, with the first call for volunteers, he unsheathed the sword, and was made lieutenant-colonel of the 42d Ohio Regiment. In the arduous campaigns of the southwest his unfaltering courage, vigorous physique, strong common sense, peculiar gift of language, and cultured mental powers, united to make him a successful soldier. He was promoted from rank to rank, until in 1863, he received a commission as major-general of volunteers, as a reward for gallant and meritorious conduct at the battle of Chickamauga.

But providence had called him to another field of labor.

In the broad territories of what was then the far west, some of the original States laid claim to large tracts of land, which they finally ceded, to the jurisdiction of the United States, reserving only the fee-simple. In what is now the northern part of the Sovereign State of Ohio, the mother of our latest Presidents, was the "Western Reserve of Connecticutt." It was sold in farm plots of a moderate size, to actual settlers, principally from New England, a hardy, liberty loving race of pioneers, whose children have furnished some of the best blood of the modern Republic. For twenty years a portion of this "Western Reserve" had the good fortune to be represented in Congress, by Joshua R. Giddings, the stern and uncompromising Abolitionist. In casting about for his successor, the popular mind turned instinctively to the western battle field, and the chief of staff under Rosecrans. General GARFIELD was greatly disinclined to leave the army: it seemed to him cowardly to desert the forefront of the battle, even for halls of legislation; but his brother officers persuaded him to take the seat, for the very purpose of shaping the "war legislation" with which in the past they had been dissatisfied. When Abraham Lincoln added his entreaty, the General threw up his commission to engage in the debates, hardly less fierce and angry than the strife of arms, which characterized the ses-

sions of Congress during the War for the Union. And
there, for eighteen years he stood, reelected again and again
by overwhelming majorities. He might at an early day
have entered the Senate, but convinced that the post of
usefulness was in the lower house, he resolutely refused
to be a candidate.

The scenes of the convention which nominated him for
the presidency are fresh in memory. By one of those
irresistible impulses, which are not infrequent in our
popular assemblies, a name never formally presented,
and receiving at first a single obscure vote, rallies about
it the conflicting elements of a divided majority, and the
great commoner is urged upon the suffrages of the
American people for the highest office in their gift.

He was elected, inaugurated, and spent a few earnest
months in office. He called to his assistance an able
Cabinet, and carried forward successfully a few of the
many plans for his country's welfare which his busy
brain had been maturing. And then—the rest is sicken-
ing—attacked in bitter diatribe by some politicians of
the baser sort in his own party, (men who would be glad
indeed could they eat their words, and have buried in
oblivion their acts and the memory of them), he stood
firmly by the principles avowed. A division in the party
was threatened; the strife preyed upon the mind of a
self-conceited, fanatical office-seeker, whose whole nature
was stirred to hate because his individual claims for preferment had not been acknowledged. He imagined himself to be the messenger of Heaven, to remove the one
obstacle to Republican unity, and at the same time avenge
his own wrongs. Coward that he is, he steals behind his
victim, in the public depot, and fires the two shots, which
go crashing through the dearest hopes of the people, and
into many anxious hearts. It was indeed, "A shot heard
'round the world."

" A wasp flew out upon our fairest son,
And stung him to the quick, with poisoned shaft.

*   *   *   *   *   *   *   *   *

And so this life amid our love begun
Envenomed by the insect's hellish craft,
Was drunk by death in one long feverish draft,
And he was lost —Our precious, priceless one !
Oh mystery of blind remorseless fate !
Oh cruel end of a most causeless hate !
That life so mean should murder life so great."

During all his long term of public service, our lamented
President stands before us the very ideal of a public
servant.

First, he always waited until *the office sought him,* but as
soon as men appreciating his worth, called him to a
service, he allowed no personal preferences to swerve
him from the path of duty.

Secondly, this course kept him entirely free from cliques
or factions, either in state or nation. He has remained
throughout an independent man, has never aspired to be
a political " boss," and has called no man master.

Thirdly, he has always done his very best, in every capacity and trust, and has served the interests of the nation
as faithfully as if they were his own. It is a marked
peculiarity of JAMES A. GARFIELD, that he did well everything he attempted to do at all. Into every work, from
canal boat to White House, he enlisted with his whole
heart. In the harvest field he could do man's work
while yet a lad; he accomplished six years' study in three,
supporting himself by arduous labors, the meanwhile;
he conquered a school full of determined boys, which
others had declared unmanageable ; he took the first honors of his college class; he raised Hiram Academy to
the dignity of a college ; without a West Point training he
fought like an old campaigner ; and no sooner was he
established as a legislator than he bent every energy to
the framing of laws, and the maintenance of the Union.
As a member of the " Military Committee," the committee
on " Ways and Means," and on " Appropriations," he has

saved to the treasury millions of money, and many a veteran on the tented field has blessed his name for comforts provided. Our country in all her century of life has never produced so versatile a genius, or one who could do well in so many departments.

Fourth, the purity and integrity of his career may well stand unchallenged. We can easily understand how his opportunities might have made him immensely rich. Let his slender means be a barrier to all criticism. We say, he was *pure* because he was *poor*, or if we reverse the proposition we record the fact to his honor, he remained poor, because too pure to make himself rich at the expense of the people who so implicitly trusted him. When calumny assailed him he went back to the Western Reserve, and put his story by the side of Oakes Ames' tale, whereupon his friends and neighbors of that Puritanic stock sent him back thoroughly vindicated to his seat in Congress. The gifts which the people are providing to place wife and children beyond the possibility of want, are no more than an honest debt to one who gave life and death to his country.

It has long been an open secret, that the motive of this noble life, and the inspiration of all these faithful services, are to be found in the deep underlying Christian principles of a character changed by the Grace of God, in the regeneration of the Holy Ghost.

Two lines of pious ancestors from two sanctified sources, seem to join in the life of JAMES A. GARFIELD. On his mother's side he is a Huguenot, and from the Ballous he inherited all the traditions of St. Bartholomew's, of the galleys, and of exile for conscience sake. Through his father he looked back to the GARFIELDS who come from Chester, England, to Massachusetts Bay, only ten years after the landing of the Pilgrims from the Mayflower.

Let us praise God his mother was a Christian, and add that gentle face with the halo of silver about the brow to the gallery of saints, where hang the mothers of great men. Even now, though bowed with sorrow, she sits in her Ohio home, she looks up with hopeful eye, assured that "God still reigns." "It is providential and all for the best." For the formation of that strong character and purpose, whose heroic patience has for three months been the world's marvel, we must go back to that humble cabin with a single room, where the bereaved but not forsaken widow gathered her children about her every day, to hear the living word of God. Four chapters a day was her portion. James treasured the precious truth, and wrought in with his manhood those principles of brotherhood, love, purity, truth and integrity which were to grow out of an unfaltering trust in God.

Theological discussion was common among the settlers in Ohio, and the cabin of Mrs. Garfield, like the house of Lydia in Philippi, was always open to the servants of God who came preaching the righteousness of Christ. The prevailing faith of the neighborhood was that of Thomas and Alexander Campbell, which had been first promulgated at the beginning of the century.

We at the East, know so little of these "Disciples of Christ," as they call themselves, that we do not realize the immense following and influence, the system has obtained throughout the West. Its membership is at present six times as large as that of our own communion, and numbers nearly half a million souls. "The Disciples" were gathered in the first instance to give expression to the thought of Christian unity. It was deemed feasible to unite all believers in the Lord Jesus upon the simple platform of the Bible as the "only rule of faith and practice, in order that in feeble settlements, a single church rather than several, might supply spiritual necessities. In this direction the movement was a failure, but gradually there was *formed*, rather than *organized*, that which its founders never intended, a new sect, to take its share in the labors of the kingdom.

In government the churches of the Disciples are Congregational. Each community elects its own elders and deacons. No ordination to the ministry is necessary, and the theory is, that any church may elect any brother of whose gifts they are satisfied, as "Presiding Elder" or "Pastor;" practically, however, a company of preachers has sprung up as distinct as in any other denomination. Their doctrines are in full accord with our evangelical churches, the statements of the creed being always couched in the simple language of Scripture. Baptism is only administered by immersion and to believers; and the outward sign is regarded as a token from the Lord of the remission of sins. Candidates for church membership are always required to confess an entire reliance upon the merits of Christ for justification, and then to exhibit a conduct becoming the Christian profession. The Lord's Supper is administered according to Apostolic example every Lord's Day, and taking the ground that the table belongs to Christ, rather than to his church, no one is excluded from participation, who desires to commune.

In this simple faith the boy was nurtured; and taught to refer all questions to the sacred oracles, he became himself a close student of the Word. In his nineteenth year "Pollock's Course of Time" fell into his hands; he read and pondered its instructive measures. At the same time, while he was studying in the academy at Chester, a sweet-tempered evangelist, who told in the most straight-forward way the simple story of the Gospel, touched his heart, and the young academician yielded his soul to his Saviour. He was baptized March, 1850, in the river near Chester; and although he thus early in life entered upon his career of Christian manhood, he never deserted the colors of his new Master, or ceased to be loyal to Jesus his Saviour.

When he began to teach after graduating from college, his rare grace of rhetoric was discovered by his old neighbors, and he was frequently called into the pulpit on the Lord's day. He was never pastor of a church, but was ever ready to speak a word in season, when the door stood open. His last act before leaving Mentor was to eat and drink in remembrance of the Lord, with his brethren in the simple Christian Church. And in Washington the President's place was so well known in the House of God, that the assassin had planned to fire the fatal shot, while his victim was seeking rest from the cares of State, in the worship of his Creator.

Of GARFIELD'S christian character his pastor thus spoke over his remains in the rotunda of the Capitol :

"The chief glory of this man, as we think of him now, was his discipleship in the school of Christ. His attainments as scholar and statesman, will be the theme of orators and historians, and they must be worthy men to speak his praise worthily. But it is as a Christian we love to think of him now. It was this which made his life to man an invaluable boon, his death to us an unspeakable loss, his eternity to himself, an inheritance incorruptible, undefiled, and that fadeth not away. He was no sectarian. His religion was broad as the religion of Christ. He was a simple Christian, bound by no sectarian ties, and wholly in fellowship with all pure spirits. He was a *Christologist* rather than a *Theologist*. He had great reverence for the family. His example as son, husband, and father is a glory to this nation."

As we think of him in comparison with others, he seems to be the most pronounced Christian believer who since Washington has occupied the Presidential chair. Would that in choosing his successors from this time forth, Christian character might weigh with the people. We would not make church membership a test of office-holding, for that would lead to arrant hypocrisy, but we do long and pray for the time, when in state and nation, only those may rule us, whose spirit Christ has ruled, and when those only may legislate for us whose lives are ordered according to the law of God.

What sadly solemn weeks have we been passing since that memorable Sabbath, July 3d, (how long ago it seems), when we hung over his fresh wound, expecting every hour to see him die. The thought of the patient sufferer at the White House and the Francklyn Cottage has cast a gloom over the summer holiday. The people have, it is true, taken their annual vacation, but few cared to get beyond the reach of newspaper and telegraph. From Maine to California each citizen has, as it were, brought

a wire from the general circuit to his own heart. We
have counted the pulse beats, measured the temperature,
noted the changing symptoms, and listened eagerly to
every word that escaped his lips. As he rallied or re-
lapsed, hope rose or fell. Now there was assurance that
God would not let him die, and then with the profound
consciousness of sin and desert, we would smite on the
breast, and cry "Lord be merciful to us sinners," as
we gave him up. And shall men now go up and down
lamenting or scoffing because God has not answered a people's earnest prayer? I tell you God HAS answered our
prayers directly, by preserving that valued life for eighty
days. Though for himself, it had been better to have taken
the "home journey" from the depot at Washington, ere the
echoes of the ball had died in silence; for his country he
has been living in the daily torture and weakness of a wasting frame. Not the least service to the Republic has JAMES
A. GARFIELD rendered, during those hours of helplessness,
when his only official act was to sign an extradition paper.
His life has kept us, from we know not what. We shudder
to think what might have been, had the change of administration occurred when by the shock of assassination men
were maddened, and the whole community in an uproar.
We have had time to rally our scattered forces, to think, to
reflect, to pray, to come forth from a baptism of blood,
tender hearted and mutually forbearing. We have had
time to prepare for the worst, to make business arrangements such as time only could mature. While he whom
we now honor as President has had time, as in a vigil of
knighthood, to get his armor ready for the new conflicts.
Ah friends! we never will know what these eighty days of
our President's sorrow have been worth to us. God gave
them to him and to us in answer to prayer.

From another standpoint, we see the value of this prolonged struggle for life. The world has looked with amazement at the sublime spectacle of a Christian man, holding
a position of eminence, looking death in the face with
calmness, yet for the sake of his country, his family, his
further usefulness, battling for life. Readiness for death

does not necessarily involve a desire to die. All who belong to Christ would better their condition by a change of worlds, but he is a coward who longs to shirk the dangers and responsibilities of life by entering into the joy of the Lord. Though to die may be gain, to live is Christ. Hence when our hero fell, and his attendants gave him "one chance in a hundred" for his life, he bravely "took that chance." He let them cut, and probe, without a murmur. When the chance is only one in a thousand, he takes it still, giving the whole of his magnificent will power to support a physical frame, which no excess has ever weakened: and through all, in sleepless nights and wearisome days, amid torrid heats and unwholesome vapors, he endures with stoical bravery, almost without a groan. From the beginning, however, he lets it be known to nurse and to physician, he is not afraid to die. In the words of the "Disciples," formula, he has been baptized "for the remission of sins," and if these sins have been washed away in atoning blood, what is there for him to fear? Such firm courage, born of Christian hope, every pastor meets from time to time in his ministry among the sick and dying, but the world at large seldom looks so intently upon such a scene. God himself has drawn aside the curtain from the dying couch, because the man belonged to the people, and he has held it long that all the world might see the power of the sustaining grace of God. Death is a mystery which many fear to try; he was never afraid, because the rod and staff of the Shepherd and Bishop of his soul comforted him. Death was only "the stretching out of the road a little longer toward his home." He has been safely carried over it; he sleeps in Jesus: and though we sorrow, we sorrow not as those without hope. What was yet lacking in him—for none claim perfection of manhood in the flesh—has now been completed. He is forever with the Lord; he knows as he is known. All that he once saw only in a mirror, he now sees face to face, and because he sees Him face to face, he shall be like his Lord.

It is to soon to ask, What meaneth this strange thing? What has our Lord in store for us?

Perhaps, the Nation, restless under the guidance of a chieftain of such consummate wisdom, at Kadesh Barnea, refused to cross at once the border land of a party reform, even for the grapes from Eshcol which his bold spies brought back over their shoulders, has been turned back to wander, until in another generation, another leader shall bring us to the Jordan crossing, and a Joshua shall arise to deliver the host.

Or perchance, just this supreme sacrifice, the life of a Christian Statesman, of rare abilities, and in the prime of life, the most excellent thing in America, was needed to show the people the hideous gap in the body politic, which the insane race for office, and self-seeking political service have made. If it be so, and if *the gap* be now closed, we we may accept the sacrifice with gratitude to God, for raising up one worthy to make it; and with a new lease of national life, go forward under him, on whom by the providence of God, the responsible duties of the Presidency now devolve.

To our new Chief Magistrate, all Christian citizens pledge their earnest prayers; they sympathize with him; they are ready to take him to their hearts, to rally about him, to stand by him, while he stands for the right. May he by no means disappoint their high and cherished hopes.

The powers that be are ordained of God, and under the divine ordination, we are ready to put aside partizanship, and enter upon an era of good feeling, which knows no North, no South, no East, no West, but one undivided country—*Christian* in very deed and purpose, as well as name. In order to accomplish this, let the people arise in majesty to put aside the self-seeking demagogues, whose only thought in connection with public service is its reward; and to seek our officials from the men of modest worth and unsullied reputation, who will not push themselves forward, but must be discovered by patient search.

But aside from statecraft, may we all learn from the the story of this life struggle and heroic death, the meaning of *true manhood*.

May our *youth* note the estimate which an aspiring boy

from a log cabin put upon *scholastic training.* His ambition was not to make money, but to get an education. How many recklessly throw away the opportunities so freely offered in our common schools, priceless opportunities which the passing years steal from them. Would that they would learn as well, the oft repeated lesson of a successful career, " Whatever is worth doing, is worth doing well." Aspire as you may for promotion, it will not come to you, until the present task has been thoroughly mastered.

Office-holders! take this man as your model, in painstaking fidelity and integrity : become the servants of the State, deeming it a higher honor to minister than to be ministered unto. Do your whole duty in every department of your work.

Citizens! imbibe some of the disinterested patriotism of your fallen leader, and may love of country lead you to devote time and talent to the service of your fellow man.

May we *all* learn the value of Christian faith, to fit us for every station, and prepare us for every emergency. In the days of his youth he remembered his Creator. Had young GARFIELD refused to hear his Father's voice before the exciting scenes opened, in which so large a portion of his life was spent, doubtless he too would have continued like so many of our public men, without formal acknowledgment of Jehovah's claims. It was his youthful allegiance, that threw the sheet anchor of his hope into the sands of life, and it held the frail bark as an anchor of the soul, sure and steadfast. It laid hold even deeper than he knew, and bound him unto that which is within the veil. You cannot at an hour too early for your present and eternal welfare, confess your Saviour ; and if you have been delaying that act which should long ago have been performed, I pray you in the hush of this solemn hour, while the nation is bathed in tears, say unto God, and the church, before your fellow men, "As for me and my house, we will serve the Lord." Then, and not till then, will you be thoroughly furnished unto all good works : ready for life, ready for death, ready for public or private service, doing all things unto the glory of God.

May we all—

" So live, that when our summons comes to join
The innumerable caravan that moves
To the pale realms of shade, where each shall take
His chamber in the silent halls of death,
We go not, like the quarry-slave at night,
Scourged to his dungeon, but, sustained and soothed
By an unfaltering trust, approach the grave
Like one who wraps the drapery of his couch
About him, and lies down to pleasant dreams."

First Congregational Church of Jersey City.

(TABERNACLE.)

Sermon by the Pastor,

REV. ADDISON P. FOSTER.

THE ELEMENTS OF GREATNESS IN THE CHARACTER OF PRESIDENT GARFIELD.

2 *Samuel* i : 19. "'The beauty of Israel is slain upon thy high places ; how are the mighty fallen."

The world is to-day in tears. Never before since human life began has there been such a universal sympathy as has been manifested during the sic ness of our President. The lonely shepherd on English moors has been eagerly inquiring the latest news. The Armenian Patriarch at Constantinople has taken pains to send assurance of his anxiety to the sufferer at Elberon. Even in the synagogues of Palestine prayer has been offered for the President. Indeed never before in the history of the world have men in all lands and of all religions united so heartily and earnestly in a common prayer. And now, in this crushing bereavement, we are asking more than aught else, What has become of our prayers ; why did not God answer them. My friends, those prayers are not lost ; they are answered. When President GARFIELD's physician exclaimed bitterly, "Why could not the President's prayers be answered? He only prayed that he might accomplish his mission," the question unconsciously replied to itself. We all prayed that Mr. GARFIELD be spared, in order that, living, he might do his work, but what if like Samson he do a greater work in his death than in his life ? He has seemed needed above all men by his country, but it is easy for God so to overrule his death as by it to bring out a greater blessing than in his

145

life. If this be God's purpose, surely in no direction can we see greater good than in the example which is given to us in the character of him, who like his Savior before him, has been held up into prominence by his suffering. President Garfield more than any other man ever known, save Him who was more than man, has come to fill the world's eye, and to attract the world's admiration, by his nobility of character. As an example he is destined to have a profound influence on the young men of this and other lands.

Our President had rare points of contact with the people and so was unusually fitted as a typical American to serve through coming ages as an example. His lowly birth, his early poverty, his courageous self-help, his familiarity with work in its most toilsome and distasteful forms, his struggles for an education, his slow but steady advance from terrace to terrace in life's ascent till he stood on its pinnacle, the very quality of his greatness, which consisted not in any one distinguishing trait of genius, but in a happy combination of a great number of excellences of character in an even and proportionate development; these things have given us a man whose greatness of character is recognized by all and yet who has come to his pre-eminence not by any paths or through any gifts which are denied to any. And especially is there encouragement in the fact that his greatness was long undiscovered and then came to be recognized in a flash, as when on a sudden the lights are turned up in a hall and disclose a great congregation which has been gathering there in the darkness.

How aptly have the lines of Tennyson which Mr. Garfield once applied to President Lincoln, been applied in turn to himself!

For surely he was

> " As some divinely gifted man,
> Whose life in low estate began,
> And on a simple village green;
>
> " Who breaks his birth's invidious bar,
> And grasps the skirts of happy chance
> And breasts the blows of circumstance
> And grapples with his evil star;

" Who makes by force his merit known,
        And lives to clutch the golden keys,
        To mould a mighty State's decrees,
    And shape the whispers of the throne.

" And moving up from high to higher
        Becomes on fortune's crowning slope
        The pillar of a nation's hope,
    The centre of a world's desire."

There is embarassment and yet advantage, in attempting
an analysis of the President's character, in the fact that all
are familiar with the incidents of his life ; embarassment,
lest there be brought before you that which seems trite ;
advantage, because this familiarity makes brevity of illustration possible, and gives an added force to the lessons
drawn.   In taking up then these threads of familiar fact
and weaving them together into a single web, it will be the
fault of him who weaves rather than of the thread upon the
spindle if there come not forth a cloth of gold.

Let us notice then some of the elements of President
GARFIELD's greatness of character.

I.   *His High Aims.*

What were the aims that controlled Mr. GARFIELD ?
They were at least three—to make the most of himself, to
do in the best way possible the thing first at hand and to
do all the good in the world that he could.   He had a pure
ambition.   Every one should desire to be all that God
made him to be, and Mr. GARFIELD, from the day that he
left home for Geauga Academy to his death, burned with a
desire to grind to the sharpest edge and finest polish
whatever qualities God might have endowed him with.
And yet in that ambition there was nothing unworthy.   He
had a rare and delicate self-respect.   His pure ambition
never degenerated into self-seeking or brazen-faced push-
ing for place.   If anything, he erred in the direction of
extreme sensitiveness.   He once left a position because a
member of his employer's family called him a servant.   At

one time seeking a position as school teacher and failing to
find it, he declared that never again would he seek a place.
The same day a place sought him and so has it been from
that day on. Every office or honor since then has come to
him unsought,—in educational work, in the army, and in
political life, even to the day when in the Chicago Convention he protested against Wisconsin's votes for him as out
of order on the ground that he refused his consent. It
may be doubted if the resolution of his boyhood, kept to
the day of his death, would not be a mistake for most, yet
it worked him no harm because he made himself so well
fitted for important trusts that others sought his aid.

Now character is founded upon aims. Here is the beginning of greatness. A man may fall below his aims ; he
never rises above them. Whoever, then, will live a noble life,
great in the truest sense, must, like him we honor to-day,
form some conception of that which he would be. In other
words, never drift, but sail with chart and compass.

In close connection as an element of our President's
greatness, we may notice—

II. *His Energy and Resolution.*

Nothing could discourage him or shake his determination when once he had resolved upon a certain course. We
see this in his boyhood, when, not content to eat the bread
of idleness, or live in dependence on a feeble mother, he
left his home at the age of twelve and ever after by brave
and faithful labor supported himself. We see it in his educational days at school and college, when he resolutely
entered on a course of study that he supposed would take
twelve years to finish, including the time he must take to
earn enough to pay his bills. Looking down this long and
painful lane of student life, where difficulties stood on either
side like Indian with tomahawk, he never once hesitated
to run the gauntlet, but went through his course without
flinching. We see the same spirit in his army life. Nothing but his dauntless energy made it possible for him with
a force of eleven hundred to drive Gen. Marshall with his

army of five thousand out of Kentucky. Nothing but this made it possible for him to take a steamer loaded with provisions up the swollen Sandy river to supply his half-starved troops. Nothing but this in fact, with the Lord's favor, kept him alive for the eleven weeks of his last sickness, when calmly taking his one chance of life, and bringing his whole resolution to bear, he kept Death at bay, when men of less iron will would long before have succumbed.

Here, then, is one secret of Mr. GARFIELD's success. There must be a will-power back of high aims. Not only must the arrow be lifted to the skies, but there must be strength in the arm that bends the bow. Men of mark and success in whatever walk of life are characterized by force of will. By this we do not mean obstinacy, but we do mean a determined purpose, that is undaunted by difficulties, expects them indeed, but proposes to overcome them. A resolute human will is the grandest, the subduing force on earth. Before it all hindrances of time and nature crumble to dust like the rocky cliff against which the surf beats day and night, through the tireless centuries. "There is nothing," a modern expert has said, "which engineering cannot accomplish." If this be true, it is because, save as opposed by the will of God, the human will is irresistible.

But high aims and a strong will may go astray without the trained intellect. And here President GARFIELD was not lacking. His greatness may be traced—

III. *To his Superior Scholarship.*

He was a man of learning. The secret of study was grasped by him in his boyhood and held fast throughout his life. He was a student, not only in school and college, but subsequently as well in the educational, military and political stages of his life. He became confessedly one of the best scholars of the country, while absolutely free from that pedantry which detracted somewhat from the influence of Everett and Sumner. At college he applied himself

resolutely to his books, improving every moment. Nor
was he a mere scholastic in his plan of work. From the
first he took up courses of reading in literature, science
and art, and afterwards in Congress used to say that to
preserve himself from ruts, he never was so busy but that
he kept by him the works of some great thinker, not only
reading them but analyzing them and making a record of
their thought. The studious disposition thus manifested
was a peculiar characteristic of his, and especially deserves
notice and imitation on the part of young men. By way of
emphasizing it, therefore, let us cite several other instan-
ces. On one occasion in college hearing a political speech
on the slavery question, he said to a friend as he went from
the meeting that he did not mean to leave that subject
until he understood all about it; so gathering his books
together from the libraries he sat down to his task until
the history of the question and the principles involved
were clear in his mind. So in the army he took up the
study of military science and filled a book with excerpts
on the subject in several languages, embracing statements
from the time of Sesostris down. So in Congress he became a great student of subjects. When in the Committee
of Ways and Means he thoroughly investigated the taxation, the national debt and the currency. When on the
Committee on Appropriations, he went into a profound
study of the history of appropriations in this country and
in England. Probably no one made more constant use of
the Congressional Library than he. He not only examined
the more common authorities, but others less known, so
that when a rare book was out, the librarian was wont to
say, "Either Mr. Sumner or Mr. GARFIELD has it."

And while we are speaking of his methods of study, let
us not omit a reference to his great use of newspaper clip-
pings. Like Agassiz, like Caleb Cushing, he set great
store by the many wise thoughts and valuable statements
of fact to be found from day to day in the newspapers. He
could not bear that their utterances should be ephemeral,
and consequently did his best to preserve them for future
reference by the use of scrap books and indexes.

We have no time to enter into an analysis of our President's scholarship. It is sufficient to say here that it was both versatile and thorough. He was master of many languages. He was conversant with many themes. As professor and college president, he could lead his pupils as far as they could follow him through the curriculum of study. As general in the army, he understood the principles of military science. As a well-bred thinker, he was familiar with the best literature of his own and other languages. As an earnest Christian, recognizing his duty to preach the gospel, he grasped the profound doctrines of our religion. As a lawyer, he had made himself acquainted with law. As a legislator, he had so studied the science of government that no man in Washington comprehended it better. And his scholarship, too, was intensely practical. It always had a bearing on matters in hand. His college education was not, as is so often the case, a mere jumble of useless facts, but he wisely stored every truth he learned where he could use it. His methods of utilizing study were shown in his habit at Hiram College of requiring observation from his students, in the thorough training of his memory, which was able to recall and quote, without a mistake, lines from the poets which he had not read for years. Above all was the practicality of his scholarship shown in his public addresses. Where a hundred can grasp great truths, only one here and there is able to set them forth with convincing clearness. This rare power had Mr. GARFIELD. He was a man of genuine eloquence, if eloquence be understood to be the art of convincing men. His brief eulogy of Lincoln, his speech at Boston, when Everett stood by his side and Everett's greater name then overshadowed his, his thrilling answer to Lamar in the House, when the House went wild with enthusiasm after it, and a million copies of it were circulated as a campaign document—these are specimens of an ability that was ever equal to the emergency. In fact, his admirable speeches on all subjects connected with politics and government, form a thesaurus of information, setting forth in the clearest, most candid and generous manner, the principles that underlie this republic. The day will surely come when a complete set of his speeches will stand in the library of every public man and careful thinker in the country as an indispensable *vade mecum* on all topics connected with good government.

Now a man to secure wide influence, must be educated. Scholarship is worthless alone, and unpractical scholarship is worse than none, but a well trained and well stored intellect is invaluable in securing influence and greatness. The training may come through college halls, as in the case of Mr. GARFIELD, or through private study and wide reading and hard knocks without the college, as in the case of Mr. Lincoln. No matter how it comes, but come it must. God endows many a man with brains, but brain without education is like iron in the ore. The iron must be extracted from the slag, hardened into steel, wrought into a shapely blade, polished and sharpened, before it become the sword that shall carve a way to fortune. So must every well-filled brain be disciplined and developed by study of some kind before it can become a power. There must be education before there can be greatness.

But there is a certain fine quality allied to scholarship and yet not obtained by education, which is essential to greatness of character. President GARFIELD was remarkable—

IV. *For his Good Judgment.*

Our President greatly admired this quality in others, and once commended it in one whom we all revere, in these words, "Whether in the camp or in the cabinet, the quality that rose above all the other great gifts of the period, was the comprehensive and unerring judgment of Washington." It was the same trait that contributed largely to the success of Mr. GARFIELD. How many have super-eminent gifts, wonderful genius, rare scholarship, quickness and energy, but lack a balance wheel, and so through some eccentricity or blunder, forfeit the confidence of their fellows, and fall back to an inferior position. There are a hundred unreliable geniuses to one cool, clear-headed, methodical man who never makes a mistake, and never misses fire. Such a man, however, was our late President. To his other surpassing gifts he added this,—which is perhaps rarest,—of being quick-witted and wise in judgment. He showed this early in life in declining a tempting offer in Troy, N. Y., that he might finish his education and locate among his own people. He showed it subsequently as chief of staff to Gen. Rosecrans, when he successfully urged a forward movement which was opposed by seventeen generals. He showed it when in Congress he chose to be on the Committee of Ways and Means rather than the Military Committee, because he saw that though the latter committee was considered more important, the former was really to take up the questions around which the future interests of the country centered. It was this shrewd, clear judgment,—not always infallible, to be sure, and yet seldom making mistakes,—which caused others to trust in him. Because of this fine quality the students of Hiram College, the soldiers under his command, his superior officers whom he was called on to advise, all believed in him. Because of this, the leadership of the House naturally fell to him after Mr. Blaine went into the Senate. Because of this more than from any other cause, he was chosen by his party, against his will, a member of the Electoral Commission.

Probably no other one thing contributes so much to success in life, as men measure success, as this quality of good judgment. Without it, many other excellences are simply waste forces. While it is a quality inborn, yet, like the eyesight, it may be trained and made stronger. It is something to be cultivated. It depends to some extent on steady nerves, still more on experience and reflection. If then we have it in only a small degree, we need not be altogether discouraged. By care, thoughtfulness and exercise, we may come to gain a quality which is always put at the helm.

Thus far we have been discussing qualities in our President which are largely intellectual. Did they stand alone he would be by no means the complete man and admirable

example which he was. But he had also moral qualities
of inestimable worth. In this analysis of his character,
then, we must instance—

V. *His Unselfishness.*

He was one of the most unselfish public men our country
has ever known. We can point, and are glad to point, amid
the prevalent selfishness of the age, to not a few of our
political leaders whom we believe to have been actuated
by higher motives than personal self-seeking. Such were
Washington, Franklin, Adams, of a past generation. Such
were Lincoln, Sumner, Wilson, Stanton, of a later day.
Such pre-eminently was our beloved and now martyred
President GARFIELD. Mr. GARFIELD was nominated for
Congress when in the army. He had just been made major-
general, and naturally preferred his military position to a
seat in Congress. He was a poor man, and the fact that
his salary as major-general was twice as large as that he
would receive in Congress was not a small consideration.
He was a favorite in military circles, was on the high road
to success, and had every prospect, if he remained, of becoming one of the leading generals of the war. But his
friends at home claimed his service in another position,
and President Lincoln urged him to sacrifice personal advantage for his country's sake, and he consented. So afterward a nomination was offered him by the Ohio Legislature, with the best prospects of election, to a seat in the
United States Senate. But here again he was urged to
sink his personal advantage for the sake of greater usefulness. President Hayes desired him to remain in the House
as leader of his party, and he cheerfully consented to hold
the lower place.

Undoubtedly this unselfishness in the end, as is always
the case, resulted to his advantage. It was a trait which
won men to him, and gave them confidence in him. No
man has ever come to the Presidency in this land who has
persistently sought it. Many and many an able man has
failed in his ambition to attain this highest place in the

nation's gift, because he has pushed himself or allowed his friends to push him so prominently as a candidate. Mr. GARFIELD was the available man and the nation's choice, because he was unselfish, and had never in any way sought the place which could not do without him.

No man who is selfish can succeed, even in politics. He may for a little while thrust himself into public notice, and obtain positions of honor, but the time will come when the millstone of his selfishness will drag him down and sink him in the waters of oblivion. Men recognize a self-seeker, distrust him, and rid themselves of him as soon as they are able. And, what is of more importance, no character can be truly great which has in it the cancer of selfishness. There may be rare beauty of form, with many qualities of surpassing excellence, but if selfishness be there it is a foul blot upon the soul, it is sending its stinging pains throughout the life, and is sure in the end to bring the highest hopes to an untimely grave.

Yet another point in our President's greatness of character was—

VI. *His Integrity.*

Without distinction of party we now in common feel a deep regret that his fair name was so unjustly villified during the presidential campaign. We may hope that all parties have learned a lesson, and that over the grave of our murdered President we shall as a nation resolve never again to descend in our political campaigns into the mire of slander and forgery for the advancement of party ends. As our tears drop on the bier of him we would emulate, let us determine like him to avoid ungenerous personalities, and to deal with underlying principles. At this hour President GARFIELD needs no vindication. He was vindicated years ago by his Ohio constituency, who in the face of trumped-up charges, sent him back to Congress by larger majorities than before. He was vindicated by the verdict of a great people. Never were charges more persistently urged; never was a man's character more thoroughly sifted. But the people, after patient and careful hearing, decided him guiltless, and committed to him their most sacred trusts. He was vindicated by his pecuniary condition at the time of his death. It is stated that he left property amounting only to the paltry sum of $25,000. But most of all is he vindicated by the conviction which has been springing up in the hearts of all men in all lands, as he has been dying through these weary weeks, that here was one of the purest and best of men. In truth, we are all now satisfied that our President was singularly free from every taint. We have seen so much corruption in political life, we have so often seen men of the best reputation suddenly smirched by some unworthy deed that it is not strange that we are suspicious of all, and too ready to believe evil of any. But our President, we are now satisfied, was pure to the core.

We may believe, and rejoice in believing, that there is a call for purity in politics. Both nominations for the presidency in the last campaign were a testimony in this direction. The choice of Mr. GARFIELD to the highest honors of the nation is an evidence of it. The people are beginning to insist that their representatives shall be clean men. President GARFIELD is a reflection of the temper of the times. His life is one of the most hopeful indications of the condition of our republic. It is worth everything to our youth that he has been held up as an example of success. True greatness is impossible without integrity, and in this land it would seem to be that it is coming true that even political success cannot be otherwise secured.

Mr. GARFIELD illustrated greatness of character—

VII. *In his Courage.*

Like many others he was physically brave. We can understand how one who had run the gauntlet of confederate sharp-shooters, spurring his horse across the open field under the enemy's fire, saying to himself as he leaped a fence and entered the deadly plain, "Now, JAMES GARFIELD,

be a man ;" we can understand how he could say as he
sank under the bullet of the assassin, "I have met Death
before and am not afraid of him." But bravery like this,
honorable as it is, was the least element in his courage.
To it was added a moral courage that made him a hero
and distinguished him from the multitude. This moral
courage appeared in his unflinching devotion to principle.
He did not hesitate to put himself in opposition to his
party if he thought it in the wrong. When that financial
heresy known as Pendletonism was rife among his constituency, he did not bow before it. Many would have
cringed and yielded their convictions at the popular clam-
our. Not so he. He argued the point at issue throughout his district. He was unwilling to represent the people
on any other basis. The result was that his bravery and
his arguments carried the day. Another instance is still
more striking. President Lincoln had vetoed a certain bill
in Congress and Senators Wade and Davis had united in a
criticism on the veto. Mr. GARFIELD justified the criticism
while his constituents disapproved it. They were met in
convention and seemed about to throw him aside for his
views in this matter, when he rose and said in a most
manly and unassuming way that he had respect for their
convictions but more for his own, that he should be glad
to serve them if he could do so independently, acting on
his own convictions, but that otherwise he did not wish for
the nomination. On this a delegate sprang to his feet, and
saying that such courage before a convention was rare and
deserved to be rewarded, moved his nomination by acclamation, and the motion was instantly carried.

Now such Christian courage, such manly devotion to
principle, is universally needed. It is an essential element in greatness. No man can be a leader among men
who has not profound convictions and is not ready to stand
by them to the death. Force of character depends in
large degree on this one element. Life is a battle with
difficulties and the successful man or the great man must
be undaunted in face of them. Success never lies for any
great length of time in the line of mere policy. Policy

always over-reaches itself. Fidelity to principle, no matter what its temporary reverses, triumphs in the end.

But a brief reference is needed to another, yet an essential element in our President's character. We must not forget—

VIII. *His Patriotism.*

This was shown throughout his public life,—when he enlisted for the war, when he left the army at the request of his commander-in-chief to serve his country elsewhere, in all his political acts, whether in speech or vote, and not least upon his sick bed when among his last utterances were those beautiful and tender words, now embalmed in the hearts of his countrymen, " O the people, the people, my trust."

No truly great man ever lived who did not recognize his obligation to his country and seek to do it good. Patriotism is a most important element in greatness of character in that it leads a man out of self and into deeds for the universal good. We are apt to live within the contracted horizon of our own home, or our own business, or our own circle of friends. Patriotism draws a man into sympathy with his fellow man, broadens his thought, leads him to reach out to benefit a land and develops in him a comprehension of great principles. Patriotism brings a man more or less into public life and so ensures, to some degree at least, that if there be elements of greatness in him they shall be brought in contact with his fellow man, and so be recognized and utilized for the common good.

A most striking element in Mr. GARFIELD's greatness of character was—

IX. *His Warmth of Affection.*

This was shown pre-eminently to his family. He was an affectionate son, a devoted husband, a good father. When at his inauguration, in the sight of all the people, he kissed his mother and his wife, the act thrilled the nation.

It was something unexpected; never had been done before on like occasion; but it struck a sympathetic chord in every heart. It was a solemn declaration on the part of the head of the nation of his allegiance to loved ones, and of his loyal acknowledgement of obligation to them. Never were the family relations of a President better known. That brave mother staggering under the load of her grief, and crying out, "God's will be done"; that gentle, self-possessed wife, watching over her beloved one, through the anxious and bitter weeks; those children of rich promise, the sons and the daughter inheriting the virtues of their parents; we know them, and pity them and love them all.

How much our President owed to his mother! We do well to believe in blood. Here was a royal mixture of strains, English, German and Huguenot. Mr. GARFIELD was endowed at his birth with a grand physique and a massive brain. Our President certainly was fortunate in father and mother. Surely few men loved mother more than he, and few ever had more reason. Her influence over him from first to last was great, and the benediction she gave him when he enlisted for the war was equally applicable when he assumed the unknown perils of the Presidency. "Go, my son! Your life belongs to your country."

His love for his wife was beautiful. Their patient waiting for five years before marriage was an omen of devotion in the future, and we are not surprised to find, as another has said, that "he was never so happy in Washington as when he had her by his side." We have only glimpses, but they are choice and rare, of their happy domestic life. We see her, now in his study, clipping and sorting for him his newspaper scraps; now in the family carriage, calming him by a word when the impudence of certain rowdies in front of him had frightened his spirited horses and roused his anger; now in the sick room, comforting him with loving touch. We wonder not that he could say, "I have been wonderfully blest by the devotion of my wife. She is one of the coolest and best balanced women I ever saw.

There has not been one solitary instance in my public career when I have suffered in the smallest degree for any
remark she ever made."

No man can estimate what these two women have done
for our President. He was fortunate in them both. They
undoubtedly largely shaped his career. He for his part
was receptive and readily open to their influence, and so
the Scripture was fulfilled for each of them.—"She will do
him good and not evil all the days of her life."

But Mr. GARFIELD had a warm heart, not only for those
of his home, but for a wide circle of friends. He was a
genial man; capable of strong friendships. He was devoted to his friends and they to him. With him there was
no assumption of interest in others, but he felt the interest
he showed. With a firmness in the right which prevented
him from going astray, he yet had a tenderness towards
others that won their hearts. The devotion of friends dur-
his last sickness,—friends whose names, Boynton, Swain,
Rockwell, will be lovingly remembered by the American
people for their consecration of service,—is but one proof
out of many of the magnetic power of our President to
attract and hold firmly to him, the love of others.

Now this is an element of greatness and an example of
excellence in character well worth our imitation. True
greatness should exist in the private life. Character
should be so pure as to bear the microscopic inspection of
the home. In the sanctities of the home lies the essential
part, if not the most sacred and deepest part of life. In
these days of indifference to home joys and infidelity to
home duties, we may well be thankful that Providence has
turned the nation's eyes to a most admirable example of
what a son, a husband and a father should be.

One more point needs our attention in this analysis.
Mr. GARFIELD was great—

X. In his Religious Convictions.

He was converted and joined the church at eighteen. He had been away from home, and on his return in the evening, found his mother on her knees before her open Bible, praying for him. He threw his arms about her neck and then and there gave his heart to God. From that time to the day of his death, according to the testimony of his pastor at Washington, "he was a faithful and diligent Christian."

It is interesting to notice the different ways in which his piety displayed itself. When a boy at school, obliged to support himself by his own labor, having worked hard in vacation and paid up his bills for sickness, he came home with a sixpence in his pocket, and the first Sabbath morning at home that sixpence, his all, was put into the contribution box. It was a characteristic act, indicative of his consecration and faith. Nor was he afraid to bear testimony for his Master. Before he went to college and after his return to Hiram, he was an acceptable lay-preacher, often occupying the pulpits in the country round. And in his later years when political cares pressed upon him, he yet found time to give occasional religious addresses in Washington and elsewhere. The claims of missions, the evidences of Christianity, the obligation of charity, were among the themes on which he spoke. He was a regular attendant at church and never failed to be present at the Lord's Supper. His utterances during his sickness, though necessarily brief, were all of them consistent with his godly life. When informed that his wound might prove fatal, he calmly said, "I know God and trust myself in His hands." When during those weary weeks he balanced his chances for life or death, he would say, "I must be ready for either." One Sabbath morning he remarked, "This is the Lord's Day. I have a great reverence for it." And at Elberon, as there came through the open window from a congregation of worshippers near by, the sweet notes of the hymn "Jesus, lover of my soul," he joined in with feeble voice, but evident feeling, and sang:

11

" Let me to thy bosom fly
While the billows near me roll,
While the tempest still is high."

But these expressions of feeling, precious as they are,
are surpassed in value by the wonderful patience, cheerfulness and Christian courage of those long weeks. "The
best patient I've ever had," said one of his physicians.
It was an unconscious testimony to the sincerity of his
piety.

It is time men understood that there is no true greatness
without religion. A trustful submission to the divine will
is absolutely necessary. The arch of character may be
built up in beauty by the addition of virtue to virtue, but
it has no strength and no guarantee of permanence, unless
the keystone of a Christian faith is set in at the top to con-
solidate the whole. Or to change the figure, religious
principle is the backbone of character. Everything else is
articulated to it and moves from it. The weakness of many
a public man, the ruin of many an otherwise admirable
character, has come from the fact that with the possession of innumerable other excellencies this central one
of consecration to God was lacking. The young men of
our land should perceive a fact which President GARFIELD's
life teaches us all, that not only is piety essential to true
greatness, but it is a help and not a hindrance to any kind
of success in this life that is worth the having.

President GARFIELD unquestionably comes the nearest
to the Christian's ideal of a true man, of any one who has
ever been before the American public. To see this let us
compare him with Washington and Lincoln, the other two
among our Presidents whom we specially revere. We
shall find them strikingly alike, yet with decided differences in Mr. GARFIELD's favor.

All three were Christian men, consistent and prayerful,
yet Washington seemed to lack that childlike humility
and that longing for the salvation of souls which characterize the most devout, and Lincoln was at first not careful
as to the purity of his speech, and never made a profession

of religion. GARFIELD, on the other hand, was humble, self-denying, and active as a Christian. His voice, his purse, his whole influence were always at the service of the church. As says his pastor: "He sought in every way to advance the interests of the cause of Christ."

These three great men were in sympathy with the people, but in unequal degree. Washington, largely from the temper of his age, and from his training in a land of slavery, was something of an aristocrat. Lincoln, at heart a scholar and a gentleman, yet from defects of early training, did not always seem in sympathy with the more cultivated class of society, and allowed himself in some gruff, quizzical and unrefined ways which gave offense where offense might easily have been avoided. But GARFIELD was thoroughly identified with both extremes of society. He had drank the cup of poverty almost to the dregs, and yet by tastes and training was in perfect sympathy with all that is most elevated in intellect and culture.

In mental ability all were unusual men. Finely endowed by nature, they had by discipline minds well stored and keen. All were marked by good judgment, by clearness of statement, and a consequent power over men. But in GARFIELD was a ripe education which neither of the others had, and consequently a scholarly sweep and grasp of mind which gave peculiarity tohisgreatness.

As to their work, it is yet too early to speak with assurance. GARFIELD's influence yet remains to be estimated. Washington's work was that of construction, Lincoln's, that of deliverance, GARFIELD's, that of consolidation. His example and his words have become a powerful influence in this country, and are destined to be lasting. His administration was brief and comparatively uneventful, yet his life and his teachings are forever imprinted on the memory of this people. Like Confucius in another land and another age, he will live for coming centuries in the hearts of a great people and shape their character.

At the Chicago Convention as the states one after another broke away from their old candidates and cast their votes for GARFIELD, those who bore the standards of the states came over and took their position beside him, while he looked on, white with amazement at the unexpected sight. Those flags concentering around our future President showed where the hearts of the people were. To-day flags and emblems of mourning fill the land, while every household and every congregation are thinking of our beloved Chief Magistrate lying at Cleveland, pale in death. What means this unwonted display? It means that we love and honor him who has gone. As in the days of his health and his wisdom the standards flocked around him, so let it be to-day. God has given us a sacred memory to cherish, a beautiful and pure example to follow. Let us study the life of the departed and imitate it so far as it is worthy. Above all let us remember that our brother, now a saint in glory, in no other point so much deserves imitation as in this—that he sought to imitate Christ, the Great Exemplar. Could he speak to-day he would turn your thoughts away from himself to Him who stands infinitely above him as an example, to the blessed and only potentate, even the Lord Jesus Christ. Our President shone only by reflection from a superior greatness, and now that the moon has set, and its departing glory is traced to the great original, let us rejoice in the beams of the Sun of Righteousness, and walk in its light.

To give voice to the feeling which, I am sure, is upper-most with us all, to-night I should speak simply words of mourning. For myself indeed I can speak none other. I cannot bring you comfort nor direct you where to seek it. Let those discourse of the purpose of an over-ruling Providence in this affliction, who think they can "fathom the Eternal Thought." To me it is all dark and inexplicable. Nor to-night is it fitting in my view to speak of the self-evident lessons this people may learn from the calamity which has fallen on us. We have just buried our dead out of our sight. On the morrow we will think of the future.

The Chief Magistrate of a great nation, whose citizens we are, has fallen. This of itself is cause for sorrow and would justify our gathering here; but even of this I do not care to speak, nor you to hear. There is nothing formal or perfunctory in our mourning. It is the man not the president we mourn. True the glare of public life and his high station made him known to us, but it was his simple manhood which attracted all and attached all to him; and that not in this land only, but in all lands. It is not merely because the President of the Republic is dead that the royal standard is to-day at half-mast on Windsor Castle, but because the Queen and her subjects feel personal loss. It is not the Queen indeed, but the woman who mourns. No event in the world's history ever so brought men together, soul to soul, as this has done. No such blotting out of race and class distinctions was ever known as that which has been manifested by the common interest in the sublime struggle for life we have all been watching, and the common sorrow at death's final victory. It is indeed a most striking fact, that we all feel the death

165

of the President so largely as a personal bereavement. It
is, say so many, "as if there were a death in my own
house."

Therefore, I wish to speak only of the *man* who is
gone, forgetting all that was adventitious; all that was
mere circumstance and accident. To his career, preg-
nant as it is with suggestive thought, I will at this time
only refer as it illustrates the man. We loved him and we
did well, for he was worthy. Let us think upon his character. Chief among the qualities which drew all to him,
were his grand simplicity—his manly humility. These were
native qualities, doubtless, but they were exercised under
most unfavorable conditions. He had not indeed the
temptation toward arrogance which comes with elevation,
sudden or gradual, to prominence and honor, from obscurity or lowly birth—the common temptation of "self-
made" men, so called. Here, as to him there is a wide-
spread error, the result of the Presidential canvass. It
needed not, by the unworthy, though common, device of a
political campaign, that his party should have attempted
to add lustre to his bright achievements by pointing
to ignoble origin and humble beginnings, and in his case
the facts did not warrant it. He came of good stock.
There is no better in this land. He was, indeed, reared
in poverty, but remember, his family were among the
Western pioneers who were all poor alike, and his father
died young, before he had had opportunity to acquire
a competency. Too much stress has been laid on young
GARFIELD'S early struggles. They were the merest inci
dents, and not at all unusual. Such struggles have been
a part of the experience of hundreds and thousands.
In all free countries the strong intellect triumphs over
difficulties, and rises to place and power. It is indeed a
glory to our nation that such a career is even common-
place with us; that we give and are able to give to every
one "a fair start and an equal chance in the race of life,"
but no especial credit is due the individual. Indeed this
youth labored under no peculiar difficulties. His devoted
mother deserves the highest meed of praise for her sac-

rifices in his behalf, but the boy no more than many
another who has worked his way through school and college, and not a tithe so much as one who in despite of
fate's stern limitations wrests knowledge from her fastnesses
without the help of school or teacher. The revered and
honored LINCOLN is a type of such a victor over adverse
circumstances; but GARFIELD's circumstances were from the
very first propitious. The few months of lowly labor,
voluntarily and needlessly taken on himself when but a
boy, of which so much has been said, were no real part of
his life. That began when he entered school with fixed
purpose to acquire an education. He took the common
road, a road fortunately in this country, open to any one of
health and strength without dependents, who is willing to
take it. Let us honor the mother who in her poverty gave
up the services of her boy that he might educate himself,
more than the boy, who doubtless found his highest pleasure in what he did. Nor was his after preferment at all
remarkable. It came by a process of natural selection, not
by conquest on his part. His greatness therefore was all
from within, not from without, and the temptation toward
proud self-assertion against which the successful man of
humble antecedents must always contend, could have had
little force with him. But he had the greater temptation of
the consciousness of inherent strength and superiority, and
yet resisted it. Consider who and what he was. By natural
gift and laborious acquisition one of the greatest of men.
In mind and body a type of perfect manhood. In faculty
and accomplishment versatile beyond precedent. He went
from the school-room to the camp and battle-field, and in
two years by sheer merit became a major-general. He was
without special training, a preacher of great renown, and
became one of the most eloquent of orators. He was a
lawyer, who without the drill of active practice, was most
effective in the very highest departments of the law, that
most artificial and recondite of sciences. He who was
hardly thought of as being a lawyer at all, had argued
some thirteen causes in the United States Supreme Court,
where eminent counsel, standing perhaps at the head

of the bar of their own states, appear but once or twice in
a life time. He had mastered and could lucidly expound
the principles of those most abtruse and delicate problems
of political science and finance which embarrass and dis-
tract the wisest statesmen, particularly in their application
to the practical affairs of life, and which in the last few
years so hardly pressed upon this people for solution. He
was a most accomplished scholar—Greek tragedy was his
recreation—and withal he was a thorough and practical
man of business and affairs. He had great sagacity and
wisdom. During the months of his presidential canvass
he went about among his fellow citizens discussing everywhere and every day off-hand, the issues of the contest, shirk-
ing no question, boldly giving his opinions; and yet he made
not one mistake, and his brief, concise utterances furnished
texts for the political speeches of his party. He had been
greatly honored and flattered all his life. His life indeed
was from the first an uninterrupted success. Acknowledged
always and everywhere a leader he went steadily upward-
Knowing human weakness of what spirit should we expect to find a man so constituted and thus environed? It
were not strange had he been proud if not arrogant, self-
complacent if not vain, patronizing or haughty as his hu-
mor might be or the occasion might prompt—but he was
none of these. He was as simple as a little child, and as
ready a learner. He was kindness personified, and he met
the humblest on equal terms. His pleasures were of the
simplest, chief among them his home-life on the farm.
His plain way of life never changed. He remained to the
last an active worker, unashamed, in the comparatively obscure religious sect whose tenets he embraced in early
youth, and whose outward surroundings were probably the
humblest in the capital. This could hardly have been, in
one of his broad mind, because of strong conviction, that
to this somewhat narrow sect were committed the oracles
of truth. A man less simple and less humble would
soon have drifted away to some church which while
it taught what he considered essential truth, also gave
greater social advantages. He was domestic, and made

his home his social center, almost his social world.
At his inauguration he turned and kissed his wife and
mother. In the light of what we know of him, that act of
questionable taste in another, was in perfect keeping with
his simple character. Then, too, his humility. He never
sought advancement. It always came to him. He never
refused duty, but it is evident that he always entered on a
new one with deep self-distrust. His words to Col. Rockwell a few days before his death, and when he knew he was
to die (indeed I think *he* knew it all along), were most pathetic, "Do you think I'll find a place in human history?"
We gladly join in the answer, "Yes, a grand one, but a
grander one in human hearts." He will fill that place
because of his humility, because of his simplicity. But
not alone because of these. Without pretence or ostentation, he exemplified the virtues good men all admire.
He was loyal, truthful, and sincere. He was honest,
faithful, and just. He was manly yet pure and chaste.
He had, too, those traits which adorn virtue. He was
singularly open, confiding, and frank. He was joyous and
buoyant of spirit, considerate and helpful of others, unselfish, and always accessible to every one who sought him.
Why should he not have been honored and loved?

But while men love a grand yet simple and kindly
nature, admire a lofty intellect, and honor a virtuous life;
yet above all do our hearts go out toward the brave man
who bears great suffering with fortitude and without complaint, and calmly faces death. Had General GARFIELD died
when the bullet pierced him our feelings would not have
been so deep as now. It was after all by that courageous
fight for life, against fearful odds, by that calm, considerate,
self-abnegating demeanor with which he bore his sufferings
that he drew the people to him. It was during those eighty
days of constant pain and strength in weakness, that we
learned to love him, and indeed learned to *know* him as he
was. He never murmured or complained. He was wonderfully patient, even cheerful. Thoughtful for others even in
those agonizing days, he wrote with his own hand as soon as
he could hold a pen, that touching letter to his mother, and

on the same day dictated his last will, by which he left to
his faithful wife (how worthy of him in all things she has
proved), his little property. He cried not for any vengeance. He only among all men seemed to give no thought
to the assassin, and his forgiveness was given unasked.

Another thing about this death-bed is significant. This
man had been a devoted Christian all his life. Most men
neglect their Maker's will through life and call loudly on
Him when they come to die. His course was the precise
reverse of this. When he was brought to the White House
dying as it seemed, it was suggested that a Christian minister should be summoned, but he forbade it. He did not
need comfort or encouragement. He was not afraid to meet
his God. All through the sad struggle he maintained the
same composure, and so far as I have heard no priestly
office was done for him or asked by him. He needed no
human shriving or intercession. His great soul went forth
naked and alone. By that death-bed all could stand of
whatever religion or of no religion, and see a brave man
die, and all could honor him.

And so I say we mourn. *For him* indeed we do not
mourn—who can? Who would not choose such a death?
At peace with God and man: in the firm belief in immortality: full of honors: at the zenith of earthly ambition,
with his powers yet unabated: safe from calumny, and the
sure reaction which must have come with many (such is
weak humanity) had he recovered, when he again should
wield the power of his great office, for envy, misconstruc-
tion, misunderstanding, and disappointed ambition would
do their evil work—a blessed martyr now—his loved ones
the cherished wards of the nation, what better time could
he choose to die?

His work is crowned. The affection of nations and the
remembrance of generations are his secure possession—
his the laurel wreath, the victors, yea the martyr's crown.

For him I say we do not mourn, but for the loss of him,
who can bring consolation?

First Presbyterian Church of Jersey City.

Sermon by the Pastor,

REV. C. K. IMBRIE, D. D.

TEXT—" The breath of our nostrils, the Anointed of the Lord was taken in their pits of whom we said, Under His shadow we shall live among the nations."—*Lamentations* 4:20

This is the wailing cry of the prophet Jeremiah over the capture and death of the King of Judah. He calls him " the breath of our nostrils ;" knowing that the very life of a nation is in a manner connected with its Head. He speaks of him as " the Anointed of the Lord ;" because in any realm civil authority is exercised by God's appointment. And in Israel's case emphatically did the king represent God's authority. He was " the Anointed of the Lord." This breath of the nation, Zedekiah, had been taken captive, had seen his sons slain before his eyes ; had himself been slain ; at the very time when the nation were hoping, that under his shadow they would dwell secure among the nations. How truly do these words of the text express to-day the sudden and sad extinction of our own hopes as a nation.

Sixteen years and five months ago I preached from this text before you, when all the nation was stunned by the cruel assassination of our lamented President Lincoln. It would be a very strange circumstance in any Christian nation that a minister of Christ, during one pastorate, should be twice called, sadly to preach over the fall of the Nation's Head, by the ruthless hand of the assassin. How passing strange is it that this should be the case in this land of freedom and prosperity.

I announce the same text to you to-day, therefore, because these two events are linked together, and will go

171

down together to posterity, in sad conjunction, as a part
of our national history. On the former occasion, indeed,
the blow was more stunning. And in a certain sense, however wicked the deed was, it was prompted by the evil
passions that grew out of our war. It roused the nation's
anger and resentment that so cowardly a blow should have
been struck. In the present case the blow fills us more
than ever with wonder. It seems so unaccountable. It is
rather poignant grief and dismay therefore, than anger,
which fills the nation's heart to-day. And there is a sadness too, that her lingering hope for the precious life so
long deferred, should be at last disappointed. And so in
the nation's depth of sorrow, the ruthless hand that caused
it has become comparatively forgotten. And there is besides a tenderness in the nation's grief, and a deep sympathy for the bereaved household, mingling with its lamentations and extending far beyond our national limits in is
universality, which is so genuine, so delicate as to be ex-
ceedingly touching and instructive.

For our departed President himself this providence
which has at last shattered our long cherished hopes has
brought a sweet rest after eleven weeks of agony and suspense. True, indeed, his heroism, his patient endurance,
his hearty cheer, even amidst his pain, towards the kind
hearts around him, his hope to the last against hope, have
drawn forth admiring comments from all, and have been
equaled only by the patient heroism of his beloved wife.
But what a bed of anguish it has been! And this has
bound him to the nation by stronger ties than aught else
could have done. But now he sleeps—sleeps, as all who
knew him testify—the sleep of a believer in Jesus. What
a blessed change for him! He has struggled upward
from obscurity and poverty by hard service. God helped
him. And he has risen with steady course to the highest
pinnacle of honor. And now the same hand has as strangely
cast him down. "Thou hast lifted me up, and cast me
down." It was a sad reverse. And yet, beyond all the joy
or the sorrow which such earthly vicissitudes could bring
to brighten or to sadden the present life, he passes now

through the open door which reveals to his vision only the brightness of eternal blessedness; and he leaves behind all the uncertainties and the losses which dim the glory of even the highest of earth's honors.

For himself, then, this rest is a blessed change. But for the *Nation!* The Providence which has brought us to this crisis is very strange. Many are startled by it. There is danger of mistake as to its meanings. May God teach us to learn right lessons at this moment, and not allow our blind natures to judge him amiss. It is a great satisfaction·to find—as is manifest in these well-worded proclamations which come to us from the highest authorities in the general and State governments; as is manifest in the felicitous, reverential, God-honoring tone displayed in the prominent editorials of the day; as is manifest in the wide-spread desire that the nation should reverently bow its head at this solemn moment in prayer—that, after all the occasional outbursts of sporadic cases of infidelity, the great body of the people are right in their views. They turn to God, and would fain be taught aright what are the great lessons of the hour.

Let us, then, endeavor to get some truths of the occasion established in our minds.

1. The *first*, and most important one is, that this stroke is from God; and, it being from God, we must bow in submission.

I put this first, because we can never too soundly learn that all things are in God's hand and under God's control and because, also, as I intimated last Sabbath, there is a strong disposition to deny God's hand in the adverse affairs among men, as though, according to the old heathen Persian notion, there were two deities in the universe—one managing all that is good, the other controlling all that is evil; and because, also, on the other hand, some men, while admitting the fact of God's rule in all things, yet find fault with God, as unfeeling, as tyrannical, as unconcerned about us, when he allows dark crimes to be perpetrated.

Both are wrong. In the first place, all is of God. He
rules universally. And equally true it is, in the second
place, that God is good and wise in all His dealings. If
ever our souls are to be kept at peace, and bound to the
right in this changing, dark world, we must get right principles on this subject.

This stroke is of God. The allegation of many is
that because some things are huge crimes, God can have
no hand in even permitting them, much less in embracing them in his plans for dealing with a nation. And the
reason given is that thereby He would be criminal. But
consider how impossible it is that God can desert any
part of His universe. The hugest actors of evil are
still God's creatures ; dependent upon Him. How could
they live ? How could they perform their evil actions if
God did not uphold their lives and strength ? You ask,
Why does not God if he is holy blot such great criminals
out of existence when He sees one about to commit an evil
deed ? You may as well ask why does He not blot *any*
sinner out of existence when He sees the sinner about to
commit sin. It is not the perpetration of only huge
crimes that creates the difficulty. Huge crimes are not
the only sins requiring God's forbearance. Why does not
God blot from existence any foul tongue about to give
vent to iniquity—any liar—any perjurer ? Indeed, to
speak on, you may as well ask why He does not blot out
of existence any sinner at all—you or me, for example,
when we are about to do or speak an evil thing. Can He
be holy and yet uphold us in life ? If he can, why can He
not be holy and yet spare more hardened and corrupt sinners ? Answer one of these questions and the other is
answered. If God permits any sinner to live on and sin in
small things and yet can Himself be clear and holy—why
can He not be clear and holy when permitting great crimes
and when preserving their actors and overruling their
wicked ways in His great counsels for wise ends ? Who
shall prescribe to the Almighty, just how much wickedness
He shall allow to exist ? You see thus, that the question
which is raised here is just, in another form, the old ques-

tion, " Why does God permit the existence of evil at all in
His universe "—a question which none can solve because
man is too weak to take in all God's designs for eternity.
The simple fact is that He does permit it—does control it
—does take it into His plan for carrying out his great designs—tells us that it is allowed for wise reasons—tells us
that He will bring good out of it—often indeed gives us
glimpses clear and satisfactory as to the way in which He
brings good out of it—tells us we shall praise Him in the
end when we see it accomplished. And meantime He
requires us to acknowledge that His hand is controlling
all, and bids us trust Him.

A man carelessly, or ignorantly, or intentionally, sets
fire to a building. The flame spreads until it consumes a
vast portion of the city. Men unwisely declare that God
can have no hand at all in such things, either for rebuking
a people or as a means of future good to them. Why God
surely could have prevented the catastrophe if he had
thought it best. That He did not do so, shows that He
allowed it for reasons good to Himself. The truth is, all
this talk about the Eternal God not being able to permit
and to embrace in His wise and deep counsels the acts of
evil men, without thereby becoming an abettor of the evil,
is just the expression of the weakness of the human mind
which would measure God by itself; which determines to
subject everything, even God himself, to its own puny reason. And because such persons cannot see how they, with
their limited powers, could permit evil without partak-
ing in the crime, they judge that the Almighty cannot
take the acts of the wicked into his plans and yet be clear.

The Scriptures are very clear on this subject. They
speak of the Almighty as He is. They declare that He
does permit evil. They declare that He does embrace the
evil actions of men in His plans for dealing with nations
and individuals. They declare that when the evil does
come and does afflict, it is His hand which uses it for
His own purposes. They say that the men of this world—
the wicked are "God's sword." " Is there evil in the city
and the Lord hath not done it?" Amos 3 : 6. " I am Je-

hovah, and there is no God besides me; I form the light
and I create darkness; I make peace and I create evil;
I the Lord do all these things." Isaiah 45: 7. "Behold
I have created the smith that bloweth the coals in the fire,
and bringeth forth an instrument for his work; and I have
created the waster to destroy." Isaiah 54: 16. They declare also that while God does take their evil acts into His
plans, yet that He Himself is pure.

Let us take one single case out of many. It is very con-
clusive. It is the case of the crucifixion of the Lord Jesus
by the hands of wicked men, in fulfillment of God's own
eternal counsels to open the way of Heaven to man. You
find it in the apostle Peter's address to these very sinners,
after the resurrection. Here are his words: "Ye men of
Israel hear these words: Jesus of Nazareth, a man ap-
proved of God among you by miracles and wonders and
signs which God did by Him in the midst of you as ye
yourselves also know; Him, being delivered up by the
DETERMINATE COUNSEL and FOREKNOWLEDGE OF GOD; ye have
taken and by *wicked hands have crucified and slain*, whom
God hath raised up," &c. Act 2: 22, 23.

Is it not plain here that God *decreed*, for the most glorious
of purposes, *the death* of Christ, because it was necessary
to our salvation,—God's sacrifice to take away the sin of
the world? Is it not just as plain here that to accomplish
this decree God took the evil deed of these vile, wicked
men into His plan of Providence, allowed these wicked
men to have their own way, and so ordered it that in having
their own way they should fulfill His gracious purposes?
Is it not plain here, that in His Providence He therefore put
Christ into their hands to this end? As the apostle states
it: "He delivered Him up" to them. Is it not plain here,
that the Christ was then "taken by them and slain by
them," and that his foreordained death was accomplished
by these wicked, brutal hands, against light and truth, with
every good reason forbidding it; God standing by and
allowing it to be done? Is it not plain here, that at the
same time the guilt of these men remained the same in all its
enormity? He charges their guilt upon them: "Ye have

taken and by *wicked* hands have crucified and slain the Holy One and the Just and desired a murderer to be granted unto you." Does not Christ himself charge them with the heinousness of their guilt and predict their certain punishment? "Daughters of Jerusalem, weep not for me, but weep for yourselves and for your children, for behold the days come when they shall say : Blessed are the barren, and the womb that never bore, and the paps that never gave suck. Then shall they begin to say to the mountains : Fall on us ! and to the hills : Cover us." Luke 23 : 28–30. Is it not clear that these wicked men were perfectly free in their actions, and accountable for them, and yet that they carried out unwittingly God's holy purpose? Is it not plain, that from this foul deed there flows, by God's wondrous counsel, life eternal to the world? And is not God holy and clear of blame in all this? Is He not praised beforehand by the Holy Ones of Heaven for this death which Jesus was to accomplish at Jerusalem? Is He not acknowledged by the angels as the Holy Lord God Almighty, who worketh all things according to the counsels of His own will? Is He not praised by the multitude of the redeemed as the only wise and Holy One, who has redeemed us out of every nation, by the blood shed on this very cross? How plainly then, does this single act declare every particular which we have asserted. Let us be sure that it is a poor, illogical and unscientific philosophy which in reality demands that God be put aside out of this universe as its All-wise Governor, in order to accommodate the strange events of this world to its own puny thinking. Admit *all* the facts before you draw your conclusion. This is imperatively necessary. And among these facts, account for them as we may, there rises one grand fact above all others which cannot be wisely ignored, and that is the fact of a personal, all-wise, ever-present, all-upholding, all-controlling God. Every theory that leaves out or impairs this fact is necessarily false and harmful.

Yes, as our own Confession of Faith so well expresses it (chap. iii. sec. 1.) "God from all eternity did, by the most wise and holy counsel of His own will, freely and unchangeably ordain whatsoever comes to pass,—yet so, as thereby, neither is God the author of sin, nor is violence offered to the will of the creatures, nor is the liberty or contingency of second causes taken away, but rather established." Both sides are true—God does permit, does ordain, and yet wicked men are all guilty—and He is holy.

The profound methods by which the Infinite God deals with men and events so as to secure the result that they are guilty, while His Holiness is unimpaired, He does not unfold. We could not wholly understand it if we did. Yet we may give an imperfect illustration. A father has a wild son whom he wishes to save. The son has formed a determination to go to a certain place and perform some evil deed. The father foresees that this evil deed will be the son's ruin. He wishes to preserve him from going to that place. At the same time the father knows (what the son does not) that a band of ruffians have decided to seize the son on his way to that place and carry him off to another distant spot for their own wicked purposes. Now the father allows those men to succeed. They seize the young man. They hurry him far off from the scene of his intended crime. At the moment of their reaching the distant place the father comes in and rescues him. At the same time his very distance from the place of his own intended iniquity saves the son from the ruin it would have ensured if he had carried out his own intentions. Now plainly the father made use of the wickedness of these ruffians to effect his own good purpose. He is blameless of their guilt. But the ruffians themselves, are they any the less guilty because their wicked act led to good? Surely not. This imperfect illustration may show how God may and does allow and use the gross crimes of men for ulterior good purposes while He Himself is blameless.

It is true, when God permits evil men to act in a given case, or when He permits a great calamity to visit a city, that we cannot decide positively that He does it to punish a man or a nation. It may be designed for the nation's good. It was so in the case of the cross. Who can look so far into the future as to determine what evils may not

thus be averted, or what good secured, by this calamity?
Or it may be sent to punish for sins. This must be decided from other reasons than the mere fact of the evil
being permitted. But whatever may be God's intention in
allowing it, we must never forget that *His* hand rules in all.
He sends the sorrow, even when it comes by careless, or
by criminal, or by crazed hands; whether it comes in
judgment or for a blessing upon the land, or for the admonition of His people. As Elihu says, "He causeth it to
come, whether for correction, or for His land, or for mercy;"
Job 37 : 13. Ah! none would more heartily have sub-
scribed to this than the honored head which lies low in
death to-day. As he said, at the fall of President Lincoln
by the assassin's hand, in words that get a new vitality to-
day from his own sad decease: "Clouds and darkness are
round about Him, but righteousness and judgment are the
habitation of His throne. Fellow-citizens, God still
reigns, and the Government at Washington still lives."

Yes! in the present sorrow, we must look beyond all
second causes to God. It is the only way to true comfort.
He has done it who is wisest and best. He has sent this
sorrow to the nation who alone could have averted it. He
has seen good to allow the bullet of the assassin to do its
destructive work beyond all medical aid. He has seen it
best to deny the earnest request of praying millions. He
has brought us as a nation to kneel all at His footstool,
and weep. It is good for the nation to sit at His feet; to
"be still, and know that He is God."

2. The second truth of the occasion to which I point
you, is that God is not *unkind* in thus allowing reckless-
ness or wickedness to have their way; or to speak more
specifically, He is not unkind in this particular providence;
nor has He in the least shown that He is not the hearer
of prayer. Ah! how many strange expressions have we
heard lately on this point from lips that should know
better. "We had great hopes of his recovery." So we
had. God has seen fit to disappoint them. "The final
blow was so long delayed." So it was, and notwithstand-

ing God has brought good out of it, He has seen fit to
let the sad ending fill us with bitterness after all. "We
prayed"—So we did—"And millions of petitions ascended
that the life (which we now see was sacrificed from the
moment the bullet struck) might still be spared." So we
did. But we prayed, I trust, with reference to God's will
after all. Indeed it was no prayer at all if it was not in
submission to his will; and God's will has been manifested
to us. It was His will that the Nation's Head should die
—and that the Nation should weep. He has not shown
that He is not good, or that he does not pity us; or that
He does not answer prayer. He has only shown us that
there are cases when it is not wise in Him to grant the
request of even a whole nation for a specific object. He
shows us that from the moment the bullet struck, the case
was put beyond all present medical skill, and it was God's
will that he should die. Now that his eyes are closed in
death, the nation did not and does not pray that he may
be raised up from the dead. No, because we all know that
this is one of the things which it is not God's will to grant
to prayer. So there are other things which it is not God's
will to grant to prayer; and when his will in any case is
known, we must submit. And in all this allowed evil, God
is not unkind or oppressive, or tyrranical. Unkindness
implies that God is unfriendly, not benevolent, not hu-
mane—but unfeeling, hard, severe, rigorous, cruel, or cal-
lous towards human sorrow. But God is none of these.
It is a reproach upon His spotless Holiness and Love to
think so. All Scripture goes to show that the Lord is good.
All earth's experience even under its sins, shows that He
is good and kind. Every year, every day, shows it.

Suppose that God sent this sorrow for our national sins.
I do not say that He did. But suppose He did. Is it unkind in God to remind a nation and humble a nation for
its sins and move it to humiliation and repentance before
sorer judgments fall? Suppose He has done it to open the
way for greater national benefits; or in some way to prevent evils which only His eye could foresee would otherwise
arise. Surely this would not be unkind. In fact we must

ourselves be gods ; we must know all God's plans and purposes, before we can anticipate what God's ultimate design
may be even in the most painful event. No : Let us bow
before Him in this event and in all things, as not only wise
but good. Eli was right in his sorrow when he cried " It
is the LORD, let Him do as seemeth Him good." Job was
right when he said " Shall we receive good from the hands
of the Lord, and shall we not receive evil ?" " The Lord
gave and the Lord hath taken away, Blessed be the name
of the Lord." Let us plead with Him that the result may
be just what His wise and holy will toward us as a Nation,
decides to be best.

3. As we stand around the coffin of our deceased President to-day, there is another lesson, I think, which God has
plainly taught us. Surely we must all be more deeply
impressed than ever with the utter evanescence and the
inferior value of the chiefest worldly honors. " Surely
every man walketh in a vain show."

What an illustration have we of this before us ! Here
is a case where a man has risen, against every adverse
circumstance , to the very highest position. It is one of
the very clearest cases we know of to prove the large possibilities of even eminent success, under the peculiar fostering influences of our happy form of government, to well-
directed, upright, conscientious and persistent effort in any
of our citizens. And as such it makes a special appeal to our
youth and young men. One steady aim towards the right
from youth up has in this case secured it all. His own exertions, his untiring industry, his steadiness of purpose, his
thrifty economy, his efforts amidst difficulties to attain useful knowledge, his kindly affections to his family, and with
all these his godly rectitude and persevering uprightness,
which displayed itself even in boyhood, by his refusal to
take an unjust advantage even in the use of a canal lock,
and that on the simple ground that it was not right—
these have been the steps of the ladder by which he
reached his proud position. Above all as a pronounced

believer in Jesus Christ, as one never ashamed to acknowledge himself a Christian, or indeed publicly to preach the
gospel of Christ, his private acts and his public acts were
all radiant, we are told by those that knew him intimately,
with a glow of heartfelt devotion to Christian truth and
Christian principle.

Now note that, in God's providence, this man was ex-
ceptionally successful in the attainment of this world's
good. At every step he was prosperous. Successful in
study, successful in academic honors and position, successful in the army, successful in Congress;—He was
finally, though unexpectedly, carried, with the greatest ap-
plause, into the supreme chair of the nation, with every
circumstance gratifying to his filial devotion as a son, or
his love as a husband and father, attending his inauguration ; mother, wife, children, friends rejoicing with the nation at his elevation; himself being in robust health;
happy in his household, happy in troops of warm personal
friends. What a picture of earthly success! Surely, it is
natural to suppose that, thus elevated, he and his looked
forward to a shining career, in which the future history of
this nation, so prominent in the earth, should be inseparably intertwined with his own successful administration.
Within four short months, this beautiful flower of earthly
happiness is blasted and falls; and this bright vision, after
weeks of weariness and pain, heroically, yes, christianly
endured, ends, within three months more, in a wreath of
fading flowers laid by royal, but alas, ineffective hands on
the coffin, amidst the unavailing sighs of the nation ; ends
in the stunning blow which strikes down the aged mother's
pride and hope, and makes the once exultant wife a widow,
and sends the once joyous household back to that home
again, fatherless and desolate, which seven months before
they had left with such gladness. "Surely every man even
at his best estate is altogether vanity." Does it not seem as
if God himself had lifted him up, step by step, and adorned
him in the sight of the whole nation with every circumstance of honor, with all that earth could confer, to prove
to us by the suddenness and the sadness with which all is

extinguished, the utter emptiness of that present, earthly
good on which alas! so many men yet center their chief
affections?

You see here, that even in the case of a Christian his
earthly surroundings are but the thin, unsubstantial drapery
cast around him and thrown off in a moment, and that his
great realities are his hopes in the world eternal. How
clear then is it in every case, that our days, and our honors
on earth are all as a shadow, and there is none abiding.

What a lesson is this to the nation, that its wealth, its
political preferments, its commerce, its chiefest honors are
but a breath! How senseless is the man who makes these
his chief aim!

Does it not show too, the littleness of the rancor and
bitterness of party politics? What are all our wranglings
and bickerings about political preferment in the presence
of that poor wasted body—in the presence of the sorrow
which oppresses the heart of the whole nation at such a
stroke?

And does it not prove to us, that in such a fleeting
world, we as a Nation are dependent on God for everything? God's hand is on all our national resources; not
on our harvests alone, to preserve us from famine; not
on the channels of trade alone, to preserve to us our
prosperity; not on the feelings and passions of our people
alone, to defend us from sectional discords; but, as He has
this day shown us, the very lives most necessary for the
peace and welfare of the nation equally lie in His hands
to preserve them or end them as He will. How plain it
is, that on his sovereign mercy alone, in this regard as
well as in all others, the hopes of the people hang. Would
that we might, as a people, learn the lesson as we ought.

But our departed President had more than all these
merely earthly honors. JAMES A. GARFIELD was, by all
accounts, as I have already intimated, a sincere Christian.
And this leads me to say—

4. Lastly. What a proof there lies in that history to the ſsorrowing nation, of the pre-eminent value of a real Christian life and Christian hope.

In the midst of all these honors, Death, inexorable Death, reaches him in a moment. What time was there to prepare for such a change then ? True his life was dragged out for eleven weeks. But what time was this—burdened with racking pains, amidst groans, that cried, " Oh! this pain, like a thousand cramps in one ;"—what time was this in which to get ready ? And after all, in spite of the combined skill of physicians, notwithstanding the prayers of the nation, and the tender sympathy of all classes ; inexorable Death comes, commissioned of God, and bears him away. What is it now, I ask, that gives comfort to the stricken hearts of this people ? Is it the fact that these high honors were heaped upon him ? Is it his own heroic endurance and playful courage and hopefulness during the ordeal ? Is it even their remembrance of his personal noble qualities ? All these have their due place. But they are nothing beside that other, supereminent source of consolation that our President died a Christian. It is Jesus Christ's hand soothing that heart, and Jesus Christ's hand smoothing that pillow, and receiving that soul to Himself which brings peace to the bereaved household and to the bereaved nation.

I ask you as men who know by experience the workings of the human heart, What recollections of that sick chamber will be the sweetest in the Nation's memory ? There is much that has come from thence to our ears which has touched a chord in every heart. But above all others, will not the sweetest recollections be those that told of the life of Christ within him ? Will they not be his ready expressions of joyful sympathy with those words sung in his sick chamber—

> " Guide me Oh Thou great Jehovah
> Pilgrim, through this barren land,
> I am weak, but Thou art mighty,
> Hold me with Thy powerful hand ;
> Bread of Heaven
> Feed me till I want no more.

" When I tread the verge of Jordan,
    Bid my anxious fears subside ;
  Death of Earth ! and Hell's Destruction !
  Land me safe on Canaan's side,
      Songs of praises
      I will ever give to Thee."

Will it not be in remembering that when those silent
lips lay in the coffin in the Capitol at Washington, and the
sweet music of the choir gave utterance to those words :

" Asleep in Jesus, blessed sleep.
  From which none ever wakes to weep,
  A calm and undisturbed repose
  Which only he who feels it knows ;"

we knew well what truth and appropriateness there was in
their application ?

Yes, it will be because we are persuaded that by Christ's
grace our lamented President's sorrow has been turned to
joy, because, in the eloquent words of one who stood by
his coffin :

" The chief glory of this man, as we think of him now,
was his discipleship in the school of Christ. His attainments as scholar and statesman will be the theme of our
orators and historians, and they must be worthy men to
speak his praise worthily. But it is as a Christian that we
love to think of him now. It was this which made his life
to man an invaluable boon, his death to us an unspeakable
loss, his eternity to himself an inheritance incorruptible,
undefiled, and that fadeth not away. He was no sectarian.
His religion was as broad as the religion of Christ. He
was a simple Christian.

" Our President rests ; he had joy in the glory of *work*,
and he loved to talk of the *leisure* that had not come to
him. Now he has it. This is the clay, precious because
of the service it rendered. He is a freed spirit ; absent
from the body, he is present with the Lord. On the
heights whence came his help he finds repose. What rest
has been his for these four days ! The brave spirit which

cried in its body : " I am tired," is where the wicked cease
from troubling, and the weary are at rest. The patient
soul which groaned under the burden of the suffering
flesh, " Oh, this pain!" is now in a world without pain.
" The Eternal God is our refuge, and underneath are the
everlasting arms."*

What a testimony have we here, that to the highest on
earth, as to the lowest there is that which a simple-hearted
faith in Jesus can give, which is beyond, infinitely beyond all
that the most profuse array of this world's honor or emoluments can confer. He that has this, whatever be his station, is rich ; rich forever. He that has not this is poor;
poor, even if he be enthroned with the mightiest upon the
earth.

May God teach this nation the true lessons of wisdom at
this grave's side. May Jesus reveal His glory to the
hearts of many as they see here how truly only He and
His kingdom can satisfy the soul forever.

* The Rev. Dr. Power.

Sermon by the Pastor,

REV. EDWARD W. FRENCH, D. D.

Never such a Sabbath as this!   A single event, in the history of man, has never before to-day aroused and sustained so intelligent concentration of thought, and so fervent and genuine sympathy from so many millions simultaneously.   The universal drapery of loss and grief is the symbol of shadow and chill in every home and heart.

Not in the United States alone!   A bewildering blow has fallen upon Humanity.   Madrid and Rome, St. Petersburgh and Berlin, Paris and Bombay, Dublin and Berne, are representatives of world-wide emulation in condolence. Canada is thrilled as those next of kin.   England tolls her parish-bells; and her noble Queen confers, by order of Court-mourning, unprecedented honor upon the memory of our murdered Magistrate-in-Chief.   Superfluous his eulogy.   The whole domain of facts, in his diversified career, has been scrupulously gleaned; and its meaning expounded with care and skill in prose and verse.   For eighty days, the tender hand of the Nation has rested upon his fevered breast, while the World reverently listened.   His tomb is prepared near the site of the cabin, where the light greeted his infant eyes; near the farm whence he mounted to topmost ambition.   In a few more heavy hours, the decree, broad as our race—"*Dust to dust*"—will be on him enforced.   Meanwhile, how wise for the "*Minister of the New Testament*" to put his devout ear to God's infallible Word, and transmit to God's people an echo of the voices thereof!

This thought shall guide us :

> "I will hear what God the Lord will speak: for He
> will speak peace unto His people and to His saints : but
> let them not turn again to folly."   (Ps., LXXXV. 8.)

Can one fairly reason from the assassin's bullet to the
conclusion that *"the foundations are out of course?"* Can
man or angel inject derangement or delay into God's counsels? Is His sovereignty even impaired by collisions, cat-
astrophies and revolutions ?

> "Who in the heavens can be compared unto the Lord?
> O Lord God of hosts, who is a strong Lord like unto
> Thee? Thou art the blessed and only potentate ; the
> King of kings, and the Lord of lords. Thy throne is
> established of old. Thy name alone is Jehovah of hosts ;
> the Most High over all the earth."

Heathen are raging in the person of the felon Guiteau.
All causeless malice, frenzied fanaticism and detestable
ambition; all the elements of anarchy, riot and ruin, by
which *"the people imagine a vain thing,"* are festering with
deadly bitterness in that imprisoned wretch.

But God is on the Throne, which

> "He hath prepared for judgment. He shall minister
> judgment to the people in uprightness."

Had lightning smitten our chief; or had disease destroyed
him, men everywhere would say—Behold the hand of God!
Is it otherwise now? Are not the incendiary's torch, the
murderer's revolver and the devil's works a part of God's
instrumental agencies? Yet, therein is no infringement
upon man's freedom, or God's headship or holiness.

> "Surely the wrath of man shall praise Thee : the re-
> mainder of wrath shalt Thou restrain."
> "Deliver my soul from the wicked, which is Thy
> sword : from men which are Thy hand, O Lord ; from
> men of the world, which have their portion in this life."

Fifty millions aghast! Mystery envelops God's way. All
the antecedents of our late President's history, indicating

singular fitness for highest office; his grand beginnings of
administration, now extinguished, in which were blended
the companion and leader, friend and ruler, statesman and
philanthrophist, scholar and Christian, do but intensify
the darkness that enshrouds human reason assuming to
explain the 2d of July, 1881. What saith the Scripture?

" Who can utter the mighty acts of the Lord ? Canst
thou by searching find out God ? He made darkness His
secret place : His pavilion round about Him were dark
waters and thick clouds of the skies."

This truth lived in the memory and ruled in the heart
of JAMES A. GARFIELD. Be it ours, likewise, to ponder the
attributes of God. A government, which we can compre-
hend, could not be Divine. Plans, which sweep "*from
everlasting to everlasting,*" cannot be compassed by the
finite mind. Our hearts, keeping mournful time with the
funeral cortege from Elberon to Cleveland, have burned
with the celestial fire of this ascription—

" How unsearchable are Thy judgments, and Thy ways
past finding out ! "

But, solution of Divine problems is never the condition
of profit by them. To no one hath God said—Understand
Me : but to every one—Obey Me. God's treasure in us is,
not knowledge, but trust.

Apply this truth to our present calamity, and we find
in it an effectual shield against the darts of perplexity
and the flames of unbelief. There is a strong and
subtle temptation now to cry out—Is the corroding suspense of eleven weeks healthful ? Only four months
instead of four years, in the Presidential chair !—Is that
just to him ? Can there be good in the reversal of a Nation's high and happy expectation : in its exposure, through
loss of its admired and trusted Head, to sectional feuds
and destructive partizanship ? Is there not fearful mistake, if not radical defect, in that system in which a life,
incalculably precious, may be the victim of a lunatic's
whim or a miscreant's hate ? Where are the corner-stones
of Divine Government, if the men, who embody principles

of liberty and equity, peace and good-will, are jostled out of being, as carelessly as a teamster whips off the heads of wayside flowers?

Listen!

> "The Lord is of infinite understanding. With whom took He counsel; and who instructed Him? O the depth of the riches both of the wisdom and knowledge of God!"

Blunder in our Chief Executive's death? Impossible! Inadvertence? Inconceivable: unless the Scriptural idea of God is mutilated beyond recognition. Even in our consternation and anguish, and tremendous protest against the incomputable crime of the assassination, we know that God will vindicate Himself as transcendently wise. Yea verily, good also. God is good inherently; good communicatively; good eternally. All the efflux of His nature is in manifold and unmingled goodness. Every act, utterance and volition has goodness as its fountain, channel and goal.

This is true of all that He allows. The vast iniquity of that pistol-shot, with its long retinue of heart-break and desolation, is the very method which infinite wisdom pronounces indispensable, and infinite benevolence pronounces blessed. Let the nation say—"*My heart is withered like grass.*" Let the Church say—"*He that spared not His own Son, but delivered Him up for us all, how shall He not with Him also freely give us all things? Though He slay me, yet will I trust in Him.*"

Is the revelation of what God is, and the enjoyment of what God gives, delayed to our land?

> "Be patient, brethren, unto the coming of the Lord. Behold! The husbandman waiteth for the precious fruit of the earth, and hath long patience for it, until he receive the early and latter rain."

There is a reminiscence of Divine character in human governments, though often and grievously blurred. The government is mightier than the governor. He perishes. It abides. The respect, which he receives, may be due, not to

character, but to office. The respect, which it receives, is
due to its Divine ordination.

"For there is no power but of God. The powers that
be are ordained of God."

Civil government is His institution. Therefore, it is not
easily shaken down. Twice has horrid violence emptied
the chair of President. But, their lawful successors were
lawfully inaugurated : and the life social, commercial and
political, of the republic, moves onward, without shock or
perceptible abatement of speed ; as the railway train, under
mighty headway, releases its exhausted locomotive to rush,
for a moment with higher speed, upon the side-track,
which replaced allows the linked cars to fly straight ahead
toward the fresh and full locomotive, which cautiously
lessens its motion, till without jar or sound, the coupling
is effected, and the complete train regains momentum.

Predictions of national dismemberment, when great
Lincoln fell, were falsified. And now a leading journal
of France, (des Debats) says—"President GARFIELD's
accession meant peace secured to the American Republic
for four years, abroad and at home : but all these hopes
have been blighted by a fanatical revolver." Another
editor on that sunny shore, writes—"It is to be feared
that death has closed for a long time that march of social
and political renovation, the general lines of which Mr.
GARFIELD traced in his message to Congress."

We dismiss fear. Human government draws elasticity
and coherence from Him who appointed it. Filial dependence upon Him, whose "*foot-stool is the earth*," brings at
once exaltation to our citizenship, and glory to His name.

Painful to the patriot's ear, and hostile to the Christian
heart is the flippancy, with which, in this day, those in civil
authority are caricatured and condemned. Oversight loses
nothing of keenness by being respectful; or censorship of
rigor by being generous. Deference to the duly constituted ruler is an essential element in right character.
For lack of it in the adult, our youth are, as a class, irreverent : and between irreverence and impudence the step is

short: and the quick and vile fruit of impudence is riot.
This is the hour to press upon the young the Divine man-
date—

> " Let every soul be subject to the higher powers.
> Whosoever resisteth the power resisteth the ordinance of
> God : and they that resist shall receive to themselves con-
> demnation.'

The civil Magistrate may forget or forbear penalty.
God, never. Either in the person of His Son or of the
offender, justice must be satisfied.

Furthermore, respect and obedience to Rulers find sanction and support in Prayer for them.

> " I exhort that, first of all, supplications, prayers, in-
> tercessions and giving of thanks be made for all men ; for
> kings and for all that are in authority."

Very intimate is the connection of their administration
and the people's prayer for them : as the Gospel Minister's
pulpit reveals the quality of prayer for him by the Congregation. Forgetfulness in prayer of Rulers is our provocation of them to treachery of trust. Prayer is more than
the forerunner of mercies. It is one of their conditions.
What is the growing crop without tillage ? Our loyalty,
without prayer ? How specific yet comprehensive, simple
yet grand, are Scriptural prayers for those beset with the
temptations, as well as entrusted with the prerogatives, of
civil office !

> " Make them, O Lord, able men, and men of truth,
> fearing God and hating covetousness. Enable our Magis-
> trates to defend the poor and the fatherless ; to do justice
> for the afflicted and needy. Let those that judge remem-
> ber that they judge not for man, but for the Lord. Give
> them a spirit of wisdom and understanding, a spirit of coun-
> sel and might."

Inestimable the benefit to the land, whose children are
taught by parents thus to pray. Such petitions must have
arisen, as sweet incense, on his behalf whose honored dust
begins to-morrow its long repose in Lake View Cemetery.

and whose name has already passed into the loving cus-
tody of every honest soul.   Who discerns not the
peculiar embarrassments of his successor? Owing his elevation not to ballot but to bullet ; measured at once by the
standard of character and the outline of policy made illustrious by President GARFIELD ; conscious that the scruti-
nizing gaze of men is fixed upon him, because of outrage
upon them : suspicious too, peradventure, that an election
to-morrow would not install him where he now sits ; and
sure that some, who gave him their votes, regard him with
distrust, if not aversion : all enthusiasm denied, though
the country is certified that he has legitimately taken the
high oath of office : compelled to be satisfied with decor-
ous silence in the land : how urgently he needs, how justly
he claims, the earnest prayers of Christendom ! Though
his career be sublime in the future, we may not lean upon
him. Our slain President preaches that lesson.

> "Thus saith the Lord : Cursed is the man that trusteth
> in man, and maketh flesh his arm, and whose heart departeth
> from the Lord. For he shall be like the heath in the desert.
> and shall not see when good cometh.

On the 30th March, 1863, Abraham Lincoln wrote these
words : " It is the duty of nations, as well as individuals,
to own their dependence upon the overruling power of
God ; to confess their sins and transgressions in humble
sorrow, yet with assured hope that genuine repentance
will lead to mercy and pardon ; and to recognize the sublime truth announced in the Holy Scriptures, and proven
by all history, that those nations only are blessed, whose
God is the Lord."

Change the view. There is a prison-cell, into which
mankind pours abhorrence or execration. We are not now
competent to decide the question of the sanity and moral
accountability of its wretched inmate. We cannot set
bounds to the atrocity or consequences of his crime. It
was without provocation ; utterly causeless except by his
own delirium or devilishness. Like all monsters, he is a
coward ; fearful for his own life, a thousand times forfeited,

detestable, worthless. He avows the murder ; and far from compunction, "*glories in his shame.*" What temper toward Guiteau should characterize us. We ought to be as far from sickly sentimentality as from savage vindictiveness. We should abhor the insipidity of the weakling, and the bloodthirstiness of the cannibal. Are we to forgive him ? Assuredly not ; while he does not wish forgiveness. We are not to cast that celestial pearl before swine. God never forgives the unrepentant. Contrition and confession always precede forgiveness by Him. We are always to cherish the spirit of forgiveness, even to him who injures us seventy times seven times ; but we may exercise that spirit only to them who own and deplore sin. Our eye should foresee, and our tongue welcome, the least evidence of penitence.

Meanwhile, may one or many retaliate ? What is the interpretation of threats, curses and rumored plots for his forcible abduction and prolonged torture ? They are the same in essence as Guiteau's own crime. He constituted himself the expounder and executioner of the Law. He insolently erected his individual will above every tribunal. Likewise do they, who long to turn their voluble imprecations into tearing him asunder with their own hands.

"Avenge not yourselves, but rather give place unto wrath: for it is written, Vengeance is Mine: I will repay, saith the Lord."

There are prominent religious Journals, which discountenance prayer for Guiteau : but we have not so "*learned Christ.*" Does loathing exempt from praying ? Who knows that this scorner is a castaway ? When and to whom has God said "*Let him alone !*" His name is in the book of "*the second death*"? Till then, be it ours to pray for him. God's rule is—"*To the uttermost.*" Did Christ's prayer, on the Cross for His murderers, palliate their guilt or obstruct justice ? Let no paltry quibbles, which make Courts contemptible, delay this traitor's doom : but let it fall upon him according to Law, and without one needless pang.

What are we now to say of the efficacy of Prayer? When, in the world's history, have so many entreated God for the same object? Amazing fact! From the pioneer's cabin and the sailor's deck, from hamlet and city, from kitchen and Court, from Synagogue, Cathedral and Church, has the same prayer, in divers languages, been pressed, times beyond human computation. The busy world has paused with upward look, every night and morning, by one heroic sufferer. Yet he is dead.

This event, in order to full vindication, may enwrap the remainder of the life of our race. Its cause, connection and consequences must abide, in vast degree, among God's "*secret things.*"

Let us remember that He has not unconditionally promised to bestow the precise favor implored. The granting of particular requests must always be limited by its suitableness to our real needs and to the government and character of God. No suppliant, individual or nation, can ever decide that question: hence, Faith invariably adds—THY WILL BE DONE!

God does answer Prayer.

> " He has never said to the seed of Jacob, Seek ye Me
> in vain."

The promise abides in honor—

> " Ask ; and it shall be given unto you."

But given in His own measure, mode and moment. Does He deny the special request? Then He bestows what is far better : for

> " He is able to do exceeding abundantly above all that
> we ask or think."

Christ's prayer for removal of the cup was unanswered as to terms, but answered as to temper. The Father's grant infinitely exceeded the Son's suit. He did "*taste of death:*" and lo! the unutterable glories of Redemption!

Likewise we deem it is to be with prayers for him, embalmed in a Nation's heart. The fair scroll of History, yet to be written, will show how much more was wrought

13

by him, and for him, in his death, than could have been by
his life. We, who prayed, "*are of yesterday.*" Our eye was
upon an inch of space and a second of time. The Uncre-
ated and Unchangeable One answered, as He looked upon
eternity.   Too soon, therefore, to trace the evo-
lution of His idea in our personal, yet universal, bereavement. Verdict as to his posthumous achievements could
now be only a happy guess. As well might one calculate
the length, volume and velocity of the Amazon by its foam-
ing eddy at his feet.

Nevertheless, even now we see that death has sealed,
with immortal lustre, the name of the twin-martyr of
Abraham Lincoln. Had JAMES A. GARFIELD lived, he
might have morally fallen ; but now amaranthine flowers are his garland. The world will never forget the intelligent cheerfulness, consummate courage and Christian
peace of his death-bed. Womanhood is ennobled ever-
more by his wife's self-mastery in her love's sacrifice.
This nation, awaking to loftier conception of the truth
that power resides rather in the ruled than the Ruler,
will henceforth hold its leaders, with gentle firmness, to a
truer ideal of patriotism and statesmanship.   North
and South again clasped hands, where Life and Death
wrestled so long. The races of men have been drawn
nearer together. We have had a ravishing hint of the
Brotherhood of Man.

> " Down the dark future, through long generations,
> The echoing sounds grow fainter and then cease :
> And like a bell, with solemn, sweet vibrations,
> I hear once more the voice of Christ say, PEACE !"

Sermon by the Pastor,

REV. HENRY SPELLMEYER, D. D.*

HELPFUL LESSONS FROM THE LIFE OF GARFIELD,

A Sermon to Young Men.

Text—"He being dead yet speaketh."—*Hebrews* xi: 4.

"I have planted four saplings in these woods. I leave them in your care." So spake a man to his weeping wife, concerning his four children, when, out in Orange, Ohio, at the age of thirty-three, he felt that he must die.

He had fought the fire that threatened to destroy his home and household, and conquered that, but now he had met that enemy no man can vanquish, and Death soon conquered him.

I am to speak to you, young men, to-night, of one of these saplings, to explain as best I can its rapid and remarkable growth, so wide spread at the last, that fifty millions of people found beneath it shelter. I am to present some helpful lessons from the life of our late President, that being dead, he yet may speak words, which shall become an inspiration to you.

First, I ask what special chance had Mr. Garfield at the beginning?

The impression very generally prevails that success in life is dependent upon the start, and that the difference between those who win and those who lose is, that the one had a better chance than the other. Some call it Fortune

* This Sermon is based on notes used at the time of delivery, and may not be an exact reproduction.

115

—a sort of imaginary divinity, like Tyche of the Greeks—
from whose cornucopia blessings are scattered blindly,
without right or reason. Others call it Genius—a heaven
born quality, which predestines a man's success despite all
obstacles. The fact is that genius may exist without great
common sense, persistent application, and dogged perseverance, and that the commoner virtues practised by an
earnest plodding spirit are often better than the brightest
genius. Buffon defines genius as "patience." Newton
describes it as "industry and patient thought." You will
find that the men who have brought great things to pass
in this world, have been men, not so much of great gifts as
of great devotion to their calling. The man you have most
to fear in the race in life, is he who does everything with
all his might, and plods on, until he brings everything he
does to its highest possible perfection.

I fail to discover any great "fortune" or "genius" in the
case of Mr. GARFIELD. In fact as the world would say, the
chances were against him. Very few of us began life so
humbly. His parents were emigrants to the West, and
poor. Their house was built of logs, consisting of two
rooms below, and a garret above. There was no school
near by, and the church was three miles away. There
were no books at hand, and few neighbors from whom to
borrow them. His father was dead. The training of the
household devolved upon a lonely woman. The little plot
of ground was mortgaged. Such were some of the external
conditions surrounding the child-life of JAMES A. GARFIELD,
well nigh fifty years ago.

To be true to history it must be recorded that Mr. GAR-
FIELD had scarcely the ordinary chance of the average
American child, at the beginning.

There were, however, two endowments with which his
early life was blessed. The first was a good mother. The
second was a good constitution.

I must speak my eulogy this hour of the widow who,
with four fatherless children, began life anew in that
Western wild. Well enough did she obey the injunction of
the dying father to take care of them. If the ground was

not fenced in, and the wheat exposed, it was she, with Thomas, then nine years old, who split the needed rails, and protected the crop against intruders. If the land was mortgaged, it was she who shrewdly sold fifty acres and paid the mortgage, reserving thirty acres free and clear, as her own. If the children needed clothes, it was she who bought the sheep and sheared them, carded the wool and wove the cloth, and with true womanly skill made them. If they needed shoes, it was she who made clothes for the shoemaker's children, while he in payment made shoes for hers. If there was no school near home, it was she who gave a corner of her own estate, had a school house built, where, on split logs for seats, her own children and others, could study the rudiments of their mother tongue. If the Church was three miles away, it was she who brought it near, by establishing Divine worship in the old log school house on the Sabbath day. If the thoughts of James turned toward life at sea, as well they might, with Lake Erie spread out before his eyes, it was she who brought him books to divert his mind, called the preacher in to tell him of the outside world, saved by the closest economy seventeen dollars, and when her strategy was all expended, gave it to him, and urged him to attend the Seminary, where he laid the foundation of that scholarship, which gave him high place among the savans of his time.

It was therefore no wonder, that after his inauguration as President, the first act of his was to turn and give a kiss to his aged mother who stood beside him, as a token of profound filial devotion and gratitude.

It *is* a blessed endowment, young men, to be honored with a good mother. Good men generally have good mothers. The mother of George Washington was "pious, pure and true." And of her, whose son has a place in the heart of the people beside that of the Father of his country, we delight to say the same.

A second blessing in the life of Mr. GARFIELD was a good constitution.

His parents gave it to him, in part, as a birth-right, and the life out in the clearing finished his physical training.

He was as fine a specimen of physical hardihood as ever
came out cf an American home. Think of those eighty
days of struggle against death; of the torrid temperature
in which he suffered; of the repeated incisions and prob-
ings; of that dreadful journey on the hottest day of the
year of two hundred and fifty miles in seven hours! Only
a man of remarkable vitality could have endured so much.

Young men, the way to be strong is to save your strength.
Mr. GARFIELD did not do violence to his body, by irregu-
larity of life. He did not poison it with alcohol. He was
never known as "a fast young man." He never sowed
wild oats. He chopped wood. He toiled along the canal.
He swung the scythe in haying time. He laid for himself
a broad foundation of muscle and fibre.

But what more had JAMES A. GARFIELD at the beginning? A good mother, and a good constitution counted
everything in. He was not "a genius." He was not fon-
dled on the lap of Fortune. He was not lifted by loving
friends into power. Money was not his inheritance. The
chances were against him from the first. And yet he arose
like the eagle from the ground, to a lofty place. No man
ever died over whom greater multitudes mourned. The
bells of the world tolled his funeral knell, and three hundred millions of people bowed their heads in tears, when
he gave up the fight.

I hold up his life and character before you, as a worthy
model for your life, young men, to show that we are not
creatures of circumstance altogether, but that on the free
soil of America we may grow into power without auspicious surroundings, build up a noble manhood by the use
of energy and the genius of honest, plodding toil, rise to
be a royal chieftain by the right of intrinsic merit, and yet
be true to one's home, and mother, one's self and God!

What then were the chief causes of Mr. GARFIELD's success in life?

It is true that success is traceable to little things, quite
as much as great things. There is no fixed and invariable
rule by which men succeed. Yet there were certain qualities about this man that may be suggestive and inspira-
tional to every man.

1. James A. Garfield had an *aim* in life.

It was not to be a Preacher, though he was. Nor a Teacher, nor a Soldier, nor a Senator, though he was in all these positions of honor. He did not, forty years ago, make up his mind to be President of the United States. If so, he might, like others, have degenerated into a mere intriguer and scheming politician.

He seems to have had no specific aim, except to fit himself by a thorough and broad education, by a perfect performance of every duty, for any position to which Providence and his country might call him.

Here he made a broad and important distinction. Many men seek to fit themselves for some special position, and go into the market as a candidate for that honor alone. This they call their aim. Mr. Garfield labored to secure such a breadth of mental and moral culture, as to make office and honor seek him. It must be said of him that his honors were thrust upon him. If he had an aim it was rather to have such a roundness of qualification as to win distinction anywhere. Those who knew, said he would have been a famous General had he remained in the army. Certain it is that he was a distinguished Senator. In a few short months he proved himself a worthy occupant of the Presidential Chair.

His aim was to be a man full of knowledge, which is power, and to make himself felt everywhere.

His early struggles for an education show that this was what his heart was set upon. He walked ten miles to the Seminary. With his two cousins he rented a room in the unpainted house of a poor widow woman, and there he lived. The Academy was two stories high, with a library of one hundred and fifty volumes. Daniel Branch was Principal and his wife Assistant. Such were his advantages. Between terms he did haying in the field, and like his Master worked at the trade of a carpenter. And thus, now teaching, now working with his hands, and always studying, he fitted himself for college, and by an almost unaccountable economy, had a saving of three hundred and fifty dollars when he entered.

In the spring of 1854 he wrote to the Presidents of Yale, Brown and Williams' Colleges. Each one answered that he was far enough advanced in his studies to enter the Junior class. President Hopkins of Williams', added, "If you come here, we shall do what we can for you." That sympathetic line decided him. To Williams' he went. His aim was to have an education!

Years afterward President Hopkins, truly said, "He was not *sent* to college ; he *came!*" That, my hearers, is the root of the matter. Most boys are *sent* to college, sent to business, sent to a trade. They go because they are thrust out, and pressure is upon them. Mr. GARFIELD went because he wanted to. He had an aim!

Too many of you young men, lead aimless lives. You live as the birds live, day by day. You go the round of your daily toil like the horse in the tread mill. Some of you will never come to much, because you have no lofty, well-defined aim. Therefore I exhort you to broaden your knowledge! Make yourselves master-workmen! Instead of waiting for something, bring something to pass! Strike so hard as to command the attention of the world! Aim to have so broad and general a fitness, that you will never need to seek a place ; the place will always seek you!

2. But in the character of General GARFIELD there was not only aim, but intense and persistent application.

I need not assure you that purpose without perseverance is an engine without steam. The men who succeed in bringing things to pass, are those who keep at it day by day, hour by hour, moment by moment! It is stroke upon stroke that makes the angel out of marble. It is drop after drop that wears holes in the hardest stone. And patient, persevering, perpetual toil ensures victory anywhere.

It is told of Carey, known in his days as "the cobbler's son," and by us as the great Missionary, that when a boy in attempting to climb a tree, he fell, and broke his arm. But the first thing he did after he recovered, was to go out and climb that tree.

And Mr. GARFIELD always did what he tried to do. It was at Hiram Institute he took up the task, for the first time, of Latin translation. Many of you know that in translating Latin, it is necessary to know something of Latin construction. The noun may begin the sentence, and the verb that comes next may be at the end of it. So JAMES GARFIELD began his task of translating a few lines of Cæsar. First from a glossary he selected a meaning for each word, and wrote these down. The result was confusion. Then he wrote a meaning for each Latin word on separate pieces of paper and tried to adjust them, as one does with a word puzzle, but it was confusion still. At last, just as the morning hours were creeping on, he discovered that each Latin word had several meanings, and by selecting the right one, translation was comparatively easy.

That was an important victory. His course of life was marked by this characteristic—doing what he proposed to do. He was quick to seize opportunity, ready to adapt himself to his surroundings, and so sure to surmount all obstacles, that in no position was he found wanting.

He was not found wanting when, at twenty-eight years of age, he was elected State Senator. Legislation was a new field, and politics a new experience. Yet he applied himself at once, and because he proposed to rise, did rise, until, for rare tact, culture, and eloquence, he was unexcelled in the Senate chamber of Ohio. A report on education, bristling with statistics, another on weights and measures, and one most comprehensive and reliable, on the geological survey of Ohio, were some of the first fruits of his labors.

Afterward he was called to the army. Now remember, he had no military training. He had not studied at West Point. He was simply a State Senator, a cultured gentleman, a patriot. But he gathered a regiment together, was commissioned as its Colonel, applied himself to his new task, by persistent study mastered the situation, and after a few short, sharp, brilliant engagements, won the title of "Major-General" at the battle of Chickamauga. It was of him General Rosecrans then said: "He possesses the energy and instinct of a great commander."

General GARFIELD was a young man when he entered
Congress. In the house were Washburn and Stevens, Bout-
well, of Masachusetts, and Fenton, of New York; Davis
and Dawes, English, of Connecticut, and Pendleton, of
Ohio; Randall and Windom, Voorhees, of Indiana, and
Wood, of New York. There were also James G. Blaine
and Roscoe Conkling.

Here was a fine chance for the young officer, untried in
national affairs, to test his metal, and if too rash or indo-
lent, to be laughed at and hooted down.

The currency question came before the people. General
GARFIELD began thoroughly to prepare himself on that important subject. As usual, if he were not ready, he applied
himself until he was ready. He read every book he could
find. He studied all that English history had to reveal.
He learned French so far at least that he might read
treatises upon the subject in the original. He armed
himself like a skilled general, and on the 16th of March,
1866, made a speech on the public debt and specie payment, which laid the foundation for a wise and honest
financial system.

Young men, there never arose an emergency in the career of Mr. GARFIELD but that he arose to meet it. He was
not a creature of circumstances, so much as the conqueror
of circumstances. He was not afraid of hard and unexpected work. He had no more hours in the day than you
and I have, but he used the time we waste. He carried an
edition of some classic in his pocket, and was often found
in his tent, during his army life, reading it. If we cannot
admit that he had marvellous genius, he had wonderful
powers of application. He had the genius of rising early
and toiling late, of using every moment as it flew by, of
absorbing information from everything he saw.

He won, young men, as the spider wins, by working
away between the corners *until* its web has bridged them.
He won, as General Grant took Richmond, by "pegging
away." He did not, as so many do, wait for the iron to
get hot. He made the iron hot, by patient, persistent,
striking.

3. A third element of inspiration in the life of Mr. GAR-
FIELD was his courage.

He had physical courage. Like Lord Nelson he seems
never to have known what fear was, and like John Knox
he did not fear "a face of clay."

I know no better illustration of this than when with a
boat loaded with provisions, he started up the Big Sandy
toward his camp. A severe freshet had occurred, the
waters raged like Niagara's rapids about the vessel, the
channel was sixty feet deep, the tree tops along the bank
were almost covered, and the boat making but three miles an
hour, trembled and shook before the flood. Every man. was
afraid to proceed but one. He grasped the deserted wheel
and for forty out of forty-eight hours stood at his post.
When his boat was forced ashore it was he who lowered
the little boat, and with rope and windlass, drew it off.
He thought not of his own danger, in his over mastering
desire to take food to his men. His courage failed not!
And at nine o'clock, on a Monday morning, amid tumultuous cheering he entered camp, by his own unparalleled
bravery having saved the command from starvation.

But Mr. GARFIELD had moral courage also. Few men
have this double blessing.

The boy who would not drive his boat into the lock
ahead of another, because it was not his right, grew to
be a man of the same sort of principle.

President GARFIELD had convictions, and while he was
tolerant with others who had convictions too, he had profound respect for his own.

He was too bold and independent, to be a politician.
He was not careful to be on the side of majorities. He
was more loyal to himself than to his constituency, and
was more apt to form than to follow popular opinion.
"There is one man," said he ; "whom I must always live
with. That man should so respect me, as to be a pleasant
and agreeable companion. And that man, whose respect
I must secure for my peace, is JAMES A. GARFIELD."

Hence, when the army of Rosecrans for six long months
had lain idle at Murfreesboro, the order came from Wash-

ington to move on. Every one of the seventeen generals opposed it. Then GARFIELD arose alone, argued against them, convinced his chief that they were wrong, and the army did move, and GARFIELD was proven a wise counsellor.

Rarely do we find a man in the heat of political contest more solicitous to be right than to be popular. This distinguishes the statesman from the politician, and is a supreme test of one's courage. General GARFIELD had this independent character.

When the tariff question came up, he wrote : " You know my views on the tariff. My own course is chosen. And it is quite probable it will throw me out of public life."

Another great question arose. He wrote: "I have examamined the testimony and reports. I shall vote against the measure. It will probably cost me my political life."

Those are courageous words, young men!

I know the opinion prevails that one cannot be a public officer and always remain true to personal convictions. And I admit that few can be, not because it is impossible, but because they lack moral courage. Public honor in this land depends so much upon the people that public men are apt to inquire first what the people want, and afterward, with a wonderful harmony, announce their own opinion, and so be loyal to their constituency.

Some politicians undoubtedly owe a great deal to their constituency. Possibly more than to merit. But from this platform, and as a moral teacher, I declare to you my conviction, that no public officer has a right to accept favor from a constituency, who, *therefore*, expect to bridle his tongue, control his hand, and violate his conscience.

The man who holds the rifle is the man whose finger should be on the trigger! Truth to principle is tantamount to truth to party.

That was the course of our lamented President. In his first debate in congress, regarding the seizure and confiscation of rebel property, his opponent taunted him by asking "if he would break the constitution to aggravate the punishment of the traitor." With undaunted courage, intense loyalty to his country, and withal profound conviction, he replied: "I do not see that this bill breaks the constitution. If the gentleman can show me that it overleaps the constitution, I will vote against it with him, though every member of my party votes for it—that makes no difference to me."

I hold up this life to you, therefore, for its courage, as well as for its aim and application.

You must learn to respect your own opinion, and while I warn you against narrowness and bigotry, I would incite you to a bold and manly independence. You pay too much for popularity, if it costs you your conscience! You have no right to represent others, if you misrepresent yourself! It is a great achievement often to utter aloud two words: "No, sir!" That may be the test, the anvil, on which you shall be made or broken! Be content sometimes to be a minority before men, remembering that you are always in the majority with God and righteousness on your side!

4. But the crowning virtue in the life of Mr. Garfield was his Christian character.

Character is power. It gives power to purpose, power to perseverance, power to courage. Let a man have the Ten Commandments stamped upon his forehead and he will be a power anywhere.

Benjamin Franklin was a poor speaker, yet everyone crowded to hear him, because of his known integrity of character.

Montaigne during the wars in France was the only man who dared to keep his castle gates unbarred. His personal character was a greater protection to him than a regiment of armed men.

Mr. Garfield was a man of character. The biographer of most great men is forced to pass rapidly over some part of their history. He comes to a black spot, and shrewdly draws the fold of the outer garment over it, when he paints the picture. There is some subtraction to be made from the sum total of the life. Milton was a great poet, *but* he was blind. Naaman was a great captain, *but* he was a leper. Paul was a great apostle, *but* he had a thorn in his flesh. William Pitt was a great prodigy, but at forty-seven died of a broken heart.

I can find neither marked physical nor moral defect in the life of our lamented chieftain. He was "every inch a man." There is nothing to cover up, no great weakness to hide under garments of charity.

He was a Christian not only in name, but in truth. He was converted at sixteen years of age. From that hour the vision of God never faded from before his eyes. He says, "That settled canal, lake, sea, everything." Genuine conversion does throw a new light upon everything.

When he came home from school one Fall, after hard work in the field and hard study in the class, he had but sixpence left, but that he dropped in the contribution box on the Sabbath day.

Seated on the hill side near the college one day near even-tide, GARFIELD took out his pocket Testament and said, "Boys, I am accustomed to read a chapter with my absent mother every night. Shall I read aloud?" He read, and a class-mate led in prayer, while God's stars crept softly out, and their faces grew bright as they looked down.

President GARFIELD was never ashamed of his religion. A member of a church recognizing no distinction between clergy and laity, he often took part in religious meetings, preached in many pulpits, presided at the Lord's table, and inside the last three years lectured in Washington, on "The Evidences of Christianity."

When every noble temple of the Capital of the Nation bade him welcome, as a bright example of the value of early Christian training, and humble, unostentatious piety, he chose the church of his boyhood, a very unpretentious structure, from which on the first day of the week he was rarely absent.

When, in 1876, his "precious little boy" died, instead of an array of brilliant and distinguished associates, he wrote his pastor, " to come and read and pray at six o'clock with a few of our brethren and sisters" . . . "in the hope of the Gospel which is so precious in this affliction."

So I am not surprised that on the 2d day of July, 1881, when the assassin's bullet severed every thread of life but one, and he, face to face himself with death, heard Doctor Sunderland say as he held his hand: "Mr. President, you are in the hands of the God you have long trusted;" he answered: "I know it, Doctor; I believe in God, and trust myself in his hands."

Thus he fell!

The ocean surf dashed against the shore at Elberon, and nearer and nearer, like the tide, came the life of our loved President to the Eternal Shore. He sat by the window. Doctor Bliss sat near. Mrs. Garfield in a room adjoining, in soft, and plaintive tones sang a stanza of that hymn of faith, commencing:

> "Guide me, O Thou Great Jehovah!"

The President turned his weary eyes away from the sea, and inquired of the Doctor: "Is that Crete?" "Yes," he answered; "it is Mrs. Garfield." "Open the door a little! softly! that I may hear her sing!" The door was opened,

> "When I tread the verge of Jordan,
> Bid my anxious fears subside;
> Bear me through the swelling current;
> Land me safe on Canaan's side."

and the tears fell fast, and eyes grew bright once again, as he said—"Glorious, Bliss, isn't it?"

Thus he died!

So to-night, young men, I place before you two characters for your choice. The one I will seat here on my left. Look at him well! He is a man *without* aim. He is a crazed adventurer, possessed of the fatal idea that the world owes him a living, and therefore leads an aimless life—a lawyer, a lecturer, a preacher, a politician—a mere thistle-down wafted about by every breath of air!

I show you a man *without* application, in whose vocabulary, plodding and perseverance do not appear, a human sponge, a mere excrescence on the body politic, a man

who seldom paid for what he got, and owes the world
more than he can ever repay, a mere hanger-on to society
like the young rag-a-muffin who steals rides on cars and
stages—a man who sought office without ever deserving it,
and is simply the spoils system gone to seed!

I show you a man *without* courage, a cowardly, pusillan-
imous villain, whose head would probably never have got-
ten turned but for the perversity and wickedness of his
heart, a man without creed, and conscience, with no aim,
no application, no courage, *no* character, the direct anti-
podes of Mr. GARFIELD, for whom it takes a righteous man
to pray—to-night pacing his little cell, carrying the anath-
emas of the world upon his shoulders, whose very name is
odium, and whose body hardly merits a place of burial in
the cemeteries of a nation he has so dreadfully wronged!

Now on my right hand, I place before you another character. Look at *him*, young men!

He was a canal boy, then a student, then a Senator, then
a General, then a Congressman, then President of fifty millions of people.

His mausoleum is the heart of a nation.

There is not a language in which prayer was not uttered
for his recovery, nor a soil on which tears did not fall at
his death.

The sun in his circuit this day has shone on no city, or
country place, where heads were not bowed down over his
departure.

Mr. Blaine by careful estimate declares that three hundred millions will weep at his grave.

Three European courts—Great Britain, Belgium, and
Spain, an unprecedented fact in royal etiquette, are in
mourning to-day.

The Emperor William, and Prince Bismarck, send auto-
graph letters expressive of their sympathy.

The King of Italy cables " profound sorrow for the death
of a chief magistrate of a great people, and our execration
of the crime of which he was a victim."

Sir Moses Montefiori telegraphs to have prayers offered
in the four holy cities of Palestine.

In London, English flags hang at half mast: commerce even has stopped to heave a sigh: the exchanges are closed: the bells of the churches are tolling: prayers arise from Westminster Abbey for the stricken family: England's Queen orders an elegant floral wreath and lays it upon his coffin: Drs. Parker and Newman Hall speak to a mournful throng in City Temple, and Antoinette Stirling, dressed in black, (strong personification of our stricken Republic,) sang "Beyond the smiling and the weeping:" while in Exeter Hall are scenes, the like of which England never saw before.

Bishop Simpson speaks. His words are calm, pathetic, paternal. The vast audience feel their power. Had not England's Queen listened to the pulse beat of our President for eighty days? Had not messages flashed daily under the sea? When Queen Lucy Garfield left her husband for the last time, did not Queen Victoria cable those memorable words: "May God bless and comfort you, as He alone can?" And shall so worthy a son of America allow such sympathy to pass unrecognized?

Bishop Simpson, when the enthusiasm was at its highest point, simply said, with indescribable feeling, "God bless Queen Victoria for her womanly sympathy and queenly courtesy."

Then the audience arose. Men shouted and waved; women wept and smiled. There never was just such a scene. England and America never came so close to each other before.

The whole world drew nearer together around the death bed of JAMES A. GARFIELD!

Which, then, of these two characters will you choose, young man? Which shall be your model, Guiteau or GARFIELD?

14

·

So fully, so appropriately, and eloquently have the gentlemen to whom you have listened interpreted the feelings
of our saddened hearts, that little further need be, or can
be, said. It is fit that the people, believing in and enjoy-
ing the largest liberty consistent with law and order, should
join in giving expression to the common sentiment which
pervades every mind, when the head of the government,
the very representative of regulated law, the very embodiment of organized order, falls the unprovoking victim of a
crime, atrocious and unparalleled. When the citadel of
law is attacked, what more natural than that we, its chosen
watchmen, should be aroused; and though, alas! too late
to shield him, should rally round the fallen chieftain whose
dancing plume made him but too shining a mark. We meet
in common sadness to join our voices to the swelling chorus of universal sympathy. We do not meet to pay homage
to a hero like those familiar to the classic period of the
world, half God, half man; not one of those huge, dim,
mysterious shapes of which we catch occasional glimpses
through the murky atmosphere of mediæval history, but
simply to pay our tribute of respect to the memory of a
great brave-hearted, just-minded, country-loving citizen;
one of the foremost names of the world to be sure, yet one
whom nearly every person in the audience has seen, and
one personally known to many of us. President GARFIELD's
life is not a matter of tradition. His character is not great
because not understood. There is no mythic greatness
about him. We venerate his name because we knew and
understood him; we love his life because we saw it unfold
day by day and year by year; and our hearts yet bleed with
all the fulness of overwhelming grief, as the tolling bells

recall to us the sad intelligence that from beside the many sounding sea that brave spirit had taken its upward flight, and that but yesterday, beneath the splendid dome that rears itself above the fair proportions of the proud Capitol, lay the remains of that heroic man, as cold, as silent, and as lifeless as the marble statues of the immortal fathers of the Republic that stood like watchful sentinels around him.

The life of the late President is to my mind the most striking illustration in all our history—of the wonderful possibilities of American life. It ought to stir like the blast of a trumpet the hot impulsive blood of every generous boy in the land. His life is an argument that batters down the fictitious partitions of social caste and aristocratic pretensions : it is an argument that gives force and illustration and reality to the declaration of the equality of man. As we have looked upon his manly form and strong, fair countenance, somewhat Teutonic in its mould, we could well believe that he traced his lineage through his Welsh ancestors back to far off dwellers of the black forests by the German Ocean, that ancient home of the English speaking people, to that broad shouldered, fierce blue-eyed, yellow haired race, no one of whom, the historian records, was ever known to cut off his thumb to avoid the service of Mars, and who drove back for ever to the soft shores of the Mediteranean the Imperial armies of the all-accomplished Roman. It is but natural that the descendants of a race so brave and warlike should be found fighting beneath the dykes in the long, bitter and doubtful struggles of the Lowlands ; it is but natural that when peace failed to bring the liberty they sought, that we find them among the hardy pilgrims of New England ; it is but natural that we find one, if not two of them, among the " embattled farmers" whose shots echoed round the world from Concord bridge ; but natural, sir, bearing the blood of such an ancestry in his veins, that he whose death to-day casts a gloom over the greatest and fairest portions of the earth, and clothes in mourning the sorrowing court of the proudest nation of the world, should have left the quiet

walks of a student and professional life, so congenial to
him, at the call of the imperilled and endangered liberties
of his country.

Born a half century ago, on the then far frontier, in the
narrowest conditions of poverty, reared amid the rude
manners of a half civilization, without the early advantages of books, or the society of the cultivated, surrounded
by circumstances and conditions more repressive to his
generous and manly impulses than those which surround
many a boy in this very city; yet through all the vicissitudes of that plastic period of his life, through all the
discouragements which "low birth and iron fortune,"
those "twin jailers of the daring heart," threw about
him, through all his varying fortunes, through all the
fluctuations of party politics, he never for a moment lost
heart, never once violated the traditional honesty of the
blood of his Puritan ancestry, and he became at last the
eloquent champion of a great cause, the trusted leader of
a great party, the chosen head of a great Government, and
I believe he had inaugurated that policy which would have
made him the recognized pacificator of the irritating animosities and sectional jealousies of a great people. He
was a statesman without a statesman's craftiness; he was
a politician without a politician's duplicity; he was a
Christian without pretensions; he had the qualities of a
great and successful ruler, without pride and without
ostentation; and over all the obstacles which adverse fortune had reared, and which lay in cold obstruction across
his path, he came to the great office in which he died better equipped to discharge its high and its delicate duties
than any of his great predecessors, with the possible exception of John Quincy Adams, who was specially trained at
home and abroad for the political service of his country.
Eminent as the late President was as a scholar, soldier,
statesman, orator, great as he was in every station of life,
he was greater yet than all, in the sublime heroism of his
death.

Somewhere I have read a legend connected with the
early history of Ireland, that in the beautiful lake of Mun-

ster there were two islands, upon one of which death could
not enter. But age, sickness and all the wearying infir-
mities of life were admitted there, and so ceaselessly did
these remorseless agents work, that the worn out inhabi-
tants, tired of life, learned to look upon the opposite island
as a haven of repose, and longed for the hour to launch
their bark upon the gloomy waters, and be borne to its
peaceful shore and be at rest. So I have thought that the
President from his bed of weary suffering, realizing the
impossibility of recovery, must have often turned toward
that peaceful, happy shore which his firm faith pictured to
him beyond life's stormy sea, and must have been glad
when the stern old ferryman bore him over the dark flood
to its calm eternal repose. And though our eyes become
misty, and our hearts grow heavy, in the recollection of
the circumstances and surroundings of his death, his devoted wife and his dear, old, gray-haired mother, it is perhaps fittest that he should die now at the zenith of his
fame, in this season of the year itself appropriately sad
with the evidences on every side of nature's decay. When

> " The withered banners of the corn are still,
> And gathered fields are growing strangely wan,
> While death, poetic death, with hands that color
> What'er they touch, weaves in the Autumn wood,
> Her tapestries of gold and brown."

It is perhaps best that he should die as he did, in that
splendid altitude, to show the world how a brave man
should die.

But from out the gloom that shrouds our hearts, let us
remember in his own words, that "God reigns, and the
government at Washington still lives," that the loss of no
one man, however great and distinguished, is sufficient to
impart even a momentary jar to the movements of the
majestic machinery of representative republican government.

And so following the mournful cortege from the lofty
scene of the President's last ambition, to the spot where
he himself chose to rest, in the heart of his much loved

"western reserve," surrounded by his neighbors and his early friends, in whose keeping his fame will be secure, and as we hear the kindly earth close over him, we may well say of him, as was said a quarter of a century ago of a very distinguished but dissimilar character :

> " Oh voice from which all men their omens drew,
> Oh iron heart to true occasion true,
> Oh fallen at length that tower of strength,
> That stood four square to all the winds that blew."

South Bergen Reformed Church, Jersey City Heights.

Sermon by the Pastor,

REV. HENRY M. COX.

"And the king said unto his servants, ' Know ye not that there is a prince and a great man fallen this day in Israel?'" 2 *Sam.*, *iii* : 38.

What a mournful significance do these words possess as we study history in the light of Providence. And how beautifully does the sweet Psalmist of Israel voice the language of our hearts to-day, as he stands at Abner's grave to pronounce the last sad tribute of honor to his memory. Then too, had an assassin's hand been lifted against a political and military chieftain, and by that single act of cowardice and madness a whole nation had been plunged in sorrow. Then too, the heart of royalty was melted. David wept, and David's people clothed with him in sackcloth, poured forth their tears of sympathy, while they sat together in silence and in sorrow to meditate upon the life and character of the dead, and to learn the lesson of a great national bereavement.

With a feeling akin to that, but more profound and universal, I doubt not, than ancient Israel knew, we come to-day to give expression to our grief, to join in the general voice of lamentation, and to hear what God the Lord shall speak to us in this dark hour of sorrow. I ask you then, to ponder for a little, the sad announcement suggested by this royal interrogative : " Know ye not," my brethren, " that there is a prince and a great man fallen this day in Israel ? " Do we need these emblems of mourning which we see about us, to emphasize the solemn truth, or to add to the bitterness of our grief ? The midnight cry is still ringing in our ears, and the tones of that sad, sad requiem

217

rung out from yonder tower, will linger long as memory lasts. They told us in language eloquent, though inarticulate, that he whom we loved was dead, and that our honored magistrate had passed at length, into the silent land.

It is only natural, at an hour like this, while we pause to give expression to our grief, that we should try to form some estimate, at least, of the character of him whose loss is so universally deplored.

To say that President GARFIELD was simply a great man whom the people loved, would be doing but faint justice to his memory. But consider

I. WHAT IT WAS THAT MADE HIM GREAT IN THE ESTIMATION OF HIS PEOPLE AND OF THE WORLD.

"A year ago," says a London paper, in commenting on the death of the President, "Not one Englishman in a thousand had heard Gen. GARFIELD's name. To-day there will scarcely be one Englishman in a thousand who will not read of his death with regret as real and as deep as if he had been a ruler of our own." We might say then, that it was the *representative character* he bore as Chief Magistrate of the Nation which made him the prince and the great man that he was among us. Exalted from a very lowly position to the highest official trust within the gift of the American people, if he had possessed no personal qualifications whatever, for the responsible duties of his office, the call of his countrymen to preside over the destinies of our Republic, would alone have made him great. But that fact, important as it may seem to us, and as it was undoubtedly in the estimation of the world, was no more than a simple incident in the life of one who brought to the proud position which he occupied, such qualities of mind and heart as would have made him conspicuous in any sphere to which the providence of God had called him.

It is one of the peculiarities of our American political life that mediocrity so often takes rank with genius. Trained statesmen are not ordinarily in demand even when the highest offices under the government are to be filled, and long years of faithful public service have sometimes been regarded as a hindrance rather than a help to the political aspirations of men. But what patriot did not recognize with satisfaction, in the late national election, an exception to that absurd rule which has so long obtained in American politics?

"Some men," it has been said, "are born great, some *achieve* greatness, while others have greatness thrust upon them." General GARFIELD was one of those who by his patient industry, and untiring devotion to principle and duty, was enabled to *achieve* no small share of the public honor and esteem which he enjoyed. The mere accident of birth was not such as to excite even a remote suspicion of future greatness. But what are the accidents of birth in a land like this, where the avenues to distinction and fortune are open alike to all who have the pluck and purpose, and the natural or acquired fitness to attain the object of their ambition? With a wealth of intellectual power and resource such as few possess, a mind broad in its natural endowments, and trained by long years of careful culture, he entered upon the duties of his last and highest office as one "thoroughly furnished" for that supreme responsibility.

He had won a reputation for statesmanship long before the voice of the nation fixed upon him as its most conspicuous representative. In the halls of Congress, in the popular assemblies of the people, in the Council Chambers of the government, his name and presence have been familiar for more than a score of years. Few men have cultivated more assiduously the arts of eloquence; none ever used the gift of speech to nobler purpose.

That little episode in his life which occurred shortly after the assassination of the lamented Lincoln, and which has been brought so vividly to mind in the light of recent events, when from the steps of the Treasury in New York, he quelled the rising tumult of the mob, by some simple, earnest word, is only an illustration of the power with which he so often seemed to sway the minds and hearts of

his countrymen at will. As an acknowledged leader, for
many years in the House of Representatives at Washington,
he afterwards found ample scope for the exercise of his
noble gift. It would be folly to deny that during that long
period of public service the President was an active and
ardent partizan. But who that is familiar with his public
utterances, has not also been impressed with that tone of
lofty patriotism which subordinated party to principle, and
made the glory of our common country the chief aim of
his political manhood? There was a Roman dignity and
simplicity about him suggestive of the very highest type
of character which prevailed in the palmiest days of the
ancient Republic. He might have rivalled Tully in his
matchless power of thought and speech, but in his life what
elements of moral and of spiritual force there were, which
combined to magnify his greatness and his glory, and to
render him, apart from these outward adornments, a very
prince in our political Israel.

From the very moment when the fatal blow was struck,
on that memorable July morning, through all the weary
weeks of suffering and of pain, what an abundant testimony has been afforded us of his *sublime heroism.* Some
one has well said that highly as we may have appreciated
his character, "we never knew before what manner of man
he was" who had been called to the helm of State for such
an hour as this. Even his military career, characterized
as it was by so many evidences of courage and bravery,
bears no comparison with that brief but bitter experience
in which suffering patience was so sorely tried, and the
nobler spirit of the man achieved its grandest triumph.
It is not always amid the din and uproar of the battle-field
that the heroic element in human nature finds its truest
expression, and we may well believe that when the name
of Chickamauga has faded from our memories, the record
of that eighty days' battle with the last enemy, and of the
heroic way in which our martyr President advanced to
death, will live enshrined securely and forever within the
nation's heart.

But President GARFIELD was distinguished for a heroism of another sort, and to which we should hardly dare to attach less significance than to that of which we have already spoken. He possessed, in a very remarkable degree, what men have sometimes called "the courage of their convictions." His life, for this reason, was a moral power among political associates, and in the State and community with which all his interests were identified. A single incident, unimportant in itself, may yet serve to illustrate this somewhat unusual trait in the character of a public man. A fellow Member of Congress, too much addicted to the language of profanity, ventured on one occasion in GARFIELD's presence to express himself in unbecoming words. The sound grated harshly upon his ear, and after enduring it for a moment, he turned kindly towards the offender and mildly reproved the fault, only, however, to receive insult in return. But the language of that reproof was not without its influence, and the man who tells the story of himself, has added but another link to the chain of golden virtues which adorned the character of the illustrious dead.

Nor can we forget in our enumeration of his nobler qualities, that *tender* and *large hearted sympathy* which made him a prince among men, a Great Heart even in the estimation of his foes. No knight of old, even in the golden age of chivalry, was ever more valiant in fight, and at the same time, more courteous and considerate of the feelings of his adversary. Defeat would at any time have been more grateful to him than a victory foully or unfairly won. Do you recall that incident of his congressional career, when on the eve of an important debate in the Hall of Representatives he disclosed to a political opponent the entire line of argument which he proposed to pursue upon the morrow, lest by withholding that he should seem to place the other at a disadvantage? Or, can we fail now to appreciate the magnanimity which he displayed more recently, when another, who had felt compelled, reluctantly, to oppose the policy of the administration, expressed the hope that he might not be regarded as entertaining any personal hostility to-

wards him. " Personal feeling," was his reply; " why not
at all, my dear fellow !" as though it were impossible for
him to cherish in his heart an uncharitable thought even
towards an enemy.   And if the record of his public life
bears testimony to such a character as that, for generosity
and goodness, we are not surprised to find that in the home
circle and among the friends he loved, these finer feelings
of his nature should have found their freest scope.   As
husband, father, son, loving and beloved, the memories
which are now associated with his name have already become a priceless part of the nation's heritage.   But when
we stop to ask ourselves the question :   What, after all,
was the crowning glory of that illustrious life ? we may
almost hear the answer in the voice which is speaking to
us now from beyond the portals of the tomb : " Not in the
proud position which he occupied as the nation's Chief ;
not in those heroic elements of character which made him
a prince and a great man in the estimation of the world ;
not in that consummate ability which he brought to the
administration of his high and holy trust ; not in that large
and tender heart which willingly or unwillingly provoked
our love—but *in his simple faith in God* we find that basal
element of character upon which rested all those outward
adornments of the heart and of the life which made him
conspicuous and beloved among his fellows."   In the long
catalogue of eminent men who have been exalted to the
Chief Magistracy of the nation, there were but two, who at
the time, bore openly and confessedly, the Christian name
—one, the Father of his country ; the other, he whose
loss the nation mourns to-day.   In his early manhood,
GARFIELD gave his heart to God, and from that hour of
consecration has never failed to witness a good confession
of his faith before the world.   Like Washington, he was a
praying man.   And as the oak at Cambridge, beneath
whose spreading branches the Father of his country poured
out his soul before God in an hour of national peril was a
monument to his piety and devotion, so that mount of
prayer at Greylock at which young GARFIELD led the devotions of a little band of collegians, will seem to us like holy

ground, and more than ever now that the leading spirit of the occasion has passed within the veil, and the spot with its hallowed and delightful associations, alone remains as a precious reminder of a truth on which the Christian heart of the nation will delight to linger—that our President, from his youth, was a man of God, and that he loved to pray. That incident of his student life at Williams was no isolated example of a spirit of devotion to which he yielded but for a moment. It was characteristic of the man, and all his later life bears testimony to the extent and power of that profound religious sentiment by which he was actuated and controlled. It found expression often, in those little gatherings for prayer, in which he loved to mingle, and where the name and voice of Brother GARFIELD, as his fellow-worshipers were wont to call him, were so familiar.

It manifested itself not unfrequently, in his more public utterances also, forming indeed, the under-current of his whole life. Not less beautiful in this respect, are the occasional glimpses which have sometimes been afforded us of the President's home life. And these furnish, after all, the truest criterion of his Christian character. Family worship, in his household, was no unheard of thing, even while he occupied the Executive Mansion at Washington. And if a near friend, tarrying with him for a night, has wisely or unwisely, drawn aside the veil of that inner sanctuary, and revealed to us the spectacle of our Chief Magistrate, upon his knees in prayer before God, surrounded only by the members of that domestic circle which he loved, is it any wonder that we treasure up that scene also, as another of the precious memories associated with his Christian character and experience?

II. But there is another truth suggested by the language of the inspired penman which we are called upon to contemplate. This prince, this great man in Israel, has fallen.

In the prime of manhood, in the full maturity of his magnificent powers, he has been laid low by the assassin's stroke. Amid the prayers and the tears of his loyal people, that lofty spirit has returned to God who gave it, and to-morrow we follow him to the tomb. His name, his life, is but a memory now. But can any living words be more tender and appropriate than those which fell from our dead hero's lips, when under the shadow of a national calamity like that which has befallen us, in his own assassination, he rose in Congress, to pay his last tribute to Lincoln's memory? These were the words he uttered then:

"Oh, sir, there are times in the history of men and nations when they stand so near the veil that separates mortals and immortals, time from eternity, and men from their God, that they can almost hear the beating and feel the pulsations of the Infinite. Through such a time this nation has passed. When 250,000 brave spirits passed from the field of honor through that thin veil to the presence of God, and when at last its parting folds admitted that martyred President to the company of the dead heroes of the Republic, the nation stood so near the veil that the whispers of God were heard by the children of men."

God has spoken again to this great nation, not in whispers but in thunder tones, as when of old the word of the Almighty first wakened the echoes of Sinai. Bowing with trembling expectation at the sound of that same voice which again has shook the earth, we may hear ringing in our ears to-day, the first sentence of that eternal law : " *I* am the Lord thy God." The death knell of our martyred President was a call to penitence and prayer. Political wickedness in high places, by his death, has been rebuked, and the nation is once more reminded that there is a God in Israel whose kingly government demands her loyal rec-

ognition, and whose laws of righteousness and purity and
truth, are eternal and supreme. But God spake from
Sinai to a people whom he loved, and may we not hope
that the voice which speaks to us from out of the midst of
this dark, overhanging cloud, is the voice of that gracious
Providence which has exalted us from nothingness to
greatness, and which, in days that are passed, has made
even our national calamities to contribute to the strength
and permanency of our religious and political institutions?

The sad fact which we have been considering, is significant again, as it emphasizes the lesson of our national dependence upon the guiding and controlling power of that
unseen hand which shapes our destinies.

Strong as our confidence may be in the sober and patriotic sentiment which governs the popular mind, who can
contemplate without a shudder, the tremendous possibilities of even a momentary withdrawal of that beneficient
influence?

Should our present Chief Magistrate be overtaken by
such a catastrophe as that which has befallen his predecessor in office, for the first time in its history the nation
would be without a head, and with no constitutional power
even to fill the vacant chair, until the national legislature
could be convened. These thoughts, my brethren, need
not excite our fears, if they but enforce the wholesome
lesson they suggest, and drive us to our knees before the
God in whom we trust. But oh! how eloquently do they
call us now to the throne of the heavenly grace, that we
may obtain mercy and find help in the dark hour of our
need.

One more brief word and I have done.

We are called upon to recognize in this calamity the
voice of God speaking to us through the life of the great man
who has fallen. Every incident in his career will be precious now, as forming a part of that historical legacy which
he has left us. But the proudest tribute that can be offered
to his memory is contained in that epitaph which Daniel
Webster once prayed might be inscribed upon his tomb-
stone: "He was a believer in the religion of Jesus." That

15

faith was the brightest jewel in his earthly crown, as it was the strongest and most enduring element of his simple yet heroic Christian character.

Surrounded as we are, by these emblems of mortality and decay, and the sad remnant of human greatness, what soul does not cry aloud for some more real and substantial good than earthly honor or ambition can bestow? Learn then, the final lesson of that life, as it falls from other lips, now cold in death, but once as eloquent as his; hear him, as from the spirit land, he seems to utter in his own behalf, the same solemn admonition: "Mortals hastening to the tomb, and once the companions of my pilgrimage, take warning and avoid my errors; cultivate the virtues I have recommended; choose the Saviour I have chosen: live disinterestedly; live for immortality; and would you rescue anything from final dissolution, lay it up in God."

SECOND PRESBYTERIAN CHURCH OF JERSEY CITY.*

Sermon by the Pastor,

REV. J. R. FISHER.

TEXT—"The Lord reigneth; let the earth rejoice; let the multitude of isles be glad thereof. Clouds and darkness are round about him : righteousness and judgment are the habitation of His throne."—*Psalm* 97 : 1-2.

What a strange week ! How like the dream of some night of sorrow !

"Is everybody dead?" asked a little girl of her mother in a distant city, as everywhere her eye met the memorials of Death's work. We certainly feel like taking firmer hold

---

* The Pastor of this Church being absent from the City on the day recommended by the Governor as a day of prayer for the President's recovery, special services were held on the Sabbath evening following. The Rev. Henry Mattice, of the Free Reformed Church, and the Rev. W. R. Esher of Emmanuel Reformed Episcopal Church took part with the Pastor in the services.

In accordance with a recommendation of a Pastors' conference called to take suitable action with reference to the death of the Chief Magistrate, a memorial service was held in the Second Presbyterian Church on Monday, the 26th of September, 1881, at two o'clock in the afternoon. The Rev. C. R. Barnes, of the Centenary M. E. Church, presided. Addresses were delivered by Hon. Wm. A. Lewis, Judge Dixon and the Rev. Mr. Nicholson of the North Baptist Church, the Rev. J. Howard Suydam of the Park Reformed Church, the Rev. Dr. Wilson of the Zion A. M. E. Church, and the Rev. J. R. Fisher of the Second Presbyterian Church took part in the exercise. The music was in charge of Prof. W. W. Keenan, organist of the Church, and was beautiful and appropriate. Especially touching was the contralto solo "The Lord is my Shepherd," sung by Mrs. Millie E. Howe.

Another meeting called by the Committee of the Mayor and Aldermen was held here in the evening. It was presided over by Jas. H. Startup, Esq., and addresses were delivered by Dr. I. N. Quimby, A. W. Dickinson, Esq., G. N. Timberman, Esq.

The Rev. Spencer M. Rice, D. D. of Grace Episcopal Church, and others also took part.

upon the objects nearest our hearts lest they too shall be taken.

In the country one morning some three weeks ago, when we awoke we were all puzzled to know what the strange and unnatural appearance of the atmosphere meant. All was dark and sallow; the gas and the lamps gave a light of peculiar whiteness: everything seemed weird and strange—the question on everybody's lips was, "Did you ever see the like of this before?" The timid were sore afraid, some of whom could not drive away the apprehension of some coming terrible judgment.

So the dark foreboding shadow into which we went with our suffering, struggling President, grew thicker and thicker, until it lay like a heavy night-mare upon our spirits, save now and again as the potency of prayer suggested the possibility of relief and deliverance—not alone the prayers of a wife, or of a family, no, nor of a great nation, but the heart-cry of unnumbered multitudes in all lands, and which appealed to the *certain mercy* of Him with whom are the issues of life, and whose goodness is not a matter of speculation, but of tangible experience.

It has seemed, that, like the half-conscious knowledge of the Disciples of our Saviour, of the purpose of God respecting the people of Israel, we have looked for a realization of hopes in a certain way, and bitter disappointment has followed. Perhaps we can appreciate the feelings of the two with whom Christ talked on the way to Emaus, when thinking of their hopes and the dead Christ in whom they were all centered, they exclaimed, "We trusted that it had been he which should have redeemed Israel." Peculiar hopes had centered in this great and good man (let not the comparison be thought irreverent) and we had grown in the familiar scenes of his sick chamber to feel, in addition to the respect and confidence due him as President, the tenderness of a brother's love. But they tell us he is dead—that these hopes can never be realized. "No, no," say our rebellious hearts, "it cannot be; his work was not done; it was but just begun—the tread of the thousands who escorted him to the highest place in the gift of the nation. has hardly died away—we have hardly laid aside our robes since returning from the solemn and impressive scenes of that unusually auspicious inaugural"—but they repeat it, "he is dead." They take us to the cottage by the sea, through the windows of which we have watched him from our distant homes; yes, alas! it is empty. The waters that laughed and sang when they brought him, as if to assure him of certain help and healing from fountains of life stored in their vast and exhaustless depths, or that gently murmured a soft, sweet lullaby when he said he was weary and longed for sleep, are sighing and moaning a sad and melancholy refrain—the requiem of departed greatness. Yes, the unwelcome fact stands out everywhere, from the black lines of the newspapers, from the national ensign at half-mast, from almost every private as well as public building, half hidden in folds of black and white, comes the silent but unwelcome voice, "he is dead." Even nature seems to have entered into sympathy with these sad voices, for she bids the clouds withhold their moisture that woodland and meadow may the earlier don their autumn dress, writing over the sere and yellow landscape the words of Holy Writ: "We all do fade as a leaf."

Yes, the President, beloved and honored is dead, and Longfellow's tender words:

> " There is no home how'er defended
> But has one vacant chair"

seems almost literally fulfilled.

Few men have been so universally loved,—so deeply mourned. No earthly ruler, not even excepting the noble but martyred Lincoln, ever had so many mourners at his funeral, representing such diverse and widely extended interests.

The unwillingness to acquiesce in the manifest fiat of the Almighty, so largely characteristic of this providence, is not because a great man has died, that an honored and useful life has closed, but because of the attending circumstances. Had he come to his grave like a shock of corn fully ripe—had we watched the strength of three-score and ten years grow feebler and feebler, until compelled with loving hands to lay him down to die, 'twere comparatively easy to say—"The will of the Lord be done." But to be stricken down like a dog, in the full meridian of his strength, at the zenith of his prosperity, nay, at the very threshhold of the most important period of his history—his hand just clutching the laurels for which he had striven in honorable contest with the noblest of the nation's sons—this is what makes an inconsolable grief. Had we the sovereign will to control, it never should be thus; indeed there would never be any sunsets while it was yet day.

Ah, well! it is an amazing mercy that the interests of even this little world are not dependent upon the limited wisdom of our finite minds—"God reigns ; let the people rejoice." "But," say our disappointed, desolate hearts, "that is but to mock us in our helplessness. If there be a God, and such a sympathizing Friend as he is claimed to be—why did he utterly ignore the wishes of fifty millions of people? If He reigns, it is as a remorseless tyrant. The widow and her fatherless children, with their pitiful appeal were disregarded ; the imperilled interests of a great people offered no hindrance, so enshrined in the hearts of this great people that no power but death could take him from them, but God heeded it not."

But a greater than our hearts assures us that though clouds and darkness are round about Him, justice and judgment are the habitation of His throne, therefore we may rejoice. Let us not therefore so summarily dismiss our confidence in God, and with Him the only hopes worth having ; yea, more, the last possible source of the heroism imperatively needed in every conflict of life. Presidents may die, but our God is from everlasting to everlasting. " Before the mountains were brought forth or ever He had formed the earth and the world even from everlasting to everlasting He is God."

As Moses was standing in the sunset of his life, that he might number his days wisely, he thought to look about him

on the desolation God had wrought, but lest he should grow
faint-hearted and unbelieving, he first wrapped the cable
of his faith around the eternity of God, and holding fast by
that, could stand unmoved in the midst of destruction he
could not measure, and as he turned away lift up one of
the sublimest prayers ever offered : " Let Thy work appear
unto Thy servants, and Thy glory unto their children.
And let the beauty of the Lord our God be upon us ; and
establish Thou the work of our hands upon us ; yea, the
work of our hands establish Thou it !" Yes, God reigneth. No assassin's work can ever dethrone Him.

But more than this, God has already and will more fully
demonstrate the fact, that not in anger, but in love, not
as a tyrant gloating over the miseries of his subjects, but
as a wise and loving Ruler He has disposed of the events
of this providence.

I think I can see already in several ways the illustration
of this truth :

1. The hearts of this great people were never so thoroughly *one* as to-day. The groans and agony of a dying
President have wrought this hopeful change.

Political strife and animosity were sadly marring the
peace and harmony of the country. Because of the pressure of widely growing and prosperous business pursuits,
multitudes of citizens had forgotten a duty owed to the
State, and she was fast falling into the hands of men who
were greedy of spoil. The crack of the assassin's pistol
silenced the strife of the partizan, and awoke the citizen to
a sense of his duty to his country.

The safety of this government is not in the ruler, but
in the citizen. It needs now and again some alarming
voice to awaken the slumbering hosts who create and preserve our institutions, to vigilance and caution. Thus
twenty years ago God spoke to us, and so again to-day.

2. I think I see another thing tinging this sad providence with mercy. We need now and again in the midst

of the absorbing interests of business life, to be assured
that the *heart* of this great people is right; and so I think,
while the noble qualities of JAMES A. GARFIELD drew all
men to him with affectionate interest, the attachment was
chiefly because he was the representative of a position the
people delighted to honor. He was the nation's ruler, and
the high office he held is after all, the center of this profound interest. At heart, as a people, we are loyal to our
rulers. I endorse the opinion which I find in one of our
metropolitan dailies. It says: "the sentiment of the public was not based on personal regard for the President, for
not one person in a hundred had ever seen him. Neither
was it inspired by the victim's good qualities, for although
these were many, only the President's personal acquain-
tances knew them well. The feeling that caused thousands to cluster around bulletin boards at an hour when
ordinarily they would have been in bed; that impelled
country farmers to neglect their work and walk miles to
buy a newspaper; that prompted even children to read the
dispatches that came daily from the wounded man's bedside, was respect for the President of the United States.
Had his name been other than GARFIELD, had he been
Democrat instead of Republican, public feeling would
have been just as apparent, warm-hearted, and steadfast.
*   *   * It is no small fault to abuse a sentiment so
honorable; it is a shameful crime. The man who seeks
public office for purposes of self aggrandizement, or to
gratify personal ambition, outrages one of the purest feelings of which the public is capable, and he who sneers at
the office-holder, as a mere creature of a party, needs to
study the first principles of a republican form of government, and the sentiments that maintain republics in their
existence."

3. I think I see another fact in the death of President
GARFIELD. It has seemed to me that the great Ruler
wished to arrest the attention of the whole world, that
He might signalize the type of character our free, chris-

tian institutions were intended to produce, and He chose this dreadful but summary method. I do not recall a character in history that more fitly represents the peculiar institutions of his country than the late President. He was a typical citizen; a specimen or illustration of what our form of government can and does produce. He was entirely without the prestige of wealth or family influence; without the safeguards, which the anxious solicitude of those jealous of an honorable and conspicuous name might throw around him, save what a loving mother, who was its sole custodian did; indeed with no capital but a stout body, a firm, steady will, and a pure, noble and honorable ambition to become somebody and to do something, he forged the instruments of his own progress—earning the money to pay for his education, and winning the respect and confidence of all men by the high sense of manly honor, the large-hearted benevolence, the indomitable perseverance, and the quiet but heroic courage that characized him. From the towpath to the highest position of duty and trust in the gift of the American people, his progress was slow, steady, but sure and certain. And all this was possible because of our peculiar institutions. His qualities of mind and heart would have been a tremendous advantage in any country but only under the fostering, helpful influence of our free, christian institutions could such unlimited results be obtained.

4. And better than all, I think I see in the calmness and heroism, and almost superhuman patience and resignation through eighty days of keen and unremitting suffering, the glory of the gospel of Jesus Christ, the triumphs of Christian faith.

The suggestive facts that reveal this are familiar to you all, in the prime of life, in the zenith of power, with the tenderest of domestic interests; in short, having everything in the world to live for, and for which he might reasonably desire to live, and then to be *shot* by a fool, causelessly, damnably! Watch the sainted sufferer during those days of mortal sickness; not a murmur, nor a complaint; cheerful even to the remonstrance of his medical advisers—himself the inspirer of hope in the hearts of his stricken wife and mother.

Some have found but little assurance of Christian triumph in his death, because of the absence of remarkable death-bed utterances and the ministrations of comfort and instruction from a Gospel minister, and the seeming desire and expectation of recovery.

But these things are in perfect harmony with the circumstances of his sickness, and at the same time agree with the spirit of entire submission to the will of God, even should death be the result. With heroism prompted not by the undaunted courage of his strong nature, but the sweet acquiescence of his own will to the Divine, should it so determine, he did say : "I am not afraid to die." You will remember that soon after the fatal bullet sped to its mark, and when they had sought in vain its location that they might determine whether it would prove fatal or not, he looked into the blanched faces of those who stood by his bedside and exclaimed; "it's all right; it's all right." " Rockwell," said he afterward to his intimate friend, " I fully realize my situation."

One day when wheeled in his chair to the window from which he looked upon the open sea, in which he had always taken so much delight, Colonel Rockwell said : " You have made this short journey so well that you can easily attempt a longer one." The answer amply assures us that he was never deluded by any false hope of recovery ; that he was sustained by an enviable and unruffled faith, that he had rested all his hopes upon the good pleasure of his Father in heaven. " Yes," said he ; " it can be easily expanded into the long, long journey home."

These sayings in the chamber of death are after all just like the man ; his death in the religious aspect of it was a fitting conclusion to the life he had lived. He had loved the Gospel with a deep and abiding affection, so much so, that in accordance with the custom of the denomination of Christians to which he belonged, it had been his delight

to preach it ; and to commend it by his own exemplary
life. Its truths he never compromised, however great the
temptation. His speeches on several occasions in Congress, were masterly illustrations of the eloquence and
pathos and power with which one may commend these
blessed principles to his fellows for their guidance and
help.

In his own ardent nature they had wrought great calmness and dignity ; their subduing power had been felt in
the provocation of business life, in the heat of debate, at
the shrine of domestic affection, and at last in the presence
of death.

The silent utterances that come back to us from that
retreating form as it vanishes in the mists of eternity,
seem to be the familiar words of Faith triumphant—
"Though I walk through the valley of the shadow of
death, I will fear no evil ; for thou art with me ; thy rod
and thy staff they comfort me."

Thus, in these and other ways, the time to-night proves
too short to note, can we trace the ruling hand of God.

Even from the clouds and thick darkness wherewith his
throne is girded, come revelations of His love and wisdom
as well as sovereignty.

Surely there cometh a time when we must put our trust
in another beside princes or men's sons in whom there is
no help.

Let us humbly deplore the sins that have made possible
such scenes as those through which we have just passed,
turning from them in penitence and faith to Him who
promises to abolish both sin and the grave, meanwhile
rejoicing in his eternal sympathy.

St. Paul's Episcopal Church, Jersey City Heights.

Services by the Pastor,

REV. FERNANDO C. PUTNAM.

On the 27th day of September, at the hour appointed for the funeral solemnities of the late President GARFIELD at Cleveland, in Ohio, the congregation of St. Paul's Church, assembled in large numbers, and after the service for the burial of the dead, together with other appropriate prayers, the entire litany was said by minister and people, amidst a hush of an unusual silence and solemnity. These devotional services being concluded, the Rector spoke substantially as follows :

My dear brethren and friends—In accordance with the appointment of the Bishop conveyed to us in his pastoral letter, we have assembled to express our sense of profound sorrow and affliction at the death of our Civil Father, and to unite our prayers with those of the whole nation, that God could sanctify this affliction to us as a people, and to supplicate the Divine mercy and consolation for the family and friends of the President, in their unspeakable affliction and sorrow.

This is not the time to pronounce the eulogy befitting the President's life and character. The words that would depict his vigorous and hearty life ; from boyhood, and through the training and discipline that developed and ripened his mind ; that would describe his work, as teacher, as soldier, as senator ; that would give us some conception of his virtues and graces in his home and among his neighbors and friends, have no place here. We are in the presence of God, and these services are a kind of holy leave-taking of him as he passes away from earth into eternity. He has gone from us. We shall see him no more in this world; and the parting is so sad, so solemn, so awful, that only the words of prayer and religious devotion seems in keeping with it. And the emotions which these words kindle in our hearts will be deepened and made more vivid, if we try to realize that at this very moment there are gathered around his coffin in the church in a distant city in Ohio near his home, and where his remains are to rest, not alone his bereaved family, his near friends and neighbors, but all the great civil officers of this Government, Cabinet Ministers, Judges, Senators, Magistrates, Officers of the Army and Navy, Representatives of Foreign Nations, men most distinguished by official honors, by the splendor of personal character—all the most eminent in this country, and of the great Powers of the world, to drop the tear of sympathy on his grave, to testify their sense of his worth as a man, his greatness as the Head of this Nation.

But while we unite with all our hearts in this solemn sadness and sympathy, our full duty will hardly be discharged without some expression of our thankfulness for the wonderful compensations which accompanied this national affliction. Never before was a nation, nay, we may say,—the civilized world—admitted to the bed-side of a sufferer, as they were in the case of the President. By ceaseless telegraphic communication, not only were the hourly experiences of this sufferer almost witnessed by millions in sympathy with him, but almost his pulse beats were audible to them; and what this people and the world saw in the chamber where he lay, was the sublime patience and the calm courage of a true man. And never before did these noble qualities of character bear such precious fruit as they have done in this instance in bringing into a common brotherhood of pure and refining sympathy the whole people of this land. Suffering GARFIELD has cemented the national unity, and linked to us the kindly friendship of the best and most exalted in all lands. You may indeed say that while the fruit of the suffering was most precious to us, it was at a terrible cost to the sufferer himself. But how do we know? He may have had himself wonderful compensations. His life was marvellously rounded off, by this sacrifice. He wrought nobly, while he suffered. His very anguish melted all discords into harmony. And it may be, that during those eighty days while he lay face to face with eternity, there were preparations of heart going on between himself and his God, which made the exchange of worlds one which we might all pray might be ours.

These thoughts, if we let them sink down into our hearts, may help us to realize that while the ways of Divine Providence are often mysterious, they are always merciful.

ADDRESS BY ISAAC N. QUIMBY. M. D..

At the Second Presbyterian Church of Jersey City.

As I stepped to-day, from the ocean, to the land, or
rather from the steamer, to this church, a strange, sad
spectacle met my view. An ominous stillness pervaded
everywhere, all business was suspended, the flags of all
nations at half-mast, the stars and stripes encircled in
mournful black, floating sadly in the breeze. Public buildings, ah yes, and every private house, draped in the habiliments of mourning. This suspension of business, this
mournful draping everywhere, and on everything fills the
mind with awe and depresses the heart and soul with an
inexpressible feeling of sadness. This peculiarly depress-
ing sensation of the soul is brought about by no ordinary
occasion.

JAMES A. GARFIELD, the newly elected President of the
United States has been stricken to the death by the hands
of a semi-lunatic or an assassin. What shall we say?
What can we say, befitting this sad occasion? Words indeed fail, utterly fail to give expression to the melancholy
feelings of the heart. We are dumb before this awful
calamity, and did we not realize the solemn fact that
JAMES A. GARFIELD had only commenced his journey beyond the grave a little while before us, our grief, and loss
would be unendurable. JAMES A. GARFIELD dead! Shot
down by a monster fiend, a wretch in human shape, in the
noon-day of his manhood, just as he was about to enjoy
some of the best fruits of his active, busy life. GARFIELD,
had been deprived of his father in his early boyhood
and brought up by his widowed mother struggling with
poverty. But by industry and sobriety, mainly through
his own exertions, he attained to the highest position in

the gift of the American people. But like Moses, after climbing this giddy political eminence, he was permitted to take but a single view of the great national panorama spread out before him. It is a singular coincidence that two of the most prominent Presidents of the United States, who came up from among the people, by their own laborious and honorable efforts, should have been shot down by the hands of the assassin. Abraham Lincoln and JAMES A. GARFIELD, were emphatically "of the people," and both were taken off while at the post of duty by the hands of violence. But history and posterity will take care of their precious names, and see that the lessons taught by their noble lives will not be lost. President GARFIELD has passed away, and beyond our view; we may look, but him we cannot see; our criticism can therefore take nothing from, nor our eulogy add anything to the useful life thus brought to its untimely end. As the dead cannot be influenced by our action here to-day, let us pause for a single moment amid our sighs and tears, and ask ourselves if there is no instructive lesson, that can be drawn from this sad calamity, that may be useful to the living.

There are three aspects of this national calamity that seem to me might profitably and briefly be considered here to-day : 1st. The religious ; 2d. The political ; and 3d. The international aspect. I may be permitted to say a word in reference to the efficacy of prayer. The statement would not be far amiss, if I should say that no man who had ever lived, had had so many and long continued prayers and supplications offered in his behalf as President GARFIELD. The throne of grace was literally besieged with the prayers of God's people. This is not only true of our own nation, but I have reason to believe, fervent prayer and supplication went up from all the civilized nations of the earth.

I was abroad during nearly the whole of our President's illness, and wherever I went in England, France, Belgium, Holland and Ireland, wherever I attended religious services in church or cathedral, after the accustomed prayers were offered for the heads of these governments, whether Chief Magistrate, King or Queen, the clergy never omitted to offer a fervent and ofttimes touching prayer, on behalf of the President of the United States, who was then lying on a bed of anguish and impending death. Yet, notwithstanding the anxious prayers of the mighty millions of the christian world, death marched steadily forward to claim his distinguished victim, just as though not a single supplication had been offered. This result has called forth the remark from some that since the death of President GARFIELD, they had *lost faith* in the efficacy of prayer. In answer to those who have thus lost faith, I would like to say that they must misunderstand the legitimate scope and application of the character of prayer, or perhaps, are tinctured with Prof. Tyndall's idea of the "prayer test." Prof. Tyndall holds out substantially the perverted idea that if prayer is worth anything, or to be efficient, should have the power when properly offered, to alter or change a fixed natural law. The world is governed by physical laws, which, if violated to any great extent, bring confusion and calamity. And thus, as the universe is governed by *fixed physical* laws, so is it, to a great extent, with the human body. If vital organs of the body are destroyed by either disease or violence, to any great extent, death follows as the necessary result, and prayer, however earnestly offered, could not reasonably be expected to preserve life, or arrest or change the physical laws of nature. If it were so, there would be an obvious, palpable, direct and instantaneous reversal of the established laws of nature, which really would be a miracle. Now, miracles have never been wrought as a personal favor, out of regard of private feelings or public usefulness, but were performed no doubt by our Lord or His Apostles to prove the great truths of christianity. We are told and believe that the fervent prayers of the righteous availeth much, and always to pray and not to faint, but we are nowhere told that through the agency of prayer, bullets were to be extracted or fractured limbs were to be set.

It is this *perverted* view of prayer which encourages or promotes atheism or unbelief, and weakens the faith of men in the divine origin and beauty of christianity. We must not lose sight of the fact that God is the Supreme Ruler of the Universe, and that his creatures cannot dictate to him the manner in which his power is to be exercised for the accomplishment of the greatest good to the greatest number. Thus GARFIELD dead, may be more powerful for universal good, than GARFIELD living. Providence may be teaching by this melancholy event a lesson to all mankind. It will evidently show to the nations of the world that the foundation and stability of our government does not rest upon the action of a single life. The assassination of President Lincoln put to the test the strength and stability of our government, at an hour of its extreme weakness, which can scarcely be repeated in the future. The subduing of the rebellion, the settling of a presidential election by an electoral commission, illustrated the power of the republic, and demonstrated to the world that the people of the United States are able to govern themselves. And now the foul murder of another Chief Magistrate has occurred, yet the wheels of our government have rolled on without interruption—without a single jar.

In considering the political aspect of this calamity, I think it would be profitable for each one of us to ask ourselves this question, are we as members of this commonwealth in any way responsible for the death of President GARFIELD?

This is a question that not only affects this country, but affects the whole civilized world. The most unobservant person among us could not but have noticed the lamentable fact, that the best men (and especially is this true of our larger municipalities), have almost entirely withdrawn from active participation in the management of the political affairs of our country. Our best business men, our best lawyers, our best physicians, our best clergymen, our best mechanics and laborers, all pay but little or no attention to the nomination of good and true men to office— they vote, but know little about the men for whom they

vote ; and by thus failing to perform what clearly should
be a sacred duty are guilty of throwing the political affairs
of city, state and nation, into the hands of the worst element of society! hence it is, that we are so often forced to
witness such unholy alliances between different political
parties, and disgraceful and disgusting efforts and scram-
bles for office. State legislatures, nay even the wheels of
the National Government at Washington have been perverted or stopped for weeks while the members of the legislature or congress have been drawn up in battle array—
fiercely contending for the flesh pots of Egypt. Corrupt,
ignorant, and incompetent men are constantly seeking and
obtaining office, with no brighter motive than *place, power*
and plunder. This condition of affairs brings into action
the vicious principles of the worst kind of men, who failing in gaining the object they seek, resort to slander or even
assassination. Cataline by *corrupting* the *youth* of the *country*
and consorting with the worst elements of the Roman republic attempted to overthrow the government by the assassination of its official heads. So we to-day, have our Cata-
lines and Guiteaus, in ever increasing numbers among us,
who maddened by their failure in obtaining their coveted
official positions resort to fraud, corruption and even murder. Thus it is, that one of the noblest men, kindest of
fathers and husbands, and the Chief Magistrate of this Republic, was assassinated. And then Guiteau, as if to add
infamy to his crime, insists that the deed was done by and
through divine inspiration, thus insulting every good citizen and the highest principles of christianity. This condition of things should strike the alarm and awake to
action the nobler manhood of our country, so that this
government, whose foundation was laid amid prayers and
tears, cemented by the blood of our forefathers, should be
preserved and perpetuated in its purity to bless mankind.
We are all, to a certain extent, responsible for the condition of society, and the habits of our people. If we stand
idly by, and see political corruption spring up in high
places and immoral and irreligious practices taught without rebuke, the evil arising therefrom will cling to our
skirts.

Great national calamities have often, by turning the eyes of the world towards the afflicted, been the means of bringing about great international good, therefore, we may draw some consolation from the fact that the death of President GARFIELD has touched the hearts of nations, and awakened more profound and universal sympathy, than has ever been accorded to any nation before in the world's history. The Queen of England, true to her affectionate and womanly nature, directs her court in mourning, and sends to the wife and mother of the departed President a floral tribute, accompanied with expressions of tender and touching sympathy. Men of all ranks and classes, nobles and the wealthy, no less than the obscure and humble, without distinction or reserve, seemed as deeply concerned and as anxious for his recovery as though he had been a member of the royal family or one of their own household. In truth, however, I am bound to say that the true sympathy that springs from the heart, and has its origin in the soul, came from the middle and lower classes—at least this seemed to be the case in England, and what is true of that country is true of every other country through which I travelled. This feeling is readily accounted for, I think, when we remember the fact that there is scarcely a country on the face of the globe that has not many friends of the middle and lower classes, who, escaping from oppression and tyranny, have found a resting place and a home upon the broad and mighty bosom of this grand republic.

It is to this class especially, that the name of the United States is like a long-looked for friend, coming to their relief,—to lighten their load and sweeten their toil. Wherever I traveled, whether in England, Ireland, France, Belgum or Holland, when it was discovered that I was an American, the first, and constant question, "How is your President?" "I hope he may recover"—and next to this would be the significant question, "What prompted this dastardly act?" When I replied that I thought it was the work of a semi-lunatic, or a disappointed demagogue and office seeker, this reply seemed to give them relief, followed often by the expression, "that they were glad to know that it was not the work of a political faction, which might be looking to the overthrow of our form of government." Thus, through the death of President GARFIELD, many queries will arise. Our form of government will be more or less investigated by other nations, which may be the means of lightening the yoke of oppression, and letting into the dark recesses of despotic governments the light of liberty and law, whereby rulers may become more considerate towards their subjects, thus abolishing Nihilism and elevating mankind.

The members of the International Medical Congress in London, were invited to attend service, on Sunday, August 7th, at Westminster Abbey, and St. Paul's Cathedral. Both of these immense edifices were thronged, to such an extent, that not even standing room was left. At Westminster Abbey Rev. Canon Farrar occupied the pulpit of the late lamented, generous and broad minded Dean Stanley; amid the profound stillness of this vast assembly Canon Farrar made some feeling and touching allusion to our President's condition, "hoping that the medical skill, then being exerted, would be, through the providence of God able to restore the President and preserve his life, so that he might again resume his official duties, which were so important to the government of the United States." At St. Paul's Cathedral, while again listening to prayer offered for the recovery of our President, my mind irresistibly reverted to the fact, that just to the right of me, beneath a beautiful and imposing monument lay the body of Lord Cornwallis, who surrendered the British forces at Yorktown! Is it possible that the Canon is really praying for the recovery of the President of a country that had been engaged in deadly conflict with this hero, whose venerated ashes are now resting within the sacred walls of this stately edifice? What a revolution in sentiment! — what a laying down of the implements of war and prejudice, twin relics of barbarism, what advancement and development of reason, what change of action in one hundred years — stupendous! Truly, "the sword is being beaten into plough-shares, and the

spear into pruning-hooks, so that nation shall not lift up
the sword against nation, neither shall we learn war any
more." What has wrought this kindly, international, feeling? Do we not see in this the bow of promise dimly
streaking the deep blue vault of heaven, bringing peace to
men and goodwill and harmony among the nations, to
elevate and bless the race? Surely enlightenment and
the higher forms of civilization are marching forward pari
passu, as christianity holds up the lamp and points the
way. Fondly do we hope, earnestly do we pray, that
while the "deep damnation" of his taking off, which so
powerfully effected the sensibilities of all christendom, will
not be lost to us, and that the winds of heaven will waft
it, as fragant incense, to the coming ages of this republic.
Yet it never would have elicited such expressions of grief,
veneration and love from all the world, *except* that *he died*
at the post of *duty* and a martyr to the *cause* of *universal
freedom.* It is this that will cause the name of " GARFIELD "
to encircle the globe, and be remembered in the palace,
and treasured and revered in the humble cottage of the
poor. The honest, sober, faithful life of JAMES A. GAR-
FIELD, thus sacrificed, has reared for him a

> " Tower of fame, more durable than gold,
>   And loftier than the royal fame
>   Of pyramid of old,
>   Which no inclemencies of clime,
>   Nor fiercest wind that blow,
>   Nor endless change, nor lapse of time,
>   Shall ever overthrow."

Sermon by the Pastor,

REV. W. W. EVERTS, D. D.

THE LATE TRAGICAL EXPERIENCE OF THE REPUBLIC ILLUSTRATING DOCTRINE, DUTY, AND PROMISE OF LIFE.

TEXT—" And the king said unto his servants, Know ye not that there is a prince and a great man fallen this day in Israel?"—2 *Sam.* iii. 38.

That is a beautiful custom observed by the City of Hamburg. When a burgomaster dies, a town trumpeter ascends a tower and pouring forth a requiem blast heralds the public calamity.

The nineteenth of September, at the midnight hour, a thousand bells pealed out over the continent the death of the Chief Magistrate of the Republic. The next morning from Maine to Florida, and from the Atlantic to the Pacific ten thousand banners floated at half-mast from national and state capitol, from ships of the navy and headquarters of the army, from public and private buildings, from palaces of the rich and cottages of the poor. Eighty days and

---

* A public meeting was held in this Church September 26th, 1881, at 7:30 P. M., called by the Mayor and Aldermen of the City, for the commemoration of the brilliant career and tragical death of JAMES A. GARFIELD. The house was filled with citizens of different political parties and different religious opinions.

The Hon. Charles Siedler was called to the chair.

Appropriate music was rendered by the Choir of the Church, and Rev. Adolos Allen, of the Claremont Presbyterian Church, offered an impressive prayer. Judge B. F. Randolph, the first speaker called upon, read an original poem (see page 259) prepared for the occasion, and then gave an eloquent tribute to the deceased President.

Similar tributes were given by Messrs. Jacob Weart, Gilbert Collins, and Charles H. Hartshorne, some of which addresses appear in this volume.

nights the nation had watched by the bed-side of their stricken chief. After the dreadful suspense was over they followed his remains from the seaside to Washington, from Washington to the shore of the lake he had loved to gaze upon from his boyhood, and there waited with uncovered head while over his last resting place was pronounced that mortal decree " Earth to earth ; dust to dust!"

The whole land draped in mourning. A hush of tender thoughtfulness rested on all marts of business, all thoroughfares of travel, all public assemblies, and upon all social circles. Every family mourned as if they had lost a near relative, and the heart of the nation swelled with the great sorrow! Messages of condolence came from rulers across the sea, foreign courts went into mourning, and three hundred and fifty millions by sympathizing word or act, joined in the greatest pageant of mourning the sun ever shone upon. The tearful adieus waived by thronging multitudes to the funeral train as it moved across the country, and the profusion of flowers scattered along the iron track which binds the union of states, was but a symbol of the honor and love of a great nation and of the civilized world.

The tributes to the dead President from pulpit and press, public hall and chamber of commerce, and from casual utterances of thoughtful men of all professions and callings, would surpass in wise counsel, beautiful sentiment, and tender pathos, those pronounced over the grave of any other man in the world's history, and gathered into a volume, would constitute a funeral wreath rich enough for the tomb of a generation or race. Leaving other lines of thought, we invite attention to a consideration of the principles regulating human life and destiny, as illustrated by the late tragical experience of the Republic.

1. In true social order, honorable *distinction* is awarded to personal virtues. In perverted society it is attained by birth, conquest or by political or social diplomacy. For centuries the fabric of society has been reared upon

the distinctions of caste, forbidding ascent from lower to higher grades. It has existed as a series of separate rings, one above the other, without communication. In natural order it is a spiral inviting ascent. Our republic is the most conspicuous example of this natural social order. Here may be realized the proverbial promise, "Seest thou a man diligent in business, he shall stand before kings ; he shall not stand before mean men." A diligent use of gifts of nature and providence opens up an indefinite promise for ultimate distinction and power. No more striking example of the possibilities of our American citizenship has appeared than in the career of JAMES A. GARFIELD.

He inherited no family name or fortune as stepping-stone to greatness. He possessed only advantages within the reach of thousands. He cherished vigorous health, industry, frugality, moral convictions, and a lofty purpose. From the menial tasks of a canal boy and a wood-chopper, he rose through industry and faithfulness to the mastery of books, the honor of the schools, the head of a college, place in the legal profession, among public lecturers, and popular preachers.

Through this many sided character and culture, he was found at the breaking out of the war, eminently fitted for the army, and after winning its glory, he rose through various civic administration to the head of the national councils.

As the chairman of the most important Congressional Committees, he contributed perhaps more than any other member of either house to the reestablishment and policy of the Government.

At the Chicago Convention after unsuccessful balloting for other illustrious names, JAMES A. GARFIELD was nominated with acclamation for the presidency of the Republic.

The President of the United States is the only civil magistrate in the world who rules fifty millions of people by their own suffrage. And considering the greatness, intelligence and virtue of the American people, their Chief Magistrate attains the highest pinnacle of fame. JAMES A. GARFIELD through exalted virtues rose from humble life to this unrivaled distinction—won a renown no other mortal has won. But the path of his ascent is as palpably traced for succeeding generations as Jacob's ladder to the aspiring patriarch. His name shall celebrate on the page of history the inspiring motto "Excelsior" to the latest generation.

2. The character of a nation or age is judged by the character of individuals. Federal headship operates beyond the condemnation of the race in Adam or its justification in Christ. A nation is credited as being and doing what its founders are and do. Her military, commercial, scientific or moral character is disclosed through the career of her generals, merchants, philosophers, artists or philanthropists.

Abraham, Moses, Christ, the Apostles represent the culture and character of the Hebrew race. Each age presents its best men as illustrating the height of its virtues, and every nation has canonized its most distinguished citizens as a roll of honor.

GARFIELD will be associated with Washington and Lincoln as illustrating the virtues of our American manhood, and when annals of the Republic are fading away and their moral significance becomes uncertain, their names will appear as symbols of the moral elevation of free institutions age after age.

As Greek culture and art were resplendent in the names of her philosophers and artists, American manhood and virtue will remain, resplendent in the lives of Washington, Lincoln, and GARFIELD. But vices of humanity have also been exemplified in individual histories. In Adam all were condemned because in the same temptations all would have disobeyed in like manner. Joseph's brethren, Korah, Achan, Saul, Absolom, Ahab, Jesebel, Judas—disclosed the vices of the Jewish civilization. A succession of bad men is traced in every land and age attesting the continual depravity of the race. In the brief annals of the Republic Arnold, Burr, Booth, and Guiteau, exemplify vices inherent in humanity, and especially fostered by free institutions.

The malignity of secession denied by partizan press, and politicians, was attested by the crime of Booth. He struck not at the just and generous Lincoln, but at his office—the sovereignty of the Republic. It was not Booth that struck, but a people blinded and misled by political fallacy, and sectional prejudice. The act of the assassin photographed the character of the rebellion, to be shown in the annals of history, as a face of a criminal in a rogue's gallery.

Guiteau's crime discloses the corruption of American politics. Thousands felt with him the President was not subservient to party policy and leaders. This feeling in him grew into bitter resentment and the desperate purpose to remove him if necessary by assassination. Others may have shared his vindictive feeling, if not his desperate purpose, and the hope of personal and party preferment through his removal.

But for the bitterness of political faction, our noble President might have been spared to the country and the age. Our Republic is dishonored by these recurring blots on her history, and other nations will be prejudiced against free institutions, as impracticable in the present condition of mankind.

3. The Christian doctrine of the Atonement is illustrated in all lines of social progress. The mother saves her orphan family, by exposing her life, as the bird shelters her brood from the rapacious hawk. The patriot offers service and sacrifice for the freedom and glory of unborn generations. Martyrs laid down their lives for the truth, the promised inheritance of the millenial age. Missionaries leave kindred and native shores to spread glad tidings of Divine love to lands shrouded in ignorance and sin. Philanthropists sacrifice time, wealth, and friends in pursuit of reforms. All moral ascendencies are gained by opposing untruthfulness, injustice and selfish ambition. Progress by sacrifice is a law of the constitution of man, eloquently taught in scripture, and illustrated on every page of history. Neither individual nor nation has risen in virtue without vicarious suffering.

Washington and his compatriots hazarded life, fortune
and sacred honor for the freedom of the new world. Was
not Lincoln "bruised" for the iniquities of the rebellion,
and the salvation of the Republic? Did not GARFIELD receive the "stripes" of political faction and suffer for the
conciliation of national brotherhood? Has not his tragic
death done more to unite all parties and sections, than a
long and brilliant administration? North, South, East
and West strike hands over the grave of the martyr.
When a yawning chasm threatened to swallow ancient
Rome, legend says, an oracle promised it should be
closed, and the world's capital spared, if the noblest
Roman would leap into the vortex. A youth, inspired
with lofty patriotism, and equipped in resplendent armor,
made the fatal plunge on horseback and Rome was saved.
So the yawning chasm of political strife, threatened to
swallow up the honor and empire of the Republic. The
noblest citizen plunged into that chasm, and our institutions are saved.

4. Another principle underlying social progress, eluci-
dated by the national trial, is the effectiveness of prayer.
No success is won in manufactures, commerce, professions,
science, or art, without importunate pursuit. Much less can
moral and religious improvement be gained without prayerful devotion. Whether the power of prayer is subject-
ive or objective—the boat is drawn to the shore, or the
shore to the boat—it is none the less real or effective.
Earnest and believing pursuit is the law and measure of
all moral achievement. The reign of law in the moral
realm is conditioned upon those affections, sentiments and
trusts, articulated and confirmed by prayer; so that progress by law would still be progress by prayer. The Nil-
ometer no more fully forecasts the harvests of Egypt, than
individual, family, and social prayer, gauges spiritual culture and reform in any land or age. But importunity of
selfish desire is not a beneficent force. It precipitates the
antagonisms of the world. Importunate desire acquies-
cing in the supreme will of God, is a beneficent force, pro-

moting peace and progress. Much of the prayer for our
stricken President, may not have been "in the name of our
Lord," and in humble acquiescence in His will. "Thy
will be done," was the addenda to all the true prayer
which arose from the anguished heart of the nation.
That prayer has been answered—is still being answered.
Sectional bitterness has been appeased, the perpetuity
and glory of the Republic have been assured. If by sheer
importunity of short-sighted and selfish mortals any specific end could be gained, the reign of law would cease,
and the creature become lord of the Creator.

Over the grave of their honored President, should not
the people repeat the scripture promise he applied to the
multitudes in Wall street, bewildered and blinded with
grief and tears at the assassination of Lincoln—"Clouds
and darkness are round about Him ; but justice and judgment are the habitation of His throne. God reigns, and
the government at Washington still lives." Prayer to
heaven is still the strength of earth.

5. The relation of religion to individual and national
greatness, is transfigured by the career of our late President. As the inspiration of virtue, the standard of discipline, and the guarantee of happy destiny to the righteous,
religion "makes vows kept"—alike, personal, domestic,
social and civic. "The fear of the Lord is the beginning"
of all wise uses and directions of life. Christianity is the
final and perfected discipline of religion. The true christian, therefore, is the highest style of man, and through
christian discipline, character and manhood are perfected.
JAMES A. GARFIELD exemplified that culture. When a boy,
in a revival meeting, he first awoke to a sense of God, religious duty, and the salvation and lordship of Christ.
After conference with the evangelist, and prayerful consideration, he was baptized into disciplineship to Christ,
and devoted himself by solemn covenant, to His service
and glory. His industry, economy, pursuits and hopes,
were all inspired by christian hope. His sympathies and
friendships, in school, army, national legislature, and in

congress, were consecrated by christian charity. Religious conversation with class-mates, invitation of companions to join in prayer, at the close of a weary day on the mountain top, personal appeal to his students, earnest Sabbath discourses, the tender address to class-mates on the eve of departure to Washington, the affectionate family prayer at the close of a day of reception at Mentor, the fellowship of the last Sabbath in the church where he had so long worshipped, the faithful attendance on the obscure church of his own faith in Washington, and his patient and hopeful suffering through eighty days and nights, of painful, personal, family and national suspense—all proclaim the eminence of his christian character.

He was more pronounced in religious conviction and observance than any who have filled the Executive chair. The highest civic office was adorned by the highest Christian virtues. At the time of his death JAMES A. GARFIELD was the most influential and distinguished Christian layman in the world. In grateful admiration, one nation has inquired of another : "Know ye not that a prince and a great man has fallen this day in Israel?"

By the Republic he will be enrolled among her most distinguished worthies and by Humanity, canonized as one of her most illustrious saints.

Rector,

REV. T. JEFFERSON DANNER.

[The concluding portion of the sermon of the rector of Christ Church, embracing an original poem, written by him, and read by the Hon. Bennington F. Randolph, at the meeting held in the Bergen Baptist Church.]

TEXT—"Yea, though I walk through the valley of the shadow of death, I will fear no evil ; for Thou art with me; Thy rod and Thy staff they comfort me."—*Psalm xxiii. 4.*

And here, in connection with what I have said as suggested by the words of the text, it seems fitting that some definite, though brief, allusion be made to the occurrence which has opened up such a wondrous stream of sympathy throughout the land—aye, throughout the civilized world.

And yet, what need I say—what can I say touching the dead President who seems to have found a living tomb in the heart of the nation? With the recollection of his sufferings, of his heroic patience, and christian fortitude before us, we stand at once humbled and strengthened.

For him "the valley of the shadow of death" had naught of fear or dread.

On the morrow his mortal remains will have reached that common home—the grave, to which he, doubtless, alluded, when, with a weary smile, he spoke of taking "the long, long journey home."

God grant that we may reach that last resting-place with as little dread : and that, at the last, "through the grave " and gate of death, we may pass to our joyful resurrec- " tion; for His merits who died, and was buried, and rose " again for us—Jesus Christ our Lord."

In the presence of death, few words are best. And so, gathering together the hopes and fears and experiences of the long, sad weeks of patient suffering, I would fain lay this simple tribute on the coffin of the "sleeping" President :—

I.

Felt is the gloom that shadows the land
As forth speeds the cry, "By murd'rous hand
The President's shot—shot to the death!"
Nay, he lives! Yet long, with bated breath,
As one appalled by a blasting breath,
Th' Nation watches the shadow of death.

II.

"Measureless" streams of "tenderness" flow,
'Sunging the pain of the fearful blow.
From North, and from South, from East, from West,
From lands beyond the billowy crest,
Th' uplifted hearts of millions in prayer
Witness the world-wide sorrow and care.

III.

The death-cloud breaking, silvering lines
Broaden and deepen as brighter shines
The sunlight of hope. And oft, in strains
Of rejoicing, each glad heart proclaims
Thanksgivings to God, o'er all supreme,
Who giveth to life each radiant beam.

IV.

But hark! on the burdened midnight air
The tolling bells say, Death has been there,
In the President's home by the sea.
Dead! O God, even so let it be—
With the wave-chanted dirge of the sea
Echoing a world's sad sympathy.

Sermon by the Pastor,

REV. CHARLES L. NOYES.

"THE LIVING SOUL IN A DYING BODY."

Text—"For we know that if the earthly house of our tabernacle be dissolved, we have a building from God, a house not made with hands, eternal in the heavens."— 2 *Cor.* v. 1.

These were the words of a dying man. I do not mean that they were by any means his last words. But when he wrote them he felt his physical powers breaking up under the hardships of his outer life and the inward strains of anxiety. He says he is pressed on every side, perplexed, smitten down. Death worketh in him; his outward man is decaying. Now in the midst of this wearing, battering, dissolving of his body, he finds the assurance of continued life for the soul. When he considers that part of his nature, though "pressed on every side," he feels that he is not "straitened," though "smitten down," not "destroyed." "Yea," he affirms "though our outward man is decaying, our inward man is renewed day by day." Then his thought brings him speedily to the confident assurance of the text. "*We know that if the earthly house of our tabernacle be dissolved, we have a building from God, eternal in the heavens.*"

What Paul observed in himself we may see going on in us and about us. The durability of our bodily mechanism is, under the best conditions, narrowly restricted. Its bands, bearings and cogs are slowly but surely being worn

down, and ere long something will give away, the wheels
will stop, and the work be done. How much is the end
hastened by disease, by toil, by anxiety, by accident! We
cannot with certainty say of any youth, he is yet wholly
free from the encroachments of death. We know that with
every full grown man the process has begun, the wrinkles
on the face, the dimming of the lustre of complexion,
the whitened hair across the temple, are water marks
which show that the life-force is subsiding. With very
many about us and near to us, it needs no keen eye or
quiet reflection to notice the change. It is going on so
rapidly that we daily mark the steps of its progress. We
almost see the movement of the process, by which the
earthly house of their tabernacle is being dissolved.

Having followed Paul thus far in his experience, is it
permitted to us to go with him to the end? To assure
ourselves as well of the living, yes, growing power of the
soul. I believe that we may, and though it may require
more patient reflection, the certainty which we reach, will
be none the less reliable.

It is not at every time that we are able or disposed to
enter thus into communion with death, and search among
its ruins for the promise of another life. There are some
occasions where a community consents, or may be even
against their choice, constrained by the force of circumstances, to hold converse with these solemn facts. Such
an occasion is now upon us. I will not then apologize for
having called your thoughts to a saddening theme. It is
not I that have summoned you into the presence of death.
I find you there, drawn together by a common national
calamity, which is yet felt by each as a personal loss.

In many gatherings to-day, the life and virtues of
our GARFIELD will be rehearsed. But already the story of
his career has become a household tale, the portrait of
his noble character, each man now carries in his heart.
It seems needless that I should here describe him whom
you know so well, or praise him whom already you both
admire and love. I would rather turn this occasion of
grief into one of promise and hope. Like the disciples of

old you crowd about to look into his open tomb, but what did they see? not the Lord Himself, only the place where the Lord lay, and they heard the angel voice confirming their rising hopes, "He is not here, for He is risen." Just such an angel voice we may hear. The voice from spirit to spirit assuring our hearts, that there is no death for such great souls as that of GARFIELD. We may behold his wasted body, lowered to the dust, but it is "only the place where he lay," the swift-dissolving tabernacle of his earthly abode, his soul has risen to dwell in the building from God, eternal in the heavens.

The value to us of such a hope is that it is a hope not for one man but for all who share the same humanity. I believe then that I may count on your willing attention, while we seize upon this precious opportunity to explain more carefully the promises of life for the soul to be found in the midst of the death of the body.

First. We may observe that in the midst of the wasting of the body, the soul shows no signs of wasting. "The inward man is renewed day by day."

This *vigor* of the soul is peculiarly wonderful, and liable to be overlooked, because we can know of the existence of a soul other than our own, only through means of the body. Only as the soul reflects itself upon the outward form of your friend, do you know that it is or what it is. This is why we so inseparably connect our thoughts of departed friends and our loves for them with their face and figure. We cannot bear to close the lid upon the form of the departed. Philosophy vainly endeavors to make us feel that this body is only cold clay and that the real object of our love is neither lost nor far away. This is why that mother, in Ohio, will not give up her last look, and cries "O I must see him. You know he was my boy." This is why the brave, all-enduring wife follows the mere dust of her departed husband from one resting place to another, and one opportunity of view to another, and gives way to grief the most uncontrollable when the relentless gates of the tomb swing together. The face, the eye, the voice, the touch is the soul for our senses. What wonder then that when the senses are clouded the soul *seems* to be failing.

The strength of evidence for the life of the soul distinct from and beyond the body lies in the fact that the soul shows itself unimpaired by every failure of the body *until* the senses are weakened, and even then as one of them fails to do its service it reaches us through another, betaking itself from speech to gesture and from gesture to look.

As long as the last scene in the cottage at Elberon is fixed in our memories, can we doubt of an existence of the soul independently of the body? GARFIELD could no longer speak. He could no longer beckon with the hand—that had been voice to him for the last time, when he pressed it to his heart. There was left only the window of his eyes through which his soul could look out. As they fastened upon his wife, in their dumbness, eloquent of his faithfulness to a life-long affection, can you yet discover any diminution in the force of that great heart, and as those eyes too fail him, do you believe, the light of life in the soul, which had burned brightly, through every advance of death upon the body, through the loss of every other agent of expression, went out in the darkness, because the eyes closed forever. No: they closed not to destroy, but only to conceal the immortal vigor of a great soul.

Secondly, we observe that amid the dissolution of the body, the soul asserts its own imperishable nature, by its *longing for life*.

GARFIELD was, as has been often said, "a representative man." So, his long grand struggle for life is a vivid utterance of that noble thirst for living which is the masterpassion of the human soul. We shall not soon forget the incidents of that heroic struggle. Distant is the day when we shall hear without a thrill of admiration, how he made his great reply—"Doctor, I will make the most of that chance." Amid the terrible depression of his weakness, and the despair of his attendants, he kept his courage

bright, and clung to every shred of life; fought the enemy
inch by inch, and gave up at last only like a commander
who drops at the head of his column, with a rallying cry
on his lips.

One is proud to be a part of a humanity capable of such
things. Yes, and joyful; for the glory of it is not merely
in the sublime courage and fortitude, but because it is the
pure upswelling of the life of the soul, proclaiming in its
fierce battle for life, that it is its nature *to live*. This
eagerness for life is universal, and characteristic of the soul.
Do you ask me how it was that GARFIELD nevertheless
yielded to death with calmness and resignation? It was
not that he undervalued life, but because he was assured,
as he again and again in life and death affirmed, of another
and higher life. He fought death but he did not fear it,
because like every *man* he loved life, and like a *Christian*
he knew he should live again.

To this universal craving there may seem to be excep-
tions in the case of men, who without such a hope as our
President claimed, have yet thought themselves willing to
l^ e life. But this contempt of life is due to their having
so little true life in the present existence. When, more-
over, they actually face the extinguishing of that little
spark they are ready to turn back. Now that Guiteau is
in prison, and the question is no longer as to the life of
another, but his own, and that brought forcibly before him,
his contempt of life is not so evident. The Philosopher
Seneca, who was, as he wrote, ready to die at any moment,
surrendered his principle that he might live.

> " No life that breathes with human breath
> Has ever truly longed for death.
> "Tis life whereof our nerves are scant,
> O life, not death, for which we pant;
> More life and fuller that we want."

The craving of the soul for life is assurance that the soul
will live. The goodness of God is pledge for this. " *He
satisfieth the desire of every living thing.*" Which means not
that every foolish wish or passing fancy is granted, but

that he, who makes the needs and aspirations of his creatures provides for their satisfaction. He does not make
them merely for their disappointment. That would be the
part of a petty tyrant. I look back to-day not with amuse-
ment, but contempt for a man who won my interest as a
boy in some ingenious plaything, lured me on to ask for
it, put it almost within my grasp, awoke all my curiosity,
expectation and eagerness, then refused even to let me hold
the toy in my hand. Some talk of believing in the goodness and wisdom of God, and yet doubt the immortality of
the soul. But as it seems to me all that the harmony of
nature, and the Gospel of Christ tell of the wisdom an
goodness of God is so much assurance that the soul's
passion for life is created that it may be gratified. This
will appear even the more clearly as we proceed to our

Third Observation. The soul is never so well fitted to
live as at the hour of death.

This is true of all men. Every faculty of the soul is
improved with each passing year. I shall, however, in
accordance with our purpose, in this discussion, speak
only of the enlarging of the soul under the circumstances
of death.

President GARFIELD was a far nobler spirit, in the estimation of the American people, at the end of his illness
than even they had supposed him to be, before he was
shot. But not only in estimation, he was in fact a purified
ennobled soul, all precious qualities courage, fidelity, dis-
interestedness were not only revealed, they were developed
in those trying hours. How could it be otherwise? Could
any susceptible soul lie so long in the very ante-chamber
of God's presence? Could he receive the love and confidence of a great people? Could he daily witness the
Christian courage and faith and cheerfulness of her, who
like an angel hovered at his side, and not receive a benediction, an inspiration from such holy influences? He was
good before. He was great before, but his goodness was
purified, his greatness was magnified in that illness. Never

before was he so endowed for heroic and God-like service for his country. Was all quenched, all thrown to waste, because his body was pierced by the sting of a miserable insect? No.

> "We doubt not that for one so true,
> There must be other nobler work to do."

The same kind of assurance breaks upon any one watching the work of death on any passing soul. When they go, there is the most in them which you would cling to and retain if you could. Has not God a place and a work for such a spirit as passed away in Bloomfield. She was but a little girl, fifteen years old, who sacrificed her life to save her brother. She was employed in the rolling mills, and when she returned to her work a week ago last Tuesday, she took her little brother, eight years old, to spend the rest of the hours of work with her. On their way home in the evening they had to cross a long trestle-work bridge, which spans the creek. When well on their way across, they saw a train approaching them. There was but a single track, and no room on either side to step out of the way. The child saw that their only refuge was to throw themselves into the waters of the creek. She gently forced her brother to the edge of the bridge, then lowered him carefully as far as her hands would reach, and allowed him to drop into the shallow stream. Her next movement would have been to jump down herself, but in her care for her brother, she had not left time for herself. The train caught her and hurled her back on the track. Such a death is the best assurance of its future life. In view of such heroism, the mind rises up in defiance of argument, leaps the slow steps of logic, and declares that such things can never die. Beings capable of such action are imperishable. Yet suffer me to draw you back to the one point which I would here maintain, it is that in her case, as in that of every departing soul, at the moment of death, she was made ready to live.

And here it is time to enlarge our view by taking one step further. I have drawn you to the bedside of our dying President, and asked you to consider that humanity is there lying. Will it live again. We have seen

First. There is no sign of the soul's decay.
Secondly. It longs to live.
Thirdly. It is just ready to live.

Now go further. All that it now is demands another life
for its completion. Unless man live again, his life is a
story begun, the characters introduced, the threads of the
plot laid in order, the exciting interweaving of destinies
set in motion, and all broken off to leave us in vexation
and disappointment.

JAMES A. GARFIELD'S was a symmetrical character. He
was nobly developed on every side of his nature, yet can
we say that on any one he was completed. He had learned.
He was a marvel of information on every topic, of thor-
oughness and accuracy in his own specialties. It was
becoming proverbial among his congressional associates,
that if one would become posted on any topic the speediest
course was to ask GARFIELD. But while the acquisitions
of such a man are our admiration and despair, we are well
aware that he had picked up but a crumb of knowledge.
We know that he longed to spread more widely over the
great domain of facts, to penetrate more deeply into the
meaning of truth, to rise higher into the mystery of God
and His purposes. He learned, but he had laid only the
foundation of that knowledge toward which he was aspiring.

Again, this man worked. He did great things. Was he
contented with what his powers had suffered him to accomplish? Had he used one tithe of that energy, of that
rowing capacity? Did he ever have, or has any human
soul ever had free scope or competent bodily instruments
through which the soul could move out and accomplish
what it knows lies within it. The soul cannot express itself, cannot make its forces felt—it falls back after its
mightiest efforts, to say as Paul did after his eloquent sermons, It is but the foolishness of preaching.

Again, this man loved. If there is anything which defies
time and death it is the love of the human heart. The
more it is true love, the more it needs eternity for its dura-

tion, spirit life for its expression. Surely words and signs
and caresses can never utter it: kindly offices cannot ex-
haust it. I have known men and women who could face the
thoughts of ceasing to be on every other score, but could not
believe that the love which they had for child or parent or
friend could be contained by mere bodily existence ; that
it could ever end ; that it never should find a truer outlet
for its intensity. There was the imprint of immortality in
the love with which his eyes parted with the dearest friend
of earth.

Finally, *this man deserved*. Yes, and his murderer has
deserved. Tell me, can either of them find their deserts
at the hands of men in this world ? There is an unhesitating answer to this question found in the conscience of
every man. Our whole sense of right demands that this
good and this evil, be crowned with its fitting recompense.
Time cannot do it. A Hereafter is needed.

Heaven and Hell, we see in these tragic moments are
not originated by theologians. That faculty at the core of
the soul which man knows is the deepest and divinest thing
within him proclaims that they must be and are. Disprove
all that the systems have taught about them. Be incon-
sistent enough to do away with the one and keep the other.
What follows ? Why, after you have torn down all the
theories, discomforted all the preachers, frightened away
all the "ghosts of superstition," the human heart will reconstruct Heaven and Hell for you. As soon as we think
seriously and in the light of actual facts, we all believe in
them practically, if not confessedly. We all acknowledge
to-day the fact of a great merit unrequited. We know
that all which a great people can do or say of praise or
tribute cannot worthily honour the great virtues of our
dead chief. Every drooping banner and every ornament
of sorrow hung over the homes of this great country, prove
that we feel a debt of obligation which we only thus vaguely
hint at. " Why all this waste," said a philosphic observer
looking down the draped streets of Boston. The answer
came out the heart of a colored boot-black who had wound
with black rags the legs and back of his chair, " He was a

friend to us black men, sir. We cannot none of us pay him back, but I thought *I ought* to do so much." Nobly said. "Out of the mouth of babes and sucklings God has ordained praise." There is an eternal ought, which the feeblest heart acknowledges, and which a just God has not ignored in the constitution of his universe. And ought is not a one-sided thing. If good is worthy of reward, guilt is worthy of punishment. One scale of the balance cannot go up unless the other comes down. However much men may let sentiment cloud their reason and befog their conscience, it only needs the thunder of great wrong to clear the air and reveal in Heaven above as in the heart within, a call for a *future* of righteous recompense.

There is an old story of how the poet Longfellow was awaked from his pleasant dream of mercy without judgment, by the rude alarm of our war, and the terrible facts of desperate and brutal wickedness in man which it revealed in the instigators of secession, and how he wrote thus to Prof. Stowe at Andover, "Sir, our tongues are tied, you must open your Bibles and give these men not only Gospel but law, if you can't find denunciation suitable in the New Testament, *bang on* with the old."

That story now belongs a passing generation. I have been startled to find history repeating herself. I picked up a few days since, a newspaper which is generally the voice of a so-called liberal class who drop from their vocabulary certain strong words of scripture, and I read this sentence : "Let us have an end of this vain talk of vengeance upon Guiteau. Can any insult, or indignity, or pain that a mob could inflict, equal the crime he has done, the loss he has brought upon us? Let the law go through its form and then leave him in the hands of the *eternal avenger.*" This is a moment in which we stand face to face with verities. And of this at least we are assured that we shall have to reconstruct man himself before we can wipe out those facts of a future life which we call Heaven and Hell.

The death of our beloved President has seemed to cast a flash of light on the world to which he has gone, and the very circumstances so harrowing at first thought, of his "taking off," are full of promise for him and for his brother man. We are assured that the unwasting energies of his mind and heart will be satisfied with fullness of life ; that he will know even as he is known, will find the joy of a service in which he shall be ruler over many things, and wear the crown of reward worthy of his endurance and deeds.

> " He is gone who seemed so great, —
> *Gone : but nothing can bereave him*
> *Of the force he made his own*
> *Being here*, and we believe him
> Something far advanced in State,
> And that he wears a truer crown
> Than any wreath that man can weave him.
> But speak no more of his renown,
> Lay your earthly fancies down.
> God accept him, Christ receive him."

PROCEEDINGS OF THE HUDSON COUNTY BAR,

COURT HOUSE IN JERSEY CITY.

On the morning of September 20th, A. D. 1881, the Hudson County Courts convened, Hon. Manning M. Knapp, Associate Justice of the Supreme Court, holding the Hudson Circuit, with Hon. A. Q. Garretson, Presiding Judge, and Hon. John Brinkerhoff, and Hon. A. W. Fry, Associate Judges of the Common Pleas on the Bench. Mr. Justice Knapp announced that by reason of the death of the President of the United States, intelligence of which had just been received, the Courts would stand adjourned until the day following the funeral.

An informal meeting of the Bar was immediately organized. Gilbert Collins, Esq., was called to the chair, and Allan L. McDermott, Esq., was named as secretary. The chairman suggested an adjournment and formal notice to the Bar of a meeting at which appropriate action could be taken; the affliction being so great and so recent as to incapacitate every one for adequate expression of feeling at that time. This was unanimously adopted, and on motion of Hon. Leon Abbett, the secretary was instructed to call a meeting for Thursday, September 22d, A. D. 1881, at the Court House, and the chairman was requested to appoint a committee of five members of the Bar of the County to report resolutions at that time. Notice was accordingly sent to all resident members of the Bar.

At the time named nearly the whole Bar of the County and many other citizens assembled at the Court House,

271

and the meeting was organized with the same officers
as before. The chairman announced as the committee
authorized at the informal meeting Messrs. Leon Abbett,
Joseph D. Bedle, Robert Gilchrist, William T. Hoffman,
and William A. Lewis; and that Mr. Lewis being absent
from the city, Mr. Washington B. Williams had been
appointed in his stead.

Mr. Alex. T. McGill, Prosecutor of the Pleas, stated
that the Grand Jury, then in session, had adopted resolutions touching the death of the President, which they
wished to present to the Courts. The chairman directed
that they be invited to attend and participate in the present meeting. The Grand Jury thereupon adjourned, and
came in a body to the Court room. Mr. Abbett, for the
committee, presented the following resolutions, and moved
their adoption, with appropriate remarks :

JAMES A. GARFIELD, President of the United States, having died by the
hand of an assassin, we deem it our duty as citizens and as members of the
Hudson County Bar to give expression to our feelings in the presence of
this national calamity.

We mourn with deep sorrow the loss of a Chief Magistrate who was so
peculiarly representative of American institutions. Beginning poor and
almost unfriended, his indomitable energy and unceasing labor made him
successively the teacher, lawyer, soldier and legislator, and won the esteem
and confidence of his fellow citizens to such a degree that he was raised to
the Presidency. While his administration, had he lived, gave promise of
equal justice to all sections and classes, and of the completion of the great
task of restoring mutual confidence and general prosperity, his tragic fate
has called the whole people, regardless of opposing beliefs and prejudices,
to sympathize with his painful struggle for existence, to render their sorrowing testimony to his manly fortitude, his serene and Christian bravery,
and to lay aside their differences, while as brethren of one afflicted nation
they gather around his grave.

Called a second time within a generation to mourn the assassination of
a President, we desire not only to express our detestation of the crime, but
to condemn the indirect incentives which led to it. While the public service which belongs to all, is used as a reward for political activity in the
victorious party, and offices are yielded to direct solicitation, all the most
selfish and violent parts of our nature are tempted to exert themselves.

Minds excited by partizan abuse, by real or fancied slights, by despair of obtaining office, or by frenzied hope that a change may secure it, are likely to resort to evil methods or even to violence and murder. The President and heads of departments are now exposed to such evils, and the catastrophe thus produced should bring to us shame as well as sorrow. Mean and selfish impulses acting on a depraved nature thus excited, have caused a tragedy, of which the only parallel our history affords was the product of the fiery passions of a great civil war. A wise statesmanship would remove these dangers by abolishing the system which makes them possible.

In this hour of national affliction we find renewed confidence in the stability of our institutions. As they rest on no one man's virtue or ability, so the death of no one, however great and useful, can seriously affect them. Our pyramid rests "broad-based upon the people's will," and in the words of him whom we now lament, uttered on a like occasion, "God reigns and the government at Washington still lives."

We recognize in the peaceful succession to the office made vacant by the death of the President, the strength of our Nation in its obedience to its constitution and laws; and the people of the United States will give to Chester A. Arthur their confidence and support, in the firm belief that he will devote his whole conscience, capacity and industry to the faithful discharge of the duties of President of the whole country.

Our horror of the crime must not permit illegal violence to the assassin. He must be legally tried and legally punished. No punishment of the criminal can lighten the national calamity, but a legal trial and a legal punishment can demonstrate the highest qualities of citizenship.

We tender our respectful sympathy to the family of the deceased President. In their great sorrow they will feel and know that they are not alone; for from every household in this vast country, from its camp fires in the wilderness, and from its ships upon the sea, the warmest sympathies of our nation are now going out to them, and the most earnest prayers are ascending that they may be supported in their grief by the arm of the merciful God and Father of us all.

We request the courts of this county to make a proper record of this meeting and to cause these resolutions to be entered on the minutes.

Mr. Gilchrist seconded the motion in some eloquent and impressive remarks.

The resolutions of the Grand Jury were then presented and read by Garret S. Boice, Esq., in the absence of the foreman Hon. John D. Carscallen. They were as follows :

WHEREAS, having learned with profound sorrow of the death of the Chief Executive of this Nation, after a long period of suffering, caused by the bullet of a vile assassin, and feeling it to be our duty as citizens of Hudson County and Members of this Grand Inquest, to give appropriate and public expression of our appreciation of his high character as a ruler, a citizen, and a christian gentleman ; therefore, be it

Resolved, That in the untimely death of President GARFIELD, almost upon the threshold of his career as a Ruler of this Great Republic, the nation has sustained a loss of a representative American citizen, who, springing from the humblest walks of life, had by his energy, perseverence, patriotism and fidelity in public service, risen to the highest position of honor in his country, and was a wise and eminent statesman, and a worthy Chief Magistrate.

Resolved, That in the patient resignation, through all the fluctuating phases of his illness, alternating between hope and despair, during many weeks of physical suffering, we recognize the sublime christian fortitude and heroic spirit which characterized the man.

Resolved, That while it is allotted to all men by nature to die, the untimely taking from life of one who has been selected by his fellow-men to preside over the destinies of a great nation, especially one who possessed the sterling qualities of JAMES A. GARFIELD, is deeply to be deplored, even when it is the result of accident or disease ; but when, as in the present instance, it is the act of an assassin, it is much more heartfelt, and over every river, steep and valley of our great country is heard the voice of sorrow, and the responsive echo of the sympathy of a great people.

Resolved, That we cannot omit to express our sincere hope that the assassin who has brought about this national calamity may be speedily brought to justice, and expiate his horrible and atrocious crime.

Resolved, That we deeply sympathize with the patient, devoted, long-suffering and heroic wife, who has so tenderly and lovingly watched by the bedside of sickness and sorrow, and with the children left fatherless, and the aged, fond mother, in their irreparable loss, and commend them to the tender mercies of Him who cares for the widow and the fatherless.

Resolve, That our Grand Jury room be draped during our session.

Resolved, That a copy of these resolutions be presented to our Court of Oyer and Terminer and General Jail delivery of Hudson County.

Resolved, That as an additional expression of our respect for the memory of the deceased President, we now adjourn.

The chairman then called for remarks on the original resolutions, and a number of gentlemen responded. The following are some of the addresses :

ADDRESS BY W. B. WILLIAMS, ESQ.

Mr. CHAIRMAN AND FELLOW-CITIZENS—It may well seem that in this great grief which we all have at heart, in presence of these sad and thoughtful faces of all the people, of the stoppage of ordinary business, of these flags everywhere at half-mast, of these funeral-draped buildings, of these cannon booming forth the national sorrow, and of these hourly messages of sympathy flashing on the electric wires from North and South and West, and from beyond the sea, any words of praise or of grief which we can utter, must be feeble and almost superfluous.

Yet, in the sense, not of measuring our loss, or gauging the depth of our sorrow, but only of giving voice to the feelings of which every heart is full, our meetings and spoken words and resolutions have their place and their fitness.

I will not try to speak now at length of the life or services of the dead President. But what a wonderful life it was ! Beginning in the poor log-cabin on the little Western farm, where his brave widowed mother struggled for existence for her four little boys, and was wise enough to give a piece of her land for the public school ; we see him even in childhood, hard at work both manual and mental, working his way to the village academy and to the college, interesting those around him by his frankness, his industry, his quickness; making his mark in the Eastern college where he sought that higher education which not only solaced his leisure but helped to train him for his future positions; and so, step by step, always advancing, losing no time in idleness or vice, until he became the disciplined scholar and teacher, the trusted adviser, the brave and energetic soldier, the thoughtful legislator, the fearless politician and statesman, the peer of the best intellects on the floor of Congress, the leader of a great political party, and until at last, the voice of the American people resounding like the mighty sea, acclaimed him as its Chief Magistrate. What an astonishing series of labors and successes, of noble ambition and great rewards, of public confidence won and justified, of growth in knowledge and ability ; and what a promise of a great and useful future !

Then, as lightning from a clear sky, came the shot which startled all our land. We felt the long and trying alternations of hope and despair. The eyes of fifty millions of people were turned to the White House, and their prayers rose from every valley and hill-side, wherever faith could find a believing heart to inspire. Then came the hoping against hope, as in spite of all that skill and love could do, we saw his life ebbing steadily away; then the removal to purer air, where we, sons of New Jersey, might fondly fancy that here so near to our hearts, and within the soothing sound and life-giving breath of the Atlantic, there was yet a stay against the destroyer's hand; and then that night, now stamped into our memories, when with the little group of friends around him, and with his eyes fixed to his last sigh on the face of his faithful wife, that great, loving soul passed silently away.

Now, all that is left us is to learn what we can from this remarkable career, and to study the secrets, or the forces, by which he not only attained high position, but got so close to the people's heart as hardly any other man has, except Lincoln and Washington.

And it seems to me that this arose from his being in his life and his personal traits, a type representing with phenomenal accuracy the leading features of our naonal character.

First, there was the inherent vigor of the time and rush of events, which made his rise so rapid. It is another of our realities stranger than romance. The poor country school-boy ranking in a few years with the statesmen of his period; the college-orator in a few years "wielding at will that fierce democracie;" the quiet civilian acquitting himself with honor on the field of battle; the unknown son of an obscure family chosen while yet in the prime of life, by the almost spontaneous voice of his countrymen, to rule as chief magistrate over one of the foremost nations of the world;—this was a miracle of fortune which might turn a man's head.

Yet, with our national readiness of adaptation to whatever turn circumstances may take, he was fit, or fitted himself quickly enough, for every demand. And through all this wonderful success and rapid elevation, he never was puffed up or unduly elated. He was master of his office; not the office of him. Personal conceit was no part of his character. He never lost, even at his highest point of elevation, his early simplicity, his hearty recognition of his humblest fellow citizen. He was like the old Scottish king:—he

> " Hath borne his faculties so meek, hath been
> So clear in his great office, that his virtues
> Do plead like angels, trumpet-tongued, against
> The deep damnation of his taking off."

Consider next his indomitable and persistent energy. Nearly every circumstance was against him. Poverty repressed him: burdens rested on him; and many an enterprising man starting as he did, might have faltered a little after overcoming some of these difficulties, and contented himself as a village teacher or lawyer. But GARFIELD's energy was irrepressible, like a mountain spring, and could not stop. Homer would have said that he was impelled by some divine energy. We might say it too, if we could venture to pronounce on things beyond our reach, and of which the outcome is as yet all dark to us.

Next, his readiness—that unhesitating promptness with which he answered the call of duty and assumed responsibility.

" There is a tide in the affairs of men
Which, taken at the flood, leads on to fortune."

He was never deficient in this, in which many a noble soul has failed. His ambition was high, and honorable, and he was ready to render service, of his best, both body and mind, and fairly earn what he might attain to. Wherever duty called, whether at home or in the field, whatever sacrifice or labor it required, he answered promptly, like the prophet of old, " Here am I, send me ! "

Next, note that this readiness with which our people have usually fronted all responsibilities, was in Mr. GARFIELD not rash or headstrong. Fools may rush in where angels fear to tread ; but in his case, there is an example of full and thorough preparation for whatever he undertook. If he was to teach, he worked all night rather than face his class without that full learning which gives confidence and inspires interest. On joining the army, he did all that study could do to learn the theory of his duties. And then, in the camp, in the field, or in front of the enemy, he drew from every emergency the practical skill which cool observant minds acquire best under such pressure.

So, in Congress, I venture to say that no great public question on which it was Mr. GARFIELD's duty to speak or vote, ever found him unprepared. He studied and loved the great classic writers, the statesmen and philosophers of antiquity ; he ransacked history, and no less studied the discussions of modern economists. And so it was, that even on those most difficult questions of finance, and public credit and taxation, to deal with which needs special knowledge and training like a profession, and on which our representative bodies represent chiefly the popular ignorance, this quondam Western school-teacher made himself the exponent of thought and leader of argument in Congress, and stood for many years at the head of one of its most important committees.

His example then, encourages that noble ambition, that interest in politics, which are essential to our system of government. But it requires also a proper valuing of the duties of the citizen as well as of the public servant. The great and difficult questions of government are not to be safely dealt with by men whose chief preparation for them is stump-speaking, or good management at the corner groggery. We are not the only generation of men that has lived, nor is our country the only one that has had public interests to protect, or laws to devise and administer. The history and experience of other systems must be our light, and the past is at least one of the safest guides in judging of the future.

Another lesson from this terrible blow is the evil tendency of our present methods of appointment to office. The habit of degrading personal solicitation has grown to be a disease of our administrative departments. As one of the resolutions properly expresses it, this possibility of obtaining office on grounds of party and personal service exposes our chief officers to all the evil passions which disappointment can excite. To put an end to this, the public service which is for the benefit of all and paid for by all, must no longer be treated as the property of the victorious party. Whatever may be the reticence of professed politicians on this point, the whole press of the country has given forth a clear and certain sound, and public opinion is on its way to a reform of this blot upon our method of government.

Finally, amid our grief, we may observe with renewed confidence how quietly the wheels of society and law continue to move, and how free from all public disturbance is the sudden change of the chief magistrate. This capacity for self-control, this respect for and willing obedience to law, is the great characteristic of the Anglo-Saxon mind. It has produced the most enlightened and freest institutions which have ever given scope to the development of human rights and happiness; and it now affords us another assurance, that government by and for the [people, will never perish from the earth.

ADDRESS BY HON. JACOB WEART.

MR. PRESIDENT—I rise to support the resolutions which contain so much food for our future study, in relation to our great national bereavement.

This government did not spring into existence by mere matter of chance, but was planted here by God; and I have no fear that He will desert this people and leave us alone and forsaken in this hour of our national sorrow. We are now cast down, as we look to our lamented GAR-FIELD, about to fill an untimely grave, cut off in the full bloom and vigor of his manhood, and our sorrowing thoughts turn inward, when we lament and say to ourselves, why has God dealt unto us this heavy blow? But we should not despair, as this nation is one of law and order, and ever has been under the guiding hand of God sufficiently strong to overcome all assaults.

If we turn to our histories, we will find that while the Pilgrim Fathers were still upon the broad ocean, and before they had set foot upon American soil, in the cabin of the Mayflower they gathered around their table with Captain Miles Standish as their leader, and entered into a compact for a government of themselves both as to their religious and civil affairs, and chose John Carver to be their governor.

This compact commenced, " In the name of God, Amen," and the whole draft of the document shows how devoutly these men reverenced God; and their simple government then and there agreed upon, was based upon the idea that God is the Great Ruler of the universe, and to that Infinite Being they must look for all needed wisdom to guide them in their affairs of state. The seed then sown took root and our magnificent form of government is the ripe fruit of their early planting. But the nation has not been without sin;

that was not to be expected in a world where the Pilgrims
were fleeing from the persecutions of the old world; and
where the peoples from whom they were separating, were
also sending out their ships to other portions of our country, with the hope of gaining wealth and worldly renown,
and without distinct religious belief and zeal.

Therefore, as the nation grew and prospered, we had a
growth alike of vice, and high religious sentiment; and we
were fast approaching a period of revolution in our national history which was to overthrow, and uproot society,
and shake the fabric of our government to its very center.

We had in 1860, existing in our republic, three great
national sins or vices, which were sapping the foundations
of our government, and they were likely to bring down
the whole fabric in ruins about our heads.

These three vices consisted of: 1. Slavery. 2. [The
principle in politics, that "to the victors belong the spoils."
3. Frauds in our elections.

It is wise that we should pause in our career for a few
moments, while our lamented President lies shrouded in
our National Capitol, and ask ourselves as to God's dealings with us, in relation to our national sins.

1. That the slaveholders rebellion was the work of God
for the destruction of slavery, and not the feeble and purile
work of men to set up a new government on the face of the
earth; no student of religious history will at this day deny.
How God led this nation and people through that great
conflict, it is not now necessary for us to pause and inquire:
the events are of too recent a date to need repetition here.
But I desire to call attention to one memorable fact, that
during that struggle President Lincoln had become so endeared to every loyal heart in the nation, that he was leaned
upon and looked to as one of the main props upon which
the government rested; and the great sin of slavery did
not pass from us notwithstanding we had lost nearly one
million of human lives in the civil war, until in the providence of God, the nation was called upon to yield up her
beloved Lincoln, and he became our first martyred Presi-

dent, and the nation was brought nearer to God by this
event, than it ever had been before ; and his death was the
crowning affliction upon this nation, when the sin of slavery was put away from us.

2. To-day we are mourning over our second martyred
President, who has fallen a victim to our second national
sin, consisting of that principle, which the nation gave
birth to some fifty years ago, and has ever since cherished and fostered, that in politics, "to the victors belong
the spoils."

At the early formation of the government no such principle existed, and for the first forty years of our political
history the principles which guided the appointing power,
were summed up in these few words, *honesty, capacity, and
faithfulness :* and no officer of the government was ever removed except for cause, and men grew old and gray in the
service of their country ; so that it came to be an adage of
the people, that among the office holders, "but few die,
and none resign ;" but about fifty years ago this rule was
abandoned and upon a change of each administration, and
particularly if that change was a political one, all the officers of the government changed with it.

President Harrison, in 1841, went down to his grave,
under the over-strain of the vast army of office hunters
who pressed around him personally and by petition.

Political campaigns have been largely waged and carried
on by large masses of our citizens entering into the struggle, without love of country, without patriotism as the
mainspring of their action, but with the selfish motive and
hope, that through the success of their party, they would
obtain some lucrative office as a reward for their party
services.

During the last canvass Guiteau entered the same with
this hope in view, and being a mere political adventurer,
a mere office seeker, when he failed in the accomplishment
of his purpose, his weak mind became frenzied, and he
wreaked the vengeance of his disappointment on the life
of our President.

We as a people should put away this national sin; we should banish it from our political canvasses, and not allow it to be possible that office seekers should spring up and assassinate our Presidents, if they fail to obtain the offices they covet.*

---

*In view of recent political events, no apology need be offered here for the publication at the present time of an editorial which appeared in the Jersey City Daily Times, February 14th, 1868.

TENURE OF OFFICE.— Upon this all absorbing question of the collection of the Revenue, and the proper enforcement of the law, and the real mode of elevating the standard of the civil service of the United States, we have had a conversation with Jacob Weart, Esq., Collector of Internal Revenue of this district, who has at our request submitted his views in writing, and we take great pleasure in laying the same before our readers, and ask that the matters set forth by him have a cordial and thoughtful consideration. He says :

That in order to have a more effectual civil service, and one that will provide for the wants of the times, it is necessary to employ good and competent men ; such cannot be procured without fair and liberal salaries; then you must hold out to them such a reasonable length of service as will warrant them in taking the positions.

Since 1830 the civil service of the country has been deteriorating, and the grade of men willing to take the offices subject to constant removals, has continually been seeking a lower level instead of a higher one.

I know of no mode of making an effectual civil service, unless you remove the officers from the arena of party politics ; prevent them by law from contributing money to any political party to be used in elections, and then make the tenure of office during good behavior, with retirement on a pension, after the person has become old and superannuated. Then the government will be able to command the best men in the country to transact its business, the compensation given will belong to the person holding the office, and not be subject to assessment to carry on political campaigns.

By this mode you would remove demagogues from political strife, who enter the field for the sole purpose of obtaining office and the emoluments thereof. Politics would then become a political science, men would enter it for the love of country, the elevation of the race, and the welfare of society. As matters have been conducted for years, politics prostituted the public service for means to carry elections, and then in turn the greed for office demoralized politics to obtain office, all at last coming from the tax-payers in some form.

Whether this change can be brought about in this country, where the practice has become settled to change all or nearly all the office holders, as one political party goes out of power and another comes in, I am not prepared to say, without the constitution is changed to meet the case.

It will be well for the nation if this principle "that to the victors belong the spoils," should go down into the grave with the body of our second martyred President, and be buried with him in his tomb at Cleveland.

The enormity of this great crime has brought this political sin to the full view of our people, and they to-day see in the death of our lamented President, this national sin, in a light more clear than they have ever been permitted to see it before, and it will be well for us if we heed and profit by the lesson. For how can we say that the nation stands guiltless in the sight of God this day, when we look at the results wrought by this sin.

3. The third of our national sins, which I have spoken of as existing in our politics at the breaking out of the civil war in 1861, that of frauds in our elections, still exists, but in a modified form. This national sin we must put away from us also. We must breathe into our elections our purest spirits; we must banish all forms of corruption from our ballot boxes, so that the result of our elections will give the honest expressions of our electors, and not the expressions of wicked men who have deposited fraudulent ballots or falsified the returns; and we must see to it, that our third martyr President (if the nation is ever again to go through this hour of anguish and grief) does not fall a victim to the national sin of frauds in elections, and involve the whole country in another civil war. This great crime against the government of the people, if allowed to grow and fester, will not end with assassination. visiting the punishment on a single individual, but the infliction must fall on all alike, if the evil should pass beyond the control of our courts to correct and restrain.

But let us look to God for guidance in this direction, How this evil is to be worked out is not now entirely visible to us, but let us trust in God, he has safely carried

---

Unless you change the constitution, any system organized and perfected by one party, I fear, will be swept away by another, if the same should become necessary to get control of the offices.

this nation through every storm; he has preserved us in every hour of peril, and while he has not spared his rod of affliction, still it is our duty to kiss the rod and not murmur, but remember that he has blessings in store for us if we will give heed to His warnings, and honestly endeavor to eschew our sins. And while we are cast down to-day, and the whole nation mourns, let us remember that the night of weeping is followed by rejoicing in the morning.

ADDRESS BY HON. WILLIAM T. HOFFMAN.

Standing in the presence of this profound grief I mingle my tears with the bereaved ones, and join in sorrow with the whole nation. JAMES A. GARFIELD, who probably entered upon his office with greater hopes and more clustering friendships than any other, who stood at the threshold of an era of good feeling never before known, is dead. Fully equipped by education and experience he and the whole nation anticipated a brilliant and historical administration.

All is sunk in darkness. Hopes like himself are dead, and the stiffened corse awaiting sepulture is all that remains to his family, to his friends and to the nation.

But only in one sense.

The memory of the affectionate son who forgot not in all his successes the one who bore him, is present with the aged mother he kissed in the presence of assembled thousands, when he ascended to the highest summit of human ambition.

The remembrance of the tender, sympathetic and helpful companionship of thirty years is now about and will ever cluster around the heroic woman who was his wife, and for whom to-day go out the prayers of the civilized world.

The memory of a careful, loving father, who rose step by step from poverty and obscurity to the grandest elevation of earth, will ever be an incentive to work, to a virtuous life, to noble living, to the children he has left as the wards of the nation.

But beyond all this, the grand example of patriotic purpose, of a life devoted to all of the best interests of his country, is for all of us.

He was a typical American. More, perhaps, did he fill the full ideal of the possible man under our institutions than any other.

His example, his memory, his history are ours—ours to point to with pride, ours to make us glad that we belong to the same nation that he helped in many ways to save and for a time ruled.

So much for his bright, buoyant, healthful life. So much and more it accomplished.

But if that was all we would not have cause for the joy, which, mingling with our sorrow, we now have—that JAMES A. GARFIELD was born and lived and died.

No man is absolutely needful to the progress of mankind. One dies and another fills his place. One ruler departs and another puts hands on the lever and the machinery of government moves on in place. The crested waves break upon the shore, but the eternal tides roll on. Above and beyond all the great King governs the universe.

"Clouds and darkness are round about Him; but righteousness and judgment are the habitation of His throne. God reigns and the government at Washington still lives."

In the sublime faith of the great man who uttered these words, the nation bows to this affliction and tries to say "not our will, but Thine be done."

But this is not all.

His life was much, but his suffering and death were more. Whatever chasm of feeling there was between sections was filled to the edge with his blood. The flash of the assassin's pistol illumined the whole country and revealed the fact that we were a nation of brethren. The noise of the shot hushed all strife, drowned all sectional and partizan bitterness. The eighty days of suffering brought fifty millions—yes, one hundred millions, to their knees. Let no man say to me now for my commendation that the South is less loyal than the North. By the blood of JAMES A. GARFIELD I deny it. Let no man say to me for my approbation that one party is less devoted to the welfare of this great land than the other. Appealing to the history of the sympathy and prayers and tears that have for three months been borne to the chamber of the martyred President, I deny it.

To-day, I repeat, this nation stands more secure—is more strongly cemented than ever before, and because the man we mourn suffered and died.

Let us then take courage. "God reigns." " He doeth all things well."

Through the parted heavens down along the bright avenues of the skies comes the spirit voice of the dead yet living President, saying, " My countrymen, for you and for your country I gave the last great test of my devotion for you and it. I died that perfect peace should come. Will ye profit by it? "

With the sorrowing ones we mingle our tears. With full hearts we realize our own bereavement. Yet as we wreathe his tomb with the immortelles of our love and veneration, we look upward and thank God that JAMES A. GARFIELD lived and suffered and died.

ADDRESS BY HON. CHAS. H. WINFIELD.

Mr. Chairman—If there are times when it may be said that speech is silvern, there are also times when silence is golden. Mourning by the side of the new made grave where beats the heart of a sorrowing people, I feel that speech is not becoming. The brook, as it goes babbling on to the sea, gives no proof of deep waters or of golden wealth that lies beneath them. The *silent* tear was the key with which the Peri opened the gates of Paradise, and through it now we see signs of a broader and a better manhood in the Republic. This is not the occasion to speak of questions still open, but it is the time, when every heart is tender with a common sorrow, to remember what is noble, to forget all else.

On the nineteenth of August, fourteen years after the Birth in Bethlehem, the then master of the world lay dying at Nola, a little village between Naples and Rome. On the day of his death he asked for a mirror that he might see himself for the last time and then had his friends admitted to his room. While they stood gathered around his dying bed he asked them whether they did not think he had played his part pretty well in the comedy of human life, and without awaiting their reply immediately added in the Greek verse with which they generally closed their plays, " Clap hands! and all applaud for joy ! "

On the nineteenth of the current month, by the deep sounding sea in our own state another master lay dying; not the master of the world in the sense that Augustus was, but the master of the great American heart, captured and made his own by heroic suffering, manly resignation, and he, too, asked for a looking-glass, looked upon his face for the last time, and if then, in imitating the great Roman, he had admitted his friends to his chamber, and put to them the query whether they did not think he had acted pretty well his part in the comedy—call it comedy, call it drama, call it tragedy, call it what you will—of human life, what more appropriate answer could have been given than the words used when the curtain was rung down on the mimic stage? "Clap hands! and all applaud for joy!" This, too, notwithstanding the fact that the poor sufferer was disappearing from sight into the Valley of the Shadow; but looking back over that wonderful course which he had traveled from the hard trodden towpath of the canal to the marbled halls of the White House as President, and now, in his last hour lying close up to the great sympathetic heart of the civilized world, which justified his audible thoughts—"The people, the people, my trust,"—would the answer not have been, "Clap hands! and all applaud for joy?" Truly he had acted his part well. He seems to have been an illustration not only of our American life struggling upward and onward but in himself embodied the very order of Divine Providence even in material things which lift themselves one rank and one tier above another;

> "From the shivering seal's low moans,
>   Up through the shining tiers and ranks of life
> To stars upon their thrones."

As in the beautiful torch-race of the Athenian youth, he lit his torch at the altar of Prometheus and then pressed on toward the goal. His torch went not out in the race; its flame was bright and steady at the end. To him, then, as of old, must the victory be adjudged. Happy man! If he was great in life, nothing in his life became him like the leaving it.

> After the shower, the tranquil sun;
>   After the snow, the emerald leaves;
> Silver stars when the day is done;
>   After the harvest, golden sheaves.

> After the clouds, the violet sky;
>   After the tempest, the lull of waves;
> Quiet woods when the winds go by;
>   After the battle, peaceful graves.

> After the burden, the blissful meed ;
> After the flight, the downy nest ;
> After the furrow, the waking seed ;
> After the shadowy river—rest !

Truly, for him is the "rest which remaineth ;" for others is the sorrow. Hear the sad wail, mingling with the voice of the many-tongued sea,—as the poor heart-broken wife bends over her dying husband, who, unable to speak yet turns his eyes so sympathetically that they remain fixed upon her even in death,—"Oh why am I called upon to suffer this cruel wrong ?" That poor, afflicted woman gave voice to more than her sorrow. A nation draped in the emblems of mourning, flags at half-mast, the sad faces we meet in the street, the solemn tolling of bells throughout the land, the royal standard of England's Queen at half-mast, and her court in mourning, all echo the said wail of the widow—"Why, why ?" You and I may not pry into the secrets of the Omniscient to seek the reason why, but the assurance comes with that promise which speaks to us out of the ages from Him who is able to comfort the heart bowed down, "What I do thou knowest not now, but thou shalt know hereafter."

That same providence which took him by the hand when a boy and led him step by step up to the high and proud office of the Chief Magistrate of this Republic, will make it all plain in His own time and way—whether man lives or dies, the purposes of the Omnipotent will be accomplished :

> " Here He exalts neglected worms,
>   To sceptre and a crown ;
> And there the following page He turns,
> And treads the monarch down."

ADDRESS BY HON. ALLAN L. McDERMOTT.

Mr. CHAIRMAN—Where the sounding sea, dashing against the shore of Elberon, seemed to echo the call of Heaven, in the possession of an unclouded mind, JAMES A. GARFIELD, our nation's chosen son, passed to another life.

> " Sustained and sooth'd by an unfaltering trust, he approached his grave
> Like one that draws the drapery of his couch about him,
> And lies down to pleasant dreams."

A great and good man has gone from our land, and, although we claimed him as our own, sorrow is not limited by national boundaries. Co-extensive with civilization is the oppression of heart and brain by the heavy hand of sorrow. As with a single tongue the old and the new world give utterance to sympathy and shame—sympathy for an afflicted family and an afflicted nation ; and shame evolved from a contemplation of the fact that the life of a scholar, a statesman and a soldier has been sacrificed to appease the brutal instincts of a murderer. In an hour when, filled with gratitude to the Creator for his gifts of peace and plenty, the people of this free land were joyful in their preparation for the observance of a great National Day, they were shocked by a stroke as unexpected as it was unmerited. President GARFIELD is dead ; his assassin is awaiting the sanction of the law ; but in this our hour of sorrow, we do not look in vain for that which will assuage our grief. It is found in the fact that the act of the assassin was conceived in his own foul mind—that he represented his own thoughts, his own desires, his own beliefs ; and only his own—that in the North, in the South, in East, in the West, there lives not a citizen whose heart would not have welcomed the bullet which took from us our beloved President, if that welcome could have spared us this overwhelming sorrow. And this, whether, twenty years ago, that heart was covered by the blue or the gray. It was the act of a disappointed man, not the act of a party—the act of an individual, not of a representative ; and those, who, but a few months since, opposed, upon political grounds, the election of General GARFIELD to the Presidency, to-day yield to none in the poignancy of their grief. He was "our President," and the banners of every political party in the land are draped with mourning for "our GARFIELD." For this at last let us be thankful.

The American heart cannot sympathize with assassination as a political factor. The hands that signed the Declaration of Independence would have withered rather than to thus attempt the life of the sovereign against whose governmental policy they protested. Assassination is dark, and of darkness. The progress of our grand republic is upward, onward—toward the light of a higher and nobler civilization—and never had we a better, truer guide that JAMES A. GARFIELD. Born in the home of poverty, and forced by labor to provide himself with intellectual implements and tools, he rose above the trials of circumstance, and placed his name among the brightest in America's Pantheon. If there are lessons to be learned from the manner of his death—from the declarations and position of his assassin, it is well that we should give expression to them ; but they are not in this hour matters of debate. The grandeur and strength of our political system is proven by its second reception of the terrible shock of assassination. It is, in all its parts, a system worth loving and living for, and, when necessary, worth dying for. And to us and our children, and our children's children, its worth, its holiness will be enhanced by the fact that it will hereafter bear upon the pages of its history, in letters of golden light, the name of GARFIELD.

The President of the United States and the Governors of the separate Commonwealths, have issued proclamations setting this day apart for special service. The hearts of all the people cry, Amen!

We meet to-day, with a pure and universal interest, with deep sympathy and profound sorrow, to pay our tributes of respect to the nation's loved dead President. I did not imagine when, a little more than a year ago, I waved the banner representing New Jersey, over GARFIELD's head at the Chicago Convention, and grasped his hand in congratulation because of his nomination to be President of the United States, that eyes would now be weeping, and hearts suffering, because of his untimely taking off. The noble man, heroic soldier, thorough statesman, and perfect President. No wonder the nation mourns him, and the old world cannot keep back its tears. The sorrow that has come upon the people because of GARFIELD's death, is felt by old and young. Its truest expression perchance, came from the mouth of a little child; who, after gazing at the mourning drapings on house and school, and public building and church, turned to her mother and said, "Mamma, is *everybody* dead?"

The present is a sad, but grand occasion; and I predict that all, who, from true motives, have taken part in it, will ever be glad that they have laid aside other duties, and have forgotten all selfish considerations.

---

* Mr. Throckmorton was absent from the city when our Memorial Services were held, and upon inquiry the committee learned that he was at Great Barrington, Mass., and that upon the invitation of the Select Men, and a special committee of that place. And that he declined an invitation to return and speak here. The committee solicited from him his address, so as to publish the same as the expression of opinion of another of our thoughtful and patriotic citizens, which he has kindly furnished.

I beg your attention to some sober reflections. Our immortal Declaration of Independence proclaims the great truth that "all men are created equal." With a noble pride every American citizen can reflect that *this* was the *first* declaration of *the equality of man* made in any state paper from the creation of the world; further, that *ours* was the first nation founded on this immortal principle! Inspired by this great truth (*which eternity must endorse*), our republic has produced men, who, in greatness of intellect, purity of thought and purpose, and grandeur of character, have represented, in life and action and in public speech, this great sentiment that has MOVED THE WORLD FORWARD!

'Tis said, "the triple cord is seldom broken." What cord could bind the hearts of Americans together like that *one* cord, the strands of which are made up out of the names of WASHINGTON, LINCOLN and GARFIELD?

WASHINGTON, embodied in public and private life, in war and in peace, this great sentiment.

LINCOLN said, that he scarcely had an inspiration to political action or speech, that he did not draw from the Declaration of Independence.

GARFIELD said, "The great doctrines of our Declaration of Independence germinated in the hearts of our fathers, and were developed under the new influences of this wilderness world, by the same subtle mystery which brings forth the rose from the germ of the rose-tree. Unconciously to themselves the great truths were growing under the new conditions, until like the century-plant, *they blossomed into the matchless* beauty of the DECLARATION OF INDEPENDENCE, *whose fruitage increased and increasing, we enjoy to-day.*"

It is a remarkable fact, that upon the anniversary of the very day the Declaration of Independence was signed, the 2d of July, 1776, (although July 4th is usually celebrated to commemorate the event), GARFIELD received his mortal wound.

Pistol and powder did not alone guide the fatal bullets. The brain of an assassin, sane enough to plan in detail the

diabolical act, guided the hand that laid JAMES A. GAR-
FIELD low, with a revolver purchased with deliberate intent
for the purpose it accomplished. Sane enough to plan
with coolness and perfection—prompted perchance by des-
pondency over failure to obtain office ; possibly by a desire
always to be remembered even though to be held in immortal detestation; my theory is this—He was sane enough
thus to plan and execute ; he is sane enough to be hung
for it.

But I trust for the credit of the nation that the majesty
of the law will be vindicated, and that the death of the
criminal, (whose very name soils the lips that pronounce
it) shall be brought about only after a fair and impartial
trial; and that our constitution will be so amended, that
any attempt to kill either the President or the Vice-President, shall be declared to be TREASON, punishable, upon
conviction, by death.

I have faith in the integrity, in the love for country ; in
the marvellous self-control of the American people. The
great rebellion, the murder of the great and good Lincoln,
and now the death by assassination of the high-minded,
noble GARFIELD, have been and are terrible things to bear,
but the nation grows the nobler by nobly bearing them.

When sixteen years ago Lincoln was shot, though the
nation's heart was sorely crushed and wounded, the people
could yet realize that the spirit that could incite and carry
on rebellion, would not hesitate at murder. But why in an
hour of profound peace and unprecedented prosperity, on
the eve of a National Anniversary, the just ruler, representing the progress, civilization and greatness of the
United States, the always unoffending gentleman, should
be waylaid and made the target for a murderer's bullet,
surpasses ordinary conjecture.

I would that I had the gift properly to express the sorrow
of this nation, united in all sections closer than ever before
by his death. To-day a whole people is burying its one
dead. How tenderly did that people watch and pray at
his sick bedside. But the prayers were not answered with
returning life to him. Still his life teaches all nations a

lesson. Day by day he suffered and lingered, until by the sea where the waters of the ocean he loved, soothed his senses, his soul took its flight. Ah! the sadness of the tolling bell which announced, "THE PRESIDENT IS DEAD!"

Although not afraid of death, there must have been deep sorrow to himself that he had to meet it. By every manly means he had lifted himself from the lowest condition in life to the summit of his ambition, namely, the United States Senate. Then the people made him their President. Such grand opportunity was before him — such grand houghts for the people were in his heart—so pure and noble was his ambition, so truly did he realize that he was President—not of section or of party, but of the whole United States—and so lofty was his desire to help the country onward, that to be rudely cut off must have brought him suffering more acute than the pain of the wound. But GARFIELD's death has revealed so much of all that is noble in man, that as long as the world shall last, pride will point its finger at the noble example of American manhood set by JAMES A. GARFIELD.

To-day the grave will hide his form from our sight. How must the hearts of his family be bowed down. But they have glorious memories to take away some of the bitterness of grief. The kiss imprinted on the lips of wife and mother, by the husband and son, in the hour of his exaltation to the presidency of the nation, meant for them from him, love that shall never fade, for such "love lives on in the eternal land."

It would be impossible to enumerate the many incidents connected with his death illness that must forever be cherished by the American people.

Two remarks of the President while sick, have impressed me strangely. On being informed of the tender interest of the whole people evinced in his condition, he turned to his faithful wife and said, "Is this not a people worth living for;" and again, bravely asking if his hurt was fatal, he said, "I am not afraid to die." It is a great thing for such a President to have believed the people who chose him their ruler, to be "worth living for"—and a great thing for such a people to have chosen a ruler who was "not afraid to die."

Perhaps the Almighty permitted death to smite him, in order to emphathize the lessons of a true man's life and death, and the beauty and strength of true womanhood, as exemplified in his wife and mother; and that GARFIELD's earthly crown and glory will be the immortalizing of those he loved. Perhaps the deed was allowed which robbed the Nation of its Chief, in order to show what depths of devilshness there can be in human nature, so as to frighten the world from a repetition of crime so terrible.

In this address I have attempted nothing more than to show my more than willingness to evince respect for him whose life was one of constant work—work which was for the developement of self and yet was unselfish work, and was for the good of mankind and country. Out of respect for him who set to all the world an example of how industry and honesty and honor can elevate any man from the humblest walks to a position as high as the world affords, by faithful work; out of respect to him who bore pain in patience, and who though wanting to live for the people, yet was ready to die if God called him—let us honor ourselves and him—and pay not only by our sorrowing veneration the tribute his memory deserves—but let us determine for the sake of our country that we will grow stronger and wiser, and more skillful in all that appertains to the duties of true American citizens. This will be the greatest honor we can pay his memory.

The seal is set upon the lips that have ever eloquently spoken words of wisdom to our people—but his written words will remain—and in the everlasting affections of the American people, and in the admiration of the world the name of GARFIELD—canal-boatman, carpenter, scholar, patriot, soldier, statesman, President, will be inseparably linked with that of Lincoln.

APPENDIX.

Special meeting of the Board of Directors of Education, held in its rooms, School-building No 5, Bay street, on Wednesday evening, September 21, 1881, at eight o'clock.

Present—President McGill, Directors Jordan, Boyd, Murphy, Adams, Finck, Cringle, Witsch and Romaine.

Absent—Directors Morris and Mason.

President McGill stated to the Board that the meeting had been called in compliance with a suggestion of his Honor Mayor Taussig, that the Board should meet and take appropriate action in reference to the death of President GARFIELD.

Director Witsch thereupon offered the following:

Resolved, That the President appoint a committee of three members, to draft appropriate resolutions and to act in conjunction with any committees that may be appointed by the other city Boards, and that pending the report of such committee the Board take a recess of fifteen minutes.

The resolution was unanimously adopted.

The President appointed as committee Directors Witsch, Jordan and Romaine.

Upon the reassembling of the Board the committee submitted the following preamble and resolution:

WHEREAS, It has been the will of Divine Providence to remove by death the Chief Magistrate of our country ; therefore

Resolved, That in the death of JAMES A. GARFIELD, the nation has lost a loved and honored Chief Magistrate, humanity a friend, Christianity a devout follower, and education a firm advocate.

That excelling in all the walks of life, we have known him best as the successful soldier, the honest statesman and the nation's President.

That to those especially bowed down in grief, to the aged mother, to the wife so ruthlessly bereft of a husband, to the fatherless children and to the relatives, we tender our sincerest sympathy, for we suffer with them in the bereavement which shrouds in profound gloom, family, friends, state and nation alike.

OTTO J. WITSCH,
ISAAC ROMAINE,
R. S. JORDAN,
Committee.

On motion of Director Finck, the report of the committee was received, the resolution adopted, and ordered to be spread in full on the minutes, by a unanimous vote.

By Director Finck, and adopted:

Resolved, That all the schools under the control of this Board be closed until Tuesday morning September 27th, 1881, out of respect for our late President, JAMES A. GARFIELD.

The Board then adjourned.

E. P. CRINGLE, *Clerk.*

RESOLUTIONS ADOPTED BY THE STUDENTS OF THE HIGH SCHOOL OF JERSEY CITY.

The Students of Jersey City High School at a meeting held this morning adopted the following resolutions:

WHEREAS, The Chief Magistrate of our nation, JAMES A. GARFIELD, who throughout his life displayed a character and on his bed of suffering a fortitude worthy of our imitation, has been stricken down by the hand of an assassin ; therefore

Resolved, That his gradual rise from humble circumstances to the Presidency of our Republic is an example of the proper appreciation and reward of true merit, which every student should keep in mind.

Resolved, That his strict honesty and faithfulness to duty in all positions of honor and trust should ever stand as a model for every American to emulate.

Resolved, That our humble sympathy be hereby tendered to the members of his deeply bereaved family ;

Resolved, That a draft of these resolutions be forwarded to Mrs. James A. Garfield as a token of our sympathy with her in her deep affliction.

JERSEY CITY HIGH SCHOOL, Sept. 20, 1881.

PUBLIC SCHOOL NO. 12, OF JERSEY CITY.

The following preamble and resolutions were adopted by Public School No. 12, Crescent avenue, after learning of the death of General GARFIELD :

WHEREAS, The honored President of our Nation, JAMES A. GARFIELD, was stealthily followed from place to place, and finally slain by a cruel and wicked assassin ; therefore,

Resolved, That in the death of General GARFIELD, the nation has lost a President endowed with rare intellect, a statesman gifted with the noblest of sentiments, and a *man* whose large, generous, and true heart was only animated with a desire for the highest interests of all classes and conditions of people.

Resolved, That we recognize in the noble and studious character manifested in his boyhood, the brave, generous and patriotic character developed in his manhood ; and we heartily recommend the study of his life both as a boy and man, and the imitation of his love and devotion to his mother, to all the children of our beloved land.

A. D. JOSLIN, Prin.

IN MEMORIAM.

BERGEN LODGE, NO. 47, F. & A. M.

dedicates this page to the memory of Brother JAMES A. GARFIELD, late President of the United States, who was stricken by the hand of an assassin July 2d, 1881, and died on the 19th day of September following, after a lingering illness, throughout which, he bore the most excruciating pain with a smiling countenance far more pathetic than tears, and an heroic fortitude and sublime faith that has never been surpassed—the only counterpart to which is found in the record made in sacred history of that Job whom our Father loved so well, yet tried so sorely.

In his life energetic and aspiring, yet self-denying and magnanimous; in his illness brave and uncomplaining beyond example, he became in his death the idol of the whole American people, enshrined in all hearts and particularly

in those of *his* brethren of the great Masonic Fraternity
who recognize in his character, a bright and shining example of that pure exalted manhood, which it is the greatest
aim of Masonry to produce.

> " His life was gentle ; and the elements
>   So mixed in him, that nature might stand up,
>   And say to all the world, This was a man."

We mourn our loss but our grief is not inconsolable ;
for it is mitigated by the hope so well expressed in the
beautiful language of the Monitor, that the loving kindness
of our Father " has translated him from this imperfect, to
that all perfect, glorious, celestial lodge, where the Supreme
Architect of the Universe presides."

EUREKA COUNCIL, NO. 32, O. OF U A. M.

At a regular meeting held September 27th, 1881, the
following preamble and resolutions were unanimously
adopted :

WHEREAS, In the inscrutible providence of an unerring and all-wise God,
our late beloved President. JAMES A. GARFIELD, was assassinated on
the second day of July last, and from the wound then received he
consequently died on the nineteenth day of the present month of
September, we, as honorary members of the Council, deem it right
and proper that *all* American Organizations, and particularly our
own, should express their deep sympathy and sorrow with the general feeling that pervades *our* entire land, as well as other countries ;
therefore be it *Resolved*,

First, That we profoundly and most sincerely lament such a *fearful* deed,
by the hand of a *notorious* villain, which in an unexpected moment struck
down our honored President and brought gloom and sadness to every true
and loyal heart throughout our far famed land, and in view of which as
tounding events, we bow meekly and submissively to the stroke that falls
so terribly upon us.

Secondly Resolved, That as patriots loving our common country, and de-
siring the promotion of her greatest good and the good of humanity everywhere, we feel the loss of that great and good man is next to irreparable,

· but trust his death may prove to be the seed of a mighty power in the land which shall make Liberty and Union one and inseparable—now and forever.

Thirdly Resolved, That while words but feebly express our deep sorrow in this our national bereavement we tender to the American Nation our sympathy in this its hour of trial with the prayer to Almighty God that He would avert further calamity from this Great Nation and comfort the sorrowing widow and fatherless children, of our now deceased Chief Magistrate.

Fourthly Resolved, That the above resolution be written in full in the book of the "Minutes of this Council."

Yours in U. I. & S.

T. V. FROST,
C. W. TUTHILL,
D. P. CHRISTIE,
Committee.
E. A. BORDEN, *Councilor.*

ADOLPH MILLER, *Rec. Sec'y.*

LETTER FROM REV. WILLIAM RANKIN DURYEE, D. D.

The committee sent a request to the Lafayette Reformed Church, requesting the Church to join in the publication and furnish their Pastor's sermon. But the committee are unable to furnish the sermon of the Rev. Dr. Duryee, for the reasons which the following letter explains:

THE PARSONAGE, LAFAYETTE REF. CHURCH,
JERSEY CITY, N. J.

Mr. JACOB WEART.   233 PACIFIC AVE., OCT. 22, '81.

My DEAR SIR—I am very sorry to be unable to unite my utterances, on the day appointed for the funeral services for President GARFIELD, with the sermons of my brethren. But my discourse on that occasion was *purely extemporaneous* and my notes are all destroyed. It would be very difficult to write out *now* what I said *then* in the rush of feeling. This is my excuse for not writing you before. I really feel sorry that the matter stands so, but I cannot give what I do not possess, and the best thing my memory contains is only a "skeleton" of what I said.

Very truly yours,

WM. RANKIN DURYEE.

LETTER FROM HON. WM. A. LEWIS.

JERSEY CITY, Nov. 17, 1881.

Messrs. JACOB WEART, JOHN J. TOFFEY and JOHN M. JONES,

Committee on the Garfield Memorial Volume:

GENTLEMEN—In reply to your communication, requesting me to furnish the committee with my address, delivered at a meeting held in the Presbyterian Church in Third Street, Jersey City, Sept. 26, 1881, on the occasion of the death of JAMES A. GARFIELD, late President of the United States, I have to inform you, my address was not written.

While I recall the heads, scope and outlines of my speech, to attempt its reproduction now, would result in writing for your committee a new address, but would fail to give you the identical address I then delivered.

Supposing it to be foreign to your purpose to print aught but what was delivered, and as delivered, I will therefore content myself with letting my address, on that occasion, pass into "history" through the indulgence of those who had the kindness to listen to it.

Thanking you, gentlemen of the committee, for your courtesy,

I remain yours truly,

WILLIAM A. LEWIS.

INDEX.

www.ingramcontent.com/pod-product-compliance
Lightning Source LLC
Chambersburg PA
CBHW060549030726
47498CB00005B/1324